THE COUNTRY
OF THE
POINTED FIRS
AND OTHER STORIES

Sarah Orne Jewett was born in 1849 in the Maine coast village of South Berwick, where she remained for most of her life. Her sketches of Maine life first appeared in *Harper's*, *The Century*, and *The Atlantic* when she was in her twenties, and in 1877 her first collection, *Deephaven*, was published. From that time, until her death in 1909, fourteen collections of her stories, several volumes of verse, and a number of children's books were published. *The Country of the Pointed Firs* was first published in 1896.

"I always think of her as of one who, hearing New England accused of being a bleak land without beauty, passes confidently over the snow, and by the gray rock, and past the dark fir tree, to a southern bank, and there, brushing away the decayed leaves, triumphantly shows to the faultfinder a spray of the trailing arbutus. And I should like, for my own part, to add this: that the fragrant, retiring, exquisite flower, which I think she would say is the symbol of New England virtue, is the symbol also of her own modest and delightful art."

Charles Miner Thompson,
"The Art of Miss Jewett,"
The Atlantic, October 1904

THE COUNTRY
OF THE
POINTED FIRS
AND OTHER STORIES

SARAH ORNE JEWETT

PREFACE BY

WILLA CATHER

ANCHOR BOOKS

DOUBLEDAY

NEW YORK LONDON TORONTO SYDNEY AUCKLAND

AN ANCHOR BOOK
PUBLISHED BY DOUBLEDAY
a division of Bantam Doubleday Dell Publishing Group, Inc.
666 Fifth Avenue, New York, New York 10103

ANCHOR BOOKS, DOUBLEDAY, and the portrayal of an anchor
are trademarks of Doubleday, a division of Bantam Doubleday
Dell Publishing Group, Inc.

The Country of the Pointed Firs and Other Stories originally
appeared in the two-volume Mayflower Edition as *The Best Stories
of Sarah Orne Jewett*. It was published in 1925 by Houghton Mifflin
Company. The Anchor Books edition is published by arrangement
with Houghton Mifflin company.

Library of Congress Cataloging-in-Publication Data
Jewett, Sarah Orne, 1849–1909.
    The country of the pointed firs and other
    stories / by Sarah Orne
    Jewett:selected and arranged with a preface
    by Willa Cather.
        p. cm.
    Reprint. Originally published:1956.
    I. Cather, Willa, 1873–1947. II. Title.
    PS2132.C64   1989   89-27686
    813'.4—dc20   CIP
    ISBN 0-385-09214-8

24 26 27 25 23

CONTENTS

PREFACE

LOUISE IMOGEN GUINEY:

*But give to thine own story
Simplicity, with glory.*

In reading over a package of letters from Sarah Orne Jewett, I find this observation: *"The thing that teases the mind over and over for years, and at last gets itself put down rightly on paper—whether little or great, it belongs to Literature."* Miss Jewett was very conscious of the fact that when a writer makes anything that belongs to Literature (limiting the term here to imaginative literature, which she of course meant), his material goes through a process very different from that by which he makes merely a good story or a good novel. No one can exactly define this process; but certainly persistence, survival, recurrence in the writer's mind, are highly characteristic of it. The shapes and scenes that have "teased" the mind for years, when they do at last get themselves rightly put down, make a very much higher order of writing, and a much more costly, than the most vivid and vigorous transfer of immediate impressions.

In some of Miss Jewett's earlier books, "Deephaven," "Country Byways," "Old Friends and New," one can find first sketches, first impressions, which later crystallized into the almost flawless examples of literary art that make up this volume. One can, as it were, watch in process the two kinds of making: the first, which is full of perception and feeling but rather fluid and formless, the second, which is so tightly built and significant in design. The design is, indeed, so happy, so right, that it seems inevitable; the design is the story and the story is the design. The "Pointed Fir" sketches are living things caught in the open, with light and freedom and air-spaces about them. They melt into the land and the life of the land until they are not stories at all, but life itself.

A great many good stories were being written upon New England themes at the same time that Miss Jewett was writing; stories that to many contemporary readers may have seemed more interesting than hers, because they dealt with more startling "situations," were more heavily accented, more elaborately costumed and posed in the studio. But most of them are not very interesting to read and re-read to-day; they have not the one thing that survives all arresting situations, all good writing and clever storymaking—inherent, individual beauty; the kind of beauty we feel when a beautiful song is sung by a beautiful voice that is exactly suited to the song.

Pater said that every truly great drama must, in the end, linger in the reader's mind as a sort of ballad. Probably the same thing might be said of every great story. It must leave in the mind of the sensitive reader an intangible residuum of pleasure; a cadence, a quality of voice that is exclusively the writer's own, individual, unique. A quality that one can remember without the volume at hand, can experience over and over again in the mind but can never absolutely define, as one can experience in memory a melody, or the summer perfume of a garden. The magnitude of the subject-matter is not of primary importance, seemingly. An idyl of Theocritus, concerned with sheep and goats and shade and pastures, is to-day as much alive as the most dramatic passages of the Iliad—stirs the reader's feeling quite as much, perhaps, if the reader is a poet.

It is a common fallacy that a writer, if he is talented enough, can achieve this poignant quality by improving upon his subject-matter, by using his "imagination" upon it and twisting it to suit his purpose. The truth is that by such a process (which is not imaginative at all!) he can at best produce only a brilliant sham, which, like a badly built and pretentious house, looks poor and shabby in a few years. If he achieves anything noble, anything enduring, it must be by giving himself absolutely to his material. And this gift of sympathy is his great gift; is the fine thing in him that alone can make his work fine. He fades away into the land and people of his heart, he dies of love only to be born again. The artist spends a life-time in loving the things that haunt him, in having his mind "teased" by them, in trying to get these conceptions down on paper exactly as they are to him and not in conventional poses supposed to reveal their character; trying this method and that, as a painter tries different lightings and different attitudes with his subject to catch the one that presents it more suggestively than any other. And at the end of a lifetime he emerges with much that is more or less happy experimenting, and comparatively little that is the very flower of himself and his genius. I have tried to gather in this volume the very best of Miss Jewett's beautiful work; the stories which, read by an eager student fifty years from now, will give him the characteristic flavor, the spirit, the cadence, of an American writer of the first order—and of a New England which will then be a thing of the past.

Even in the stories that fall a little short of being Miss Jewett's finest, there are many delightful characters and there is much beautiful writing. Take, for instance, the first part of "A Second Spring," or the chapter from "Deephaven" called "In Shadow"; or glance at this clear, daybreak passage at the beginning of "By the Morning Boat":

On the coast of Maine, where many green islands and salt inlets fringe the deep-cut shore line; where balsam firs and bayberry bushes send their fragrance far seaward, and song-sparrows sing all day, and the tide runs plashing in and out among the weedy ledges; where cowbells tinkle on the hills and herons stand in the shady coves—on the lonely coast of Maine stood a small gray house facing the morning light. All the weather-beaten houses of that region face the sea apprehensively, like the women who live in them.

Or consider the closing paragraph of "Marsh Rosemary," which might stand as a tender apology for the art of all new countries, which must grow out of a thin new soil and bear its fate:

Who can laugh at my Marsh Rosemary, or who can cry, for that matter? The gray primness of the plant is made up from a hundred colors if you look close enough to find them. This Marsh Rosemary stands in her own place, and holds her dry leaves and tiny blossoms steadily toward the same sun that the pink lotus blooms for, and the white rose.

The stories chosen vary little in quality, though one may

have one's favorites among them. Personally, I like "The Flight of Betsey Lane" better than "The Hiltons' Holiday," though the latter story was especially dear to Miss Jewett herself. I think I know why; that story simply *is* *the look*—shy, kind, a little wistful—that shines out at one from good country faces on remote farms; it is the look *itself*—and therefore is a little miracle. To have got it down upon the printed page is like bringing the tenderest of early spring flowers from the deep wood into the hot light of summer noon without bruising its petals. The story "William's Wedding" at the end of the "Pointed Fir" volume was uncompleted at the time of Miss Jewett's death, and while all the essentials of the picture are there, the writing is in places a little vague, lacks the last coördinating touch of the writer's hand.

To note an artist's limitations is but to define his genius. A reporter can write equally well about everything that is presented to his view, but a creative writer can do his best only with what lies within the range and character of his talent. These stories of Miss Jewett's have much to do with fisher-folk and seaside villages; with juniper pastures and lonely farms, neat gray country houses and delightful, well-seasoned old men and women. That, when one thinks of it in a flash, is New England. I remember hearing an English actor say that until he made a motor trip through New England he had supposed that the Americans killed their aged in some merciful fashion, for he saw none in the cities where he played.

There are many kinds of people in the State of Maine, and its neighboring States, who are not in Miss Jewett's books. There may be Othellos and Iagos and Don Juans, but they are not highly characteristic of the country, they do not come up spontaneously in the juniper pastures as the everlasting does. Miss Jewett wrote of the people who grew out of the soil and the life of the country near her heart, not about exceptional individuals at war with their environment. This was not a creed with her, but an instinctive preference. She once laughingly told me that her head was full of dear old houses and dear old women, and that when an old house and an old woman came together in her brain with a click, she knew that a story was under way.

Born within the scent of the sea but not within sight of it, in a beautiful old house full of strange and lovely things brought home from all over the globe by seafaring ancestors, she spent much of her girlhood driving about the country with her doctor father on his professional rounds among the farms. She early learned to love her country for what it was. What is quite as important, she saw it as it was. She happened to have the right nature, the right temperament, to see it so—and to understand by intuition the deeper meaning of all she saw.

She had not only the eye, she had the ear. From childhood she must have treasured up those pithy bits of local speech, of native idiom, which enrich and enliven her pages. The language her people speak to each other is a native tongue. No writer can invent it. It is made in the hard school of experience, in communities where language has been undisturbed long enough to take on color and character from the nature and experiences of the people. The "sayings" of a community, its proverbs, are its characteristic comment upon life; they imply its history, suggest its attitude toward the world, and its way of accepting life. Such an idiom makes the finest language any writer can have; and he can never get it with a notebook. He himself must be able to think and feel in that speech—it is a gift from heart to heart.

Much of Miss Jewett's delightful humor comes from her delicate and tactful handling of this native language of the waterside and countryside, never overdone, never pushed a shade too far; from this, and from her own fine attitude toward her subject-matter. This attitude in itself, though unspoken, is everywhere felt, and constitutes one of the most potent elements of grace and charm in her stories. She had with her own stories and her own characters a very charming relation; spirited, gay, tactful, noble in its essence and a little arch in its expression. In this particular relationship many of our most gifted writers are unfortunate. If a writer's attitude toward his characters and his scene is as vulgar as a showman's, as mercenary as an auctioneer's, vulgar and meretricious will his product remain forever. *attractive in a flashy way*

Gilbert Murray has illustrated the two kinds of beauty

in writing by a happy similitude. There is a kind of beauty, he says, which comes from rich ornamentation; like the splendor one might admire on a Chinese junk, gorgeously gilded and painted, hung with rich embroideries and tapestries. Then there is the beauty of a modern yacht, where there is no ornamentation at all; our whole sensation of pleasure in watching a yacht under sail comes from the fact that every line of the craft is designed for one purpose, that everything about it furthers that purpose, so that it has an organic, living simplicity and directness. This, he says, is the beauty for which the Greek writers strove; it is certainly that for which Miss Jewett strove.

If I were asked to name three American books which have the possibility of a long, long life, I would say at once, "The Scarlet Letter," "Huckleberry Finn," and "The Country of the Pointed Firs." I can think of no others that confront time and change so serenely. The latter book seems to me fairly to shine with the reflection of its long, joyous future. It is so tightly yet so lightly built, so little encumbered with heavy materialism that deteriorates and grows old-fashioned. I like to think with what pleasure, with what a sense of rich discovery, the young student of American literature in far distant years to come will take up this book and say, "A masterpiece!" as proudly as if he himself had made it. It will be a message to the future, a message in a universal language, like the tuft of meadow flowers in Robert Frost's fine poem, which the mower abroad in the early morning left standing, just skirted by the scythe, for the mower of the afternoon to gaze upon and wonder at—the one message that even the scythe of Time spares.

Willa Cather

New York
February, 1925

THE COUNTRY OF
THE POINTED FIRS

1 *The Return* There was something about the coast town of Dunnet which made it seem more attractive than other maritime villages of eastern Maine. Perhaps it was the simple fact of acquaintance with that neighborhood which made it so attaching, and gave such interest to the rocky shore and dark woods, and the few houses which seemed to be securely wedged and tree-nailed in among the ledges by the Landing. These houses made the most of their seaward view, and there was a gayety and determined floweriness in their bits of garden ground; the small-paned high windows in the peaks of their steep gables were like knowing eyes that watched the harbor and the far sea-line beyond, or looked northward all along the shore and its background of spruces and balsam firs. When one really knows a village like this and its surroundings, it is like becoming acquainted with a single person. The process of falling in love at first sight is as final as it is swift in such a case, but the growth of true friendship may be a lifelong affair.

After a first brief visit made two or three summers before in the course of a yachting cruise, a lover of Dunnet Landing returned to find the unchanged shores of the pointed firs, the same quaintness of the village with its elaborate conventionalities; all that mixture of remoteness, and childish certainty of being the centre of civilization of which her affectionate dreams had told. One evening in June, a single passenger landed upon the steamboat wharf. The tide was high, there was a fine crowd of spectators, and the younger portion of the company followed her with subdued excitement up the narrow street of the salt-aired, white-clap-boarded little town.

2 *Mrs. Todd* Later, there was only one fault to find with this choice of a summer lodging-place, and that was

its complete lack of seclusion. At first the tiny house of
Mrs. Almira Todd, which stood with its end to the street,
appeared to be retired and sheltered enough from the busy
world, behind its bushy bit of a green garden, in which all
the blooming things, two or three gay hollyhocks and some
London-pride, were pushed back against the gray-shingled
wall. It was a queer little garden and puzzling to a stranger,
the few flowers being put at a disadvantage by so much
greenery; but the discovery was soon made that Mrs. Todd
was an ardent lover of herbs, both wild and tame, and the
sea-breezes blew into the low end-window of the house
laden with not only sweet-brier and sweet-mary, but balm
and sage and borage and mint, wormwood and southernwood. If Mrs. Todd had occasion to step into the far corner
of her herb plot, she trod heavily upon thyme, and made its
fragrant presence known with all the rest. Being a very large
person, her full skirts brushed and bent almost every slender
stalk that her feet missed. You could always tell when she
was stepping about there, even when you were half awake
in the morning, and learned to know, in the course of a
few weeks' experience, in exactly which corner of the garden
she might be.

At one side of this herb plot were other growths of a
rustic pharmacopœia, great treasures and rarities among
the commoner herbs. There were some strange and pungent odors that roused a dim sense and remembrance of
something in the forgotten past. Some of these might once
have belonged to sacred and mystic rites, and have had
some occult knowledge handed with them down the cen-
turies; but now they pertained only to humble compounds
brewed at intervals with molasses or vinegar or spirits in a
small caldron on Mrs. Todd's kitchen stove. They were dis-
pensed to suffering neighbors, who usually came at night as
if by stealth, bringing their own ancient-looking vials to
be filled. One nostrum was called the Indian remedy, and
its price was but fifteen cents; the whispered directions
could be heard as customers passed the windows. With most
remedies the purchaser was allowed to depart unadmon-
ished from the kitchen, Mrs. Todd being a wise saver of
steps; but with certain vials she gave cautions, standing in
the doorway, and there were other doses which had to be

accompanied on their healing way as far as the gate, while she muttered long chapters of directions, and kept up an air of secrecy and importance to the last. It may not have been only the common ails of humanity with which she tried to cope; it seemed sometimes as if love and hate and jealousy and adverse winds at sea might also find their proper remedies among the curious wild-looking plants in Mrs. Todd's garden.

The village doctor and this learned herbalist were upon the best of terms. The good man may have counted upon the unfavorable effect of certain potions which he should find his opportunity in counteracting; at any rate, he now and then stopped and exchanged greetings with Mrs. Todd over the picket fence. The conversation became at once professional after the briefest preliminaries, and he would stand twirling a sweet-scented sprig in his fingers, and make suggestive jokes, perhaps about her faith in a too persistent course of thoroughwort elixir, in which my landlady professed such firm belief as sometimes to endanger the life and usefulness of worthy neighbors.

To arrive at this quietest of seaside villages late in June, when the busy herb-gathering season was just beginning, was also to arrive in the early prime of Mrs. Todd's activity in the brewing of old-fashioned spruce beer. This cooling and refreshing drink had been brought to wonderful perfection through a long series of experiments; it had won immense local fame, and the supplies for its manufacture were always giving out and having to be replenished. For various reasons, the seclusion and uninterrupted days which had been looked forward to proved to be very rare in this otherwise delightful corner of the world. My hostess and I had made our shrewd business agreement on the basis of a simple cold luncheon at noon, and liberal restitution in the matter of hot suppers, to provide for which the lodger might sometimes be seen hurrying down the road, late in the day, with cunner line in hand. It was soon found that this arrangement made large allowance for Mrs. Todd's slow herb-gathering progresses through woods and pastures. The spruce-beer customers were pretty steady in hot weather, and there were many demands for different soothing syrups and elixirs with which the unwise curiosity of my early *be cannot that delayed.*

residence had made me acquainted. Knowing Mrs. Todd to be a widow, who had little beside this slender business and the income from one hungry lodger to maintain her, one's energies and even interest were quickly bestowed, until it became a matter of course that she should go afield every pleasant day, and that the lodger should answer all peremptory knocks at the side door.

In taking an occasional wisdom-giving stroll in Mrs. Todd's company, and in acting as business partner during her frequent absences, I found the July days fly fast, and it was not until I felt myself confronted with too great pride and pleasure in the display, one night, of two dollars and twenty-seven cents which I had taken in during the day, that I remembered a long piece of writing, sadly belated now, which I was bound to do. To have been patted kindly on the shoulder and called "darlin'," to have been offered a surprise of early mushrooms for supper, to have had all the glory of making two dollars and twenty-seven cents in a single day, and then to renounce it all and withdraw from these pleasant successes, needed much resolution. Literary employments are so vexed with uncertainties at best, and it was not until the voice of conscience sounded louder in my ears than the sea on the nearest pebble beach that I said unkind words of withdrawal to Mrs. Todd. She only became more wistfully affectionate than ever in her expressions, and looked as disappointed as I expected when I frankly told her that I could no longer enjoy the pleasure of what we called "seein' folks." I felt that I was cruel to a whole neighborhood in curtailing her liberty in this most important season for harvesting the different wild herbs that were so much counted upon to ease their winter ails.

"Well, dear," she said sorrowfully, "I've took great advantage o' your bein' here. I ain't had such a season for years, but I have never had nobody I could so trust. All you lack is a few qualities, but with time you'd gain judgment an' experience, an' be very able in the business. I'd stand right here an' say it to anybody."

Mrs. Todd and I were not separated or estranged by the change in our business relations; on the contrary, a deeper intimacy seemed to begin. I do not know what herb of the night it was that used sometimes to send out a penetrating odor late in the evening, after the dew had fallen, and the moon was high, and the cool air came up from the sea. Then Mrs. Todd would feel that she must talk to somebody, and I was only too glad to listen. We both fell under the spell, and she either stood outside the window, or made an errand to my sitting-room, and told, it might be very commonplace news of the day, or, as happened one misty summer night, all that lay deepest in her heart. It was in this way that I came to know that she had loved one who was far above her.

"No, dear, him I speak of could never think of me," she said. "When we was young together his mother didn't favor the match, an' done everything she could to part us; and folks thought we both married well, but 't wa'n't what either one of us wanted most; an' now we're left alone again, an' might have had each other all the time. He was above bein' a seafarin' man, an' prospered more than most; he come of a high family, an' my lot was plain an' hard-workin'. I ain't seen him for some years; he's forgot our youthful feelin's, I expect, but a woman's heart is different; them feelin's comes back when you think you've done with 'em, as sure as spring comes with the year. An' I've always had ways of hearin' about him."

She stood in the centre of a braided rug, and its rings of black and gray seemed to circle about her feet in the dim light. Her height and massiveness in the low room gave her the look of a huge sibyl, while the strange fragrance of the mysterious herb blew in from the little garden.

3 *The Schoolhouse* For some days after this, Mrs. Todd's customers came and went past my windows, and, haying-time being nearly over, strangers began to arrive from the inland country, such was her widespread reputation. Sometimes I saw a pale young creature like a white windflower left over into midsummer, upon whose face consumption had set its bright and wistful mark; but oftener two stout, hard-worked women from the farms came together, and detailed their symptoms to Mrs. Todd in loud and cheerful voices, combining the satisfactions of a friendly gossip with the medical opportunity. They seemed to give much from their own store of therapeutic learning. I became aware of the school in which my landlady had strengthened her natural gift; but hers was always the governing mind, and the final command, "Take of hy'sop one handful" (or whatever herb it was), was received in respectful silence. One afternoon, when I had listened,—it was impossible not to listen, with cottonless ears,—and then laughed and listened again, with an idle pen in my hand, during a particularly spirited and personal conversation, I reached for my hat, and, taking blotting-book and all under my arm, I resolutely fled further temptation, and walked out past the fragrant green garden and up the dusty road. The way went straight uphill, and presently I stopped and turned to look back.

The tide was in, the wide harbor was surrounded by its dark woods, and the small wooden houses stood as near as they could get to the landing. Mrs. Todd's was the last house on the way inland. The gray ledges of the rocky shore were well covered with sod in most places, and the pasture bayberry and wild roses grew thick among them. I could see the higher inland country and the scattered farms. On the brink of the hill stood a little white schoolhouse, much wind-blown and weather-beaten, which was a landmark to seagoing folk; from its door there was a most beautiful view of sea and shore. The summer vacation now prevailed, and after finding the door unfastened, and taking a long look through one of the seaward windows, and reflecting afterward for some time in a shady place near by among the bayberry bushes, I returned to the chief place of business in the village, and, to the amusement of two of the selectmen, brothers and autocrats of Dunnet Landing, I hired the schoolhouse for the rest of the vacation for fifty cents a week.

Selfish as it may appear, the retired situation seemed to possess great advantages, and I spent many days there quite undisturbed, with the sea-breeze blowing through the small, high windows and swaying the heavy outside shutters to and fro. I hung my hat and luncheon-basket on an entry nail as if I were a small scholar, but I sat at the teacher's desk as if I were that great authority, with all the timid empty

benches in rows before me. Now and then an idle sheep
came and stood for a long time looking in at the door. At
sundown I went back, feeling most businesslike, down toward the village again, and usually met the flavor, not of the
herb garden, but of Mrs. Todd's hot supper, halfway up
the hill. On the nights when there were evening meetings
or other public exercises that demanded her presence we
had tea very early, and I was welcomed back as if from a
long absence.

Once or twice I feigned excuses for staying at home,
while Mrs. Todd made distant excursions, and came home
late with both hands full and a heavily laden apron. This
was in pennyroyal time, and when the rare lobelia was in
its prime and the elecampane was coming on. One day she
appeared at the schoolhouse itself, partly out of amused
curiosity about my industries; but she explained that there
was no tansy in the neighborhood with such snap to it as
some that grew about the schoolhouse lot. Being scuffed
down all the spring made it grow so much the better, like
some folks that had it hard in their youth, and were bound
to make the most of themselves before they died.

4 At the Schoolhouse Window   One day I reached the
schoolhouse very late, owing to attendance upon the funeral of an acquaintance and neighbor, with whose sad
decline in health I had been familiar, and whose last days
both the doctor and Mrs. Todd had tried in vain to ease.
The services had taken place at one o'clock, and now, at
quarter past two, I stood at the schoolhouse window, looking down at the procession as it went along the lower road
close to the shore. It was a walking funeral, and even at
that distance I could recognize most of the mourners as
they went their solemn way. Mrs. Begg had been very much
respected, and there was a large company of friends following to her grave. She had been brought up on one of the
neighboring farms, and each of the few times that I had
seen her she professed great dissatisfaction with town life.
The people lived too close together for her liking, at the
Landing, and she could not get used to the constant sound
of the sea. She had lived to lament three seafaring hus-

bands, and her house was decorated with West Indian curiosities, specimens of conch shells and fine coral which they had brought home from their voyages in lumber-laden ships. Mrs. Todd had told me all our neighbor's history. They had been girls together, and, to use her own phrase, had "both seen trouble till they knew the best and worst on 't." I could see the sorrowful, large figure of Mrs. Todd as I stood at the window. She made a break in the procession by walking slowly and keeping the after-part of it back. She held a handkerchief to her eyes, and I knew, with a pang of sympathy, that hers was not affected grief.

Beside her, after much difficulty, I recognized the one strange and unrelated person in all the company, an old man who had always been mysterious to me. I could see his thin, bending figure. He wore a narrow, long-tailed coat and walked with a stick, and had the same "cant to leeward" as the wind-bent trees on the height above.

This was Captain Littlepage, whom I had seen only once or twice before, sitting pale and old behind a closed window; never out of doors until now. Mrs. Todd always shook her head gravely when I asked a question, and said that he wasn't what he had been once, and seemed to class him with her other secrets. He might have belonged with a simple which grew in a certain slug-haunted corner of the garden, whose use she could never be betrayed into telling me, though I saw her cutting the tops by moonlight once, as if it were a charm, and not a medicine, like the great fading bloodroot leaves.

I could see that she was trying to keep pace with the old captain's lighter steps. He looked like an aged grasshopper of some strange human variety. Behind this pair was a short, impatient, little person, who kept the captain's house, and gave it what Mrs. Todd and others believed to be no proper sort of care. She was usually called "that Mari' Harris" in subdued conversation between intimates, but they treated her with anxious civility when they met her face to face.

The bay-sheltered islands and the great sea beyond stretched away to the far horizon southward and eastward; the little procession in the foreground looked futile and helpless on the edge of the rocky shore. It was a glorious day early in July, with a clear, high sky; there were no clouds, there was no noise of the sea. The song sparrows sang and sang, as if with joyous knowledge of immortality, and contempt for those who could so pettily concern themselves with death. I stood watching until the funeral procession had crept round a shoulder of the slope below and disappeared from the great landscape as if it had gone into a cave.

An hour later I was busy at my work. Now and then a bee blundered in and took me for an enemy; but there was a useful stick upon the teacher's desk, and I rapped to call the bees to order as if they were unruly scholars, or waved them away from their riots over the ink, which I had bought at the Landing store, and discovered too late to be scented with bergamot, as if to refresh the labors of anxious scribes. One anxious scribe felt very dull that day; a sheep-bell tinkled near by, and called her wandering wits after it. The sentences failed to catch these lovely summer cadences. For the first time I began to wish for a companion and for news from the outer world, which had been, half unconsciously, forgotten. Watching the funeral gave one a sort of pain. I began to wonder if I ought not to have walked with the rest, instead of hurrying away at the end of the services. Perhaps the Sunday gown I had put on for the occasion was making this disastrous change of feeling, but I had now made myself and my friends remember that I did not really belong to Dunnet Landing.

I sighed, and turned to the half-written page again.

5 *Captain Littlepage* It was a long time after this; an hour was very long in that coast town where nothing stole away the shortest minute. I had lost myself completely in work, when I heard footsteps outside. There was a steep footpath between the upper and the lower road, which I climbed to shorten the way, as the children had taught me, but I believed that Mrs. Todd would find it inaccessible, unless she had occasion to seek me in great haste. I wrote on, feeling like a besieged miser of time, while the footsteps came nearer, and the sheep-bell tinkled away in haste as if some one had shaken a stick in its wearer's face. Then I looked, and saw Captain Littlepage passing the nearest window; the next moment he tapped politely at the door.

"Come in, sir," I said, rising to meet him; and he entered, bowing with much courtesy. I stepped down from the desk and offered him a chair by the window, where he seated himself at once, being sadly spent by his climb. I returned to my fixed seat behind the teacher's desk, which gave him the lower place of a scholar.

"You ought to have the place of honor, Captain Littlepage," I said.

"A happy, rural seat of various views,"

he quoted, as he gazed out into the sunshine and up the long wooded shore. Then he glanced at me, and looked all about him as pleased as a child.

"My quotation was from Paradise Lost: the greatest of poems, I suppose you know?" and I nodded. "There's nothing that ranks, to my mind, with Paradise Lost; it's all lofty, all lofty," he continued. "Shakespeare was a great poet; he copied life, but you have to put up with a great deal of low talk."

had been accused of plagiarism

I now remembered that Mrs. Todd had told me one day that Captain Littlepage had overset his mind with too much reading; she had also made dark reference to his having "spells" of some unexplainable nature. I could not help wondering what errand had brought him out in search of me. There was something quite charming in his appearance: it was a face thin and delicate with refinement, but worn into appealing lines, as if he had suffered from loneliness and misapprehension. He looked, with his careful precision of dress, as if he were the object of cherishing care on the part of elderly unmarried sisters, but I knew Mari' Harris to be a very commonplace, inelegant person, who would have no such standards; it was plain that the captain was his own attentive valet. He sat looking at me expectantly. I could not help thinking that, with his queer head and length of thinness, he was made to hop along the road of life rather than to walk. The captain was very grave indeed, and I bade my inward spirit keep close to discretion.

"Poor Mrs. Begg has gone," I ventured to say. I still wore my Sunday gown by way of showing respect.

"She has gone," said the captain,—"very easy at the last, I was informed; she slipped away as if she were glad of the opportunity."

I thought of the Countess of Carberry and felt that history repeated itself.

"She was one of the old stock," continued Captain Littlepage, with touching sincerity. "She was very much looked up to in this town, and will be missed."

I wondered, as I looked at him, if he had sprung from a line of ministers; he had the refinement of look and air of command which are the heritage of the old ecclesiastical families of New England. But as Darwin says in his autobiography, "there is no such king as a sea-captain; he is greater even than a king or a schoolmaster!"

Captain Littlepage moved his chair out of the wake of the sunshine, and still sat looking at me. I began to be very eager to know upon what errand he had come.

"It may be found out some o' these days," he said earnestly. "We may know it all, the next step; where Mrs. Begg is now, for instance. Certainty, not conjecture, is what we all desire."

"I suppose we shall know it all some day," said I.

"We shall know it while yet below," insisted the captain, with a flush of impatience on his thin cheeks. "We have not looked for truth in the right direction. I know what I speak of; those who have laughed at me little know how much reason my ideas are based upon." He waved his hand toward the village below. "In that handful of houses they fancy that they comprehend the universe."

I smiled, and waited for him to go on.

"I am an old man, as you can see," he continued, "and I have been a shipmaster the greater part of my life,—forty-three years in all. You may not think it, but I am above eighty years of age."

He did not look so old, and I hastened to say so.

"You must have left the sea a good many years ago, then, Captain Littlepage?" I said.

"I should have been serviceable at least five or six years more," he answered. "My acquaintance with certain—my experience upon a certain occasion, I might say, gave rise to prejudice. I do not mind telling you that I chanced to learn of one of the greatest discoveries that man has ever made."

Now we were approaching dangerous ground, but a sudden sense of his sufferings at the hands of the ignorant came to my help, and I asked to hear more with all the deference I really felt. A swallow flew into the schoolhouse at this moment as if a kingbird were after it, and beat itself against the walls for a minute, and escaped again to the open air; but Captain Littlepage took no notice whatever of the flurry.

"I had a valuable cargo of general merchandise from the London docks to Fort Churchill, a station of the old company on Hudson's Bay," said the captain earnestly. "We were delayed in lading, and baffled by head winds and a heavy tumbling sea all the way north-about and across. Then the fog kept us off the coast; and when I made port at last, it was too late to delay in those northern waters with such a vessel and such a crew as I had. They cared for nothing, and idled me into a fit of sickness; but my first mate was a good, excellent man, with no more idea of being frozen in there until spring than I had, so we made what speed we could to get clear of Hudson's Bay and off the coast. I owned an eighth of the vessel, and he owned a sixteenth of her. She was a full-rigged ship, called the Minerva, but she was getting old and leaky. I meant it should be my last v'y'ge in her, and so it proved. She had been an excellent vessel in her day. Of the cowards aboard her I can't say so much."

"Then you were wrecked?" I asked, as he made a long pause.

"I wa'n't caught astern o' the lighter by any fault of mine," said the captain gloomily. "We left Fort Churchill and run out into the Bay with a light pair o' heels; but I had been vexed to death with their red-tape rigging at the company's office, and chilled with stayin' on deck an' tryin' to hurry up things, and when we were well out o' sight o' land, headin' for Hudson's Straits, I had a bad turn o' some sort o' fever, and had to stay below. The days were getting short, and we made good runs, all well on board but me, and the crew done their work by dint of hard driving."

I began to find this unexpected narrative a little dull. Captain Littlepage spoke with a kind of slow correctness that lacked the longshore high flavor to which I had grown used; but I listened respectfully while he explained the winds having become contrary, and talked on in a dreary sort of way about his voyage, the bad weather, and the disadvantages he was under in the lightness of his ship, which bounced about like a chip in a bucket, and would not answer the rudder or properly respond to the most careful setting of sails.

"So there we were blowin' along anyways," he complained; but looking at me at this moment, and seeing that my thoughts were unkindly wandering, he ceased to speak.

"It was a hard life at sea in those days, I am sure," said I, with redoubled interest.

"It was a dog's life," said the poor old gentleman, quite reassured, "but it made men of those who followed it. I see a change for the worse even in our own town here; full of loafers now, small and poor as 't is, who once would have followed the sea, every lazy soul of 'em. There is no occupation so fit for just that class o' men who never get beyond the fo'cas'le. I view it, in addition, that a community narrows down and grows dreadful ignorant when it is shut up to its own affairs, and gets no knowledge of the outside world except from a cheap, unprincipled newspaper. In the old days, a good part o' the best men here knew a hundred ports and something of the way folks lived in them. They saw the world for themselves, and like's not their wives and children saw it with them. They may not have had the best of knowledge to carry with 'em sight-seein', but they were some acquainted with foreign lands an' their laws, an' could see outside the battle for town clerk here in Dunnet; they got some sense o' proportion. Yes, they lived more dignified, and their houses were better within an' without. Shipping's a terrible loss to this part o' New England from a social point o' view, ma'am."

"I have thought of that myself," I returned, with my interest quite awakened. "It accounts for the change in a great many things,—the sad disappearance of sea-captains, —doesn't it?"

"A shipmaster was apt to get the habit of reading," said my companion, brightening still more, and taking on a most touching air of unreserve. "A captain is not expected to be

familiar with his crew, and for company's sake in dull days
and nights he turns to his book. Most of us old shipmasters
came to know 'most everything about something; one would
take to readin' on farming topics, and some were great on
medicine,—but Lord help their poor crews!—or some were
all for history, and now and then there'd be one like me
that gave his time to the poets. I was well acquainted with a
shipmaster that was all for bees an' bee-keepin'; and if you
met him in port and went aboard, he'd sit and talk a terrible while about their havin' so much information, and
the money that could be made out of keepin' 'em. He was
one of the smartest captains that ever sailed the seas, but
they used to call the Newcastle, a great bark he commanded
for many years, Tuttle's beehive. There was old Cap'n
Jameson: he had notions of Solomon's Temple, and made a
very handsome little model of the same, right from the
Scripture measurements, same's other sailors make little
ships and design new tricks of rigging and all that. No,
there's nothing to take the place of shipping in a place like
ours. These bicycles offend me dreadfully; they don't afford
no real opportunities of experience such as a man gained on
a voyage. No: when folks left home in the old days they
left it to some purpose, and when they got home they
stayed there and had some pride in it. There's no large-
minded way of thinking now: the worst have got to be best
and rule everything; we're all turned upside down and going
back year by year."

"Oh no, Captain Littlepage, I hope not," said I, trying
to soothe his feelings.

There was a silence in the schoolhouse, but we could hear
the noise of the water on a beach below. It sounded like the
strange warning wave that gives notice of the turn of the
tide. A late golden robin, with the most joyful and eager
of voices, was singing close by in a thicket of wild roses.

6 *The Waiting Place* "How did you manage with the
rest of that rough voyage on the Minerva?" I asked.

"I shall be glad to explain to you," said Captain Littlepage, forgetting his grievances for the moment. "If I had a
map at hand I could explain better. We were driven to and

fro 'way up toward what we used to call Parry's Discoveries, and lost our bearings. It was thick and foggy, and at last I lost my ship; she drove on a rock, and we managed to get ashore on what I took to be a barren island, the few of us that were left alive. When she first struck, the sea was somewhat calmer than it had been, and most of the crew, against orders, manned the long-boat and put off in a hurry, and were never heard of more. Our own boat upset, but the carpenter kept himself and me above water, and we drifted in. I had no strength to call upon after my recent fever, and laid down to die; but he found the tracks of a man and dog the second day, and got along the shore to one of those far missionary stations that the Moravians support. They were very poor themselves, and in distress; 't was a useless place. There were but few Esquimaux left in that region. There we remained for some time, and I became acquainted with strange events."

The captain lifted his head and gave me a questioning glance. I could not help noticing that the dulled look in his eyes had gone, and there was instead a clear intentness that made them seem dark and piercing.

"There was a supply ship expected, and the pastor, an excellent Christian man, made no doubt that we should get passage in her. He was hoping that orders would come to break up the station; but everything was uncertain, and we got on the best we could for a while. We fished, and helped the people in other ways; there was no other way of paying our debts. I was taken to the pastor's house until I got better; but they were crowded, and I felt myself in the way, and made excuse to join with an old seaman, a Scotchman, who had built him a warm cabin, and had room in it for another. He was looked upon with regard, and had stood by the pastor in some troubles with the people. He had been on one of those English exploring parties that found one end of the road to the north pole, but never could find the other. We lived like dogs in a kennel, or so you'd thought if you had seen the hut from the outside; but the main thing was to keep warm; there were piles of birdskins to lie on, and he'd made him a good bunk, and there was another for me. 'T was dreadful dreary waitin' there; we begun to think the supply steamer was lost, and my poor ship broke up and strewed herself all along the shore. We got to watching on the headlands; my men and me knew the people were short of supplies and had to pinch themselves. It ought to read in the Bible, 'Man cannot live by fish alone,' if they'd told the truth of things; 'tain't bread that wears the worst on you! First part of the time, old Gaffett, that I lived with, seemed speechless, and I didn't know what to make of him, nor he of me, I dare say; but as we got acquainted, I found he'd been through more disasters than I had, and had troubles that wa'n't going to let him live a great while. It used to ease his mind to talk to an understanding person, so we used to sit and talk together all day, if it rained or blew so that we couldn't get out. I'd got a bad blow on the back of my head at the time we came ashore, and it pained me at times, and my strength was broken, anyway; I've never been so able since."

Captain Littlepage fell into a reverie.

"Then I had the good of my reading," he explained presently. "I had no books; the pastor spoke but little English, and all his books were foreign; but I used to say over all I could remember. The old poets little knew what comfort they could be to a man. I was well acquainted with the works of Milton, but up there it did seem to me as if Shakespeare was the king; he has his sea terms very accurate, and some beautiful passages were calming to the mind. I could say them over until I shed tears; there was nothing beautiful to me in that place but the stars above and those passages of verse.

"Gaffett was always brooding and brooding, and talking to himself; he was afraid he should never get away, and it preyed upon his mind. He thought when I got home I could interest the scientific men in his discovery: but they're all taken up with their own notions; some didn't even take pains to answer the letters I wrote. You observe that I said this crippled man Gaffett had been shipped on a voyage of discovery. I now tell you that the ship was lost on its return, and only Gaffett and two officers were saved off the Greenland coast, and he had knowledge later that those men never got back to England; the brig they shipped on was run down in the night. So no other living soul had the facts, and he gave them to me. There is a strange sort of a country 'way up north beyond the ice, and strange folks living in it. Gaffett believed it was the next world to this."

"What do you mean, Captain Littlepage?" I exclaimed. The old man was bending forward and whispering; he looked over his shoulder before he spoke the last sentence.

"To hear old Gaffett tell about it was something awful," he said, going on with his story quite steadily after the moment of excitement had passed. " 'T was first a tale of dogs and sledges, and cold and wind and snow. Then they begun to find the ice grow rotten; they had been frozen in, and got into a current flowing north, far up beyond Fox Channel, and they took to their boats when the ship got crushed, and this warm current took them out of sight of the ice, and into a great open sea; and they still followed it due north, just the very way they had planned to go. Then they struck a coast that wasn't laid down or charted, but the cliffs were such that no boat could land until they found a bay and struck across under sail to the other side where the shore looked lower; they were scant of provisions and out of water, but they got sight of something that looked like a great town. 'For God's sake, Gaffett!' said I, the first time he told me. 'You don't mean a town two degrees farther north than ships had ever been?' for he'd got their course marked on an old chart that he'd pieced out at the top; but he insisted upon it, and told it over and over again, to be sure I had it straight to carry to those who would be interested. There was no snow and ice, he said, after they had sailed some days with that warm current, which seemed to come right from under the ice that they'd been pinched up in and had been crossing on foot for weeks."

"But what about the town?" I asked. "Did they get to the town?"

"They did," said the captain, "and found inhabitants; 't was an awful condition of things. It appeared, as near as Gaffett could express it, like a place where there was neither living nor dead. They could see the place when they were approaching it by sea pretty near like any town, and thick with habitations; but all at once they lost sight of it altogether, and when they got close inshore they could see the shapes of folks, but they never could get near them,—all

blowing gray figures that would pass along alone, or sometimes gathered in companies as if they were watching. The
men were frightened at first, but the shapes never came
near them,—it was as if they blew back; and at last they all
got bold and went ashore, and found birds' eggs and sea
fowl, like any wild northern spot where creatures were
tame and folks had never been, and there was good water.
Gaffett said that he and another man came near one o' the
fog-shaped men that was going along slow with the look of
a pack on his back, among the rocks, an' they chased him;
but, Lord! he flittered away out o' sight like a leaf the wind
takes with it, or a piece of cobweb. They would make as if
they talked together, but there was no sound of voices,
and 'they acted as if they didn't see us, but only felt us
coming towards them,' says Gaffett one day, trying to tell
the particulars. They couldn't see the town when they were
ashore. One day the captain and the doctor were gone till
night up across the high land where the town had seemed
to be, and they came back at night beat out and white as
ashes, and wrote and wrote all next day in their notebooks,
and whispered together full of excitement, and they were
sharp-spoken with the men when they offered to ask any
questions.

"Then there came a day," said Captain Littlepage,
leaning toward me with a strange look in his eyes, and
whispering quickly. "The men all swore they wouldn't stay
any longer; the man on watch early in the morning gave the
alarm, and they all put off in the boat and got a little way
out to sea. Those folks, or whatever they were, come about
'em like bats; all at once they raised incessant armies, and
come as if to drive 'em back to sea. They stood thick at the
edge o' the water like the ridges o' grim war; no thought o'
flight, none of retreat. Sometimes a standing fight, then
soaring on main wing tormented all the air. And when
they'd got the boat out o 'reach o' danger, Gaffet said they
looked back, and there was the town again, standing up just
as they'd seen it first, comin' on the coast. Say what you
might, they all believed 't was a kind of waiting-place between this world an' the next."

The captain had sprung to his feet in his excitement, and
made excited gestures, but he still whispered huskily.

"Sit down, sir," I said as quietly as I could, and he sank into his chair quite spent.

"Gaffett thought the officers were hurrying home to report and to fit out a new expedition when they were all lost. At the time, the men got orders not to talk over what they had seen," the old man explained presently in a more natural tone.

"Weren't they all starving, and wasn't it a mirage or something of that sort?" I ventured to ask. But he looked at me blankly.

"Gaffett had got so that his mind ran on nothing else," he went on. "The ship's surgeon let fall an opinion to the captain, one day, that 't was some condition o' the light and the magnetic currents that let them see those folks. 'T wa'n't a right-feeling part of the world, anyway; they had to battle with the compass to make it serve, an' everything seemed to go wrong. Gaffett had worked it out in his own mind that they was all common ghosts, but the conditions were unusual favorable for seeing them. He was always talking about the Ge'graphical Society, but he never took proper steps, as I view it now, and stayed right there at the mission. He was a good deal crippled, and thought they'd confine him in some jail of a hospital. He said he was waiting to find the right men to tell, somebody bound north. Once in a while they stopped there to leave a mail or something. He was set in his notions, and let two or three proper explorin' expeditions go by him because he didn't like their looks; but when I was there he had got restless, fearin' he might be taken away or something. He had all his directions written out straight as a string to give the right ones. I wanted him to trust 'em to me, so I might have something to show, but he wouldn't. I suppose he's dead now. I wrote to him, an' I done all I could. 'T will be a great exploit some o' these days."

I assented absent-mindedly, thinking more just then of my companion's alert, determined look and the seafaring, ready aspect that had come to his face; but at this moment there fell a sudden change, and the old, pathetic, scholarly look returned. Behind me hung a map of North America, and I saw, as I turned a little, that his eyes were fixed upon

the northernmost regions and their careful recent outlines
with a look of bewilderment.

7 *The Outer Island* Gaffett with his good bunk and the
birdskins, the story of the wreck of the Minerva, the hu-
man-shaped creatures of fog and cobweb, the great words of
Milton with which he described their onslaught upon the
crew, all this moving tale had such an air of truth that I
could not argue with Captain Littlepage. The old man
looked away from the map as if it had vaguely troubled him,
and regarded me appealingly.

"We were just speaking of"—and he stopped. I saw that
he had suddenly forgotten his subject.

"There were a great many persons at the funeral," I
hastened to say.

"Oh yes," the captain answered, with satisfaction. "All
showed respect who could. The sad circumstances had for
a moment slipped my mind. Yes, Mrs. Begg will be very
much missed. She was a capital manager for her husband
when he was at sea. Oh yes, shipping is a very great loss."
And he sighed heavily. "There was hardly a man of any
standing who didn't interest himself in some way in navi-
gation. It always gave credit to a town. I call it low-water
mark now here in Dunnet."

He rose with dignity to take leave, and asked me to stop
at his house some day, when he would show me some outlandish things that he had brought home from sea. I was
familiar with the subject of the decadence of shipping interests in all its affecting branches, having been already
some time in Dunnet, and I felt sure that Captain Littlepage's mind had now returned to a safe level.

As we came down the hill toward the village our ways
divided, and when I had seen the old captain well started
on a smooth piece of sidewalk which would lead him to
his own door, we parted, the best of friends. "Step in some
afternoon," he said, as affectionately as if I were a fellow-
shipmaster wrecked on the lee shore of age like himself. I
turned toward home, and presently met Mrs. Todd coming
toward me with an anxious expression.

"I see you sleevin' the old gentleman down the hill," she suggested.

"Yes. I've had a very interesting afternoon with him," I answered; and her face brightened.

"Oh, then he's all right. I was afraid 't was one o' his flighty spells, an' Mari' Harris wouldn't"—

"Yes," I returned, smiling, "he has been telling me some old stories, but we talked about Mrs. Begg and the funeral beside, and Paradise Lost."

"I expect he got tellin' of you some o' his great narratives," she answered, looking at me shrewdly. "Funerals always sets him goin'. Some o' them tales hangs together toler'ble well," she added, with a sharper look than before. "An' he's been a great reader all his seafarin' days. Some thinks he overdid, and affected his head, but for a man o' his years he's amazin' now when he's at his best. Oh, he used to be a beautiful man!"

We were standing where there was a fine view of the harbor and its long stretches of shore all covered by the great army of the pointed firs, darkly cloaked and standing as if they waited to embark. As we looked far seaward among the outer islands, the trees seemed to march seaward still, going steadily over the heights and down to the water's edge.

It had been growing gray and cloudy, like the first evening of autumn, and a shadow had fallen on the darkening shore. Suddenly, as we looked, a gleam of golden sunshine struck the outer islands, and one of them shone out clear in the light, and revealed itself in a compelling way to our eyes. Mrs. Todd was looking off across the bay with a face full of affection and interest. The sunburst upon that outermost island made it seem like a sudden revelation of the world beyond this which some believe to be so near.

"That's where mother lives," said Mrs. Todd. "Can't we see it plain? I was brought up out there on Green Island. I know every rock an' bush on it."

"Your mother!" I exclaimed, with great interest.

"Yes, dear, cert'in; I've got her yet, old's I be. She's one of them spry, light-footed little women; always was, an'

light-hearted, too," answered Mrs. Todd, with satisfaction.
"She's seen all the trouble folks can see, without it's her
last sickness; an' she's got a word of courage for everybody.
Life ain't spoilt her a mite. She's eighty-six an' I'm sixty-
seven, and I've seen the time I've felt a good sight the
oldest. 'Land sakes alive!' says she, last time I was out to see
her. 'How you do lurch about steppin' into a bo't!' I laughed
so I liked to have gone right over into the water; an' we
pushed off, an' left her laughin' there on the shore."

The light had faded as we watched. Mrs. Todd had
mounted a gray rock, and stood there grand and architec-
tural, like a *caryatide*. Presently she stepped down, and we
continued our way homeward.

"You an' me, we'll take a bo't an' go out some day and
see mother," she promised me. "'T would please her very
much, an' there's one or two sca'ce herbs grows better on
the island than anywheres else. I ain't seen their like no-
wheres here on the main.

"Now I'm goin' right down to get us each a mug o' my
beer," she announced as we entered the house, "an' I believe I'll sneak in a little mite o' camomile. Goin' to the funeral an' all, I feel to have had a very wearin' afternoon."

I heard her going down into the cool little cellar, and then
there was considerable delay. When she returned, mug in
hand, I noticed the taste of camomile, in spite of my protest; but its flavor was disguised by some other herb that I
did not know, and she stood over me until I drank it all
and said that I liked it.

"I don't give that to everybody," said Mrs. Todd kindly;
and I felt for a moment as if it were part of a spell and in-
cantation, and as if my enchantress would now begin to
look like the cobweb shapes of the arctic town. Nothing
happened but a quiet evening and some delightful plans
that we made about going to Green Island, and on the
morrow there was the clear sunshine and blue sky of
another day.

8 *Green Island* One morning, very early, I heard Mrs.
Todd in the garden outside my window. By the unusual
loudness of her remarks to a passer-by, and the notes of a

familiar hymn which she sang as she worked among the
herbs, and which came as if directed purposely to the sleepy
ears of my consciousness, I knew that she wished I would
wake up and come and speak to her.

In a few minutes she responded to a morning voice from
behind the blinds. "I expect you're goin' up to your schoolhouse to pass all this pleasant day; yes, I expect you're goin'
to be dreadful busy," she said despairingly.

"Perhaps not," said I. "Why, what's going to be the
matter with you, Mrs. Todd?" For I supposed that she was
tempted by the fine weather to take one of her favorite
expeditions along the shore pastures to gather herbs and
simples, and would like to have me keep the house.

"No, I don't want to go nowhere by land," she answered
gayly,—"no, not by land; but I don't know's we shall have
a better day all the rest of the summer to go out to Green
Island an' see mother. I waked up early thinkin' of her.
The wind's light northeast,—'t will take us right straight
out; an' this time o' year it's liable to change round southwest an' fetch us home pretty, 'long late in the afternoon.
Yes, it's goin' to be a good day."

"Speak to the captain and the Bowden boy, if you see
anybody going by toward the landing," said I. "We'll take
the big boat."

"Oh, my sakes! now you let me do things my way," said
Mrs. Todd scornfully. "No, dear, we won't take no big
bo't. I'll just git a handy dory, an' Johnny Bowden an'
me, we'll man her ourselves. I don't want no abler bo't
than a good dory, an' a nice light breeze ain't goin' to make
no sea; an' Johnny's my cousin's son,—mother'll like to have
him come; an' he'll be down to the herrin' weirs all the
time we're there, anyway; we don't want to carry no men
folks havin' to be considered every minute an' takin' up all
our time. No, you let me do; we'll just slip out an' see
mother by ourselves. I guess what breakfast you'll want's
about ready now."

I had become well acquainted with Mrs. Todd as landlady, herb-gatherer, and rustic philosopher; we had been
discreet fellow-passengers once or twice when I had sailed
up the coast to a larger town than Dunnet Landing to do
some shopping; but I was yet to become acquainted with

her as a mariner. An hour later we pushed off from the
landing in the desired dory. The tide was just on the turn,
beginning to fall, and several friends and acquaintances
stood along the side of the dilapidated wharf and cheered us
by their words and evident interest. Johnny Bowden and
I were both rowing in haste to get out where we could catch
the breeze and put up the small sail which lay clumsily
furled along the gunwale. Mrs. Todd sat aft, a stern and
unbending lawgiver.

"You better let her drift; we'll get there 'bout as quick;
the tide 'll take her right out from under these old buildin's;
there's plenty wind outside."

"Your bo't ain't trimmed proper, Mis' Todd!" exclaimed
a voice from shore. "You're lo'ded so the bo't'll drag; you
can't git her before the wind, ma'am. You set 'midships,
Mis' Todd, an' let the boy hold the sheet 'n' steer after he
gits the sail up; you won't never git out to Green Island
that way. She's lo'ded bad, your bo't is,—she's heavy behind 's she is now!"

Mrs. Todd turned with some difficulty and regarded the
anxious adviser, my right oar flew out of water, and we
seemed about to capsize. "That you, Asa? Good-mornin',"
she said politely. "I al'ays liked the starn seat best. When'd
you git back from up country?"

This allusion to Asa's origin was not lost upon the rest of
the company. We were some little distance from shore, but
we could hear a chuckle of laughter, and Asa, a person
who was too ready with his criticism and advice on every
possible subject, turned and walked indignantly away.

When we caught the wind we were soon on our seaward
course, and only stopped to underrun a trawl, for the floats
of which Mrs. Todd looked earnestly, explaining that her
mother might not be prepared for three extra to dinner;
it was her brother's trawl, and she meant to just run her
eye along for the right sort of a little haddock. I leaned over
the boat's side with great interest and excitement, while she
skillfully handled the long line of hooks, and made scornful remarks upon worthless, bait-consuming creatures of
the sea as she reviewed them and left them on the trawl or
shook them off into the waves. At last we came to what she

pronounced a proper haddock, and having taken him on board and ended his life resolutely, we went our way.

As we sailed along I listened to an increasingly delightful commentary upon the islands, some of them barren rocks, or at best giving sparse pasturage for sheep in the early summer. On one of these an eager little flock ran to the water's edge and bleated at us so affectingly that I would willingly have stopped; but Mrs. Todd steered away from the rocks, and scolded at the sheep's mean owner, an acquaintance of hers, who grudged the little salt and still less care which the patient creatures needed. The hot midsummer sun makes prisons of these small islands that are a paradise in early June, with their cool springs and short thick-growing grass. On a larger island, farther out to sea, my entertaining companion showed me with glee the small houses of two farmers who shared the island between them, and declared that for three generations the people had not spoken to each other even in times of sickness or death or birth. "When the news come that the war was over, one of 'em knew it a week, and never stepped across his wall to tell the others," she said. "There, they enjoy it: they've got to have somethin' to interest 'em in such a place; 't is a good deal more tryin' to be tied to folks you don't like than 't is to be alone. Each of 'em tells the neighbors their wrongs; plenty likes to hear and tell again; them as fetch a bone 'll carry one, an' so they keep the fight a-goin'. I must say I like variety myself; some folks washes Monday an' irons Tuesday the whole year round, even if the circus is goin' by!"

A long time before we landed at Green Island we could see the small white house, standing high like a beacon, where Mrs. Todd was born and where her mother lived, on a green slope above the water, with dark spruce woods still higher. There were crops in the fields, which we presently distinguished from one another. Mrs. Todd examined them while we were still far at sea. "Mother's late potatoes looks backward; ain't had rain enough so far," she pronounced her opinion. "They look weedier than what they call Front Street down to Cowper Centre. I expect brother William is so occupied with his herrin' weirs an' servin' out bait to the schooners that he don't think once a day of the land."

"What's the flag for, up above the spruces there behind the house?" I inquired, with eagerness.

"Oh, that's the sign for herrin'," she explained kindly, while Johnny Bowden regarded me with contemptuous surprise. "When they get enough for schooners they raise that flag; an' when 't is a poor catch in the weir pocket they just fly a little signal down by the shore, an' then the small bo'ts comes and get enough an' over for their trawls. There, look! there she is: mother sees us; she's wavin' somethin' out o' the fore door! She'll be to the landin'-place quick's we are."

I looked, and could see a tiny flutter in the doorway, but a quicker signal had made its way from the heart on shore to the heart on the sea.

"How do you suppose she knows it's me?" said Mrs. Todd, with a tender smile on her broad face. "There, you never get over bein' a child long's you have a mother to go to. Look at the chimney, now; she's gone right in an' brightened up the fire. Well, there, I'm glad mother's well; you'll enjoy seein' her very much."

Mrs. Todd leaned back into her proper position, and the boat trimmed again. She took a firmer grasp of the sheet, and gave an impatient look up at the gaff and the leech of the little sail, and twitched the sheet as if she urged the wind like a horse. There came at once a fresh gust, and we seemed to have doubled our speed. Soon we were near enough to see a tiny figure with handkerchiefed head come down across the field and stand waiting for us at the cove above a curve of pebble beach.

Presently the dory grated on the pebbles, and Johnny Bowden, who had been kept in abeyance during the voyage, sprang out and used manful exertions to haul us up with the next wave, so that Mrs. Todd could make a dry landing.

"You done that very well," she said, mounting to her feet, and coming ashore somewhat stiffly, but with great dignity, refusing our outstretched hands, and returning to possess herself of a bag which had lain at her feet.

"Well, mother, here I be!" she announced with indifference; but they stood and beamed in each other's faces.

"Lookin' pretty well for an old lady, ain't she?" said Mrs. Todd's mother, turning away from her daughter to speak to me. She was a delightful little person herself, with bright eyes and an affectionate air of expectation like a child on a holiday. You felt as if Mrs. Blackett were an old and dear friend before you let go her cordial hand. We all started together up the hill.

"Now don't you haste too fast, mother," said Mrs. Todd warningly; "'t is a far reach o' risin' ground to the fore door, and you won't set an' get your breath when you're once there, but go trotting about. Now don't you go a mite faster than we proceed with this bag an' basket. Johnny, there, 'll fetch up the haddock. I just made one stop to underrun William's trawl till I come to jes' such a fish 's I thought you'd want to make one o' your nice chowders of. I've brought an onion with me that was layin' about on the window-sill at home."

"That's just what I was wantin'," said the hostess. "I give a sigh when you spoke o' chowder, knowin' my onions was out. William forgot to replenish us last time he was to the Landin'. Don't you haste so yourself, Almiry, up this risin' ground. I hear you commencin' to wheeze a'ready."

This mild revenge seemed to afford great pleasure to both giver and receiver. They laughed a little, and looked at each other affectionately, and then at me. Mrs. Todd considerately paused, and faced about to regard the wide sea view. I was glad to stop, being more out of breath than either of my companions, and I prolonged the halt by asking the names of the neighboring islands. There was a fine breeze blowing, which we felt more there on the high land than when we were running before it in the dory.

"Why, this ain't that kitten I saw when I was out last, the one that I said didn't appear likely?" exclaimed Mrs. Todd as we went our way.

"That's the one, Almiry," said her mother. "She always had a likely look to me, an' she's right after her business. I never see such a mouser for one of her age. If 't wan't for William, I never should have housed that other dronin' old thing so long; but he sets by her on account of her havin' a bob tail. I don't deem it advisable to maintain cats just on account of their havin' bob tails; they're like all other

curiosities, good for them that wants to see 'em twice.
This kitten catches mice for both, an' keeps me respectable
as I ain't been for a year. She's a real understandin' little
help, this kitten is. I picked her from among five Miss
Augusta Pennell had over to Burnt Island," said the old
woman, trudging along with the kitten close at her skirts.
"Augusta, she says to me, 'Why, Mis' Blackett, you've took
the homeliest;' an' says I, 'I've got the smartest; I'm satisfied.' "

"I'd trust nobody sooner'n you to pick out a kitten,
mother," said the daughter handsomely, and we went on in
peace and harmony.

The house was just before us now, on a green level that
looked as if a huge hand had scooped it out of the long
green field we had been ascending. A little way above, the
dark spruce woods began to climb the top of the hill and
cover the seaward slopes of the island. There was just room
for the small farm and the forest; we looked down at the
fish-house and its rough sheds, and the weirs stretching far
out into the water. As we looked upward, the tops of the
firs came sharp against the blue sky. There was a great
stretch of rough pasture-land round the shoulder of the island to the eastward, and here were all the thick-scattered
gray rocks that kept their places, and the gray backs of many
sheep that forever wandered and fed on the thin sweet
pasturage that fringed the ledges and made soft hollows
and strips of green turf like growing velvet. I could see the
rich green of bayberry bushes here and there, where the
rocks made room. The air was very sweet; one could not
help wishing to be a citizen of such a complete and tiny
continent and home of fisherfolk.

The house was broad and clean, with a roof that looked
heavy on its low walls. It was one of the houses that seem
firm-rooted in the ground, as if they were two-thirds below
the surface, like icebergs. The front door stood hospitably
open in expectation of company, and an orderly vine grew
at each side; but our path led to the kitchen door at the
house-end, and there grew a mass of gay flowers and greenery, as if they had been swept together by some diligent
garden broom into a tangled heap: there were portulacas all
along under the lower step and straggling off into the grass,

and clustering mallows that crept as near as they dared, like poor relations. I saw the bright eyes and brainless little heads of two half-grown chickens who were snuggled down among the mallows as if they had been chased away from the door more than once, and expected to be again.

"It seems kind o' formal comin' in this way," said Mrs. Todd impulsively, as we passed the flowers and came to the front doorstep; but she was mindful of the proprieties, and walked before us into the best room on the left.

"Why, mother, if you haven't gone an' turned the carpet!" she exclaimed, with something in her voice that spoke of awe and admiration. "When'd you get to it? I s'pose Mis' Addicks come over an' helped you, from White Island Landing?"

"No, she didn't," answered the old woman, standing proudly erect, and making the most of a great moment. "I done it all myself with William's help. He had a spare day, an' took right holt with me; an' 't was all well beat on the grass, an' turned, an' put down again afore we went to bed. I ripped an' sewed over two o' them long breadths. I ain't had such a good night's sleep for two years."

"There, what do you think o' havin' such a mother as that for eighty-six year old?" said Mrs. Todd, standing before us like a large figure of Victory.

As for the mother, she took on a sudden look of youth; you felt as if she promised a great future, and was beginning, not ending, her summers and their happy toils.

"My, my!" exclaimed Mrs. Todd. "I couldn't ha' done it myself, I've got to own it."

"I was much pleased to have it off my mind," said Mrs. Blackett, humbly; "the more so because along at the first of the next week I wasn't very well. I suppose it may have been the change of weather."

Mrs. Todd could not resist a significant glance at me, but, with charming sympathy, she forbore to point the lesson or to connect this illness with its apparent cause. She loomed larger than ever in the little old-fashioned best room, with its few pieces of good furniture and pictures of national interest. The green paper curtains were stamped with conventional landscapes of a foreign order,—castles on inaccessible crags, and lovely lakes with steep wooded shores;

under-foot the treasured carpet was covered thick with home-made rugs. There were empty glass lamps and crystallized bouquets of grass and some fine shells on the narrow mantelpiece.

"I was married in this room," said Mrs. Todd unexpectedly; and I heard her give a sigh after she had spoken, as if she could not help the touch of regret that would forever come with all her thoughts of happiness.

"We stood right there between the windows," she added, "and the minister stood here. William wouldn't come in. He was always odd about seein' folks, just 's he is now. I run to meet 'em from a child, an' William, he'd take an' run away."

"I've been the gainer," said the old mother cheerfully. "William has been son an' daughter both since you was married off the island. He's been 'most too satisfied to stop at home 'long o' his old mother, but I always tell 'em I'm the gainer."

We were all moving toward the kitchen as if by common instinct. The best room was too suggestive of serious occasions, and the shades were all pulled down to shut out the summer light and air. It was indeed a tribute to Society to find a room set apart for her behests out there on so apparently neighborless and remote an island. Afternoon visits and evening festivals must be few in such a bleak situation at certain seasons of the year, but Mrs. Blackett was of those who do not live to themselves, and who have long since passed the line that divides mere self-concern from a valued share in whatever Society can give and take. There were those of her neighbors who never had taken the trouble to furnish a best room, but Mrs. Blackett was one who knew the uses of a parlor.

"Yes, do come right out into the old kitchen; I shan't make any stranger of you," she invited us pleasantly, after we had been properly received in the room appointed to formality. "I expect Almiry, here, 'll be driftin' out 'mongst the pasture-weeds quick's she can find a good excuse. 'T is hot now. You'd better content yourselves till you get nice an' rested, an' 'long after dinner the sea-breeze'll spring up, an' then you can take your walks, an' go up an' see the prospect from the big ledge. Almiry'll want to show off everything there is. Then I'll get you a good cup o' tea before you start to go home. The days are plenty long now."

While we were talking in the best room the selected fish had been mysteriously brought up from the shore, and lay all cleaned and ready in an earthen crock on the table.

"I think William might have just stopped an' said a word," remarked Mrs. Todd, pouting with high affront as she caught sight of it. "He's friendly enough when he comes ashore, an' was remarkable social the last time, for him."

"He ain't disposed to be very social with the ladies," explained William's mother, with a delightful glance at me, as if she counted upon my friendship and tolerance. "He's very particular, and he's all in his old fishin'-clothes to-day. He'll want me to tell him everything you said and done, after you've gone. William has very deep affections. He'll want to see you, Almiry. Yes, I guess he'll be in by an' by."

"I'll search for him by 'n' by, if he don't," proclaimed Mrs. Todd, with an air of unalterable resolution. "I know all of his burrows down 'long the shore. I'll catch him by hand 'fore he knows it. I've got some business with William, anyway. I brought forty-two cents with me that was due him for them last lobsters he brought in."

"You can leave it with me," suggested the little old mother, who was already stepping about among her pots and pans in the pantry, and preparing to make the chowder.

I became possessed of a sudden unwonted curiosity in regard to William, and felt that half the pleasure of my visit would be lost if I could not make his interesting acquaintance.

9 *William*   Mrs. Todd had taken the onion out of her basket and laid it down upon the kitchen table. "There's Johnny Bowden come with us, you know," she reminded her mother. "He'll be hungry enough to eat his size."

"I've got new doughnuts, dear," said the little old lady. "You don't often catch William 'n' me out o' provisions. I expect you might have chose a somewhat larger fish, but I'll try an' make it do. I shall have to have a few extra potatoes, but there's a field full out there, an' the hoe's leanin' against the well-house, in 'mongst the climbin'-beans." She smiled, and gave her daughter a commanding nod.

"Land sakes alive! Le' 's blow the horn for William," insisted Mrs. Todd, with some excitement. "He needn't break his spirit so far's to come in. He'll know you need him for something particular, an' then we can call to him as he comes up the path. I won't put him to no pain."

Mrs. Blackett's old face, for the first time, wore a look of trouble, and I found it necessary to counteract the teasing spirit of Almira. It was too pleasant to stay indoors altogether, even in such rewarding companionship; besides, I might meet William; and, straying out presently, I found the hoe by the well-house and an old splint basket at the woodshed door, and also found my way down to the field where there was a great square patch of rough, weedy potato-tops and tall ragweed. One corner was already dug, and I chose a fat-looking hill where the tops were well withered. There is all the pleasure that one can have in gold-digging in finding one's hopes satisfied in the riches of a good hill of potatoes. I longed to go on; but it did not seem frugal to dig any longer after my basket was full, and at last I took my hoe by the middle and lifted the basket to go back up the hill. I was sure that Mrs. Blackett must be waiting impatiently to slice the potatoes into the chowder, layer after layer, with the fish.

"You let me take holt o' that basket, ma'am," said a pleasant, anxious voice behind me.

I turned, startled in the silence of the wide field, and saw an elderly man, bent in the shoulders as fishermen often are, gray-headed and clean-shaven, and with a timid air. It was William. He looked just like his mother, and I had been imagining that he was large and stout like his sister, Almira Todd; and, strange to say, my fancy had led me to picture him not far from thirty and a little loutish. It was necessary instead to pay William the respect due to age.

I accustomed myself to plain facts on the instant, and we said good-morning like old friends. The basket was really heavy, and I put the hoe through its handle and offered him one end; then we moved easily toward the house together, speaking of the fine weather and of mackerel which were

reported to be striking in all about the bay. William had
been out since three o'clock, and had taken an extra fare of
fish. I could feel that Mrs. Todd's eyes were upon us as we
approached the house, and although I fell behind in the
narrow path, and let William take the basket alone and
precede me at some little distance the rest of the way, I
could plainly hear her greet him.

"Got round to comin' in, didn't you?" she inquired, with
amusement. "Well, now, that's clever. Didn't know 's I
should see you to-day, William, an' I wanted to settle an
account."

I felt somewhat disturbed and responsible, but when I
joined them they were on most simple and friendly terms.
It became evident that, with William, it was the first step
that cost, and that, having once joined in social interests,
he was able to pursue them with more or less pleasure. He
was about sixty, and not young-looking for his years, yet so
undying is the spirit of youth, and bashfulness has such a
power of survival, that I felt all the time as if one must
try to make the occasion easy for some one who was young
and new to the affairs of social life. He asked politely if I
would like to go up to the great ledge while dinner was getting ready; so, not without a deep sense of pleasure, and a
delighted look of surprise from the two hostesses, we started,
William and I, as if both of us felt much younger than we
looked. Such was the innocence and simplicity of the moment that when I heard Mrs. Todd laughing behind us in
the kitchen I laughed too, but William did not even blush.
I think he was a little deaf, and he stepped along before me
most businesslike and intent upon his errand.

We went from the upper edge of the field above the
house into a smooth, brown path among the dark spruces.
The hot sun brought out the fragrance of the pitchy bark,
and the shade was pleasant as we climbed the hill. William
stopped once or twice to show me a great wasps'-nest close
by, or some fishhawks'-nests below in a bit of swamp. He
picked a few sprigs of late-blooming linnæa as we came out
upon an open bit of pasture at the top of the island, and
gave them to me without speaking, but he knew as well
as I that one could not say half he wished about linnæa.
Through this piece of rough pasture ran a huge shape of

stone like the great backbone of an enormous creature. At the end, near the woods, we could climb up on it and walk along to the highest point; there above the circle of pointed firs we could look down over all the island, and could see the ocean that circled this and a hundred other bits of island-ground, the mainland shore and all the far horizons. It gave a sudden sense of space, for nothing stopped the eye or hedged one in,—that sense of liberty in space and time which great prospects always give.

"There ain't no such view in the world, I expect," said William proudly, and I hastened to speak my heartfelt tribute of praise: it was impossible not to feel as if an untraveled boy had spoken, and yet one loved to have him value his native heath. ~ *open woodland*

10 *Where Pennyroyal Grew* We were a little late to dinner, but Mrs. Blackett and Mrs. Todd were lenient, and we all took our places after William had paused to wash his hands, like a pious Brahmin, at the well, and put on a neat blue coat which he took from a peg behind the kitchen door. Then he resolutely asked a blessing in words that I could not hear, and we ate the chowder and were thankful. The kitten went round and round the table, quite erect, and, holding on by her fierce young claws, she stopped to mew with pathos at each elbow, or darted off to the open door when a song sparrow forgot himself and lit in the grass too near. William did not talk much, but his sister Todd occupied the time and told all the news there was to tell of Dunnet Landing and its coasts, while the old mother listened with delight. Her hospitality was something exquisite; she had the gift which so many women lack, of being able to make themselves and their houses belong entirely to a guest's pleasure,—that charming surrender for the moment of themselves and whatever belongs to them, so that they make a part of one's own life that can never be forgotten. Tact is after all a kind of mind-reading, and my hostess held the golden gift. Sympathy is of the mind as well as the heart, and Mrs. Blackett's world and mine were one from the moment we met. Besides, she had that final, that highest gift of heaven, a perfect self-forget-

fulness. Sometimes, as I watched her eager, sweet old face,
I wondered why she had been set to shine on this lonely island of the northern coast. It must have been to keep the
balance true, and make up to all her scattered and depend-
ing neighbors for other things which they may have lacked.

When we had finished clearing away the old blue plates,
and the kitten had taken care of her share of the fresh
haddock, just as we were putting back the kitchen chairs
in their places, Mrs. Todd said briskly that she must go up
into the pasture now to gather the desired herbs.

"You can stop here an' rest, or you can accompany me,"
she announced. "Mother ought to have her nap, and when
we come back she an' William'll sing for you. She admires
music," said Mrs. Todd, turning to speak to her mother.

But Mrs. Blackett tried to say that she couldn't sing as
she used, and perhaps William wouldn't feel like it. She
looked tired, the good old soul, or I should have liked to sit
in the peaceful little house while she slept; I had had much
pleasant experience of pastures already in her daughter's
company. But it seemed best to go with Mrs. Todd, and off
we went.

Mrs. Todd carried the gingham bag which she had
brought from home, and a small heavy burden in the bottom made it hang straight and slender from her hand. The
way was steep, and she soon grew breathless, so that we
sat down to rest awhile on a convenient large stone among
the bayberry.

"There, I wanted you to see this,—'t is mother's picture,"
said Mrs. Todd; "'t was taken once when she was up to
Portland, soon after she was married. That's me," she
added, opening another worn case, and displaying the full
face of the cheerful child she looked like still in spite of
being past sixty. "And here's William an' father together.
I take after father, large and heavy, an' William is like
mother's folks, short an' thin. He ought to have made something o' himself, bein' a man an' so like mother; but though
he's been very steady to work, an' kept up the farm, an'
done his fishin' too right along, he never had mother's snap
an' power o' seein' things just as they be. He's got excellent
judgment, too," meditated William's sister, but she could
not arrive at any satisfactory decision upon what she evi-

dently thought his failure in life. "I think it is well to see any one so happy an' makin' the most of life just as it falls to hand," she said as she began to put the daguerreotypes away again; but I reached out my hand to see her mother's once more, a most flower-like face of a lovely young woman in quaint dress. There was in the eyes a look of anticipation and joy, a far-off look that sought the horizon; one often sees it in seafaring families, inherited by girls and boys alike from men who spend their lives at sea, and are always watching for distant sails or the first loom of the land. At sea there is nothing to be seen close by, and this has its counterpart in a sailor's character, in the large and brave and patient traits that are developed, the hopeful pleasantness that one loves so in a seafarer.

When the family pictures were wrapped again in a big handkerchief, we set forward in a narrow footpath and made our way to a lonely place that faced northward, where there was more pasturage and fewer bushes, and we went down to the edge of short grass above some rocky cliffs where the deep sea broke with a great noise, though the wind was down and the water looked quiet a little way from shore. Among the grass grew such pennyroyal as the rest of the world could not provide. There was a fine fragrance in the air as we gathered it sprig by sprig and stepped along carefully, and Mrs. Todd pressed her aromatic nosegay between her hands and offered it to me again and again. *small bouquet*

"There's nothin' like it," she said; "oh no, there's no such pennyr'yal as this in the State of Maine. It's the right pattern of the plant, and all the rest I ever see is but an imitation. Don't it do you good?" And I answered with enthusiasm.

"There, dear, I never showed nobody else but mother where to find this place; 't is kind of sainted to me. Nathan, my husband, an' I used to love this place when we was courtin', and"—she hesitated, and then spoke softly—"when he was lost, 't was just off shore tryin' to get in by the short channel out there between Squaw Islands, right in sight o' this headland where we'd set an' made our plans all summer long."

I had never heard her speak of her husband before, but

The love and use of the land
mrs. Todd draws her "in" helps to become
part of Dunnet Landing

I felt that we were friends now since she had brought me to
this place.

" 'T was but a dream with us," Mrs. Todd said. "I knew
it when he was gone. I knew it"—and she whispered as if
she were at confession—"I knew it afore he started to go to
sea. My heart was gone out o' my keepin' before I ever
saw Nathan; but he loved me well, and he made me real
happy, and he died before he ever knew what he'd had to
know if we'd lived long together. 'T is very strange about
love. No, Nathan never found out, but my heart was troubled when I knew him first. There's more women likes to
be loved than there is of those that loves. I spent some
happy hours right here. I always liked Nathan, and he never
knew. But this pennyr'yal always reminded me, as I'd sit
and gather it and hear him talkin'—it always would remind
me of—the other one."

She looked away from me, and presently rose and went
on by herself. There was something lonely and solitary about
her great determined shape. She might have been Antigone
alone on the Theban plain. It is not often given in a noisy
world to come to the places of great grief and silence. An
absolute, archaic grief possessed this countrywoman; she
seemed like a renewal of some historic soul, with her sorrows and the remoteness of a daily life busied with rustic
simplicities and the scents of primeval herbs.

I was not incompetent at herb-gathering, and after a
while, when I had sat long enough waking myself to new
thoughts, and reading a page of remembrance with new
pleasure, I gathered some bunches, as I was bound to do,
and at last we met again higher up the shore, in the plain
every-day world we had left behind when we went down to
the pennyroyal plot. As we walked together along the high
edge of the field we saw a hundred sails about the bay and
farther seaward; it was mid-afternoon or after, and the day
was coming to an end.

"Yes, they're all makin' towards the shore,—the small
craft an' the lobster smacks an' all," said my companion.
"We must spend a little time with mother now, just to
have our tea, an' then put for home."

"No matter if we lose the wind at sundown; I can row in

with Johnny," said I; and Mrs. Todd nodded reassuringly and kept to her steady plod, not quickening her gait even when we saw William come round the corner of the house as if to look for us, and wave his hand and disappear.

"Why, William's right on deck; I didn't know's we should see any more of him!" exclaimed Mrs. Todd. "Now mother'll put the kettle right on; she's got a good fire goin'." I too could see the blue smoke thicken, and then we both walked a little faster, while Mrs. Todd groped in her full bag of herbs to find the daguerreotypes and be ready to put them in their places.

11 *The Old Singers* William was sitting on the side door step, and the old mother was busy making her tea; she gave into my hand an old flowered-glass tea-caddy.

"William thought you'd like to see this, when he was settin' the table. My father brought it to my mother from the island of Tobago; an' here's a pair of beautiful mugs that came with it." She opened the glass door of a little cupboard beside the chimney. "These I call my best things, dear," she said. "You'd laugh to see how we enjoy 'em Sunday nights in winter: we have a real company tea 'stead o' livin' right along just the same, an' I make somethin' good for a s'prise an' put on some o' my preserves, an' we get a-talkin' together an' have real pleasant times."

Mrs. Todd laughed indulgently, and looked to see what I thought of such childishness.

"I wish I could be here some Sunday evening," said I.

"William an' me'll be talkin' about you an' thinkin' o' this nice day," said Mrs. Blackett affectionately, and she glanced at William, and he looked up bravely and nodded. I began to discover that he and his sister could not speak their deeper feelings before each other.

"Now I want you an' mother to sing," said Mrs. Todd abruptly, with an air of command, and I gave William much sympathy in his evident distress.

"After I've had my cup o' tea, dear," answered the old hostess cheerfully; and so we sat down and took our cups and made merry while they lasted. It was impossible not to wish to stay on forever at Green Island, and I could not help saying so.

"I'm very happy here, both winter an' summer," said old Mrs. Blackett. "William an' I never wish for any other home, do we, William? I'm glad you find it pleasant; I wish you'd come an' stay, dear, whenever you feel inclined. But here's Almiry; I always think Providence was kind to plot an' have her husband leave her a good house where she really belonged. She'd been very restless if she'd had to continue here on Green Island. You wanted more scope, didn't you, Almiry, an' to live in a large place where more things grew? Sometimes folks wonders that we don't live together; perhaps we shall some time," and a shadow of sadness and apprehension flitted across her face. "The time o' sickness an' failin' has got to come to all. But Almiry's got an herb that's good for everything." She smiled as she spoke, and looked bright again.

"There's some herb that's good for everybody, except for them that thinks they're sick when they ain't," announced Mrs. Todd, with a truly professional air of finality. "Come, William, let's have Sweet Home, an' then mother'll sing Cupid an' the Bee for us."

Then followed a most charming surprise. William mastered his timidity and began to sing. His voice was a little faint and frail, like the family daguerreotypes, but it was a tenor voice, and perfectly true and sweet. I have never heard Home, Sweet Home sung as touchingly and seriously as he sang it; he seemed to make it quite new; and when he paused for a moment at the end of the first line and began the next, the old mother joined him and they sang together, she missing only the higher notes, where he seemed to lend his voice to hers for the moment and carry on her very note and air. It was the silent man's real and only means of expression, and one could have listened forever, and have asked for more and more songs of old Scotch and English inheritance and the best that have lived from the ballad music of the war. Mrs. Todd kept time visibly, and sometimes audibly, with her ample foot. I saw the tears in her eyes sometimes, when I could see beyond the tears in mine. But at last the songs ended and the time came to say good-by; it was the end of a great pleasure.

Mrs. Blackett, the dear old lady, opened the door of her bedroom while Mrs. Todd was tying up the herb bag, and William had gone down to get the boat ready and to blow the horn for Johnny Bowden, who had joined a roving boat party who were off the shore lobstering.

I went to the door of the bedroom, and thought how pleasant it looked, with its pink-and-white patchwork quilt and the brown unpainted paneling of its woodwork.

"Come right in, dear," she said. "I want you to set down in my old quilted rockin'-chair there by the window; you'll say it's the prettiest view in the house. I set there a good deal to rest me and when I want to read."

There was a worn red Bible on the lightstand, and Mrs. Blackett's heavy silver-bowed glasses; her thimble was on the narrow window-ledge, and folded carefully on the table was a thick striped-cotton shirt that she was making for her son. Those dear old fingers and their loving stitches, that heart which had made the most of everything that needed love! Here was the real home, the heart of the old house on Green Island! I sat in the rocking-chair, and felt that it was a place of peace, the little brown bedroom, and the quiet outlook upon field and sea and sky.

I looked up, and we understood each other without speaking. "I shall like to think o' your settin' here to-day," said Mrs. Blackett. "I want you to come again. It has been so pleasant for William."

The wind served us all the way home, and did not fall or let the sail slacken until we were close to the shore. We had a generous freight of lobsters in the boat, and new potatoes which William had put aboard, and what Mrs. Todd proudly called a full "kag" of prime number one salted mackerel; and when we landed we had to make business arrangements to have these conveyed to her house in a wheelbarrow.

I never shall forget the day at Green Island. The town of Dunnet Landing seemed large and noisy and oppressive as we came ashore. Such is the power of contrast; for the village was so still that I could hear the shy whippoorwills singing that night as I lay awake in my downstairs bedroom, and the scent of Mrs. Todd's herb garden under

the window blew in again and again with every gentle rising
of the sea-breeze.

12 *A Strange Sail* Except for a few stray guests, island-
ers or from the inland country, to whom Mrs. Todd offered
the hospitalities of a single meal, we were quite by ourselves all summer; and when there were signs of invasion,
late in July, and a certain Mrs. Fosdick appeared like a
strange sail on the far horizon, I suffered much from apprehension. I had been living in the quaint little house
with as much comfort and unconsciousness as if it were a
larger body, or a double shell, in whose simple convolutions
Mrs. Todd and I had secreted ourselves, until some wandering hermit crab of a visitor marked the little spare room
for her own. Perhaps now and then a castaway on a lonely
desert island dreads the thought of being rescued. I heard
of Mrs. Fosdick for the first time with a selfish sense of
objection; but after all, I was still vacation-tenant of the
schoolhouse, where I could always be alone, and it was
impossible not to sympathize with Mrs. Todd, who, in
spite of some preliminary grumbling, was really delighted
with the prospect of entertaining an old friend.

For nearly a month we received occasional news of Mrs.
Fosdick, who seemed to be making a royal progress from
house to house in the inland neighborhood, after the fashion
of Queen Elizabeth. One Sunday after another came and
went, disappointing Mrs. Todd in the hope of seeing her
guest at church and fixing the day for the great visit to begin; but Mrs. Fosdick was not ready to commit herself to a
date. An assurance of "some time this week" was not
sufficiently definite from a free-footed housekeeper's point
of view, and Mrs. Todd put aside all herb-gathering plans,
and went through the various stages of expectation, prov-
ocation, and despair. At last she was ready to believe that
Mrs. Fosdick must have forgotten her promise and returned
to her home, which was vaguely said to be over Thomaston
way. But one evening, just as the supper-table was cleared
and "readied up," and Mrs. Todd had put her large apron
over her head and stepped forth for an evening stroll in
the garden, the unexpected happened. She heard the

sound of wheels, and gave an excited cry to me, as I sat by
the window, that Mrs. Fosdick was coming right up the
street.

"She may not be considerate, but she's dreadful good
company," said Mrs. Todd hastily, coming back a few steps
from the neighborhood of the gate. "No, she ain't a mite
considerate, but there's a small lobster left over from your
tea; yes, it's a real mercy there's a lobster. Susan Fosdick
might just as well have passed the compliment o' comin' an
hour ago."

"Perhaps she has had her supper," I ventured to suggest,
sharing the housekeeper's anxiety, and meekly conscious of
an inconsiderate appetite for my own supper after a long
expedition up the bay. There were so few emergencies of
any sort at Dunnet Landing that this one appeared over-
whelming.

"No, she's rode 'way over from Nahum Brayton's place.
I expect they were busy on the farm, and couldn't spare
the horse in proper season. You just sly out an' set the tea-
kittle on again, dear, an' drop in a good han'ful o' chips;
the fire's all alive. I'll take her right up to lay off her things,
an' she'll be occupied with explanations an' gettin' her bunnit off, so you'll have plenty o' time. She's one I shouldn't
like to have find me unprepared."

Mrs. Fosdick was already at the gate, and Mrs. Todd
now turned with an air of complete surprise and delight
to welcome her.

"Why, Susan Fosdick," I heard her exclaim in a fine
unhindered voice, as if she were calling across a field, "I
come near giving of you up! I was afraid you'd gone an'
'portioned out my visit to somebody else. I s'pose you've
been to supper?"

"Lor', no, I ain't, Almiry Todd," said Mrs. Fosdick
cheerfully, as she turned, laden with bags and bundles,
from making her adieux to the boy driver. "I ain't had a
mite o' supper, dear. I've been lottin' all the way on a cup
o' that best tea o' yourn,—some o' that Oolong you keep
in the little chist. I don't want none o' your useful herbs."

"I keep that tea for ministers' folks," gayly responded
Mrs. Todd. "Come right along in, Susan Fosdick. I declare
if you ain't the same old sixpence!"

As they came up the walk together, laughing like girls, I fled, full of cares, to the kitchen, to brighten the fire and be sure that the lobster, sole dependence of a late supper, was well out of reach of the cat. There proved to be fine reserves of wild raspberries and bread and butter, so that I regained my composure, and waited impatiently for my own share of this illustrious visit to begin. There was an instant sense of high festivity in the evening air from the moment when our guest had so frankly demanded the Oolong tea.

The great moment arrived. I was formally presented at the stair-foot, and the two friends passed on to the kitchen, where I soon heard a hospitable clink of crockery and the brisk stirring of a tea-cup. I sat in my high-backed rocking-chair by the window in the front room with an unreasonable feeling of being left out, like the child who stood at the gate in Hans Andersen's story. Mrs. Fosdick did not look, at first sight, like a person of great social gifts. She was a serious-looking little bit of an old woman, with a birdlike nod of the head. I had often been told that she was the "best hand in the world to make a visit,"—as if to visit were the highest of vocations; that everybody wished for her, while few could get her; and I saw that Mrs. Todd felt a comfortable sense of distinction in being favored with the company of this eminent person who "knew just how." It was certainly true that Mrs. Fosdick gave both her hostess and me a warm feeling of enjoyment and expectation, as if she had the power of social suggestion to all neighboring minds.

The two friends did not reappear for at least an hour. I could hear their busy voices, loud and low by turns, as they ranged from public to confidential topics. At last Mrs. Todd kindly remembered me and returned, giving my door a ceremonious knock before she stepped in, with the small visitor in her wake. She reached behind her and took Mrs. Fosdick's hand as if she were young and bashful, and gave her a gentle pull forward.

"There, I don't know whether you're goin' to take to each other or not; no, nobody can't tell whether you'll suit each other, but I expect you'll get along some way, both having seen the world," said our affectionate hostess. "You can inform Mis' Fosdick how we found the folks out to Green Island the other day. She's always been well acquainted with mother. I'll slip out now an' put away the supper things an' set my bread to rise, if you'll both excuse me. You can come out an' keep me company when you get ready, either or both." And Mrs. Todd, large and amiable, disappeared and left us.

Being furnished not only with a subject of conversation, but with a safe refuge in the kitchen in case of incompatibility, Mrs. Fosdick and I sat down, prepared to make the best of each other. I soon discovered that she, like many of the elder women of that coast, had spent a part of her life at sea, and was full of a good traveler's curiosity and enlightenment. By the time we thought it discreet to join our hostess we were already sincere friends.

You may speak of a visit's setting in as well as a tide's, and it was impossible, as Mrs. Todd whispered to me, not to be pleased at the way this visit was setting in; a new impulse and refreshing of the social currents and seldom visited bays of memory appeared to have begun. Mrs. Fosdick had been the mother of a large family of sons and daughters,—sailors and sailors' wives,—and most of them had died before her. I soon grew more or less acquainted with the histories of all their fortunes and misfortunes, and subjects of an intimate nature were no more withheld from my ears than if I had been a shell on the mantelpiece. Mrs. Fosdick was not without a touch of dignity and elegance; she was fashionable in her dress, but it was a curiously well-preserved provincial fashion of some years back. In a wider sphere one might have called her a woman of the world, with her unexpected bits of modern knowledge, but Mrs. Todd's wisdom was an intimation of truth itself. She might belong to any age, like an idyl of Theocritus; but while she always understood Mrs. Fosdick, that entertaining pilgrim could not always understand Mrs. Todd.

That very first evening my friends plunged into a borderless sea of reminiscences and personal news. Mrs. Fosdick had been staying with a family who owned the farm where she was born, and she had visited every sunny knoll and shady field corner; but when she said that it might be for

the last time, I detected in her tone something expectant
of the contradiction which Mrs. Todd promptly offered.

"Almiry," said Mrs. Fosdick, with sadness, "you may
say what you like, but I am one of nine brothers and sisters
brought up on the old place, and we're all dead but me."

"Your sister Dailey ain't gone, is she? Why, no, Louisa
ain't gone!" exclaimed Mrs. Todd, with surprise. "Why, I
never heard of that occurrence!"

"Yes'm; she passed away last October, in Lynn. She had
made her distant home in Vermont State, but she was making a visit to her youngest daughter. Louisa was the only
one of my family whose funeral I wasn't able to attend,
but 't was a mere accident. All the rest of us were settled
right about home. I thought it was very slack of 'em in Lynn
not to fetch her to the old place; but when I came to hear
about it, I learned that they'd recently put up a very
elegant monument, and my sister Dailey was always great
for show. She'd just been out to see the monument the
week before she was taken down, and admired it so much
that they felt sure of her wishes."

"So she's really gone, and the funeral was up to Lynn!"
repeated Mrs. Todd, as if to impress the sad fact upon her
mind. "She was some years younger than we be, too. I recollect the first day she ever came to school; 't was that first
year mother sent me inshore to stay with aunt Topham's
folks and get my schooling. You fetched little Louisa to
school one Monday mornin' in a pink dress an' her long
curls, and she set between you an' me, and got cryin' after
a while, so the teacher sent us home with her at recess."

"She was scared of seeing so many children about her;
there was only her and me and brother John at home then;
the older boys were to sea with father, an' the rest of us
wa'n't born," explained Mrs. Fosdick. "That next fall we all
went to sea together. Mother was uncertain till the last
minute, as one may say. The ship was waiting orders, but
the baby that then was, was born just in time, and there
was a long spell of extra bad weather, so mother got about
again before they had to sail, an' we all went. I remember
my clothes were all left ashore in the east chamber in a
basket where mother'd took them out o' my chist o' drawers an' left 'em ready to carry aboard. She didn't have noth-

ing aboard, of her own, that she wanted to cut up for me,
so when my dress wore out she just put me into a spare suit
o' John's, jacket and trousers. I wasn't but eight years old
an' he was most seven and large of his age. Quick as we
made a port she went right ashore an' fitted me out pretty,
but we was bound for the East Indies and didn't put in
anywhere for a good while. So I had quite a spell o' freedom.
Mother made my new skirt long because I was growing,
and I poked about the deck after that, real discouraged,
feeling the hem at my heels every minute, and as if youth
was past and gone. I liked the trousers best; I used to climb
the riggin' with 'em and frighten mother till she said an'
vowed she'd never take me to sea again."

I thought by the polite absent-minded smile on Mrs.
Todd's face this was no new story.

"Little Louisa was a beautiful child; yes, I always thought
Louisa was very pretty," Mrs. Todd said. "She was a dear
little girl in those days. She favored your mother; the rest
of you took after your father's folks."

"We did certain," agreed Mrs. Fosdick, rocking steadily.
"There, it does seem so pleasant to talk with an old acquaintance that knows what you know. I see so many of
these new folks nowadays, that seem to have neither past
nor future. Conversation's got to have some root in the
past, or else you've got to explain every remark you make,
an' it wears a person out."

Mrs. Todd gave a funny little laugh. "Yes'm, old friends
is always best, 'less you can catch a new one that's fit to
make an old one out of, she said, and we gave an affectionate glance at each other which Mrs. Fosdick could not have
understood, being the latest comer to the house.

13 *Poor Joanna* One evening my ears caught a mysterious allusion which Mrs. Todd made to Shell-heap Island.
It was a chilly night of cold northeasterly rain, and I made
a fire for the first time in the Franklin stove in my room,
and begged my two housemates to come in and keep me
company. The weather had convinced Mrs. Todd that it
was time to make a supply of cough-drops, and she had been
bringing forth herbs from dark and dry hiding-places, until

now the pungent dust and odor of them had resolved themselves into one mighty flavor of spearmint that came from a simmering caldron of syrup in the kitchen. She called it done, and well done, and had ostentatiously left it to cool, and taken her knitting-work because Mrs. Fosdick was busy with hers. They sat in the two rocking-chairs, the small woman and the large one, but now and then I could see that Mrs. Todd's thoughts remained with the cough-drops. The time of gathering herbs was nearly over, but the time of syrups and cordials had begun.

The heat of the open fire made us a little drowsy, but something in the way Mrs. Todd spoke of Shell-heap Island waked my interest. I waited to see if she would say any more, and then took a roundabout way back to the subject by saying what was first in my mind: that I wished the Green Island family were there to spend the evening with us,—Mrs. Todd's mother and her brother William.

Mrs. Todd smiled, and drummed on the arm of the rocking-chair. "Might scare William to death," she warned me; and Mrs. Fosdick mentioned her intention of going out to Green Island to stay two or three days, if this wind didn't make too much sea.

"Where is Shell-heap Island?" I ventured to ask, seizing the opportunity.

"Bears nor'east somewheres about three miles from Green Island; right off-shore, I should call it about eight miles out," said Mrs. Todd. "You never was there, dear; 't is off the thoroughfares, and a very bad place to land at best."

"I should think 't was," agreed Mrs. Fosdick, smoothing down her black silk apron. "'T is a place worth visitin' when you once get there. Some o' the old folks was kind o' fearful about it. 'T was 'counted a great place in old Indian times; you can pick up their stone tools 'most any time if you hunt about. There's a beautiful spring o' water, too. Yes, I remember when they used to tell queer stories about Shell-heap Island. Some said 't was a great bangeing-place for the Indians, and an old chief resided there once that ruled the winds; and others said they'd always heard that once the Indians come down from up country an' left a captive there without any bo't, an' 't was too far to swim across to Black Island, so called, an' he lived there till he perished."

"I've heard say he walked the island after that, and sharp-sighted folks could see him an' lose him like one o' them citizens Cap'n Littlepage was acquainted with up to the north pole," announced Mrs. Todd grimly. "Anyway, there was Indians,—you can see their shell-heap that named the island; and I've heard myself that 't was one o' their cannibal places, but I never could believe it. There never was no cannibals on the coast o' Maine. All the Indians o' these regions are tame-looking folks."

"Sakes alive, yes!" exclaimed Mrs. Fosdick. "Ought to see them painted savages I've seen when I was young out in the South Sea Islands! That was the time for folks to travel, 'way back in the old whalin' days!"

"Whalin' must have been dull for a lady, hardly ever makin' a lively port, and not takin' in any mixed cargoes," said Mrs. Todd. "I never desired to go a whalin' v'y'ge myself."

"I used to return feelin' very slack an' behind the times, 't is true," explained Mrs. Fosdick, "but 't was excitin', an' we always done extra well, and felt rich when we did get ashore. I liked the variety. There, how times have changed; how few seafarin' families there are left! What a lot o' queer folks there used to be about here, anyway, when we was young, Almiry. Everybody's just like everybody else, now; nobody to laugh about, and nobody to cry about."

It seemed to me that there were peculiarities of character in the region of Dunnet Landing yet, but I did not like to interrupt.

"Yes," said Mrs. Todd after a moment of meditation, "there was certain a good many curiosities of human natur' in this neighborhood years ago. There was more energy then, and in some the energy took a singular turn. In these days the young folks is all copy-cats, 'fraid to death they won't be all just alike; as for the old folks, they pray for the advantage o' bein' a little different."

"I ain't heard of a copy-cat this great many years," said Mrs. Fosdick, laughing; "'t was a favorite term o' my grandmother's. No, I wa'n't thinking o' those things, but of them strange straying creatur's that used to rove the country. You don't see them now, or the ones that used to hive away in their own houses with some strange notion or other."

I thought again of Captain Littlepage, but my companions were not reminded of his name; and there was brother William at Green Island, whom we all three knew.

"I was talking o' poor Joanna the other day. I hadn't thought of her for a great while," said Mrs. Fosdick abruptly. "Mis' Brayton an' I recalled her as we sat together sewing. She was one o' your peculiar persons, wa'n't she? Speaking of such persons," she turned to explain to me, "there was a sort of a nun or hermit person lived out there for years all alone on Shell-heap Island. Miss Joanna Todd, her name was,—a cousin o' Almiry's late husband."

I expressed my interest, but as I glanced at Mrs. Todd I saw that she was confused by sudden affectionate feeling and unmistakable desire for reticence. ~ *disinclined to speak / taciturn*

"I never want to hear Joanna laughed about," she said anxiously.

"Nor I," answered Mrs. Fosdick reassuringly. "She was crossed in love,—that was all the matter to begin with; but as I look back, I can see that Joanna was one doomed from the first to fall into a melancholy. She retired from the world for good an' all, though she was a well-off woman. All she wanted was to get away from folks; she thought she wasn't fit to live with anybody, and wanted to be free. Shell-heap Island come to her from her father, and first thing folks knew she'd gone off out there to live, and left word she didn't want no company. 'T was a bad place to get to, unless the wind an' tide were just right; 't was hard work to make a landing."

"What time of year was this?" I asked.

"Very late in the summer," said Mrs. Fosdick. "No, I never could laugh at Joanna, as some did. She set everything by the young man, an' they were going to marry in about a month, when he got bewitched with a girl 'way up the bay, and married her, and went off to Massachusetts. He wasn't well thought of,—there were those who thought Joanna's money was what had tempted him; but she'd given him her whole heart, an' she wa'n't so young as she had been. All her hopes were built on marryin', an' havin' a real home and somebody to look to; she acted just like a

bird when its nest is spoilt. The day after she heard the
news she was in dreadful woe, but the next she came to
herself very quiet, and took the horse and wagon, and drove
fourteen miles to the lawyer's, and signed a paper givin'
her half of the farm to her brother. They never had got
along very well together, but he didn't want to sign it, till
she acted so distressed that he gave in. Edward Todd's wife
was a good woman, who felt very bad indeed, and used
every argument with Joanna; but Joanna took a poor old
boat that had been her father's and lo'ded in a few things,
and off she put all alone, with a good land breeze, right out
to sea. Edward Todd ran down to the beach, an' stood there
cryin' like a boy to see her go, but she was out o' hearin'.
She never stepped foot on the mainland again long as she
lived."

"How large an island is it? How did she manage in
winter?" I asked.

"Perhaps thirty acres, rocks and all," answered Mrs.
Todd, taking up the story gravely. "There can't be much of
it that the salt spray don't fly over in storms. No, 't is a
dreadful small place to make a world of; it has a different
look from any of the other islands, but there's a sheltered
cove on the south side, with mud-flats across one end of it
at low water where there's excellent clams, and the big
shell-heap keeps some o' the wind off a little house her
father took the trouble to build when he was a young man.
They said there was an old house built o' logs there before
that, with a kind of natural cellar in the rock under it. He
used to stay out there days to a time, and anchor a little
sloop he had, and dig clams to fill it, and sail up to Portland. They said the dealers always gave him an extra price,
the clams were so noted. Joanna used to go out and stay
with him. They were always great companions, so she knew
just what 't was out there. There was a few sheep that belonged to her brother an' her, but she bargained for him to
come and get them on the edge o' cold weather. Yes, she
desired him to come for the sheep; an' his wife thought perhaps Joanna'd return, but he said no, an' lo'ded the bo't
with warm things an' what he thought she'd need through
the winter. He come home with the sheep an' left the other
things by the house, but she never so much as looked out

o' the window. She done it for a penance. She must have wanted to see Edward by that time."

Mrs. Fosdick was fidgeting with eagerness to speak.

"Some thought the first cold snap would set her ashore, but she always remained," concluded Mrs. Todd soberly.

"Talk about the men not having any curiosity!" exclaimed Mrs. Fosdick scornfully. "Why, the waters round Shell-heap Island were white with sails all that fall. 'T was never called no great of a fishin'-ground before. Many of 'em made excuse to go ashore to get water at the spring; but at last she spoke to a bo't-load, very dignified and calm, and said that she'd like it better if they'd make a practice of getting water to Black Island or somewheres else and leave her alone, except in case of accident or trouble. But there was one man who had always set everything by her from a boy. He'd have married her if the other hadn't come about an' spoilt his chance, and he used to get close to the island, before light, on his way out fishin', and throw a little bundle 'way up the green slope front o' the house. His sister told me she happened to see, the first time, what a pretty choice he made o' useful things that a woman would feel lost without. He stood off fishin', and could see them in the grass all day, though sometimes she'd come out and walk right by them. There was other bo'ts near, out after mackerel. But early next morning his present was gone. He didn't presume too much, but once he took her a nice firkin o' things he got up to Portland, and when spring come he landed her a hen and chickens in a nice little coop. There was a good many old friends had Joanna on their minds."

"Yes," said Mrs. Todd, losing her sad reserve in the growing sympathy of these reminiscences. "How everybody used to notice whether there was smoke out of the chimney! The Black Island folks could see her with their spy-glass, and if they'd ever missed getting some sign o' life they'd have sent notice to her folks. But after the first year or two Joanna was more and more forgotten as an every-day charge. Folks lived very simple in those days, you know," she continued, as Mrs. Fosdick's knitting was taking much thought at the moment. "I expect there was always plenty of driftwood thrown up, and a poor failin' patch of spruces covered all the north side of the island, so she always had something to burn. She was very fond of workin' in the garden ashore, and that first summer she began to till the little field out there, and raised a nice parcel o' potatoes. She could fish, o' course, and there was all her clams an' lobsters. You can always live well in any wild place by the sea when you'd starve to death up country, except 't was berry time. Joanna had berries out there, blackberries at least, and there was a few herbs in case she needed them. Mullein in great quantities and a plant o' wormwood I remember seeing once when I stayed there, long before she fled out to Shell-heap. Yes, I recall the wormwood, which is always a planted herb, so there must have been folks there before the Todds' day. A growin' bush makes the best gravestone; I expect that wormwood always stood for some-body's solemn monument. Catnip, too, is a very endurin' herb about an old place."

"But what I want to know is what she did for other things," interrupted Mrs. Fosdick. "Almiry, what did she do for clothin' when she needed to replenish, or risin' for her bread, or the piece-bag that no woman can live long without?"

"Or company," suggested Mrs. Todd. "Joanna was one that loved her friends. There must have been a terrible sight o' long winter evenin's that first year."

"There was her hens," suggested Mrs. Fosdick, after re-viewing the melancholy situation. "She never wanted the sheep after that first season. There wa'n't no proper pas-ture for sheep after the June grass was past, and she ascer-tained the fact and couldn't bear to see them suffer; but the chickens done well. I remember sailin' by one spring after-noon, an' seein' the coops out front o' the house in the sun. How long was it before you went out with the minister? You were the first ones that ever really got ashore to see Joanna."

I had been reflecting upon a state of society which ad-mitted such personal freedom and a voluntary hermitage. There was something mediæval in the behavior of poor Joanna Todd under a disappointment of the heart. The two women had drawn closer together, and were talking on, quite unconscious of a listener.

"Poor Joanna!" said Mrs. Todd again, and sadly

shook her head as if there were things one could not speak about.

"I called her a great fool," declared Mrs. Fosdick, with spirit, "but I pitied her then, and I pity her far more now. Some other minister would have been a great help to her, —one that preached self-forgetfulness and doin' for others to cure our own ills; but Parson Dimmick was a vague person, well meanin', but very numb in his feelin's. I don't suppose at that troubled time Joanna could think of any way to mend her troubles except to run off and hide."

"Mother used to say she didn't see how Joanna lived without having nobody to do for, getting her own meals and tending her own poor self day in an' day out," said Mrs. Todd sorrowfully.

"There was the hens," repeated Mrs. Fosdick kindly. "I expect she soon came to makin' folks o' them. No, I never went to work to blame Joanna, as some did. She was full o' feeling, and her troubles hurt her more than she could bear. I see it all now as I couldn't when I was young."

"I suppose in old times they had their shut-up convents for just such folks," said Mrs. Todd, as if she and her friend had disagreed about Joanna once, and were now in happy harmony. She seemed to speak with new openness and freedom. "Oh yes, I was only too pleased when the Reverend Mr. Dimmick invited me to go out with him. He hadn't been very long in the place when Joanna left home and friends. 'T was one day that next summer after she went, and I had been married early in the spring. He felt that he ought to go out and visit her. She was a member of the church, and might wish to have him consider her spiritual state. I wa'n't so sure o' that, but I always liked Joanna, and I'd come to be her cousin by marriage. Nathan an' I had conversed about goin' out to pay her a visit, but he got his chance to sail sooner'n he expected. He always thought everything of her, and last time he come home, knowing nothing of her change, he brought her a beautiful coral pin from a port he'd touched at somewheres up the Mediterranean. So I wrapped the little box in a nice piece of paper and put it in my pocket, and picked her a bunch of fresh lemon balm, and off we started."

Mrs. Fosdick laughed. "I remember hearin' about your trials on the v'y'ge," she said.

"Why, yes," continued Mrs. Todd in her company manner. "I picked her the balm, an' we started. Why, yes, Susan, the minister liked to have cost me my life that day. He would fasten the sheet, though I advised against it. He said the rope was rough an' cut his hand. There was a fresh breeze, an' he went on talking rather high flown, an' I felt some interested. All of a sudden there come up a gust, and he give a screech and stood right up and called for help, 'way out there to sea. I knocked him right over into the bottom o' the bo't, getting by to catch hold of the sheet an' untie it. He wasn't but a little man; I helped him right up after the squall passed, and made a handsome apology to him, but he did act kind o' offended."

"I do think they ought not to settle them landlocked folks in parishes where they're liable to be on the water," insisted Mrs. Fosdick. "Think of the families in our parish that was scattered all about the bay, and what a sight o' sails you used to see, in Mr. Dimmick's day, standing across to the mainland on a pleasant Sunday morning, filled with church-going folks, all sure to want him some time or other! You couldn't find no doctor that would stand up in the boat and screech if a flaw struck her."

"Old Dr. Bennett had a beautiful sailboat, didn't he?" responded Mrs. Todd. "And how well he used to brave the weather! Mother always said that in time o' trouble that tall white sail used to look like an angel's wing comin' over the sea to them that was in pain. Well, there's a difference in gifts. Mr. Dimmick was not without light."

" 'T was light o' the moon, then," snapped Mrs. Fosdick; "he was pompous enough, but I never could remember a single word he said. There, go on, Mis' Todd; I forget a great deal about that day you went to see poor Joanna."

"I felt she saw us coming, and knew us a great way off; yes, I seemed to feel it within me," said our friend, laying down her knitting. "I kept my seat, and took the bo't in shore without saying a word; there was a short channel that I was sure Mr. Dimmick wasn't acquainted with, and the tide was very low. She never came out to warn us off nor anything, and I thought, as I hauled the bo't up on a wave and let the Reverend Mr. Dimmick step out, that it was somethin' gained to be safe ashore. There was a little smoke out o' the chimney o' Joanna's house, and it did look sort of homelike and pleasant with wild mornin'-glory vines trained up; an' there was a plot o' flowers under the front window, portulacas and things. I believe she'd made a garden once, when she was stopping there with her father, and some things must have seeded in. It looked as if she might have gone over to the other side of the island. 'T was neat and pretty all about the house, and a lovely day in July. We walked up from the beach together very sedate, and I felt for poor Nathan's little pin to see if 't was safe in my dress pocket. All of a sudden Joanna come right to the fore door and stood there, not sayin' a word."

14 *The Hermitage* My companions and I had been so intent upon the subject of the conversation that we had not heard any one open the gate, but at this moment, above the noise of the rain, we heard a loud knocking. We were all startled as we sat by the fire, and Mrs. Todd rose hastily and went to answer the call, leaving her rocking-chair in violent motion. Mrs. Fosdick and I heard an anxious voice at the door speaking of a sick child, and Mrs. Todd's kind, motherly voice inviting the messenger in: then we waited in silence. There was a sound of heavy dropping of rain from the eaves, and the distant roar and undertone of the sea. My thoughts flew back to the lonely woman on her outer island; what separation from humankind she must have felt, what terror and sadness, even in a summer storm like this!

"You send right after the doctor if she ain't better in half an hour," said Mrs. Todd to her worried customer as they parted; and I felt a warm sense of comfort in the evident resources of even so small a neighborhood, but for the poor hermit Joanna there was no neighbor on a winter night.

"How did she look?" demanded Mrs. Fosdick, without preface, as our large hostess returned to the little room with a mist about her from standing long in the wet doorway, and the sudden draught of her coming beat out the smoke and flame from the Franklin stove. "How did poor Joanna look?"

"She was the same as ever, except I thought she looked smaller," answered Mrs. Todd after thinking a moment; perhaps it was only a last considering thought about her patient. "Yes, she was just the same, and looked very nice, Joanna did. I had been married since she left home, an' she treated me like her own folks. I expected she'd look strange, with her hair turned gray in a night or somethin', but she wore a pretty gingham dress I'd often seen her wear before she went away; she must have kept it nice for best in the afternoons. She always had beautiful, quiet manners. I remember she waited till we were close to her, and then kissed me real affectionate, and inquired for Nathan before she shook hands with the minister, and then she invited us both in. 'T was the same little house her father had built him when he was a bachelor, with one livin'-room, and a little mite of a bedroom out of it where she slept, but 't was neat as a ship's cabin. There was some old chairs, an' a seat made of a long box that might have held boat tackle an' things to lock up in his fishin' days, and a good enough stove so anybody could cook and keep warm in cold weather. I went over once from home and stayed 'most a week with Joanna when we was girls, and those young happy days rose up before me. Her father was busy all day fishin' or clam-min'; he was one o' the pleasantest men in the world, but Joanna's mother had the grim streak, and never knew what 't was to be happy. The first minute my eyes fell upon Joanna's face that day I saw how she had grown to look like Mis' Todd. 'T was the mother right over again."

"Oh dear me!" said Mrs. Fosdick.

"Joanna had done one thing very pretty. There was a little piece o' swamp on the island where good rushes grew plenty, and she'd gathered 'em, and braided some beautiful mats for the floor and a thick cushion for the long bunk. She'd showed a good deal of invention; you see there was a nice chance to pick up pieces o' wood and boards that drove ashore, and she'd made good use o' what she found. There wasn't no clock, but she had a few dishes on a shelf, and flowers set about in shells fixed to the walls, so it did look sort of homelike, though so lonely and poor. I couldn't keep the tears out o' my eyes, I felt so sad. I said to myself, I must get mother to come over an' see Joanna; the love in mother's heart would warm her, an' she might be able to advise."

"Oh no, Joanna was dreadful stern," said Mrs. Fosdick.

"We were all settin' down very proper, but Joanna would keep stealin' glances at me as if she was glad I come. She had but little to say; she was real polite an' gentle, and yet forbiddin'. The minister found it hard," confessed Mrs. Todd; "he got embarrassed, an' when he put on his authority and asked her if she felt to enjoy religion in her present situation, an' she replied that she must be excused from answerin', I thought I should fly. She might have made it easier for him; after all, he was the minister and had taken some trouble to come out, though 't was kind of cold an' unfeelin' the way he inquired. I thought he might have seen the little old Bible a-layin' on the shelf close by him, an' I wished he knew enough to just lay his hand on it an' read somethin' kind an' fatherly 'stead of accusin' her, an' then given poor Joanna his blessin' with the hope she might be led to comfort. He did offer prayer, but 't was all about hearin' the voice o' God out o' the whirlwind; and I thought while he was goin' on that anybody that had spent the long cold winter all alone out on Shell-heap Island knew a good deal more about those things than he did. I got so provoked I opened my eyes and stared right at him.

"She didn't take no notice, she kep' a nice respectful manner towards him, and when there come a pause she asked if he had any interest about the old Indian remains, and took down some queer stone gouges and hammers off of one of her shelves and showed them to him same's if he was a boy. He remarked that he'd like to walk over an' see the shell-heap; so she went right to the door and pointed him the way. I see then that she'd made her some kind o' sandal-shoes out o' the fine rushes to wear on her feet; she stepped light an' nice in 'em as shoes."

Mrs. Fosdick leaned back in her rocking-chair and gave a heavy sigh.

"I didn't move at first, but I'd held out just as long as I could," said Mrs. Todd, whose voice trembled a little.

"When Joanna returned from the door, an' I could see that man's stupid back departin' among the wild rose bushes, I just ran to her an' caught her in my arms. I wasn't so big as I be now, and she was older than me, but I hugged her tight, just as if she was a child. 'Oh, Joanna dear,' I says, 'won't you come ashore an' live 'long o' me at the Landin', or go over to Green Island to mother's when winter comes? Nobody shall trouble you, an' mother finds it hard bein' alone. I can't bear to leave you here'—and I burst right out crying. I'd had my own trials, young as I was, an' she knew it. Oh, I did entreat her; yes, I entreated Joanna."

"What did she say then?" asked Mrs. Fosdick, much moved.

"She looked the same way, sad an' remote through it all," said Mrs. Todd mournfully. "She took hold of my hand, and we sat down close together; 't was as if she turned round an' made a child of me. 'I haven't got no right to live with folks no more,' she said. 'You must never ask me again, Almiry: I've done the only thing I could do, and I've made my choice. I feel a great comfort in your kindness, but I don't deserve it. I have committed the unpardonable sin; you don't understand,' says she humbly. 'I was in great wrath and trouble, and my thoughts was so wicked towards God that I can't expect ever to be forgiven. I have come to know what it is to have patience, but I have lost my hope. You must tell those that ask how 't is with me,' she said, 'an' tell them I want to be alone.' I couldn't speak; no, there wa'n't anything I could say, she seemed so above everything common. I was a good deal younger then than I be now, and I got Nathan's little coral pin out o' my pocket and put it into her hand; and when she saw it and I told her where it come from, her face did really light up for a minute, sort of bright an' pleasant. 'Nathan an' I was always good friends; I'm glad he don't think hard of me,' says she. 'I want you to have it, Almiry, an' wear it for love o' both o' us,' and she handed it back to me. 'You give my love to Nathan,—he's a dear good man,' she said; 'an' tell your mother, if I should be sick she mustn't wish I could get well, but I want her to be the one to come.' Then she seemed to have said all she wanted to, as if she was done with the world, and we sat there a few minutes longer together. It was real sweet and quiet except for a good many birds and the sea rollin' up on the beach; but at last she rose, an' I did too, and she kissed me and held my hand in hers a minute, as if to say good-by; then she turned and went right away out o' the door and disappeared.

"The minister come back pretty soon, and I told him I was all ready, and we started down to the bo't. He had picked up some round stones and things and was carrying them in his pocket-handkerchief; an' he sat down amidships without making any question, and let me take the rudder an' work the bo't, an' made no remarks for some time, until we sort of eased it off speaking of the weather, an' subjects that arose as we skirted Black Island, where two or three families lived belongin' to the parish. He preached next Sabbath as usual, somethin' high soundin' about the creation, and I couldn't help thinkin' he might never get no further; he seemed to know no remedies, but he had a great use of words."

Mrs. Fosdick sighed again. "Hearin' you tell about Joanna brings the time right back as if 't was yesterday," she said. "Yes, she was one o' them poor things that talked about the great sin; we don't seem to hear nothing about the unpardonable sin now, but you may say 't was not uncommon then."

"I expect that if it had been in these days, such a person would be plagued to death with idle folks," continued Mrs. Todd, after a long pause. "As it was, nobody trespassed on her; all the folks about the bay respected her an' her feelings; but as time wore on, after you left here, one after another ventured to make occasion to put somethin' ashore for her if they went that way. I know mother used to go to see her sometimes, and send William over now and then with something fresh an' nice from the farm. There is a point on the sheltered side where you can lay a boat close to shore an' land anything safe on the turf out o' reach o' the water. There were one or two others, old folks, that she would see, and now an' then she'd hail a passin' boat an' ask for somethin'; and mother got her to promise that she would make some sign to the Black Island folks if she wanted help. I never saw her myself to speak to after that day."

"I expect nowadays, if such a thing happened, she'd have gone out West to her uncle's folks or up to Massachusetts and had a change, an' come home good as new. The world's bigger an' freer than it used to be," urged Mrs. Fosdick.

"No," said her friend. "'T is like bad eyesight, the mind of such a person: if your eyes don't see right there may be a remedy, but there's no kind of glasses to remedy the mind. No, Joanna was Joanna, and there she lays on her island where she lived and did her poor penance. She told mother the day she was dyin' that she always used to want to be fetched inshore when it come to the last; but she'd thought it over, and desired to be laid on the island, if 't was thought right. So the funeral was out there, a Saturday afternoon in September. 'T was a pretty day, and there wa'n't hardly a boat on the coast within twenty miles that didn't head for Shell-heap cram-full o' folks, an' all real respectful, same's if she'd always stayed ashore and held her friends. Some went out o' mere curiosity, I don't doubt,—there's always such to every funeral; but most had real feelin', and went purpose to show it. She'd got most o' the wild sparrows as tame as could be, livin' out there so long among 'em, and one flew right in and lit on the coffin an' begun to sing while Mr. Dimmick was speakin'. He was put out by it, an' acted as if he didn't know whether to stop or go on. I may have been prejudiced, but I wa'n't the only one thought the poor little bird done the best of the two."

"What became o' the man that treated her so, did you ever hear?" asked Mrs. Fosdick. "I know he lived up to Massachusetts for a while. Somebody who came from the same place told me that he was in trade there an' doin' very well, but that was years ago."

"I never heard anything more than that; he went to the war in one o' the early rigiments. No, I never heard any more of him," answered Mrs. Todd. "Joanna was another sort of person, and perhaps he showed good judgment in marryin' somebody else, if only he'd behaved straightforward and manly. He was a shifty-eyed, coaxin' sort of man, that got what he wanted out o' folks, an' only gave when he wanted to buy, made friends easy and lost 'em without knowin' the difference. She'd had a piece o' work tryin' to make him walk accordin' to her right ideas, but she'd have had too much variety ever to fall into a melancholy. Some is meant to be the Joannas in this world, an' 't was her poor lot."

15 *On Shell-heap Island* Some time after Mrs. Fosdick's visit was over and we had returned to our former quietness, I was out sailing alone with Captain Bowden in his large boat. We were taking the crooked northeasterly channel seaward, and were well out from shore while it was still early in the afternoon. I found myself presently among some unfamiliar islands, and suddenly remembered the story of poor Joanna. There is something in the fact of a hermitage that cannot fail to touch the imagination; the recluses are a sad kindred, but they are never commonplace. Mrs. Todd had truly said that Joanna was like one of the saints in the desert; the loneliness of sorrow will forever keep alive their sad succession.

"Where is Shell-heap Island!" I asked eagerly.

"You see Shell-heap now, layin' 'way out beyond Black Island there," answered the captain, pointing with outstretched arm as he stood, and holding the rudder with his knee.

"I should like very much to go there," said I, and the captain, without comment, changed his course a little more to the eastward and let the reef out of his mainsail.

"I don't know's we can make an easy landin' for ye," he remarked doubtfully. "May get your feet wet; bad place to land. Trouble is I ought to have brought a tagboat; but they clutch on to the water so, an' I do love to sail free. This gre't boat gets easy bothered with anything trailin'. 'T ain't breakin' much on the meetin'-house ledges; guess I can fetch in to Shell-heap."

"How long is it since Miss Joanna Todd died?" I asked, partly by way of explanation.

"Twenty-two years come September," answered the captain, after reflection. "She died the same year my oldest boy was born, an' the town house was burnt over to the Port. I didn't know but you merely wanted to hunt for some o' them Indian relics. Long 's you want to see where Joanna lived— No, 't ain't breakin' over the ledges; we'll manage to fetch across the shoals somehow, 't is such a distance to go

74

'way round, and tide's a-risin'," he ended hopefully, and we
sailed steadily on, the captain speechless with intent watching of a difficult course, until the small island with its
low whitish promontory lay in full view before us under the
bright afternoon sun.

The month was August, and I had seen the color of the
islands change from the fresh green of June to a sunburnt
brown that made them look like stone, except where the
dark green of the spruces and fir balsam kept the tint that
even winter storms might deepen, but not fade. The few
wind-bent trees on Shell-heap Island were mostly dead and
gray, but there were some low-growing bushes, and a stripe
of light green ran along just above the shore, which I knew
to be wild morning-glories. As we came close I could see the
high stone walls of a small square field, though there were
no sheep left to assail it; and below, there was a little
harbor-like cove where Captain Bowden was boldly running
the great boat in to seek a landing-place. There was a
crooked channel of deep water which led close up against
the shore.

"There, you hold fast for'ard there, an' wait for her to
lift on the wave. You'll make a good landin' if you're smart;
right on the port-hand side!" the captain called excitedly;
and I, standing ready with high ambition, seized my chance
and leaped over to the grassy bank.

"I'm beat if I ain't aground after all!" mourned the captain despondently.

But I could reach the bowsprit, and he pushed with the
boat-hook, while the wind veered round a little as if on
purpose and helped with the sail; so presently the boat was
free and began to drift out from shore.

"Used to call this p'int Joanna's wharf privilege, but 't
has worn away in the weather since her time. I thought
one or two bumps wouldn't hurt us none,—paint's got to be
renewed, anyway,—but I never thought she'd tetch. I
figured on shyin' by," the captain apologized. "She's too
gre't a boat to handle well in here; but I used to sort of shy
by in Joanna's day, an' cast a little somethin' ashore—some
apples or a couple o' pears if I had 'em—on the grass, where
she'd be sure to see."

I stood watching while Captain Bowden cleverly found

his way back to deeper water. "You needn't make no haste," he called to me; "I'll keep within call. Joanna lays right up there in the far corner o' the field. There used to be a path led to the place. I always knew her well. I was out here to the funeral."

I found the path; it was touching to discover that this lonely spot was not without its pilgrims. Later generations will know less and less of Joanna herself, but there are paths trodden to the shrines of solitude the world over,—the world cannot forget them, try as it may; the feet of the young find them out because of curiosity and dim foreboding, while the old bring hearts full of remembrance. This plain anchorite had been one of those whom sorrow made too lonely to brave the sight of men, too timid to front the simple world she knew, yet valiant enough to live alone with her poor insistent human nature and the calms and passions of the sea and sky.

The birds were flying all about the field; they fluttered up out of the grass at my feet as I walked along, so tame that I liked to think they kept some happy tradition from summer to summer of the safety of nests and good fellowship of mankind. Poor Joanna's house was gone except the stones of its foundations, and there was little trace of her flower garden except a single faded sprig of much-enduring French pinks, which a great bee and a yellow butterfly were befriending together. I drank at the spring, and thought that now and then some one would follow me from the busy, hard-worked, and simple-thoughted countryside of the mainland, which lay dim and dreamlike in the August haze, as Joanna must have watched it many a day. There was the world, and here was she with eternity well begun. In the life of each of us, I said to myself, there is a place remote and islanded, and given to endless regret or secret happiness; we are each the uncompanioned hermit and recluse of an hour or a day; we understand our fellows of the cell to whatever age of history they may belong.

But as I stood alone on the island, in the sea-breeze, suddenly there came a sound of distant voices; gay voices and laughter from a pleasure-boat that was going seaward full of boys and girls. I knew, as if she had told me, that poor Joanna must have heard the like on many and many a summer afternoon, and must have welcomed the good cheer in spite of hopelessness and winter weather, and all the sorrow and disappointment in the world.

16 *The Great Expedition* Mrs. Todd never by any chance gave warning over night of her great projects and adventures by sea and land. She first came to an understanding with the primal forces of nature, and never trusted to any preliminary promise of good weather, but examined the day for herself in its infancy. Then, if the stars were propitious, and the wind blew from a quarter of good inheritance whence no surprises of sea-turns or southwest sultriness might be feared, long before I was fairly awake I used to hear a rustle and knocking like a great mouse in the walls, and an impatient tread on the steep garret stairs that led to Mrs. Todd's chief place of storage. She went and came as if she had already started on her expedition with utmost haste and kept returning for something that was forgotten. When I appeared in quest of my breakfast, she would be absent-minded and sparing of speech, as if I had displeased her, and she was now, by main force of principle, holding herself back from altercation and strife of tongues.

These signs of a change became familiar to me in the course of time, and Mrs. Todd hardly noticed some plain proofs of divination one August morning when I said, without preface, that I had just seen the Beggs' best chaise go by, and that we should have to take the grocery. Mrs. Todd was alert in a moment.

"There! I might have known!" she exclaimed. "It's the 15th of August, when he goes and gets his money. He heired an annuity from an uncle o' his on his mother's side. I understood the uncle said none o' Sam Begg's wife's folks should make free with it, so after Sam's gone it'll all be past an' spent, like last summer. That's what Sam prospers on now, if you can call it prosperin'. Yes, I might have known. 'T is the 15th o' August with him, an' he gener'ly stops to dinner with a cousin's widow on the way home. Feb'uary an' August is the times. Takes him 'bout all day to go an' come."

I heard this explanation with interest. The tone of Mrs. Todd's voice was complaining at the last.

"I like the grocery just as well as the chaise," I hastened to say, referring to a long-bodied high wagon with a canopy-top, like an attenuated four-posted bedstead on wheels, in which we sometimes journeyed. "We can put things in behind—roots and flowers and raspberries, or anything you are going after—much better than if we had the chaise."

Mrs. Todd looked stony and unwilling. "I counted upon the chaise," she said, turning her back to me, and roughly pushing back all the quiet tumblers on the cupboard shelf as if they had been impertinent. "Yes, I desired the chaise for once. I ain't goin' berryin' nor to fetch home no more wilted vegetation this year. Season's about past, except for a poor few o' late things," she added in a milder tone. "I'm goin' up country. No, I ain't intendin' to go berryin'. I've been plottin' for it the past fortnight and hopin' for a good day."

"Would you like to have me go too?" I asked frankly, but not without a humble fear that I might have mistaken the purpose of this latest plan.

"Oh certain, dear!" answered my friend affectionately. "Oh no, I never thought o' any one else for comp'ny, if it's convenient for you, long's poor mother ain't come. I ain't nothin' like so handy with a conveyance as I be with a good bo't. Comes o' my early bringing-up. I expect we've got to make that great high wagon do. The tires want settin' and 't is all loose-jointed, so I can hear it shackle the other side o' the ridge. We'll put the basket in front. I ain't goin' to have it bouncin' an' twirlin' all the way. Why, I've been makin' some nice hearts and rounds to carry."

These were signs of high festivity, and my interest deepened moment by moment.

"I'll go down to the Beggs' and get the horse just as soon as I finish my breakfast," said I. "Then we can start whenever you are ready."

Mrs. Todd looked cloudy again. "I don't know but you look nice enough to go just as you be," she suggested doubtfully. "No, you wouldn't want to wear that pretty blue dress o' yourn 'way up country. 'T ain't dusty now, but it may be comin' home. No, I expect you'd rather not wear that and the other hat."

"Oh yes. I shouldn't think of wearing these clothes," said I, with sudden illumination. "Why, if we're going up country and are likely to see some of your friends, I'll put on my blue dress, and you must wear your watch; I am not going at all if you mean to wear the big hat."

"Now you're behavin' pretty," responded Mrs. Todd, with a gay toss of her head and a cheerful smile, as she came across the room, bringing a saucerful of wild raspberries, a pretty piece of salvage from supper-time. "I was cast down when I see you come to breakfast. I didn't think 't was just what you'd select to wear to the reunion, where you're goin' to meet everybody."

"What reunion do you mean?" I asked, not without amazement. "Not the Bowden Family's? I thought that was going to take place in September."

"To-day's the day. They sent word the middle o' the week. I thought you might have heard of it. Yes, they changed the day. I been thinkin' we'd talk it over, but you never can tell beforehand how it's goin' to be, and 't ain't worth while to wear a day all out before it comes." Mrs. Todd gave no place to the pleasures of anticipation, but she spoke like the oracle that she was. "I wish mother was here to go," she continued sadly. "I did look for her last night, and I couldn't keep back the tears when the dark really fell and she wa'n't here, she does so enjoy a great occasion. If William had a mite o' snap an' ambition, he'd take the lead at such a time. Mother likes variety, and there ain't but a few nice opportunities 'round here, an' them she has to miss 'less she contrives to get ashore to me. I do re'lly hate to go to the reunion without mother, an' 't is a beautiful day; everybody'll be asking where she is. Once she'd have got here anyway. Poor mother's beginnin' to feel her age."

"Why, there's your mother now!" I exclaimed with joy, I was so glad to see the dear old soul again. "I hear her voice at the gate." But Mrs. Todd was out of the door before me.

There, sure enough, stood Mrs. Blackett, who must have left Green Island before daylight. She had climbed the steep road from the water-side so eagerly that she was out of

breath, and was standing by the garden fence to rest. She
held an old-fashioned brown wicker cap-basket in her hand,
as if visiting were a thing of every day, and looked up at us
as pleased and triumphant as a child.

"Oh, what a poor, plain garden! Hardly a flower in it
except your bush o' balm!" she said. "But you do keep your
garden neat, Almiry. Are you both well, an' goin' up
country with me?" She came a step or two closer to meet
us, with quaint politeness and quite as delightful as if she
were at home. She dropped a quick little curtsey before Mrs.
Todd.

"There, mother, what a girl you be! I am so pleased! I
was just bewailin' you," said the daughter, with unwonted
feeling. "I was just bewailin' you, I was so disappointed, an'
I kep' myself awake a good piece o' the night scoldin' poor
William. I watched for the boat till I was ready to shed
tears yesterday, and when 't was comin' dark I kep' making
errands out to the gate an' down the road to see if you
wa'n't in the doldrums somewhere down the bay."

"There was a head wind, as you know," said Mrs. Blackett, giving me the cap-basket, and holding my hand affectionately as we walked up the clean-swept path to the door.
"I was partly ready to come, but dear William said I should
be all tired out and might get cold, havin' to beat all the
way in. So we give it up, and set down and spent the evenin'
together. It was a little rough and windy outside, and I
guess 't was better judgment; we went to bed very early and
made a good start just at daylight. It's been a lovely mornin'
on the water. William thought he'd better fetch across beyond Bird Rocks, rowin' the greater part o' the way; then
we sailed from there right over to the Landin', makin' only
one tack. William'll be in again for me to-morrow, so I can
come back here an' rest me over night, an' go to meetin'
to-morrow, and have a nice, good visit."

"She was just havin' her breakfast," said Mrs. Todd, who
had listened eagerly to the long explanation without a
word of disapproval, while her face shone more and more
with joy. "You just sit right down an' have a cup of tea
and rest you while we make our preparations. Oh, I am so
gratified to think you've come! Yes, she was just havin' her
breakfast, and we were speakin' of you. Where's William?"

"He went right back; he said he expected some schooners in about noon after bait, but he'll come an' have his dinner with us to-morrow, unless it rains; then next day. I laid his best things out all ready," explained Mrs. Blackett, a little anxiously. "This wind will serve him nice all the way home. Yes, I will take a cup of tea, dear,—a cup of tea is always good; and then I'll rest a minute and be all ready to start."

"I do feel condemned for havin' such hard thoughts o' William," openly confessed Mrs. Todd. She stood before us so large and serious that we both laughed and could not find it in our hearts to convict so rueful a culprit. "He shall have a good .dinner to-morrow, if it can be got, and I shall be real glad to see William," the confession ended handsomely, while Mrs. Blackett smiled approval and made haste to praise the tea. Then I hurried away to make sure of the grocery wagon. Whatever might be the good of the reunion, I was going to have the pleasure and delight of a day in Mrs. Blackett's company, not to speak of Mrs. Todd's.

The early morning breeze was still blowing, and the warm, sunshiny air was of some ethereal northern sort, with a cool freshness as if it came over new-fallen snow. The world was filled with a fragrance of fir-balsam and the faintest flavor of seaweed from the ledges, bare and brown at low tide in the little harbor. It was so still and so early that the village was but half awake. I could hear no voices but those of the birds, small and great,—the constant song sparrows, the clink of a yellow-hammer over in the woods, and the far conversation of some deliberate crows. I saw William Blackett's escaping sail already far from land, and Captain Littlepage was sitting behind his closed window as I passed by, watching for some one who never came. I tried to speak to him, but he did not see me. There was a patient look on the old man's face, as if the world were a great mistake and he had nobody with whom to speak his own language or find companionship.

17 *A Country Road* Whatever doubts and anxieties I may have had about the inconvenience of the Beggs' high wagon for a person of Mrs. Blackett's age and shortness,

they were happily overcome by the aid of a chair and her own valiant spirit. Mrs. Todd bestowed great care upon seating us as if we were taking passage by boat, but she finally pronounced that we were properly trimmed. When we had gone only a little way up the hill she remembered that she had left the house door wide open, though the large key was safe in her pocket. I offered to run back, but my offer was met with lofty scorn, and we lightly dismissed the matter from our minds, until two or three miles further on we met the doctor, and Mrs. Todd asked him to stop and ask her nearest neighbor to step over and close the door if the dust seemed to blow in the afternoon.

"She'll be there in her kitchen; she'll hear you the minute you call; 't won't give you no delay," said Mrs. Todd to the doctor. "Yes, Mis' Dennett's right there, with the windows all open. It isn't as if my fore door opened right on the road, anyway." At which proof of composure Mrs. Blackett smiled wisely at me.

The doctor seemed delighted to see our guest; they were evidently the warmest friends, and I saw a look of affectionate confidence in their eyes. The good man left his carriage to speak to us, but as he took Mrs. Blackett's hand he held it a moment, and, as if merely from force of habit, felt her pulse as they talked; then to my delight he gave the firm old wrist a commending pat.

"You're wearing well: good for another ten years at this rate," he assured her cheerfully, and she smiled back. "I like to keep a strict account of my old stand-bys," and he turned to me. "Don't you let Mrs. Todd overdo to-day,— old folks like her are apt to be thoughtless;" and then we all laughed, and, parting, went our ways gayly.

"I suppose he puts up with your rivalry the same as ever?" asked Mrs. Blackett. "You and he are as friendly as ever, I see, Almiry," and Almira sagely nodded.

"He's got too many long routes now to stop to 'tend to all his door patients," she said, "especially them that takes pleasure in talkin' themselves over. The doctor and me have got to be kind of partners; he's gone a good deal, far an' wide. Looked tired, didn't he? I shall have to advise with him an' get him off for a good rest. He'll take the big boat from Rockland an' go off up to Boston an' mouse round among the other doctors, once in two or three years, and come home fresh as a boy. I guess they think consider'ble of him up there." Mrs. Todd shook the reins and reached determinedly for the whip, as if she were compelling public opinion.

Whatever energy and spirit the white horse had to begin with were soon exhausted by the steep hills and his discernment of a long expedition ahead. We toiled slowly along. Mrs. Blackett and I sat together, and Mrs. Todd sat alone in front with much majesty and the large basket of provisions. Part of the way the road was shaded by thick woods, but we also passed one farmhouse after another on the high uplands, which we all three regarded with deep interest, the house itself and the barns and garden-spots and poultry all having to suffer an inspection of the shrewdest sort. This was a highway quite new to me; in fact, most of my journeys with Mrs. Todd had been made afoot and between the roads, in open pasturelands. My friends stopped several times for brief dooryard visits, and made so many promises of stopping again on the way home that I began to wonder how long the expedition would last. I had often noticed how warmly Mrs. Todd was greeted by her friends, but it was hardly to be compared to the feeling now shown toward Mrs. Blackett. A look of delight came to the faces of those who recognized the plain, dear old figure beside me; one revelation after another was made of the constant interest and intercourse that had linked the far island and these scattered farms into a golden chain of love and dependence.

"Now, we mustn't stop again if we can help it," insisted Mrs. Todd at last. "You'll get tired, mother, and you'll think the less o' reunions. We can visit along here any day. There, if they ain't frying doughnuts in this next house, too! These are new folks, you know, from over St. George way; they took this old Talcot farm last year. 'T is the best water on the road, and the checkrein's come undone—yes, we'd best delay a little and water the horse."

We stopped, and seeing a party of pleasure-seekers in holiday attire, the thin, anxious mistress of the farmhouse came out with wistful sympathy to hear what news we might have to give. Mrs. Blackett first spied her at the half-closed door, and asked with such cheerful directness if we were trespassing that, after a few words, she went back to her kitchen and reappeared with a plateful of doughnuts.

"Entertainment for man and beast," announced Mrs. Todd with satisfaction. "Why, we've perceived there was new doughnuts all along the road, but you're the first that has treated us."

Our new acquaintance flushed with pleasure, but said nothing.

"They're very nice; you've had good luck with 'em," pronounced Mrs. Todd. "Yes, we've observed there was doughnuts all the way along; if one house is frying all the rest is; 't is so with a great many things."

"I don't suppose likely you're goin' up to the Bowden reunion?" asked the hostess as the white horse lifted his head and we were saying good-by.

"Why, yes," said Mrs. Blackett and Mrs. Todd and I, all together.

"I am connected with the family. Yes, I expect to be there this afternoon. I've been lookin' forward to it," she told us eagerly.

"We shall see you there. Come and sit with us if it's convenient," said dear Mrs. Blackett, and we drove away.

"I wonder who she was before she was married?" said Mrs. Todd, who was usually unerring in matters of genealogy. "She must have been one of that remote branch that lived down beyond Thomaston. We can find out this afternoon. I expect that the families'll march together, or be sorted out some way. I'm willing to own a relation that has such proper ideas of doughnuts."

"I seem to see the family looks," said Mrs. Blackett. "I wish we'd asked her name. She's a stranger, and I want to help make it pleasant for all such."

"She resembles Cousin Pa'lina Bowden about the forehead," said Mrs. Todd with decision.

We had just passed a piece of woodland that shaded the road, and come out to some open fields beyond, when Mrs. Todd suddenly reined in the horse as if somebody had stood on the roadside and stopped her. She even gave that quick reassuring nod of her head which was usually made to answer for a bow, but I discovered that she was looking

eagerly at a tall ash-tree that grew just inside the field
fence.

"I thought 't was goin' to do well," she said complacently
as we went on again. "Last time I was up this way that
tree was kind of drooping and discouraged. Grown trees
act that way sometimes, same's folks; then they'll put right
to it and strike their roots off into new ground and start all
over again with real good courage. Ash-trees is very likely to
have poor spells; they ain't got the resolution of other
trees."

I listened hopefully for more; it was this peculiar wisdom
that made one value Mrs. Todd's pleasant company.

"There's sometimes a good hearty tree growin' right out
of the bare rock, out o' some crack that just holds the roots,"
she went on to say, "right on the pitch o' one o' them bare
stony hills where you can't seem to see a wheel-barrowful
o' good earth in a place, but that tree'll keep a green top in
the driest summer. You lay your ear down to the ground an'
you'll hear a little stream runnin'. Every such tree has got
its own livin' spring; there's folks made to match 'em."

I could not help turning to look at Mrs. Blackett, close
beside me. Her hands were clasped placidly in their thin
black woolen gloves, and she was looking at the flowery
wayside as we went slowly along, with a pleased, expectant
smile. I do not think she had heard a word about the
trees.

"I just saw a nice plant o' elecampane growin' back
there," she said presently to her daughter.

"I haven't got my mind on herbs today," responded Mrs.
Todd, in the most matter-of-fact way. "I'm bent on seeing
folks," and she shook the reins again.

I for one had no wish to hurry, it was so pleasant in the
shady roads. The woods stood close to the road on the
right; on the left were narrow fields and pastures where
there were as many acres of spruces and pines as there
were acres of bay and juniper and huckleberry, with a little
turf between. When I thought we were in the heart of the
inland country, we reached the top of a hill, and suddenly
there lay spread out before us a wonderful great view of
well-cleared fields that swept down to the wide water of a
bay. Beyond this were distant shores like another country

in the midday haze which half hid the hills beyond, and
the far-away pale blue mountains on the northern horizon.
There was a schooner with all sails set coming down the
bay from a white village that was sprinkled on the shore,
and there were many sailboats flitting about. It was a noble
landscape, and my eyes, which had grown used to the narrow inspection of a shaded roadside, could hardly take it in.

"Why, it's the upper bay," said Mrs. Todd. "You can
see 'way over into the town of Fessenden. Those farms 'way
over there are all in Fessenden. Mother used to have a sister
that lived up that shore. If we started as early 's we could on
a summer mornin', we couldn't get to her place from Green
Island till late afternoon, even with a fair, steady breeze,
and you had to strike the time just right so as to fetch up
'long o' the tide and land near the flood. 'T was ticklish
business, an' we didn't visit back an' forth as much as
mother desired. You have to go 'way down the co'st to
Cold Spring Light an' round that long point,—up here's
what they call the Back Shore."

"No, we were 'most always separated, my dear sister
and me, after the first year she was married," said Mrs.
Blackett. "We had our little families an' plenty o' cares.
We were always lookin' forward to the time we could see
each other more. Now and then she'd get out to the island
for a few days while her husband'd go fishin'; and once he
stopped with her an' two children, and made him some
flakes right there and cured all his fish for winter. We did
have a beautiful time together, sister an' me; she used to
look back to it long's she lived."

"I do love to look over there where she used to live,"
Mrs. Blackett went on as we began to go down the hill.
"It seems as if she must still be there, though she's long
been gone. She loved their farm,—she didn't see how I got
so used to our island; but somehow I was always happy from
the first."

"Yes, it's very dull to me up among those slow farms,"
declared Mrs. Todd. "The snow troubles 'em in winter.
They're all besieged by winter, as you may say; 't is far
better by the shore than up among such places. I never
thought I should like to live up country."

"Why, just see the carriages ahead of us on the next

rise!" exclaimed Mrs. Blackett. "There's going to be a great gathering, don't you believe there is, Almiry? It hasn't seemed up to now as if anybody was going but us. An' 't is such a beautiful day, with yesterday cool and pleasant to work an' get ready, I shouldn't wonder if everybody was there, even the slow ones like Phebe Ann Brock."

Mrs. Blackett's eyes were bright with excitement, and even Mrs. Todd showed remarkable enthusiasm. She hurried the horse and caught up with the holiday-makers ahead. "There's all the Dep'fords goin', six in the wagon," she told us joyfully; "an' Mis' Alva Tilley's folks are now risin' the hill in their new carryall."

Mrs. Blackett pulled at the neat bow of her black bonnet-strings, and tied them again with careful precision. "I believe your bonnet's on a little bit sideways, dear," she advised Mrs. Todd as if she were a child; but Mrs. Todd was too much occupied to pay proper heed. We began to feel a new sense of gayety and of taking part in the great occasion as we joined the little train.

18 *The Bowden Reunion* It is very rare in country life, where high days and holidays are few, that any occasion of general interest proves to be less than great. Such is the hidden fire of enthusiasm in the New England nature that, once given an outlet, it shines forth with almost volcanic light and heat. In quiet neighborhoods such inward force does not waste itself upon those petty excitements of every day that belong to cities, but when, at long intervals, the altars to patriotism, to friendship, to the ties of kindred, are reared in our familiar fields, then the fires glow, the flames come up as if from the inexhaustible burning heart of the earth; the primal fires break through the granite dust in which our souls are set. Each heart is warm and every face shines with the ancient light. Such a day as this has transfiguring powers, and easily makes friends of those who have been cold-hearted, and gives to those who are dumb their chance to speak, and lends some beauty to the plainest face.

"Oh, I expect I shall meet friends today that I haven't seen in a long while," said Mrs. Blackett with deep satisfaction. "'T will bring out a good many of the old folks, 't is such a lovely day. I'm always glad not to have them disappointed."

"I guess likely the best of 'em'll be there," answered Mrs. Todd with gentle humor, stealing a glance at me. "There's one thing certain: there's nothing takes in this whole neighborhood like anything related to the Bowdens. Yes, I do feel that when you call upon the Bowdens you may expect most families to rise up between the Landing and the far end of the Back Cove. Those that aren't kin by blood are kin by marriage."

"There used to be an old story goin' about when I was a girl," said Mrs. Blackett, with much amusement. "There was a great many more Bowdens then than there are now, and the folks was all setting in meeting a dreadful hot Sunday afternoon, and a scatter-witted little bound girl came running to the meetin'-house door all out o' breath from somewheres in the neighborhood. 'Mis' Bowden, Mis' Bowden!' says she. 'Your baby's in a fit!' They used to tell that the whole congregation was up on its feet in a minute and right out into the aisles. All the Mis' Bowdens was setting right out for home; the minister stood there in the pulpit tryin' to keep sober, an' all at once he burst right out laughin'. He was a very nice man, they said, and he said he'd better give 'em the benediction, and they could hear the sermon next Sunday, so he kept it over. My mother was there, and she thought certain 't was me."

"None of our family was ever subject to fits," interrupted Mrs. Todd severely. "No, we never had fits, none of us, and 't was lucky we didn't 'way out there to Green Island. Now these folks right in front: dear sakes knows the bunches o' soothing catnip an' yarrow I've had to favor old Mis' Evins with dryin'! You can see it right in their expressions, all them Evins folks. There, just you look up to the cross-roads, mother," she suddenly exclaimed. "See all the teams ahead of us. And oh, look down on the bay; yes, look down on the bay! See what a sight o' boats, all headin' for the Bowden place cove!"

"Oh, ain't it beautiful!" said Mrs. Blackett, with all the delight of a girl. She stood up in the high wagon to see everything, and when she sat down again she took fast hold of my hand.

"Hadn't you better urge the horse a little, Almiry?" she asked. "He's had it easy as we came along, and he can rest when we get there. The others are some little ways ahead, and I don't want to lose a minute."

We watched the boats drop their sails one by one in the cove as we drove along the high land. The old Bowden house stood, low-storied and broad-roofed, in its green fields as if it were a motherly brown hen waiting for the flock that came straying toward it from every direction. The first Bowden settler had made his home there, and it was still the Bowden farm; five generations of sailors and farmers and soldiers had been its children. And presently Mrs. Blackett showed me the stone-walled burying-ground that stood like a little fort on a knoll overlooking the bay, but, as she said, there were plenty of scattered Bowdens who were not laid there,—some lost at sea, and some out West, and some who died in the war; most of the home graves were those of women.

We could see now that there were different footpaths from along shore and across country. In all these there were straggling processions walking in single file, like old illustrations of the Pilgrim's Progress. There was a crowd about the house as if huge bees were swarming in the lilac bushes. Beyond the fields and cove a higher point of land ran out into the bay, covered with woods which must have kept away much of the northwest wind in winter. Now there was a pleasant look of shade and shelter there for the great family meeting.

We hurried on our way, beginning to feel as if we were very late, and it was a great satisfaction at last to turn out of the stony highroad into a green lane shaded with old apple-trees. Mrs. Todd encouraged the horse until he fairly pranced with gayety as we drove round to the front of the house on the soft turf. There was an instant cry of rejoicing, and two or three persons ran toward us from the busy group.

"Why, dear Mis' Blackett!—here's Mis' Blackett!" I heard them say, as if it were pleasure enough for one day to have a sight of her. Mrs. Todd turned to me with a lovely look of triumph and self-forgetfulness. An elderly man who wore

the look of a prosperous sea-captain put up both arms and
lifted Mrs. Blackett down from the high wagon like a child,
and kissed her with hearty affection. "I was master afraid
she wouldn't be here," he said, looking at Mrs. Todd with
a face like a happy sunburnt schoolboy, while everybody
crowded round to give their welcome.

"Mother's always the queen," said Mrs. Todd. "Yes,
they'll all make everything of mother; she'll have a lovely
time to-day. I wouldn't have had her miss it, and there
won't be a thing she'll ever regret, except to mourn because William wa'n't here."

Mrs. Blackett having been properly escorted to the house,
Mrs. Todd received her own full share of honor, and some
of the men, with a simple kindness that was the soul of
chivalry, waited upon us and our baskets and led away the
white horse. I already knew some of Mrs. Todd's friends
and kindred, and felt like an adopted Bowden in this happy
moment. It seemed to be enough for any one to have arrived by the same conveyance as Mrs. Blackett, who presently had her court inside the house, while Mrs. Todd,
large, hospitable, and pre-eminent, was the centre of a rap-
idly increasing crowd about the lilac bushes. Small companies were continually coming up the long green slope
from the water, and nearly all the boats had come to shore.
I counted three or four that were baffled by the light breeze,
but before long all the Bowdens, small and great, seemed
to have assembled, and we started to go up to the grove
across the field.

Out of the chattering crowd of noisy children, and large-
waisted women whose best black dresses fell straight to
the ground in generous folds, and sunburnt men who looked
as serious as if it were town-meeting day, there suddenly
came silence and order. I saw the straight, soldierly little
figure of a man who bore a fine resemblance to Mrs. Blackett, and who appeared to marshal us with perfect ease. He
was imperative enough, but with a grand military sort of
courtesy, and bore himself with solemn dignity of importance. We were sorted out according to some clear design
of his own, and stood as speechless as a troop to await his
orders. Even the children were ready to march together, a
pretty flock, and at the last moment Mrs. Blackett and a few

distinguished companions, the ministers and those who were very old, came out of the house together and took their places. We ranked by fours, and even then we made a long procession.

There was a wide path mowed for us across the field, and, as we moved along, the birds flew up out of the thick second crop of clover, and the bees hummed as if it still were June. There was a flashing of white gulls over the water where the fleet of boats rode the low waves together in the cove, swaying their small masts as if they kept time to our steps. The plash of the water could be heard faintly, yet still be heard; we might have been a company of ancient Greeks going to celebrate a victory, or to worship the god of harvests in the grove above. It was strangely moving to see this and to make part of it. The sky, the sea, have watched poor humanity at its rites so long; we were no more a New England family celebrating its own existence and simple progress; we carried the tokens and inheritance of all such households from which this had descended, and were only the latest of our line. We possessed the instincts of a far, forgotten childhood; I found myself thinking that we ought to be carrying green branches and singing as we went. So we came to the thick shaded grove still silent, and were set in our places by the straight trees that swayed together and let sunshine through here and there like a single golden leaf that flickered down, vanishing in the cool shade.

The grove was so large that the great family looked far smaller than it had in the open field; there was a thick growth of dark pines and firs with an occasional maple or oak that gave a gleam of color like a bright window in the great roof. On three sides we could see the water, shining behind the tree-trunks, and feel the cool salt breeze that began to come up with the tide just as the day reached its highest point of heat. We could see the green sunlit field we had just crossed as if we looked out at it from a dark room, and the old house and its lilacs standing placidly in the sun, and the great barn with a stockade of carriages from which two or three care-taking men who had lingered were coming across the field together. Mrs. Todd had taken off her warm gloves and looked the picture of content.

"There!" she exclaimed. "I've always meant to have you

see this place, but I never looked for such a beautiful opportunity—weather an' occasion both made to match. Yes, it suits me: I don't ask no more. I want to know if you saw mother walkin' at the head! It choked me right up to see mother at the head, walkin' with the ministers," and Mrs. Todd turned away to hide the feelings she could not instantly control.

"Who was the marshal?" I hastened to ask. "Was he an old soldier?"

"Don't he do well?" answered Mrs. Todd with satisfaction.

"He don't often have such a chance to show off his gifts," said Mrs. Caplin, a friend from the Landing who had joined us. "That's Sant Bowden; he always takes the lead, such days. Good for nothing else most o' his time; trouble is, he"—

I turned with interest to hear the worst. Mrs. Caplin's tone was both zealous and impressive.

"Stim'lates," she explained scornfully.

"No, Santin never was in the war," said Mrs. Todd with lofty indifference. "It was a cause of real distress to him. He kep' enlistin', and traveled far an' wide about here, an' even took the bo't and went to Boston to volunteer: but he ain't a sound man, an' they wouldn't have him. They say he knows all their tactics, an' can tell all about the battle o' Waterloo well's he can Bunker Hill. I told him once the country'd lost a great general, an' I meant it, too."

"I expect you're near right," said Mrs. Caplin, a little crestfallen and apologetic.

"I be right," insisted Mrs. Todd with much amiability. "'T was most too bad to cramp him down to his peaceful trade, but he's a most excellent shoemaker at his best, an' he always says it's a trade that gives him time to think an' plan his manœuvres. Over to the Port they always invite him to march Decoration Day, same as the rest, an' he does look noble; he comes of soldier stock."

I had been noticing with great interest the curiously French type of face which prevailed in this rustic company. I had said to myself before that Mrs. Blackett was plainly of French descent, in both her appearance and her charming gifts, but this is not surprising when one has learned how large a proportion of the early settlers on this northern coast of New England were of Huguenot blood, and that it is the Norman Englishman, not the Saxon, who goes adventuring to a new world.

"They used to say in old times," said Mrs. Todd modestly, "that our family came of very high folks in France, and one of 'em was a great general in some o' the old wars. I sometimes think that Santin's ability has come 'way down from then. 'T ain't nothin' he's ever acquired; 't was born in him. I don't know's he ever saw a fine parade, or met with those that studied up such things. He's figured it all out an' got his papers so he knows how to aim a cannon right for William's fish-house five miles out on Green Island, or up there on Burnt Island where the signal is. He had it all over to me one day, an' I tried hard to appear interested. His life's all in it, but he will have those poor gloomy spells come over him now an' then, an' then he has to drink."

Mrs. Caplin gave a heavy sigh.

"There's a great many such strayaway folks, just as there is plants," continued Mrs. Todd, who was nothing if not botanical. "I know of just one sprig of laurel that grows over back here in a wild spot, an' I never could hear of no other on this coast. I had a large bunch brought me once from Massachusetts way, so I know it. This piece grows in an open spot where you'd think 't would do well, but it's sort o' poor-lookin'. I've visited it time an' again, just to notice its poor blooms. 'T is a real Sant Bowden, out of its own place."

Mrs. Caplin looked bewildered and blank. "Well, all I know is, last year he worked out some kind of a plan so's to parade the county conference in platoons, and got 'em all flustered up tryin' to sense his ideas of a holler square," she burst forth. "They was holler enough anyway after ridin' 'way down from up country into the salt air, and they'd been treated to a sermon on faith an' works from old Fayther Harlow that never knows when to cease. 'T wa'n't no time for tactics then,—they wa'n't a-thinkin' of the church military. Sant, he couldn't do nothin' with 'em. All he thinks of, when he sees a crowd, is how to march 'em. 'T is all very well when he don't 'tempt too much. He never did act like other folks."

"Ain't I just been maintainin' that he ain't like 'em?" urged Mrs. Todd decidedly. "Strange folks has got to have strange ways for what I see."

"Somebody observed once that you could pick out the likeness of 'most every sort of a foreigner when you looked about you in our parish," said Sister Caplin, her face brightening with sudden illumination. "I didn't see the bearin' of it then quite so plain. I always did think Mari' Harris resembled a Chinee."

"Mari' Harris was pretty as a child, I remember," said the pleasant voice of Mrs. Blackett, who, after receiving the affectionate greetings of nearly the whole company, came to join us,—to see, as she insisted, that we were out of mischief.

"Yes, Mari' was one o' them pretty little lambs that make dreadful homely old sheep," replied Mrs. Todd with energy. "Cap'n Littlepage never'd look so disconsolate if she was any sort of a proper person to direct things. She might divert him; yes, she might divert the old gentleman, an' let him think he had his own way, 'stead o' arguing everything down to the bare bone. 'T wouldn't hurt her to sit down an' hear his great stories once in a while."

"The stories are very interesting," I ventured to say.

"Yes, you always catch yourself a-thinkin' what if they was all true, and he had the right of it," answered Mrs. Todd. "He's a good sight better company, though dreamy, than such sordid creatur's as Mari' Harris."

"Live and let live," said dear old Mrs. Blackett gently. "I haven't seen the captain for a good while, now that I ain't so constant to meetin'," she added wistfully. "We always have known each other."

"Why, if it is a good pleasant day tomorrow, I'll get William to call an' invite the capt'in to dinner. William'll be in early so's to pass up the street without meetin' anybody."

"There, they're callin' out it's time to set the tables," said Mrs. Caplin, with great excitement.

"Here's Cousin Sarah Jane Blackett! Well, I am pleased, certain!" exclaimed Mrs. Todd, with unaffected delight; and these kindred spirits met and parted with the promise of a good talk later on. After this there was no more time for

conversation until we were seated in order at the long
tables.

"I'm one that always dreads seeing some o' the folks
that I don't like, at such a time as this," announced Mrs.
Todd privately to me after a season of reflection. We were
just waiting for the feast to begin. "You wouldn't think
such a great creatur' 's I be could feel all over pins an'
needles. I remember, the day I promised to Nathan, how
it come over me, just 's I was feelin' happy 's I could, that
I'd got to have an own cousin o' his for my near relation all
the rest o' my life, an' it seemed as if die I should. Poor
Nathan saw somethin' had crossed me,—he had very nice
feelings,—and when he asked me what 't was, I told him.
'I never could like her myself,' said he. 'You sha'n't be
bothered, dear,' he says; an' 't was one o' the things that
made me set a good deal by Nathan, he didn't make a habit
of always opposin', like some men. 'Yes,' says I, 'but think o'
Thanksgivin' times an' funerals; she's our relation, an' we've
got to own her.' Young folks don't think o' those things.
There she goes now, do let's pray her by!" said Mrs. Todd,
with an alarming transition from general opinions to particular animosities. "I hate her just the same as I always did;
but she's got on a real pretty dress. I do try to remember
that she's Nathan's cousin. Oh dear, well; she's gone by
after all, an' ain't seen me. I expected she'd come pleasantin'
round just to show off an' say afterwards she was acquainted."

This was so different from Mrs. Todd's usual largeness of
mind that I had a moment's uneasiness; but the cloud
passed quickly over her spirit, and was gone with the of-
fender.

There never was a more generous out-of-door feast along
the coast than the Bowden family set forth that day. To
call it a picnic would make it seem trivial. The great tables
were edged with pretty oak-leaf trimming, which the boys
and girls made. We brought flowers from the fence-thickets
of the great field; and out of the disorder of flowers and
provisions suddenly appeared as orderly a scheme for the
feast as the marshal had shaped for the procession. I began
to respect the Bowdens for their inheritance of good taste

and skill and a certain pleasing gift of formality. Something
made them do all these things in a finer way than most
country people would have done them. As I looked up and
down the tables there was a good cheer, a grave soberness
that shone with pleasure, a humble dignity of bearing.
There were some who should have sat below the salt for
lack of this good breeding; but they were not many. So, I
said to myself, their ancestors may have sat in the great hall
of some old French house in the Middle Ages, when battles
and sieges and processions and feasts were familiar things.
The ministers and Mrs. Blackett, with a few of their rank
and age, were put in places of honor, and for once that I
looked any other way I looked twice at Mrs. Blackett's face,
serene and mindful of privilege and responsibility, the mistress by simple fitness of this great day.

Mrs. Todd looked up at the roof of green trees, and then
carefully surveyed the company. "I see 'em better now
they're all settin' down," she said with satisfaction. "There's
old Mr. Gilbraith and his sister. I wish they were settin'
with us; they're not among folks they can parley with, an'
they look disappointed."

As the feast went on, the spirits of my companion steadily
rose. The excitement of an unexpectedly great occasion was
a subtle stimulant to her disposition, and I could see that
sometimes when Mrs. Todd had seemed limited and heavily domestic, she had simply grown sluggish for lack of
proper surroundings. She was not so much reminiscent now
as expectant, and as alert and gay as a girl. We who were
her neighbors were full of gayety, which was but the reflected light from her beaming countenance. It was not the
first time that I was full of wonder at the waste of human
ability in this world, as a botanist wonders at the waste-
fulness of nature, the thousand seeds that die, the unused
provision of every sort. The reserve force of society grows
more and more amazing to one's thought. More than one
face among the Bowdens showed that only opportunity and
stimulus were lacking,—a narrow set of circumstances had
caged a fine able character and held it captive. One sees
exactly the same types in a country gathering as in the most
brilliant city company. You are safe to be understood if the

spirit of your speech is the same for one neighbor as for the other.

19 *The Feast's End*   The feast was a noble feast, as has already been said. There was an elegant ingenuity displayed in the form of pies which delighted my heart. Once acknowledge that an American pie is far to be preferred to its humble ancestor, the English tart, and it is joyful to be reassured at a Bowden reunion that invention has not yet failed. Beside a delightful variety of material, the decorations went beyond all my former experience; dates and names were wrought in lines of pastry and frosting on the tops. There was even more elaborate reading matter on an excellent early-apple pie which we began to share and eat, precept upon precept. Mrs. Todd helped me generously to the whole word *Bowden*, and consumed *Reunion* herself, save an undecipherable fragment; but the most renowned essay in cookery on the tables was a model of the old Bowden house made of durable gingerbread, with all the windows and doors in the right places, and sprigs of genuine lilac set at the front. It must have been baked in sections, in one of the last of the great brick ovens, and fastened together on the morning of the day. There was a general sigh when this fell into ruin at the feast's end, and it was shared by a great part of the assembly, not without seriousness, and as if it were a pledge and token of loyalty. I met the maker of the gingerbread house, which had called up lively remembrances of a childish story. She had the gleaming eye of an enthusiast and a look of high ideals.

"I could just as well have made it all of frosted cake," she said, "but 't wouldn't have been the right shade; the old house as you observe, was never painted, and I concluded that plain gingerbread would represent it best. It wasn't all I expected it would be," she said sadly, as many an artist had said before her of his work.

There were speeches by the ministers; and there proved to be a historian among the Bowdens, who gave some fine anecdotes of the family history; and then appeared a poetess, whom Mrs. Todd regarded with wistful compassion and indulgence, and when the long faded garland of verses came to an appealing end, she turned to me with words of praise.

"Sounded pretty," said the generous listener. "Yes, I thought she did very well. We went to school together, an' Mary Anna had a very hard time; trouble was, her mother thought she'd given birth to a genius, an' Mary Anna's come to believe it herself. There, I don't know what we should have done without her; there ain't nobody else that can write poetry between here and 'way up towards Rockland; it adds a great deal at such a time. When she speaks o' those that are gone, she feels it all, and so does everybody else, but she harps too much. I'd laid half of that away for next time, if I was Mary Anna. There comes mother to speak to her, an' old Mr. Gilbraith's sister; now she'll be heartened right up. Mother'll say just the right thing."

The leave-takings were as affecting as the meetings of these old friends had been. There were enough young persons at the reunion, but it is the old who really value such opportunities; as for the young, it is the habit of every day to meet their comrades,—the time of separation has not come. To see the joy with which these elder kinsfolk and acquaintances had looked in one another's faces, and the lingering touch of their friendly hands; to see these affectionate meetings and then the reluctant partings, gave one a new idea of the isolation in which it was possible to live in that after all thinly settled region. They did not expect to see one another again very soon; the steady, hard work on the farms, the difficulty of getting from place to place, especially in winter when boats were laid up, gave double value to any occasion which could bring a large number of families together. Even funerals in this country of the pointed firs were not without their social advantages and satisfactions. I heard the words "next summer" repeated many times, though summer was still ours and all the leaves were green.

The boats began to put out from shore, and the wagons to drive away. Mrs. Blackett took me into the old house when we came back from the grove: it was her father's birthplace and early home, and she had spent much of her own childhood there with her grandmother. She spoke of those days as if they had but lately passed; in fact, I could imagine that the house looked almost exactly the same to her. I could see the brown rafters of the unfinished roof as I looked up the steep staircase, though the best room was as handsome with its good wainscoting and touch of ornament on the cornice as any old room of its day in a town.

Some of the guests who came from a distance were still sitting in the best room when we went in to take leave of the master and mistress of the house. We all said eagerly what a pleasant day it had been, and how swiftly the time had passed. Perhaps it is the great national anniversaries which our country has lately kept, and the soldiers' meetings that take place everywhere, which have made reunions of every sort the fashion. This one, at least, had been very interesting. I fancied that old feuds had been overlooked, and the old saying that blood is thicker than water had again proved itself true, though from the variety of names one argued a certain adulteration of the Bowden traits and belongings. Clannishness is an instinct of the heart,—it is more than a birthright, or a custom; and lesser rights were forgotten in the claim to a common inheritance.

We were among the very last to return to our proper lives and lodgings. I came near to feeling like a true Bowden, and parted from certain new friends as if they were old friends; we were rich with the treasure of a new remembrance.

At last we were in the high wagon again; the old white horse had been well fed in the Bowden barn, and we drove away and soon began to climb the long hill toward the wooded ridge. The road was new to me, as roads always are, going back. Most of our companions had been full of anxious thoughts of home,—of the cows, or of young children likely to fall into disaster,—but we had no reasons for haste, and drove slowly along, talking and resting by the way. Mrs. Todd said once that she really hoped her front door had been shut on account of the dust blowing in, but added that nothing made any weight on her mind except not to forget to turn a few late mullein leaves that were drying on a newspaper in the little loft. Mrs. Blackett and I gave our word of honor that we would remind her of this heavy responsibility. The way seemed short, we had so much to talk about. We climbed hills where we could see the great bay and the islands, and then went down into shady valleys where the air began to feel like evening, cool and damp with a fragrance of wet ferns. Mrs. Todd alighted once or twice, refusing all assistance in securing some boughs of a rare shrub which she valued for its bark, though she proved incommunicative as to her reasons. We passed the house where we had been so kindly entertained with doughnuts earlier in the day, and found it closed and deserted, which was a disappointment.

"They must have stopped to tea somewheres and thought they'd finish up the day," said Mrs. Todd. "Those that enjoyed it best'll want to get right home so's to think it over."

"I didn't see the woman there after all, did you?" asked Mrs. Blackett as the horse stopped to drink at the trough.

"Oh yes, I spoke with her," answered Mrs. Todd, with but scant interest or approval. "She ain't a member o' our family."

"I thought you said she resembled Cousin Pa'lina Bowden about the forehead," suggested Mrs. Blackett.

"Well, she don't," answered Mrs. Todd impatiently. "I ain't one that's ord'narily mistaken about family likenesses, and she didn't seem to meet with friends, so I went square up to her. 'I expect you're a Bowden by your looks,' says I. 'Yes, I take it you're one o' the Bowdens.' 'Lor', no,' says she. 'Dennett was my maiden name, but I married a Bowden for my first husband. I thought I'd come an' just see what was a-goin' on'!"

Mrs. Blackett laughed heartily. "I'm goin' to remember to tell William o' that," she said. "There, Almiry, the only thing that's troubled me all this day is to think how William would have enjoyed it. I do so wish William had been there."

"I sort of wish he had, myself," said Mrs. Todd frankly.

"There wa'n't many old folks there, somehow," said Mrs. Blackett, with a touch of sadness in her voice. "There ain't so many to come as there used to be, I'm aware, but I expected to see more."

"I thought they turned out pretty well, when you come to think of it; why, everybody was sayin' so an' feelin' gratified," answered Mrs. Todd hastily with pleasing unconsciousness; then I saw the quick color flash into her cheek, and presently she made some excuse to turn and steal an anxious look at her mother. Mrs. Blackett was smiling and thinking about her happy day, though she began to look a little tired. Neither of my companions was troubled by her burden of years. I hoped in my heart that I might be like them as I lived on into age, and then smiled to think that I too was no longer very young. So we always keep the same hearts, though our outer framework fails and shows the touch of time.

"'T was pretty when they sang the hymn, wasn't it?" asked Mrs. Blackett at suppertime, with real enthusiasm. "There was such a plenty o' men's voices; where I sat it did sound beautiful. I had to stop and listen when they came to the last verse."

I saw that Mrs. Todd's broad shoulders began to shake. "There was good singers there; yes, there was excellent singers," she agreed heartily, putting down her teacup, "but I chanced to drift alongside Mis' Peter Bowden o' Great Bay, an' I couldn't help thinkin' if she was as far out o' town as she was out o' tune, she wouldn't get back in a day."

20 *Along Shore*   One day as I went along the shore beyond the old wharves and the newer, high-stepped fabric of the steamer landing, I saw that all the boats were beached, and the slack water period of the early afternoon prevailed. Nothing was going on, not even the most leisurely of occupations, like baiting trawls or mending nets, or repairing lobster pots; the very boats seemed to be taking an afternoon nap in the sun. I could hardly discover a distant sail as I looked seaward, except a weather-beaten lobster smack, which seemed to have been taken for a plaything by the light airs that blew about the bay. It drifted and turned about so aimlessly in the wide reach off Burnt Island, that I suspected there was nobody at the wheel, or that she might have parted her rusty anchor chain while all the crew were asleep.

I watched her for a minute or two; she was the old Miranda, owned by some of the Caplins, and I knew her by *add or eccentric action*

an odd shaped patch of newish duck that was set into the peak of her dingy mainsail. Her vagaries offered such an exciting subject for conversation that my heart rejoiced at the sound of a hoarse voice behind me. At that moment, before I had time to answer, I saw something large and shapeless flung from the Miranda's deck that splashed the water high against her black side, and my companion gave a satisfied chuckle. The old lobster smack's sail caught the breeze again at this moment, and she moved off down the bay. Turning, I found old Elijah Tilley, who had come softly out of his dark fish house, as if it were a burrow.

"Boy got kind o' drowsy steerin' of her; Monroe he hove him right overboard; 'wake now fast enough," explained Mr. Tilley, and we laughed together.

I was delighted, for my part, that the vicissitudes and dangers of the Miranda, in a rocky channel, should have given me this opportunity to make acquaintance with an old fisherman to whom I had never spoken. At first he had seemed to be one of those evasive and uncomfortable persons who are so suspicious of you that they make you almost suspicious of yourself. Mr. Elijah Tilley appeared to regard a stranger with scornful indifference. You might see him standing on the pebble beach or in a fish-house doorway, but when you came nearer he was gone. He was one of the small company of elderly, gaunt-shaped great fishermen whom I used to like to see leading up a deep-laden boat by the head, as if it were a horse, from the water's edge to the steep slope of the pebble beach. There were four of these large old men at the Landing, who were the survivors of an earlier and more vigorous generation. There was an alliance and understanding between them, so close that it was apparently speechless. They gave much time to watching one another's boats go out or come in; they lent a ready hand at tending one another's lobster traps in rough weather; they helped to clean the fish, or to sliver porgies for the trawls, as if they were in close partnership; and when a boat came in from deep-sea fishing they were never far out of the way, and hastened to help carry it ashore, two by two, splashing alongside, or holding its steady head, as if it were a willful sea colt. As a matter of fact no boat could help being steady and way-wise under their instant direction and companionship. Abel's boat and Jonathan Bowden's boat were as distinct and experienced personalities as the men themselves, and as inexpressive. Arguments and opinions were unknown to the conversation of these ancient friends; you would as soon have expected to hear small talk in a company of elephants as to hear old Mr. Bowden or Elijah Tilley and their two mates waste breath upon any form of trivial gossip. They made brief statements to one another from time to time. As you came to know them you wondered more and more that they should talk at all. Speech seemed to be a light and elegant accomplishment, and their unexpected acquaintance with its arts made them of new value to the listener. You felt almost as if a landmark pine should suddenly address you in regard to the weather, or a lofty-minded old camel make a remark as you stood respectfully near him under the circus tent.

I often wondered a great deal about the inner life and thought of these self-contained old fishermen; their minds seemed to be fixed upon nature and the elements rather than upon any contrivances of man, like politics or theology. My friend, Captain Bowden, who was the nephew of the eldest of this group, regarded them with deference; but he did not belong to their secret companionship, though he was neither young nor talkative.

"They've gone together ever since they were boys, they know most everything about the sea amon'st them," he told me once. "They was always just as you see 'em now since the memory of man."

These ancient seafarers had houses and lands not outwardly different from other Dunnet Landing dwellings, and two of them were fathers of families, but their true dwelling places were the sea, and the stony beach that edged its familiar shore, and the fishhouses, where much salt brine from the mackerel kits had soaked the very timbers into a state of brown permanence and petrifaction. It had also affected the old fishermen's hard complexions, until one fancied that when Death claimed them it could only be with the aid, not of any slender modern dart, but the good serviceable harpoon of a seventeenth century woodcut.

Elijah Tilley was such an evasive, discouraged-looking person, heavy-headed, and stooping so that one could never look him in the face, that even after his friendly exclamation about Monroe Pennell, the lobster smack's skipper, and the sleepy boy, I did not venture at once to speak again. Mr. Tilley was carrying a small haddock in one hand, and presently shifted it to the other hand lest it might touch my skirt. I knew that my company was accepted, and we walked together a little way.

"You mean to have a good supper," I ventured to say, by way of friendliness.

"Goin' to have this 'ere haddock an' some o' my good baked potatoes; must eat to live," responded my companion with great pleasantness and open approval. I found that I had suddenly left the forbidding coast and come into a smooth little harbor of friendship.

"You ain't never been up to my place," said the old man. "Folks don't come now as they used to; no, 't ain't no use to ask folks now. My poor dear she was a great hand to draw young company."

I remembered that Mrs. Todd had once said that this old fisherman had been sore stricken and unconsoled at the death of his wife.

"I should like very much to come," said I. "Perhaps you are going to be at home later on?"

Mr. Tilley agreed, by a sober nod, and went his way bent-shouldered and with a rolling gait. There was a new patch high on the shoulder of his old waistcoat, which corresponded to the renewing of the Miranda's mainsail down the bay, and I wondered if his own fingers, clumsy with much deep-sea fishing, had set it in.

"Was there a good catch to-day?" I asked, stopping a moment. "I didn't happen to be on the shore when the boats came in."

"No; all come in pretty light," answered Mr. Tilley. "Addicks an' Bowden they done the best; Abel an' me we had but a slim fare. We went out 'arly, but not so 'arly as sometimes; looked like a poor mornin'. I got nine haddick, all small, and seven fish; the rest on 'em got more fish than haddick. Well, I don't expect they feel like bitin' every day; we l'arn to humor 'em a little, an' let 'em have their way 'bout it. These plaguey dog-fish kind of worry 'em." Mr. Tilley pronounced the last sentence with much sympathy, as if he looked upon himself as a true friend of all the haddock and codfish that lived on the fishing grounds, and so we parted.

Later in the afternoon I went along the beach again until I came to the foot of Mr. Tilley's land, and found his rough track across the cobble-stones and rocks to the field edge, where there was a heavy piece of old wreck timber, like a ship's bone, full of treenails. From this a little footpath, narrow with one man's treading, led up across the small green field that made Mr. Tilley's whole estate, except a straggling pasture that tilted on edge up the steep hillside beyond the house and road. I could hear the tinkle-tankle of a cow-bell somewhere among the spruces by which the pasture was being walked over and forested from every side; it was likely to be called the wood lot before long, but the field was unmolested. I could not see a bush or a brier anywhere within its walls, and hardly a stray pebble showed itself. This was most surprising in that country of firm ledges, and scattered stones which all the walls that industry could devise had hardly begun to clear away off the land. In the narrow field I noticed some stout stakes, apparently planted at random in the grass and among the hills of potatoes, but carefully painted yellow and white to match the house, a neat sharp-edged little dwelling, which looked strangely modern for its owner. I should have much sooner believed that the smart young wholesale egg merchant of the Landing was its occupant than Mr. Tilley, since a man's house is really but his larger body, and expresses in a way his nature and character.

I went up the field, following the smooth little path to the side door. As for using the front door, that was a matter of great ceremony; the long grass grew close against the high stone step, and a snowberry bush leaned over it, top-heavy with the weight of a morning-glory vine that had managed to take what the fishermen might call a half hitch about the door-knob. Elijah Tilley came to the side door to receive me; he was knitting a blue yarn stocking without looking on, and was warmly dressed for the season in a

thick blue flannel shirt with white crockery buttons, a faded
waistcoat and trousers heavily patched at the knees. These
were not his fishing clothes. There was something delightful in the grasp of his hand, warm and clean, as if it never
touched anything but the comfortable woolen yarn, instead
of cold sea water and slippery fish.

"What are the painted stakes for, down in the field?"
I hastened to ask, and he came out a step or two along the
path to see; and looked at the stakes as if his attention were
called to them for the first time.

"Folks laughed at me when I first bought this place an'
come here to live," he explained. "They said 't wa'n't no
kind of a field privilege at all; no place to raise anything,
all full o' stones. I was aware 't was good land, an' I worked
some on it—odd times when I didn't have nothin' else on
hand—till I cleared them loose stones all out. You never
see a prettier piece than 't is now; now did ye? Well, as
for them painted marks, them 's my buoys. I struck on to
some heavy rocks that didn't show none, but a plow'd be
liable to ground on 'em, an' so I ketched holt an' buoyed
'em same's you see. They don't trouble me no more 'n if
they wa'n't there."

"You haven't been to sea for nothing," I said laughing.

"One trade helps another," said Elijah with an amiable
smile. "Come right in an' set down. Come in an' rest ye,"
he exclaimed, and led the way into his comfortable kitchen.
The sunshine poured in at the two further windows, and
a cat was curled up sound asleep on the table that stood
between them. There was a new-looking light oilcloth of a
tiled pattern on the floor, and a crockery teapot, large for a
household of only one person, stood on the bright stove.
I ventured to say that somebody must be a very good housekeeper.

"That's me," acknowledged the old fisherman with frank-
ness. "There ain't nobody here but me. I try to keep things
looking right, same's poor dear left 'em. You set down
here in this chair, then you can look off an' see the water.
None on 'em thought I was goin' to get along alone, no
way, but I wa'n't goin' to have my house turned upsi' down
an' all changed about; no, not to please nobody. I was the
only one knew just how she liked to have things set, poor

dear, an' I said I was goin' to make shift, and I have made shift. I'd rather tough it out alone." And he sighed heavily, as if to sigh were his familiar consolation.

We were both silent for a minute; the old man looked out of the window, as if he had forgotten I was there.

"You must miss her very much?" I said at last.

"I do miss her," he answered, and sighed again. "Folks all kep' repeatin' that time would ease me, but I can't find it does. No, I miss her just the same every day."

"How long is it since she died?" I asked.

"Eight year now, come the first of October. It don't seem near so long. I've got a sister that comes and stops 'long o' me a little spell, spring an' fall, an' odd times if I send after her. I ain't near so good a hand to sew as I be to knit, and she's very quick .to set everything to rights. She's a married woman with a family; her son's folks lives at home, an' I can't make no great claim on her time. But it makes me a kind o' good excuse, when I do send, to help her a little; she ain't none too well off. Poor dear always liked her, and we used to contrive our ways together. 'T is full as easy to be alone. I set here an' think it all over, an' think considerable when the weather's bad to go outside. I get so some days it feels as if poor dear might step right back into this kitchen. I keep a-watchin' them doors as if she might step in to ary one. Yes, ma'am, I keep a-lookin' off an' droppin' o' my stitches; that's just how it seems. I can't git over losin' of her no way nor no how. Yes, ma'am, that's just how it seems to me."

I did not say anything, and he did not look up.

"I git feelin' so sometimes I have to lay everything by an' go out door. She was a sweet pretty creatur' long 's she lived," the old man added mournfully. "There's that little rockin' chair o' her'n, I set an' notice it an' think how strange 't is a creatur' like her should be gone an' that chair be here right in its old place."

"I wish I had known her; Mrs. Todd told me about your wife one day," I said.

"You'd have liked to come and see her; all the folks did," said poor Elijah. "She'd been so pleased to hear everything and see somebody new that took such an int'rest. She had a kind o' gift to make it pleasant for folks. I guess likely

Almiry Todd told you she was a pretty woman, especially
in her young days; late years, too, she kep' her looks and
come to be so pleasant lookin'. There, 't ain't so much matter, I shall be done afore a great while. No; I sha'n't trouble
the fish a great sight more."

The old widower sat with his head bowed over his knitting, as if he were hastily shortening the very thread of time.
The minutes went slowly by. He stopped his work and
clasped his hands firmly together. I saw he had forgotten
his guest, and I kept the afternoon watch with him. At
last he looked up as if but a moment had passed of his
continual loneliness.

"Yes, ma'am, I'm one that has seen trouble," he said,
and began to knit again.

The visible tribute of his careful housekeeping, and the
clean bright room which had once enshrined his wife, and
now enshrined her memory, was very moving to me; he
had no thought for any one else or for any other place.
I began to see her myself in her home,—a delicate-looking,
faded little woman, who leaned upon his rough strength
and affectionate heart, who was always watching for his
boat out of this very window, and who always opened the
door and welcomed him when he came home.

"I used to laugh at her, poor dear," said Elijah, as if he
read my thought. "I used to make light of her timid notions. She used to be fearful when I was out in bad weather
or baffled about gettin' ashore. She used to say the time
seemed long to her, but I've found out all about it now.
I used to be dreadful thoughtless when I was a young man
and the fish was bitin' well. I'd stay out late some o'
them days, an' I expect she'd watch an' watch an' lose
heart a-waitin'. My heart alive! what a supper she'd git,
an' be right there watchin' from the door, with somethin'
over her head if 't was cold, waitin' to hear all about it as
I come up the field. Lord, how I think o' all them little
things!

"This was what she called the best room; in this way,"
he said presently, laying his knitting on the table, and leading the way across the front entry and unlocking a door,
which he threw open with an air of pride. The best room
seemed to me a much sadder and more empty place than

the kitchen; its conventionalities lacked the simple perfection of the humbler room and failed on the side of poor ambition; it was only when one remembered what patient saving, and what high respect for society in the abstract go to such furnishing that the little parlor was interesting at all. I could imagine the great day of certain purchases, the bewildering shops of the next large town, the aspiring anxious woman, the clumsy sea-tanned man in his best clothes, so eager to be pleased, but at ease only when they were safe back in the sail-boat again, going down the bay with their precious freight, the hoarded money all spent and nothing to think of but tiller and sail. I looked at the unworn carpet, the glass vases on the mantelpiece with their prim bunches of bleached swamp grass and dusty marsh rosemary, and I could read the history of Mrs. Tilley's best room from its very beginning.

"You see for yourself what beautiful rugs she could make; now I'm going to show you her best tea things she thought so much of," said the master of the house, opening the door of a shallow cupboard. "That's real chiny, all of it on those two shelves," he told me proudly. "I bought it all myself, when we was first married, in the port of Bordeaux. There never was one single piece of it broke until— Well, I used to say, long as she lived, there never was a piece broke, but long at the last I noticed she'd looked kind o' distressed, an' I thought 't was 'count o' me boastin'. When they asked if they should use it when the folks was here to supper, time o' her funeral, I knew she'd want to have everything nice, and I said 'certain.' Some o' the women they come runnin' to me an' called me, while they was takin' of the chiny down, an' showed me there was one o' the cups broke an' the pieces wropped in paper and pushed way back here, corner o' the shelf. They didn't want me to go an' think they done it. Poor dear! I had to put right out o' the house when I see that. I knowed in one minute how 't was. We'd got so used to sayin' 't was all there just 's I fetched it home, an' so when she broke that cup somehow or 'nother she couldn't frame no words to come an' tell me. She couldn't think 't would vex me, 't was her own hurt pride. I guess there wa'n't no other secret ever lay between us."

The French cups with their gay sprigs of pink and blue, the best tumblers, an old flowered bowl and tea caddy, and a japanned waiter or two adorned the shelves. These, with a few daguerreotypes in a little square pile, had the closet to themselves, and I was conscious of much pleasure in seeing them. One is shown over many a house in these days where the interest may be more complex, but not more definite.

"Those were her best things, poor dear," said Elijah as he locked the door again. "She told me that last summer before she was taken away that she couldn't think o' anything more she wanted, there was everything in the house, an' all her rooms was furnished pretty. I was goin' over to the Port, an' inquired for errands. I used to ask her to say what she wanted, cost or no cost—she was a very reasonable woman, an' 't was the place where she done all but her extra shopping. It kind o' chilled me up when she spoke so satisfied."

"You don't go out fishing after Christmas?" I asked, as we came back to the bright kitchen.

"No; I take stiddy to my knitting after January sets in," said the old seafarer. " 'T ain't worth while, fish make off into deeper water an' you can't stand no such perishin' for the sake o' what you get. I leave out a few traps in sheltered coves an' do a little lobsterin' on fair days. The young fellows braves it out, some on 'em; but, for me, I lay in my winter's yarn an' set here where 't is warm, an' knit an' take my comfort. Mother learnt me once when I was a lad; she was a beautiful knitter herself. I was laid up with a bad knee, an' she said 't would take up my time an' help her; we was a large family. They'll buy all the folks can do down here to Addicks' store. They say our Dunnet stockin's is gettin' to be celebrated up to Boston,—good quality o' wool an' even knittin' or somethin'. I've always been called a pretty hand to do nettin', but seines is master cheap to what they used to be when they was all hand worked. I change off to nettin' long towards spring, and I piece up my trawls and lines and get my fishin' stuff to rights. Lobster pots they require attention, but I make 'em up in spring weather when it's warm there in the barn. No; I ain't one o' them that likes to set an' do nothin'.

"You see the rugs, poor dear did them; she wa'n't very partial to knittin'," old Elijah went on, after he had counted his stitches. "Our rugs is beginnin' to show wear, but I can't master none o' them womanish tricks. My sister, she tinkers 'em up. She said last time she was here that she guessed they'd last my time."

"The old ones are always the prettiest," I said.

"You ain't referrin' to the braided ones now?" answered Mr. Tilley. "You see ours is braided for the most part, an' their good looks is all in the beginnin'. Poor dear used to say they made an easier floor. I go shufflin' round the house same 's if 't was a bo't, and I always used to be stubbin' up the corners o' the hooked kind. Her an' me was always havin' our jokes together same 's a boy an' girl. Outsiders never'd know nothin' about it to see us. She had nice manners with all, but to me there was nobody so entertainin'. She'd take off anybody's natural talk winter evenin's when we set here alone, so you'd think 't was them a-speakin'. There, there!"

I saw that he had dropped a stitch again, and was snarling the blue yarn round his clumsy fingers. He handled it and threw it off at arm's length as if it were a cod line; and frowned impatiently, but I saw a tear shining on his cheek.

I said that I must be going, it was growing late, and asked if I might come again, and if he would take me out to the fishing grounds some day.

"Yes, come any time you want to," said my host, "'t ain't so pleasant as when poor dear was here. Oh, I didn't want to lose her an' she didn't want to go, but it had to be. Such things ain't for us to say; there's no yes an' no to it."

"You find Almiry Todd one o' the best o' women?" said Mr. Tilley as we parted. He was standing in the doorway and I had started off down the narrow green field. "No, there ain't a better hearted woman in the State o' Maine. I've known her from a girl. She's had the best o' mothers. You tell her I'm liable to fetch her up a couple or three nice good mackerel early tomorrow," he said. "Now don't let it slip your mind. Poor dear, she always thought a sight o' Almiry, and she used to remind me there was nobody to fish for her; but I don't rec'lect it as I ought to. I see you drop a line yourself very handy now an' then."

We laughed together like the best of friends, and I spoke again about the fishing grounds, and confessed that I had no fancy for a southerly breeze and a ground swell.

"Nor me neither," said the old fisherman. "Nobody likes 'em, say what they may. Poor dear was disobliged by the mere sight of a bo't. Almiry's got the best o' mothers, I expect you know; Mis' Blackett out to Green Island; and we was always plannin' to go out when summer come; but there, I couldn't pick no day's weather that seemed to suit her just right. I never set out to worry her neither, 't wa'n't no kind o' use; she was so pleasant we couldn't have no fret nor trouble. 'T was never 'you dear an' you darlin'' afore folks, an' 'you divil' behind the door!"

As I looked back from the lower end of the field I saw him still standing, a lonely figure in the doorway. "Poor dear," I repeated to myself half aloud; "I wonder where she is and what she knows of the little world she left. I wonder what she has been doing these eight years!"

I gave the message about the mackerel to Mrs. Todd.

"Been visitin' with 'Lijah?" she asked with interest. "I expect you had kind of a dull session; he ain't the talkin' kind; dwellin' so much long o' fish seems to make 'em lose the gift o' speech." But when I told her that Mr. Tilley had been talking to me that day, she interrupted me quickly.

"Then 't was all about his wife, an' he can't say nothin' too pleasant neither. She was modest with strangers, but there ain't one o' her old friends can ever make up her loss. For me, I don't want to go there no more. There's some folks you miss and some folks you don't, when they're gone, but there ain't hardly a day I don't think o' dear Sarah Tilley. She was always right there; yes, you knew just where to find her like a plain flower. 'Lijah's worthy enough; I do esteem 'Lijah, but he's a ploddin' man."

21 *A Dunnet Shepherdess* Early one morning at Dunnet Landing, as if it were still night, I waked, suddenly startled by a spirited conversation beneath my window. It was not one of Mrs. Todd's morning soliloquies; she was not addressing her plants and flowers in words of either praise

to recite or speak in a dramatic or impassioned way

or blame. Her voice was declamatory though perfectly good-humored, while the second voice, a man's, was of lower pitch and somewhat deprecating. — *belittle*

The sun was just above the sea, and struck straight across my room through a crack in the blind. It was a strange hour for the arrival of a guest, and still too soon for the general run of business, even in that tiny eastern haven where day-break fisheries and early tides must often rule the day.

The man's voice suddenly declared itself to my sleepy ears. It was Mr. William Blackett's.

"Why, sister Almiry," he protested gently, "I don't need none o' your nostrums!"

"Pick me a small han'ful," she commanded. "No, no, a *small* han'ful, I said,—o' them large pennyr'yal sprigs! I go to all the trouble an' cossetin' of 'em just so as to have you ready to meet such occasions, an' last year, you may remember, you never stopped here at all the day you went up country. An' the frost come at last an' blacked it. I never saw any herb that so objected to gardin ground; might as well try to flourish mayflowers in a common front yard. There, you can come in now, an' set and eat what breakfast you've got patience for. I've found everything I want, an' I'll mash 'em up an' be all ready to put 'em on."

I heard such a pleading note of appeal as the speakers went round the corner of the house, and my curiosity was so demanding, that I dressed in haste, and joined my friends a little later, with two unnoticed excuses of the beauty of the morning, and the early mail boat. William's breakfast had been slighted; he had taken his cup of tea and merely pushed back the rest on the kitchen table. He was now sitting in a helpless condition by the side window, with one of his sister's purple calico aprons pinned close about his neck. Poor William was meekly submitting to being smeared, as to his countenance, with a most pungent and unattractive lotion of pennyroyal and other green herbs which had been hastily pounded and mixed with cream in the little white stone mortar.

I had to cast two or three straightforward looks at William to reassure myself that he really looked happy and expectant in spite of his melancholy circumstances, and was not being overtaken by retribution. The brother and sister seemed to be on delightful terms with each other for once, and there was something of cheerful anticipation in their morning talk. I was reminded of Medea's anointing Jason before the great episode of the iron bulls, but to-day William really could not be going up country to see a railroad for the first time. I knew this to be one of his great schemes, but he was not fitted to appear in public, or to front an observing world of strangers. As I appeared he essayed to rise, but Mrs. Todd pushed him back into the chair.

"Set where you be till it dries on," she insisted. "Land sakes, you'd think he'd get over bein' a boy some time or 'nother, gettin' along in years as he is. An' you'd think he'd seen full enough o' fish, but once a year he has to break loose like this, an' travel off way up back o' the Bowden place—far out o' my beat, 't is—an' go a trout fishin'!"

Her tone of amused scorn was so full of challenge that William changed color even under the green streaks.

"I want some change," he said, looking at me and not at her. " 'T is the prettiest little shady brook you ever saw."

"If he ever fetched home more'n a couple o' minnies, 't would seem worth while," Mrs. Todd concluded, putting a last dab of the mysterious compound so perilously near her brother's mouth that William flushed again and was silent.

A little later I witnessed his escape, when Mrs. Todd had taken the foolish risk of going down cellar. There was a horse and wagon outside the garden fence, and presently we stood where we could see him driving up the hill with thoughtless speed. Mrs. Todd said nothing, but watched him affectionately out of sight.

"It serves to keep the mosquitoes off," she said, and a moment later it occurred to my slow mind that she spoke of the pennyroyal lotion. "I don't know sometimes but William's kind of poetical," she continued, in her gentlest voice. "You'd think if anything could cure him of it, 't would be the fish business."

It was only twenty minutes past six on a summer morning, but we both sat down to rest as if the activities of the day were over. Mrs. Todd rocked gently for a time, and seemed to be lost, though not poorly, like Macbeth, in her thoughts. At last she resumed relations with her actual surroundings. "I shall now put my lobsters on. They'll make us a good supper," she announced. "Then I can let the fire out for all day; give it a holiday, same's William. You can have a little one now, nice an' hot, if you ain't got all the breakfast you want. Yes, I'll put the lobsters on. William was very thoughtful to bring 'em over; William *is* thoughtful; if he only had a spark o' ambition, there be few could match him."

This unusual concession was afforded a sympathetic listener from the depths of the kitchen closet. Mrs. Todd was getting out her old iron lobster pot, and began to speak of prosaic affairs. I hoped that I should hear something more about her brother and their island life, and sat idly by the kitchen window looking at the morning glories that shaded it, believing that some flaw of wind might set Mrs. Todd's mind on its former course. Then it occurred to me that she had spoken about our supper rather than our dinner, and I guessed that she might have some great scheme before her for the day.

When I had loitered for some time and there was no further word about William, and at last I was conscious of receiving no attention whatever, I went away. It was something of a disappointment to find that she put no hindrance in the way of my usual morning affairs, of going up to the empty little white schoolhouse on the hill where I did my task of writing. I had been almost sure of a holiday when I discovered that Mrs. Todd was likely to take one herself; we had not been far afield to gather herbs and pleasures for many days now, but a little later she had silently vanished. I found my luncheon ready on the table in the little entry, wrapped in its shining old homespun napkin, and as if by way of special consolation, there was a stone bottle of Mrs. Todd's best spruce beer, with a long piece of cod line wound round it by which it could be lowered for coolness into the deep schoolhouse well.

I walked away with a dull supply of writing-paper and these provisions, feeling like a reluctant child who hopes to be called back at every step. There was no relenting voice to be heard, and when I reached the schoolhouse, I found that I had left an open window and a swinging shutter the day before, and the sea wind that blew at evening had fluttered my poor sheaf of papers all about the room.

So the day did not begin very well, and I began to recognize that it was one of the days when nothing could be done without company. The truth was that my heart had gone trouting with William, but it would have been too selfish to say a word even to one's self about spoiling his day. If there is one way above another of getting so close to nature that one simply is a piece of nature, following a primeval instinct with perfect self-forgetfulness and forgetting everything except the dreamy consciousness of pleasant freedom, it is to take the course of a shady trout brook. The dark pools and the sunny shallows beckon one on; the wedge of sky between the trees on either bank, the speaking, companioning noise of the water, the amazing importance of what one is doing, and the constant sense of life and beauty make a strange transformation of the quick hours. I had a sudden memory of all this, and another, and another. I could not get myself free from "fishing and wishing."

At that moment I heard the unusual sound of wheels, and I looked past the high-growing thicket of wild-roses and straggling sumach to see the white nose and meagre shape of the Caplin horse; then I saw William sitting in the open wagon, with a small expectant smile upon his face.

"I've got two lines," he said. "I was quite apiece up the road. I thought perhaps 't was so you'd feel like going."

There was enough excitement for most occasions in hearing William speak three sentences at once. Words seemed but vain to me at that bright moment. I stepped back from the schoolhouse window with a beating heart. The spruce-beer bottle was not yet in the well, and with that and my luncheon, and Pleasure at the helm, I went out into the happy world. The land breeze was blowing, and, as we turned away, I saw a flutter of white go past the window as I left the schoolhouse and my morning's work to their neglected fate.

II One seldom gave way to a cruel impulse to look at an ancient seafaring William, but one felt as if he were a growing boy; I only hope that he felt much the same about me. He did not wear the fishing clothes that belonged to his sea-going life, but a strangely shaped old suit of tea-colored linen garments that might have been brought home years ago from Canton or Bombay. William had a peculiar way of giving silent assent when one spoke, but of answering your unspoken thoughts as if they reached him better than words. "I find them very easy," he said, frankly referring to the clothes. "Father had them in his old sea-chest."

The antique fashion, a quaint touch of foreign grace and even imagination about the cut were very pleasing; if ever Mr. William Blackett had faintly resembled an old beau, it was upon that day. He now appeared to feel as if everything had been explained between us, as if everything were quite understood; and we drove for some distance without finding it necessary to speak again about anything. At last, when it must have been a little past nine o'clock, he stopped the horse beside a small farmhouse, and nodded when I asked if I should get down from the wagon. "You can steer about northeast right across the pasture," he said, looking from under the eaves of his hat with an expectant smile. "I always leave the team here."

I helped to unfasten the harness, and William led the horse away to the barn. It was a poor-looking little place, and a forlorn woman looked at us through the window before she appeared at the door. I told her that Mr. Blackett and I came up from the Landing to go fishing. "He keeps a-comin', don't he?" she answered, with a funny little laugh, to which I was at a loss to find answer. When he joined us, I could not see that he took notice of her presence in any way, except to take an armful of dried salt fish from a corded stack in the back of the wagon which had been carefully covered with a piece of old sail. We had left a wake of their pungent flavor behind us all the way. I wondered what was going to become of the rest of them and some fresh lobsters which were also disclosed to view, but he laid the present gift on the doorstep without a word, and a few minutes later, when I looked back as we crossed the pasture, the fish were being carried into the house.

I could not see any signs of a trout brook until I came close upon it in the bushy pasture, and presently we struck into the low woods of straggling spruce and fir mixed into a tangle of swamp maples and alders which stretched away on either hand up and down stream. We found an open place in the pasture where some taller trees seemed to have been overlooked rather than spared. The sun was bright and hot by this time, and I sat down in the shade while William produced his lines and cut and trimmed us each a slender rod. I wondered where Mrs. Todd was spending the morning, and if later she would think that pirates had landed and captured me from the schoolhouse.

III   The brook was giving that live, persistent call to a listener that trout brooks always make; it ran with a free, swift current even here, where it crossed an apparently level piece of land. I saw two unpromising, quick barbel chase each other upstream from bank to bank as we solemnly arranged our hooks and sinkers. I felt that William's glances changed from anxiety to relief when he found that I was used to such gear; perhaps he felt that we must stay together if I could not bait my own hook, but we parted happily, full of a pleasing sense of companionship.

William had pointed me up the brook, but I chose to go down, which was only fair because it was his day, though one likes as well to follow and see where a brook goes as to find one's way to the places it comes from, and its tiny springs and headwaters, and in this case trout were not to be considered. William's only real anxiety was lest I might suffer from mosquitoes. His own complexion was still strangely impaired by its defenses, but I kept forgetting it, and looking to see if we were treading fresh pennyroyal underfoot, so efficient was Mrs. Todd's remedy. I was conscious, after we parted, and I turned to see if he were already fishing, and saw him wave his hand gallantly as he went away, that our friendship had made a great gain.

The moment that I began to fish the brook, I had a sense of its emptiness; when my bait first touched the water and went lightly down the quick stream, I knew that there was nothing to lie in wait for it. It is the same certainty that comes when one knocks at the door of an empty house, a lack of answering consciousness and of possible response; it is quite different if there is any life within. But it was a lovely brook, and I went a long way through woods and breezy open pastures, and found a forsaken house and overgrown farm, and laid up many pleasures for future joy and remembrance. At the end of the morning I came back to

118

our meeting-place hungry and without any fish. William was already waiting, and we did not mention the matter of trout. We ate our luncheons with good appetites, and William brought our two stone bottles of spruce beer from the deep place in the brook where he had left them to cool. Then we sat awhile longer in peace and quietness on the green banks.

As for William, he looked more boyish than ever, and kept a more remote and juvenile sort of silence. Once I wondered how he had come to be so curiously wrinkled, forgetting, absent-mindedly, to recognize the effects of time. He did not expect any one else to keep up a vain show of conversation, and so I was silent as well as he. I glanced at him now and then, but I watched the leaves tossing against the sky and the red cattle moving in the pasture. "I don't know's we need head for home. It's early yet," he said at last, and I was as startled as if one of the gray firs had spoken.

"I guess I'll go up-along and ask after Thankful Hight's folks," he continued. "Mother'd like to get word;" and I nodded a pleased assent.

IV William led the way across the pasture, and I followed with a deep sense of pleased anticipation. I do not believe that my companion had expected me to make any objection, but I knew that he was gratified by the easy way that his plans for the day were being seconded. He gave a look at the sky to see if there were any portents, but the sky was frankly blue; even the doubtful morning haze had disappeared.

We went northward along a rough, clayey road, across a bare-looking, sunburnt country full of tiresome long slopes where the sun was hot and bright, and I could not help observing the forlorn look of the farms. There was a great deal of pasture, but it looked deserted, and I wondered afresh why the people did not raise more sheep when that seemed the only possible use to make of their land. I said so to Mr. Blackett, who gave me a look of pleased surprise.

"That's what She always maintains," he said eagerly. "She's right about it, too; well, you'll see!" I was glad to find myself approved, but I had not the least idea whom he meant, and waited until he felt like speaking again.

A few minutes later we drove down a steep hill and entered a large tract of dark spruce woods. It was delightful to be sheltered from the afternoon sun, and when we had gone some distance in the shade, to my great pleasure William turned the horse's head toward some bars, which he let down, and I drove through into one of those narrow, still, sweet-scented by-ways which seem to be paths rather than roads. Often we had to put aside the heavy drooping branches which barred the way, and once, when a sharp twig struck William in the face, he announced with such spirit that somebody ought to go through there with an axe, that I felt unexpectedly guilty. So far as I now remember, this was William's only remark all the way through the woods to Thankful Hight's folks, but from time to time he pointed or nodded at something which I might have missed: a sleepy little owl snuggled into the bend of a branch, or a tall stalk of cardinal flowers where the sunlight came down at the edge of a small, bright piece of marsh. Many times, being used to the company of Mrs. Todd and other friends who were in the habit of talking, I came near making an idle remark to William, but I was for the most part happily preserved; to be with him only for a short time was to live on a different level, where thoughts served best because they were thoughts in common; the primary effect upon our minds of the simple things and beauties that we saw. Once when I caught sight of a lovely gay pigeon-woodpecker eyeing us curiously from a dead branch, and instinctively turned toward William, he gave an indulgent, comprehending nod which silenced me all the rest of the way. The wood-road was not a place for common noisy conversation; one would interrupt the birds and all the still little beasts that belonged there. But it was mortifying to find how strong the habit of idle speech may become in one's self. One need not always be saying something in this noisy world. I grew conscious of the difference between William's usual fashion of life and mine; for him there were long days of silence in a sea-going boat, and I could believe that he and his mother usually spoke very little because they so perfectly understood each other. There was something peculiarly unresponding about their quiet island in the sea, solidly fixed into the still foundations of the world, against whose rocky shores the sea beats and calls and is unanswered.

We were quite half an hour going through the woods; the horse's feet made no sound on the brown, soft track under the dark evergreens. I thought that we should come out at last into more pastures, but there was no half-wooded strip of land at the end; the high woods grew squarely against an old stone wall and a sunshiny open field, and we came out suddenly into broad daylight that startled us and even startled the horse, who might have been napping as he walked, like an old soldier. The field sloped up to a low unpainted house that faced the east. Behind it were long, frost-whitened ledges that made the hill, with strips of green turf and bushes between. It was the wildest, most Titanic sort of pasture country up there; there was a sort of daring in putting a frail wooden house before it, though it might have the homely field and honest woods to front against. You thought of the elements and even of possible volcanoes as you looked up the stony heights. Suddenly I saw that a region of what I had thought gray stones was slowly moving, as if the sun was making my eyesight unsteady.

"There's the sheep!" exclaimed William, pointing eagerly. "You see the sheep?" and sure enough, it was a great company of woolly backs, which seemed to have taken a mysterious protective resemblance to the ledges themselves. I could discover but little chance for pasturage on that high sunburnt ridge, but the sheep were moving steadily in a satisfied way as they fed along the slopes and hollows.

"I never have seen half so many sheep as these, all summer long!" I cried with admiration.

"There ain't so many," answered William soberly. "It's a great sight. They do so well because they're shepherded, but you can't beat sense into some folks."

"You mean that somebody stays and watches them?" I asked.

"She observed years ago in her readin' that they don't turn out their flocks without protection anywhere but in the State o' Maine," returned William. "First thing that put it into her mind was a little old book mother's got; she read it one time when she come out to the Island. They call it the 'Shepherd o' Salisbury Plain.' 'T wasn't the purpose o' the book to most, but when she read it, 'There, Mis' Blackett!' she said, 'that's where we've all lacked sense; our Bibles ought to have taught us that what sheep need is a shepherd.' You see most folks about here gave up sheep-raisin' years ago 'count o' the dogs. So she gave up school-teachin' and went out to tend her flock, and has shepherded ever since, an' done well."

For William, this approached an oration. He spoke with enthusiasm, and I shared the triumph of the moment. "There she is now!" he exclaimed, in a different tone, as the tall figure of a woman came following the flock and stood still on the ridge, looking toward us as if her eyes had been quick to see a strange object in the familiar emptiness of the field. William stood up in the wagon, and I thought he was going to call or wave his hand to her, but he sat down again more clumsily than if the wagon had made the familiar motion of a boat, and we drove on toward the house.

It was a most solitary place to live,—a place where one might think that a life could hide itself. The thick woods were between the farm and the main road, and as one looked up and down the country, there was no other house in sight.

"Potatoes look well," announced William. "The old folks used to say that there wa'n't no better land outdoors than the Hight field."

I found myself possessed of a surprising interest in the shepherdess, who stood far away in the hill pasture with her great flock, like a figure of Millet's, high against the sky.

v Everything about the old farmhouse was clean and orderly, as if the green dooryard were not only swept, but dusted. I saw a flock of turkeys stepping off carefully at a distance, but there was not the usual untidy flock of hens about the place to make everything look in disarray. William helped me out of the wagon as carefully as if I had been his mother, and nodded toward the open door with a reassuring look at me; but I waited until he had tied the horse and could lead the way, himself. He took off his hat just as we were going in, and stopped for a moment to smooth his thin gray hair with his hand, by which I saw that we had an affair of some ceremony. We entered an old-fashioned country kitchen, the floor scrubbed into unevenness, and the doors well polished by the touch of hands. In a large chair facing the window there sat a masterful-looking old woman with the features of a warlike Roman emperor, emphasized by a bonnet-like black cap with a band of green ribbon. Her sceptre was a palm-leaf fan.

William crossed the room toward her, and bent his head close to her ear.

"Feelin' pretty well to-day, Mis' Hight?" he asked, with all the voice his narrow chest could muster.

"No, I ain't, William. Here I have to set," she answered coldly, but she gave an inquiring glance over his shoulder at me.

"This is the young lady who is stopping with Almiry this summer," he explained, and I approached as if to give the countersign. She offered her left hand with considerable dignity, but her expression never seemed to change for the better. A moment later she said that she was pleased to meet me, and I felt as if the worst were over. William must have felt some apprehension, while I was only ignorant, as we had come across the field. Our hostess was more than disapproving, she was forbidding; but I was not long in suspecting that she felt the natural resentment of a strong energy that has been defeated by illness and made the spoil of captivity.

"Mother well as usual since you was up last year?" and William replied by a series of cheerful nods. The mention of dear Mrs. Blackett was a help to any conversation.

"Been fishin', ashore," he explained, in a somewhat conciliatory voice. "Thought you'd like a few for winter," which explained at once the generous freight we had brought in the back of the wagon. I could see that the offering was no surprise, and that Mrs. Hight was interested.

"Well, I expect they're good as the last," she said, but did not even approach a smile. She kept a straight, discerning eye upon me.

"Give the lady a cheer," she admonished William, who hastened to place close by her side one of the straight-backed chairs that stood against the kitchen wall. Then he lingered for a moment like a timid boy. I could see that he wore a look of resolve, but he did not ask the permission for which he evidently waited.

"You can go search for Esther," she said, at the end of a long pause that became anxious for both her guests. "Esther'd like to see her;" and William in his pale nankeens disappeared with one light step and was off.

VI   "Don't speak too loud, it jars a person's head," directed Mrs. Hight plainly. "Clear an' distinct is what reaches me best. Any news to the Landin'?"

I was happily furnished with the particulars of a sudden death, and an engagement of marriage between a Caplin, a seafaring widower home from his voyage, and one of the younger Harrises; and now Mrs. Hight really smiled and settled herself in her chair. We exhausted one subject completely before we turned to the other. One of the returning turkeys took an unwarrantable liberty, and, mounting the doorstep, came in and walked about the kitchen without being observed by its strict owner; and the tin dipper slipped off its nail behind us and made an astonishing noise, and jar enough to reach Mrs. Hight's inner ear and make her turn her head to look at it; but we talked straight on. We came at last to understand each other upon such terms of friendship that she unbent her majestic port and complained to me as any poor old woman might of the hardships of her illness. She had already fixed various dates upon the sad certainty of the year when she had the shock, which had left her perfectly helpless except for a clumsy left hand which fanned and gestured, and settled and re-settled the folds of her dress, but could do no comfortable time-shortening work.

"Yes'm, you can feel sure I use it what I can," she said severely. " 'T was a long spell before I could let Esther go forth in the mornin' till she'd got me up an' dressed me, but now she leaves things ready overnight and I get 'em as I want 'em with my light pair o' tongs, and I feel very able about helpin' myself to what I once did. Then when

Esther returns, all she has to do is to push me out here into the kitchen. Some parts o' the year Esther stays out all night, them moonlight nights when the dogs are apt to be after the sheep, but she don't use herself as hard as she once had to. She's well able to hire somebody, Esther is, but there, you can't find no hired man that wants to git up before five o'clock nowadays; 't ain't as 't was in my time. They're liable to fall asleep, too, and them moonlight nights she's so anxious she can't sleep, and out she goes. There's a kind of a fold, she calls it, up there in a sheltered spot, and she sleeps up in a little shed she's got,—built it herself for lambin' time and when the poor foolish creatur's gets hurt or anything. I've never seen it, but she says it's in a lovely spot and always pleasant in any weather. You see off, other side of the ridge, to the south'ard, where there's houses. I used to think some time I'd get up to see it again, and all them spots she lives in, but I sha'n't now. I'm beginnin' to go back; an' 't ain't surprisin'. I've kind of got used to disappointments," and the poor soul drew a deep sigh.

VII It was long before we noticed the lapse of time; I not only told every circumstance known to me of recent events among the households of Mrs. Todd's neighborhood at the shore, but Mrs. Hight became more and more communicative on her part, and went carefully into the genealogical descent and personal experience of many acquaintances, until between us we had pretty nearly circumnavigated the globe and reached Dunnet Landing from an opposite direction to that in which we had started. It was long before my own interest began to flag; there was a flavor of the best sort in her definite and descriptive fashion of speech. It may be only a fancy of my own that in the sound and value of many words, with their lengthened vowels and doubled cadences, there is some faint survival on the Maine coast of the sound of English speech of Chaucer's time.

At last Mrs. Thankful Hight gave a suspicious look through the window.

"Where do you suppose they be?" she asked me. "Esther must ha' been off to the far edge o' everything. I doubt

William ain't been able to find her; can't he hear their bells? His hearin' all right?"

William had heard some herons that morning which were beyond the reach of my own ears, and almost beyond eyesight in the upper skies, and I told her so. I was luckily preserved by some unconscious instinct from saying that we had seen the shepherdess so near as we crossed the field. Unless she had fled faster than Atalanta, William must have been but a few minutes in reaching her immediate neighborhood. I now discovered with a quick leap of amusement and delight in my heart that I had fallen upon a serious chapter of romance. The old woman looked suspiciously at me, and I made a dash to cover with a new piece of information; but she listened with lofty indifference, and soon interrupted my eager statements.

"Ain't William been gone some considerable time?" she demanded, and then in a milder tone: "The time has re'lly flown; I do enjoy havin' company. I set here alone a sight o' long days. Sheep is dreadful fools; I expect they heard a strange step, and set right off through bush an' brier, spite of all she could do. But William might have the sense to return, 'stead o' searchin' about. I want to inquire of him about his mother. What was you goin' to say? I guess you'll have time to relate it."

My powers of entertainment were on the ebb, but I doubled my diligence and we went on for another half-hour at least with banners flying, but still William did not reappear. Mrs. Hight frankly began to show fatigue.

"Somethin' 's happened, an' he's stopped to help her," groaned the old lady, in the middle of what I had found to tell her about a rumor of disaffection with the minister of a town I merely knew by name in the weekly newspaper to which Mrs. Todd subscribed. "You step to the door, dear, an' look if you can't see 'em." I promptly stepped, and once outside the house I looked anxiously in the direction which William had taken.

To my astonishment I saw all the sheep so near that I wonder we had not been aware in the house of every bleat and tinkle. And there, within a stone's-throw, on the first long gray ledge that showed above the juniper, were William and the shepherdess engaged in pleasant conversation.

At first I was provoked and then amused, and a thrill of sympathy warmed my whole heart. They had seen me and risen as if by magic; I had a sense of being the messenger of Fate. One could almost hear their sighs of regret as I appeared; they must have passed a lovely afternoon. I hurried into the house with the reassuring news that they were not only in sight but perfectly safe, with all the sheep.

VIII Mrs. Hight, like myself, was spent with conversation, and had ceased even the one activity of fanning herself. I brought a desired drink of water, and happily remembered some fruit that was left from my luncheon. She revived with splendid vigor, and told me the simple history of her later years since she had been smitten in the prime of her life by the stroke of paralysis, and her husband had died and left her alone with Esther and a mortgage on their farm. There was only one field of good land, but they owned a great region of sheep pasture and a little woodland. Esther had always been laughed at for her belief in sheep-raising when one by one their neighbors were giving up their flocks, and when everything had come to the point of despair she had raised all the money and bought all the sheep she could, insisting that Maine lambs were as good as any, and that there was a straight path by sea to Boston market. And by tending her flock herself she had managed to succeed; she had made money enough to pay off the mortgage five years ago, and now what they did not spend was safe in the bank. "It has been stubborn work, day and night, summer and winter, an' now she's beginnin' to get along in years," said the old mother sadly. "She's tended me 'long o' the sheep, an' she's been a good girl right along, but she ought to have been a teacher;" and Mrs. Hight sighed heavily and plied the fan again.

We heard voices, and William and Esther entered; they did not know that it was so late in the afternoon. William looked almost bold, and oddly like a happy young man rather than an ancient boy. As for Esther, she might have been Jeanne d'Arc returned to her sheep, touched with age and gray with the ashes of a great remembrance. She wore the simple look of sainthood and unfeigned devotion. My heart was moved by the sight of her plain sweet face, weatherworn and gentle in its looks, her thin figure in its close dress, and the strong hand that clasped a shepherd's staff, and I could only hold William in new reverence; this silent farmer-fisherman who knew, and he alone, the noble and patient heart that beat within her breast. I am not sure that they acknowledged even to themselves that they had always been lovers; they could not consent to anything so definite or pronounced but they were happy in being together in the world. Esther was untouched by the fret and fury of life; she had lived in sunshine and rain among her silly sheep, and been refined instead of coarsened, while her touching patience with a ramping old mother, stung by the sense of defeat and mourning her lost activities, had given back a lovely self-possession, and habit of sweet temper. I had seen enough of old Mrs. Hight to know that nothing a sheep might do could vex a person who was used to the uncertainties and severities of her companionship.

IX   Mrs. Hight told her daughter at once that she had enjoyed a beautiful call, and got a great many new things to think of. This was said so frankly in my hearing that it gave a consciousness of high reward, and I was indeed recompensed by the grateful look in Esther's eyes. We did not speak much together, but we understood each other. For the poor old woman did not read, and could not sew or knit with her helpless hand, and they were far from any neighbors, while her spirit was as eager in age as in youth, and expected even more from a disappointing world. She had lived to see the mortgage paid and money in the bank, and Esther's success acknowledged on every hand, and there were still a few pleasures left in life. William had his mother, and Esther had hers, and they had not seen each other for a year, though Mrs. Hight had spoken of a year's making no change in William even at his age. She must have been in the far eighties herself, but of a noble courage and persistence in the world she ruled from her stiff-backed rocking-chair.

William unloaded his gift of dried fish, each one chosen with perfect care, and Esther stood by, watching him, and then she walked across the field with us beside the wagon. I believed that I was the only one who knew their happy secret, and she blushed a little as we said good-by.

"I hope you ain't goin' to feel too tired, mother's so deaf; no, I hope you won't be tired," she said kindly, speaking as if she well knew what tiredness was. We could hear the neglected sheep bleating on the hill in the next moment's silence. Then she smiled at me, a smile of noble patience, of uncomprehended sacrifice, which I can never forget. There was all the remembrance of disappointed hopes, the hardships of winter, the loneliness of single-handedness in her look, but I understood, and I love to remember her worn face and her young blue eyes.

"Good-by, William," she said gently, and William said good-by, and gave her a quick glance, but he did not turn to look back, though I did, and waved my hand as she was putting up the bars behind us. Nor did he speak again until we had passed through the dark woods and were on our way homeward by the main road. The grave yearly visit had been changed from a hope into a happy memory.

"You can see the sea from the top of her pasture hill," said William at last.

"Can you?" I asked, with surprise.

"Yes, it's very high land; the ledges up there show very plain in clear weather from the top of our island, and there's a high upstandin' tree that makes a landmark for the fishin' grounds." And William gave a happy sigh.

When we had nearly reached the Landing, my companion looked over into the back of the wagon and saw that the piece of sailcloth was safe, with which he had covered the dried fish. "I wish we had got some trout," he said wistfully. "They always appease Almiry, and make her feel 't was worth while to go."

I stole a glance at William Blackett. We had not seen a solitary mosquito, but there was a dark stripe across his mild face, which might have been an old scar won long ago in battle.

22 *The Queen's Twin* The coast of Maine was in former years brought so near to foreign shores by its busy fleet of ships that among the older men and women one

still finds a surprising proportion of travelers. Each sea-
ward-stretching headland with its high-set houses, each island of a single farm, has sent its spies to view many a
Land of Eshcol; one may see plain, contented old faces at
the windows, whose eyes have looked at far-away ports and
known the splendors of the Eastern world. They shame
the easy voyager of the North Atlantic and the Mediterranean; they have rounded the Cape of Good Hope and
braved the angry seas of Cape Horn in small wooden ships;
they have brought up their hardy boys and girls on narrow
decks; they were among the last of the Northmen's children
to go adventuring to unknown shores. More than this one
cannot give to a young State for its enlightenment; the sea
captains and the captains' wives of Maine knew something
of the wide world, and never mistook their native parishes
for the whole instead of a part thereof; they knew not only
Thomaston and Castine and Portland, but London and
Bristol and Bordeaux, and the strange-mannered harbors
of the China Sea.

One September day, when I was nearly at the end of my
summer at Dunnet Landing, Mrs. Todd came home from
a long, solitary stroll in the wild pastures, with an eager
look as if she were just starting on a hopeful quest instead
of returning. She brought a little basket with blackberries
enough for supper, and held it towards me so that I could
see that there were also some late and surprising raspberries
sprinkled on top, but she made no comment upon her way-
faring. I could tell plainly that she had something very important to say.

"You haven't brought home a leaf of anything," I ventured to this practiced herb-gatherer. "You were saying yesterday that the witch hazel might be in bloom."

"I dare say, dear," she answered in a lofty manner; "I
ain't goin' to say it wasn't; I ain't much concerned either
way 'bout the facts o' witch hazel. Truth is, I've been off
visitin'; there's an old Indian footpath leadin' over towards
the Back Shore through the great heron swamp that anybody can't travel over all summer. You have to seize your
time some day just now, while the low ground's summer-
dried as it is to-day, and before the fall rains set in. I never
thought of it till I was out o' sight o' home, and I says to

myself, 'To-day's the day, certain!' and stepped along smart as I could. Yes, I've been visitin'. I did get into one spot that was wet underfoot before I noticed; you wait till I get me a pair o' dry woolen stockings, in case of cold, and I'll come an' tell ye."

Mrs. Todd disappeared. I could see that something had deeply interested her. She might have fallen in with either the sea-serpent or the lost tribes of Israel, such was her air of mystery and satisfaction. She had been away since just before mid-morning, and as I sat waiting by my window I saw the last red glow of autumn sunshine flare along the gray rocks of the shore and leave them cold again, and touch the far sails of some coastwise schooners so that they stood like golden houses on the sea.

I was left to wonder longer than I liked. Mrs. Todd was making an evening fire and putting things in train for supper; presently she returned, still looking warm and cheerful after her long walk.

"There's a beautiful view from a hill over where I've been," she told me; "yes, there's a beautiful prospect of land and sea. You wouldn't discern the hill from any distance, but 't is the pretty situation of it that counts. I sat there a long spell, and I did wish for you. No, I didn't know a word about goin' when I set out this morning" (as if I had openly reproached her!); "I only felt one o' them travelin' fits comin' on, an' I ketched up my little basket; I didn't know but I might turn and come back time for dinner. I thought it wise to set out your luncheon for you in case I didn't. Hope you had all you wanted; yes, I hope you had enough."

"Oh, yes, indeed," said I. My landlady was always peculiarly bountiful in her supplies when she left me to fare for myself, as if she made a sort of peace-offering or affectionate apology.

"You know that hill with the old house right on top, over beyond the heron swamp? You'll excuse me for explainin'," Mrs. Todd began, "but you ain't so apt to strike inland as you be to go right along shore. You know that hill; there's a path leadin' right over to it that you have to look sharp to find nowadays; it belonged to the up-country Indians when they had to make a carry to the landing here to get to

the out' islands. I've heard the old folks say that there used
to be a place across a ledge where they'd worn a deep track
with their moccasin feet, but I never could find it. 'T is so
overgrown in some places that you keep losin' the path in
the bushes and findin' it as you can; but it runs pretty
straight considerin' the lay o' the land, and I keep my eye
on the sun and the moss that grows one side o' the tree
trunks. Some brook's been choked up and the swamp's bigger than it used to be. Yes; I did get in deep enough, one
place!"

I showed the solicitude that I felt. Mrs. Todd was no
longer young, and in spite of her strong, great frame and
spirited behavior, I knew that certain ills were apt to seize
upon her, and would end some day by leaving her lame and
ailing.

"Don't you go to worryin' about me," she insisted, "settin' still's the only way the Evil One'll ever get the upper
hand o' me. Keep me movin' enough, an' I'm twenty year
old summer an' winter both. I don't know why 't is, but
I've never happened to mention the one I've been to see. I
don't know why I never happened to speak the name of
Abby Martin, for I often give her a thought, but 't is a
dreadful out-o'-the-way place where she lives, and I haven't
seen her myself for three or four years. She's a real good
interesting woman, and we're well acquainted; she's nigher
mother's age than mine, but she's very young feeling. She
made me a nice cup o' tea, and I don't know but I should
have stopped all night if I could have got word to you not
to worry."

Then there was a serious silence before Mrs. Todd spoke
again to make a formal announcement.

"She is the Queen's Twin," and Mrs. Todd looked
steadily to see how I might bear the great surprise.

"The Queen's Twin?" I repeated.

"Yes, she's come to feel a real interest in the Queen, and
anybody can see how natural 't is. They were born the very
same day, and you would be astonished to see what a number o' other things have corresponded. She was speaking o'
some o' the facts to me to-day, an' you'd think she'd never
done nothing but read history. I see how earnest she was
about it as I never did before. I've often and often heard her

allude to the facts, but now she's got to be old and the hurry's over with her work, she's come to live a good deal in her thoughts, as folks often do, and I tell you 't is a sight o' company for her. If you want to hear about Queen Victoria, why Mis' Abby Martin'll tell you everything. And the prospect from that hill I spoke of is as beautiful as anything in this world; 't is worth while your goin' over to see her just for that."

"When can you go again?" I demanded eagerly.

"I should say to-morrow," answered Mrs. Todd; "yes, I should say to-morrow; but I expect 't would be better to take one day to rest, in between. I considered that question as I was comin' home, but I hurried so that there wa'n't much time to think. It's a dreadful long way to go with a horse; you have to go 'most as far as the old Bowden place an' turn off to the left, a master long, rough road, and then you have to turn right round as soon as you get there if you mean to get home before nine o'clock at night. But to strike across country from here, there's plenty o' time in the shortest day, and you can have a good hour or two's visit beside; 't ain't but a very few miles, and it's pretty all the way along. There used to be a few good families over there, but they've died and scattered, so now she's far from neighbors. There, she really cried, she was so glad to see anybody comin'. You'll be amused to hear her talk about the Queen, but I thought twice or three times as I set there 't was about all the company she'd got."

"Could we go day after to-morrow?" I asked eagerly.

" 'T would suit me exactly," said Mrs. Todd.

II One can never be so certain of good New England weather as in the days when a long easterly storm has blown away the warm late-summer mists, and cooled the air so that however bright the sunshine is by day, the nights come nearer and nearer to frostiness. There was a cold freshness in the morning air when Mrs. Todd and I locked the house-door behind us; we took the key of the fields into our own hands that day, and put out across country as one puts out to sea. When we reached the top of the ridge behind the town it seemed as if we had anxiously passed the harbor bar and were comfortably in open sea at last.

"There, now!" proclaimed Mrs. Todd, taking a long breath, "now I do feel safe. It's just the weather that's liable to bring somebody to spend the day; I've had a feeling of Mis' Elder Caplin from North Point bein' close upon me ever since I waked up this mornin', an' I didn't want to be hampered with our present plans. She's a great hand to visit; she'll be spendin' the day somewhere from now till Thanksgivin', but there's plenty o' places at the Landin' where she goes, an' if I ain't there she'll just select another. I thought mother might be in, too, 't is so pleasant; but I run up the road to look off this mornin' before you was awake, and there was no sign o' the boat. If they hadn't started by that time they wouldn't start, just as the tide is now; besides, I see a lot o' mackerel-men headin' Green Island way, and they'll detain William. No, we're safe now, an' if mother should be comin' in to-morrow we'll have all this to tell her. She an' Mis' Abby Martin's very old friends."

We were walking down the long pasture slopes towards the dark woods and thickets of the low ground. They stretched away northward like an unbroken wilderness; the early mists still dulled much of the color and made the uplands beyond look like a very far-off country.

"It ain't so far as it looks from here," said my companion reassuringly, "but we've got no time to spare either," and she hurried on, leading the way with a fine sort of spirit in her step; and presently we struck into the old Indian footpath, which could be plainly seen across the long-unploughed turf of the pastures, and followed it among the thick, low-growing spruces. There the ground was smooth and brown under foot, and the thin-stemmed trees held a dark and shadowy roof overhead. We walked a long way without speaking; sometimes we had to push aside the branches, and sometimes we walked in a broad aisle where the trees were larger. It was a solitary wood, birdless and beastless; there was not even a rabbit to be seen, or a crow high in air to break the silence.

"I don't believe the Queen ever saw such a lonesome trail as this," said Mrs. Todd, as if she followed the thoughts that were in my mind. Our visit to Mrs. Abby Martin seemed in some strange way to concern the high affairs of royalty. I had just been thinking of English landscapes, and of the solemn hills of Scotland with their lonely cottages and stone-walled sheepfolds, and the wandering flocks on high cloudy pastures. I had often been struck by the quick interest and familiar allusion to certain members of the royal house which one found in distant neighborhoods of New England; whether some old instincts of personal loyalty have survived all changes of time and national vicissitudes, or whether it is only that the Queen's own character and disposition have won friends for her so far away, it is impossible to tell. But to hear of a twin sister was the most surprising proof of intimacy of all, and I must confess that there was something remarkably exciting to the imagination in my morning walk. To think of being presented at Court in the usual way was for the moment quite commonplace.

III Mrs. Todd was swinging her basket to and fro like a schoolgirl as she walked, and at this moment it slipped from her hand and rolled lightly along the ground as if there were nothing in it. I picked it up and gave it to her, whereupon she lifted the cover and looked in with anxiety.

"'T is only a few little things, but I don't want to lose 'em," she explained humbly. "'T was lucky you took the other basket if I was goin' to roll it round. Mis' Abby Martin complained o' lacking some pretty pink silk to finish one o' her little frames, an' I thought I'd carry her some, and I had a bunch o' gold thread that had been in a box o' mine this twenty year. I never was one to do much fancy work, but we're all liable to be swept away by fashion. And then there's a small packet o' very choice herbs that I gave a good deal of attention to; they'll smarten her up and give her the best of appetites, come spring. She was tellin' me that spring weather is very wiltin' an' tryin' to her, and she was beginnin' to dread it already. Mother's just the same way; if I could prevail on mother to take some o' these remedies in good season 't would make a world o' difference, but she gets all down hill before I have a chance to hear of it, and then William comes in to tell me, sighin' and bewailin', how feeble mother is. 'Why can't you remember 'bout them good herbs that I never let her be without?' I say to him—he does provoke me so; and then off he goes, sulky enough, down to his boat. Next thing I know, she comes in to go to meetin', wantin' to speak to everybody and feelin' like a girl. Mis' Martin's case is very much the same; but she's nobody to watch her. William's kind o' slow-moulded; but there, any William's better than none when you get to be Mis' Martin's age."

"Hadn't she any children?" I asked.

"Quite a number," replied Mrs. Todd grandly, "but some are gone and the rest are married and settled. She never was a great hand to go about visitin'. I don't know but Mis' Martin might be called a little peculiar. Even her own folks has to make company of her; she never slips in and lives right along with the rest as if 't was at home, even in her own children's houses. I heard one o' her sons' wives say once she'd much rather have the Queen to spend the day if she could choose between the two, but I never thought Abby was so difficult as that. I used to love to have her come; she may have been sort o' ceremonious, but very pleasant and sprightly if you had sense enough to treat her her own way. I always think she'd know just how to live with great folks, and feel easier 'long of them an' their ways. Her son's wife's a great driver with farm-work, boards a great tableful o' men in hayin' time, an' feels right in her element. I don't say but she's a good woman an' smart, but sort o' rough. Anybody that's gentle-mannered an' precise like Mis' Martin would be a sort o' restraint.

"There's all sorts o' folks in the country, same's there is in the city," concluded Mrs. Todd gravely, and I as gravely agreed. The thick woods were behind us now, and the sun was shining clear overhead, the morning mists were gone, and a faint blue haze softened the distance; as we climbed the hill where we were to see the view, it seemed like a summer day. There was an old house on the height, facing southward,—a mere forsaken shell of an old house, with empty windows that looked like blind eyes. The frost-bitten grass grew close about it like brown fur, and there was a single crooked bough of lilac holding its green leaves close by the door.

"We'll just have a good piece of bread-an'-butter now," said the commander of the expedition, "and then we'll hang up the basket on some peg inside the house out o' the way o' the sheep, and have a han'some entertainment as we're comin' back. She'll be all through her little dinner when we get there, Mis' Martin will; but she'll want to make us some tea, an' we must have our visit an' be startin' back pretty soon after two. I don't want to cross all that low ground again after it's begun to grow chilly. An' it looks to me as if the clouds might begin to gather late in the afternoon."

Before us lay a splendid world of sea and shore. The autumn colors already brightened the landscape; and here and there at the edge of a dark tract of pointed firs stood a row of bright swamp-maples like scarlet flowers. The blue sea and the great tide inlets were untroubled by the lightest winds.

"Poor land, this is!" sighed Mrs. Todd as we sat down to rest on the worn doorstep. "I've known three good hard-workin' families that come here full o' hope an' pride and tried to make something o' this farm, but it beat 'em all. There's one small field that's excellent for potatoes if you let half of it rest every year; but the land's always hungry. Now, you see them little peakéd-topped spruces an' fir balsams comin' up over the hill all green an' hearty; they've got it all their own way! Seems sometimes as if wild Natur' got jealous over a certain spot, and wanted to do just as she'd a mind to. You'll see here; she'll do her own ploughin' an' harrowin' with frost an' wet, an' plant just what she wants and wait for her own crops. Man can't do nothin' with it, try as he may. I tell you those little trees means business!"

I looked down the slope, and felt as if we ourselves were likely to be surrounded and overcome if we lingered too long. There was a vigor of growth, a persistence and savagery about the sturdy little trees that put weak human nature at complete defiance. One felt a sudden pity for the men and women who had been worsted after a long fight in that lonely place; one felt a sudden fear of the unconquerable, immediate forces of Nature, as in the irresistible moment of a thunderstorm.

"I can recollect the time when folks were shy o' these woods we just come through," said Mrs. Todd seriously. "The men-folks themselves never'd venture into 'em alone; if their cattle got strayed they'd collect whoever they could get, and start off all together. They said a person was liable to get bewildered in there alone, and in old times folks had been lost. I expect there was considerable fear left over from the old Indian times, and the poor days o' witchcraft; anyway, I've seen bold men act kind o' timid. Some women o' the Asa Bowden family went out one afternoon berryin' when I was a girl, and got lost and was out all night; they found 'em middle o' the mornin' next day, not half a mile from home, scared most to death, an' sayin' they'd heard wolves and other beasts sufficient for a caravan. Poor creatur's! they'd strayed at last into a kind of low place amongst some alders, an' one of 'em was so overset she never got over it, an' went off in a sort o' slow decline. 'T was like them victims that drowns in a foot o' water; but their minds did suffer dreadful. Some folks is born afraid of the woods and all wild places, but I must say they've always been like home to me."

I glanced at the resolute, confident face of my companion. Life was very strong in her, as if some force of Nature were personified in this simple-hearted woman and gave her cousinship to the ancient deities. She might have walked the primeval fields of Sicily; her strong gingham skirts might at that very moment bend the slender stalks of asphodel and be fragrant with trodden thyme, instead of the brown wind-brushed grass of New England and frost-bitten goldenrod. She was a great soul, was Mrs. Todd, and I her humble follower, as we went our way to visit the Queen's Twin, leaving the bright view of the sea behind us, and descending to a lower country-side through the dry pastures and fields.

The farms all wore a look of gathering age, though the settlement was, after all, so young. The fences were already fragile, and it seemed as if the first impulse of agriculture had soon spent itself without hope of renewal. The better houses were always those that had some hold upon the riches of the sea; a house that could not harbor a fishing-boat in some neighboring inlet was far from being sure of every-day comforts. The land alone was not enough to live upon in that stony region; it belonged by right to the forest, and to the forest it fast returned. From the top of the hill where we had been sitting we had seen prosperity in the dim distance, where the land was good and the sun shone upon fat barns, and where warm-looking houses with three or four chimneys apiece stood high on their solid ridge above the bay.

As we drew nearer to Mrs. Martin's it was sad to see what poor bushy fields, what thin and empty dwelling-places had been left by those who had chosen this disappointing part of the northern country for their home. We crossed the last field and came into a narrow rain-washed road, and Mrs. Todd looked eager and expectant and said that we were almost at our journey's end. "I do hope Mis' Martin'll ask you into her best room where she keeps all the Queen's pictures. Yes, I think likely she will ask you; but 't ain't everybody she deems worthy to visit 'em, I can tell you!" said Mrs. Todd warningly. "She's been collectin' 'em an' cuttin' 'em out o' newspapers an' magazines time out o' mind, and if she heard of anybody sailin' for an English port she'd contrive to get a little money to 'em and ask to have the last likeness there was. She's most covered her best-room wall now; she keeps that room shut up sacred as a meetin'-house! 'I won't say but I have my favorites amongst 'em,' she told me t' other day, 'but they're all beautiful to me as they can be!' And she's made some kind o' pretty little frames for 'em all—you know there's always a new fashion o' frames comin' round; first 't was shell-work, and then 't was pine-cones, and bead-work's had its day, and now she's much concerned with perforated cardboard worked with silk. I tell you that best room's a sight to see! But you mustn't look for anything elegant," continued Mrs. Todd, after a moment's reflection. "Mis' Martin's always been in very poor, strugglin' circumstances. She had ambition for her children, though they took right after their father an' had little for themselves; she wa'n't over an' above well married, however kind she may see fit to speak. She's been patient an' hardworkin' all her life, and always high above makin' mean complaints of other folks. I expect all this business about the Queen has buoyed her over many a shoal place in life. Yes, you might say that Abby'd been a slave, but there ain't any slave but has some freedom."

IV Presently I saw a low gray house standing on a grassy bank close to the road. The door was at the side, facing us, and a tangle of snowberry bushes and cinnamon roses grew to the level of the window-sills. On the doorstep stood a bent-shouldered, little old woman; there was an air of welcome and of unmistakable dignity about her.

"She sees us coming," exclaimed Mrs. Todd in an excited whisper. "There, I told her I might be over this way again if the weather held good, and if I came I'd bring you. She said right off she'd take great pleasure in havin' a visit from you; I was surprised, she's usually so retirin'."

Even this reassurance did not quell a faint apprehension on our part; there was something distinctly formal in the occasion, and one felt that consciousness of inadequacy which is never easy for the humblest pride to bear. On the way I had torn my dress in an unexpected encounter with a little thornbush, and I could now imagine how it felt to be going to Court and forgetting one's feathers or her Court train.

The Queen's Twin was oblivious of such trifles; she stood waiting with a calm look until we came near enough to take her kind hand. She was a beautiful old woman, with clear eyes and a lovely quietness and genuineness of manner; there was not a trace of anything pretentious about her, or high-flown, as Mrs. Todd would say comprehensively. Beauty in age is rare enough in women who have spent their lives in the hard work of a farmhouse; but autumnlike and withered as this woman may have looked, her features had kept, or rather gained, a great refinement. She led us into her old kitchen and gave us seats, and took one of the little straight-backed chairs herself and sat a short distance away, as if she were giving audience to an ambassador. It seemed as if we should all be standing; you could not help feeling that the habits of her life were more ceremonious, but that for the moment she assumed the simplicities of the occasion.

Mrs. Todd was always Mrs. Todd, too great and self-possessed a soul for any occasion to ruffle. I admired her calmness, and presently the slow current of neighborhood talk carried one easily along; we spoke of the weather and the small adventures of the way, and then, as if I were after all not a stranger, our hostess turned almost affectionately to speak to me.

"The weather will be growing dark in London now. I expect that you've been in London, dear?" she said.

"Oh, yes," I answered. "Only last year."

"It is a great many years since I was there, along in the forties," said Mrs. Martin. "'T was the only voyage I ever made; most of my neighbors have been great travelers. My brother was master of a vessel, and his wife usually sailed with him; but that year she had a young child more frail than the others, and she dreaded the care of it at sea. It happened that my brother got a chance for my husband to go as supercargo, being a good accountant, and came one day to urge him to take it; he was very ill-disposed to the sea, but he had met with losses, and I saw my own opportunity and persuaded them both to let me go too. In those days they didn't object to a woman's being aboard to wash and mend, the voyages were sometimes very long. And that was the way I come to see the Queen."

Mrs. Martin was looking straight in my eyes to see if I showed any genuine interest in the most interesting person in the world.

"Oh, I am very glad you saw the Queen," I hastened to say. "Mrs. Todd has told me that you and she were born the very same day."

"We were indeed, dear!" said Mrs. Martin, and she leaned back comfortably and smiled as she had not smiled before. Mrs. Todd gave a satisfied nod and glance, as if to say that things were going on as well as possible in this anxious moment.

"Yes," said Mrs. Martin again, drawing her chair a little nearer, "'t was a very remarkable thing; we were born the same day, and at exactly the same hour, after you allowed for all the difference in time. My father figured it out sea-fashion. Her Royal Majesty and I opened our eyes upon this world together; say what you may, 't is a bond between us."

Mrs. Todd assented with an air of triumph, and untied

her hat-strings and threw them back over her shoulders
with a gallant air.

"And I married a man by the name of Albert, just the
same as she did, and all by chance, for I didn't get the news
that she had an Albert too till a fortnight afterward; news
was slower coming then than it is now. My first baby was a
girl, and I called her Victoria after my mate; but the next
one was a boy, and my husband wanted the right to name
him, and took his own name and his brother Edward's, and
pretty soon I saw in the paper that the little Prince o' Wales
had been christened just the same. After that I made excuse
to wait till I knew what she'd named her children. I didn't
want to break the chain, so I had an Alfred, and my darling
Alice that I lost long before she lost hers, and there I stopped.
If I'd only had a dear daughter to stay at home with me,
same's her youngest one, I should have been so thankful!
But if only one of us could have a little Beatrice, I'm glad
't was the Queen; we've both seen trouble, but she's had
the most care."

I asked Mrs. Martin if she lived alone all the year, and
was told that she did except for a visit now and then from
one of her grandchildren, "the only one that really likes to
come an' stay quiet 'long o' grandma. She always says quick
as she's through her schoolin' she's goin' to live with me all
the time, but she's very pretty an' has taking ways," said
Mrs. Martin, looking both proud and wistful, "so I can tell
nothing at all about it! Yes, I've been alone most o' the time
since my Albert was taken away, and that's a great many
years; he had a long time o' failing and sickness first."
(Mrs. Todd's foot gave an impatient scuff on the floor.)
"An' I've always lived right here. I ain't like the Queen's
Majesty, for this is the only palace I've got," said the dear
old thing, smiling again. "I'm glad of it too, I don't like
changing about, an' our stations in life are set very different.
I don't require what the Queen does, but sometimes I've
thought 't was left to me to do the plain things she don't
have time for. I expect she's a beautiful housekeeper, nobody couldn't have done better in her high place, and she's
been as good a mother as she's been a queen."

"I guess she has, Abby," agreed Mrs. Todd instantly.
"How was it you happened to get such a good look at her?

I meant to ask you again when I was here t' other day."

"Our ship was layin' in the Thames, right there above Wapping. We was dischargin' cargo, and under orders to clear as quick as we could for Bordeaux to take on an excellent freight o' French goods," explained Mrs. Martin eagerly. "I heard that the Queen was goin' to a great review of her army, and would drive out o' her Buckin'ham Palace about ten o'clock in the mornin', and I run aft to Albert, my husband, and brother Horace where they was standin' together by the hatchway, and told 'em they must one of 'em take me. They laughed, I was in such a hurry, and said they couldn't go; and I found they meant it and got sort of impatient when I began to talk, and I was 'most broken-hearted; 't was all the reason I had for makin' that hard voyage. Albert couldn't help often reproachin' me, for he did so resent the sea, an' I'd known how 't would be before we sailed; but I'd minded nothing all the way till then, and I just crep' back to my cabin an' begun to cry. They was disappointed about their ship's cook, an' I'd cooked for fo'c's'le an' cabin myself all the way over; 't was dreadful hard work, specially in rough weather; we'd had head winds an' a six weeks' voyage. They'd acted sort of ashamed o' me when I pled so to go ashore, an' that hurt my feelin's most of all. But Albert come below pretty soon; I'd never given way so in my life, an' he begun to act frightened, and treated me gentle just as he did when we was goin' to be married, an' when I got over sobbin' he went on deck and saw Horace an' talked it over what they could do; they really had their duty to the vessel, and couldn't be spared that day. Horace was real good when he understood everything, and he come an' told me I'd more than worked my passage an' was goin' to do just as I liked now we was in port. He'd engaged a cook, too, that was comin' aboard that mornin', and he was goin' to send the ship's carpenter with me—a nice fellow from up Thomaston way; he'd gone to put on his ashore clothes as quick's he could. So then I got ready, and we started off in the small boat and rowed up river. I was afraid we were too late, but the tide was setting up very strong, and we landed an' left the boat to a keeper, and I run all the way up those great streets and across a park. 'T was a great day, with sights o' folks everywhere, but 't was just as if they was nothin' but wax images to me. I kep' askin' my way an' runnin' on, with the carpenter comin' after as best he could, and just as I worked to the front o' the crowd by the palace, the gates was flung open and out she came; all prancin' horses and shinin' gold, and in a beautiful carriage there she sat; 't was a moment o' heaven to me. I saw her plain, and she looked right at me so pleasant and happy, just as if she knew there was somethin' different between us from other folks."

There was a moment when the Queen's Twin could not go on and neither of her listeners could ask a question.

"Prince Albert was sitting right beside her in the carriage," she continued. "Oh, he was a beautiful man! Yes, dear, I saw 'em both together just as I see you now, and then she was gone out o' sight in another minute, and the common crowd was all spread over the place pushin' an' cheerin'. 'T was some kind o' holiday, an' the carpenter and I got separated, an' then I found him again after I didn't think I should, an' he was all for makin' a day of it, and goin' to show me all the sights; he'd been in London before, but I didn't want nothin' else, an' we went back through the streets down to the waterside an' took the boat. I remember I mended an old coat o' my Albert's as good as I could, sittin' on the quarter-deck in the sun all that afternoon, and 't was all as if I was livin' in a lovely dream. I don't know how to explain it, but there hasn't been no friend I've felt so near to me ever since."

One could not say much—only listen. Mrs. Todd put in a discerning question now and then, and Mrs. Martin's eyes shone brighter and brighter as she talked. What a lovely gift of imagination and true affection was in this fond old heart! I looked about the plain New England kitchen, with its wood-smoked walls and homely braided rugs on the worn floor, and all its simple furnishings. The loud-ticking clock seemed to encourage us to speak; at the other side of the room was an early newspaper portrait of Her Majesty the Queen of Great Britain and Ireland. On a shelf below were some flowers in a little glass dish, as if they were put before a shrine.

"If I could have had more to read, I should have known 'most everything about her," said Mrs. Martin wistfully. "I've made the most of what I did have, and thought it over and over till it came clear. I sometimes seem to have her all my own, as if we'd lived right together. I've often walked out into the woods alone and told her what my troubles was, and it always seemed as if she told me 't was all right, an' we must have patience. I've got her beautiful book about the Highlands; 't was dear Mis' Todd here that found out about her printing it and got a copy for me, and it's been a treasure to my heart, just as if 't was written right to me. I always read it Sundays now, for my Sunday treat. Before that I used to have to imagine a good deal, but when I come to read her book, I knew what I expected was all true. We do think alike about so many things," said the Queen's Twin with affectionate certainty. "You see, there is something between us, being born just at the same time; 't is what they call a birthright. She's had great tasks put upon her, being the Queen, an' mine has been the humble lot; but she's done the best she could, nobody can say to the contrary, and there's something between us; she's been the great lesson I've had to live by. She's been everything to me. An' when she had her Jubilee, oh, how my heart was with her!

"There, 't wouldn't play the part in her life it has in mine," said Mrs. Martin generously, in answer to something one of her listeners had said. "Sometimes I think, now she's older, she might like to know about us. When I think how few old friends anybody has left at our age, I suppose it may be just the same with her as it is with me; perhaps she would like to know how we came into life together. But I've had a great advantage in seeing her, an' I can always fancy her goin' on, while she don't know nothin' yet about me, except she may feel my love stayin' her heart sometimes an' not know just where it comes from. An' I dream about our being together out in some pretty fields, young as ever we was, and holdin' hands as we walk along. I'd like to know if she ever has that dream too. I used to have days when I made believe she did know, an' was comin' to see me," confessed the speaker shyly, with a little flush on her cheeks; "and I'd plan what I could have nice for supper, and I wasn't goin' to let anybody know she was here havin' a good rest, except I'd wish you, Almira Todd, or dear Mis' Blackett would happen in, for you'd know just how to talk with her. You see, she likes to be up in

Scotland, right out in the wild country, better than she does anywhere else."

"I'd really love to take her out to see mother at Green Island," said Mrs. Todd with a sudden impulse.

"Oh, yes! I should love to have you," exclaimed Mrs. Martin, and then she began to speak in a lower tone. "One day I got thinkin' so about my dear Queen," she said, "an' livin' so in my thoughts, that I went to work an' got all ready for her, just as if she was really comin'. I never told this to a livin' soul before, but I feel you'll understand. I put my best fine sheets and blankets I spun an' wove myself on the bed, and I picked some pretty flowers and put 'em all round the house, an' I worked as hard an' happy as I could all day, and had as nice a supper ready as I could get, sort of telling myself a story all the time. She was comin' an' I was goin' to see her again, an' I kep' it up until nightfall; an' when I see the dark an' it come to me I was all alone, the dream left me, an' I sat down on the doorstep an' felt all foolish an' tired. An', if you'll believe it, I heard steps comin', an' an old cousin o' mine come wanderin' along, one I was apt to be shy of. She wasn't all there, as folks used to say, but harmless enough and a kind of poor old talking body. And I went right to meet her when I first heard her call, 'stead o' hidin' as I sometimes did, an' she come in dreadful willin', an' we sat down to supper together; 't was a supper I should have had no heart to eat alone."

"I don't believe she ever had such a splendid time in her life as she did then. I heard her tell all about it afterwards," exclaimed Mrs. Todd compassionately. "There, now I hear all this it seems just as if the Queen might have known and couldn't come herself, so she sent that poor old creatur' that was always in need!"

Mrs. Martin looked timidly at Mrs. Todd and then at me. " 'T was childish o' me to go an' get supper," she confessed.

"I guess you wa'n't the first one to do that," said Mrs. Todd. "No, I guess you wa'n't the first one who's got supper that way, Abby," and then for a moment she could say no more.

Mrs. Todd and Mrs. Martin had moved their chairs a little so that they faced each other, and I, at one side, could see them both.

"No, you never told me o' that before, Abby," said Mrs. Todd gently. "Don't it show that for folks that have any fancy in 'em, such beautiful dreams is the real part o' life? But to most folks the common things that happens outside 'em is all in all."

Mrs. Martin did not appear to understand at first, strange to say, when the secret of her heart was put into words; then a glow of pleasure and comprehension shone upon her face. "Why, I believe you're right, Almira!" she said, and turned to me.

"Wouldn't you like to look at my pictures of the Queen?" she asked, and we rose and went into the best room.

v The mid-day visit seemed very short. September hours are brief to match the shortening days. The great subject was dismissed for a while after our visit to the Queen's pictures, and my companions spoke much of lesser persons until we drank the cup of tea which Mrs. Todd had foreseen. I happily remembered that the Queen herself is said to like a proper cup of tea, and this at once seemed to make her Majesty kindly join so remote and reverent a company. Mrs. Martin's thin cheeks took on a pretty color like a girl's. "Somehow I always have thought of her when I made it extra good," she said. "I got a real china cup that belonged to my grandmother, and I believe I shall call it hers now."

"Why don't you?" responded Mrs. Todd warmly, with a delightful smile.

Later they spoke of a promised visit which was to be made in the Indian summer to the Landing and Green Island, but I observed that Mrs. Todd presented the little parcel of dried herbs, with full directions, for a cure-all in the spring, as if there were no real chance of their meeting again first. As we looked back from the turn of the road the Queen's Twin was still standing on the doorstep watching us away, and Mrs. Todd stopped, and stood still for a moment before she waved her hand again.

"There's one thing certain, dear," she said to me with great discernment; "it ain't as if we left her all alone!"

Then we set out upon our long way home over the hill, where we lingered in the afternoon sunshine, and through the dark woods across the heron-swamp.

23 *William's Wedding* The hurry of life in a large town, the constant putting aside of preference to yield to a most unsatisfactory activity, began to vex me, and one day I took the train, and only left it for the eastward-bound boat. Carlyle says somewhere that the only happiness a man ought to ask for is happiness enough to get his work done; and against this the complexity and futile ingenuity of social life seems a conspiracy. But the first salt wind from the east, the first sight of a lighthouse set boldly on its outer rock, the flash of a gull, the waiting procession of seaward-bound firs on an island, made me feel solid and definite again, instead of a poor, incoherent being. Life was resumed, and anxious living blew away as if it had not been. I could not breathe deep enough or long enough. It was a return to happiness.

The coast had still a wintry look; it was far on in May, but all the shore looked cold and sterile. One was conscious of going north as well as east, and as the day went on the sea grew colder, and all the warmer air and bracing strength and stimulus of the autumn weather, and storage of the heat of summer, were quite gone. I was very cold and very tired when I came at evening up the lower bay, and saw the white houses of Dunnet Landing climbing the hill. They had a friendly look, these little houses, not as if they were climbing up the shore, but as if they were rather all coming down to meet a fond and weary traveler, and I could hardly wait with patience to step off the boat. It was not the usual eager company on the wharf. The coming-in of the mailboat was the one large public event of a summer day, and I was disappointed at seeing none of my intimate friends but Johnny Bowden, who had evidently done nothing all winter but grow, so that his short sea-smitten clothes gave him a look of poverty.

Johnny's expression did not change as we greeted each other, but I suddenly felt that I had shown indifference and inconvenient delay by not coming sooner; before I could make an apology he took my small portmanteau, and walking before me in his old fashion he made straight up the hilly road toward Mrs. Todd's. Yes, he was much grown—

it had never occurred to me the summer before that Johnny was likely, with the help of time and other forces, to grow into a young man; he was such a well-framed and well-settled chunk of a boy that nature seemed to have set him aside as something finished, quite satisfactory, and entirely completed.

The wonderful little green garden had been enchanted away by winter. There were a few frost-bitten twigs and some thin shrubbery against the fence, but it was a most unpromising small piece of ground. My heart was beating like a lover's as I passed it on the way to the door of Mrs. Todd's house, which seemed to have become much smaller under the influence of winter weather.

"She hasn't gone away?" I asked Johnny Bowden with a sudden anxiety just as we reached the doorstep.

"Gone away!" he faced me with blank astonishment,— "I see her settin' by Mis' Caplin's window, the one nighest the road, about four o'clock!" And eager with suppressed news of my coming he made his entrance as if the house were a burrow.

Then on my homesick heart fell the voice of Mrs. Todd. She stopped, through what I knew to be excess of feeling, to rebuke Johnny for bringing in so much mud, and I dallied without for one moment during the ceremony; then we met again face to face.

II   "I dare say you can advise me what shapes they are goin' to wear. My meetin'-bunnit ain't goin' to do me again this year; no! I can't expect 't would do me forever," said Mrs. Todd, as soon as she could say anything. "There! do set down and tell me how you have been! We've got a weddin' in the family, I s'pose you know?"

"A wedding!" said I, still full of excitement.

"Yes; I expect if the tide serves and the line storm don't overtake him they'll come in and appear out on Sunday. I shouldn't have concerned me about the bunnit for a month yet, nobody would notice, but havin' an occasion like this I shall show consider'ble. 'T will be an ordeal for William!"

"For *William!*" I exclaimed. "What do you mean, Mrs. Todd?"

She gave a comfortable little laugh. "Well, the Lord's seen reason at last an' removed Mis' Cap'n Hight up to the farm, an' I don't know but the weddin's goin' to be this week. Esther's had a great deal of business disposin' of her flock, but she's done extra well—the folks that owns the next place goin' up country are well off. 'T is elegant land north side o' that bleak ridge, an' one o' the boys has been Esther's right-hand man of late. She instructed him in all matters, and after she markets the early lambs he's goin' to take the farm on halves, an' she's give the refusal to him to buy her out within two years. She's reserved the buryin'-lot, an' the right o' way in, an'——"

I couldn't stop for details. I demanded reassurance of the central fact.

"William going to be married?" I repeated; whereat Mrs. Todd gave me a searching look that was not without scorn.

"Old Mis' Hight's funeral was a week ago Wednesday, and 't was very well attended," she assured me after a moment's pause.

"Poor thing!" said I, with a sudden vision of her helplessness and angry battle against the fate of illness; "it was very hard for her."

"I thought it was hard for Esther!" said Mrs. Todd without sentiment.

III   I had an odd feeling of strangeness: I missed the garden, and the little rooms, to which I had added a few things of my own the summer before, seemed oddly unfamiliar. It was like the hermit crab in a cold new shell,—and with the windows shut against the raw May air, and a strange silence and grayness of the sea all that first night and day of my visit, I felt as if I had after all lost my hold of that quiet life.

Mrs. Todd made the apt suggestion that city persons were prone to run themselves to death, and advised me to stay and get properly rested now that I had taken the trouble to come. She did not know how long I had been homesick for the conditions of life at the Landing the autumn before—it was natural enough to feel a little unsupported by compelling incidents on my return.

Some one has said that one never leaves a place, or arrives

at one, until the next day! But on the second morning I woke with the familiar feeling of interest and ease, and the bright May sun was streaming in, while I could hear Mrs. Todd's heavy footsteps pounding about in the other part of the house as if something were going to happen. There was the first golden robin singing somewhere close to the house, and a lovely aspect of spring now, and I looked at the garden to see that in the warm night some of its treasures had grown a hand's breadth; the determined spikes of yellow daffies stood tall against the doorsteps, and the bloodroot was unfolding leaf and flower. The belated spring which I had left behind farther south had overtaken me on this northern coast. I even saw a presumptuous dandelion in the garden border.

It is difficult to report the great events of New England; expression is so slight, and those few words which escape us in moments of deep feeling look but meagre on the printed page. One has to assume too much of the dramatic fervor as one reads; but as I came out of my room at breakfast-time I met Mrs. Todd face to face, and when she said to me, "This weather'll bring William in after her; 't is their happy day!" I felt something take possession of me which ought to communicate itself to the least sympathetic reader of this cold page. It is written for those who have a Dunnet Landing of their own: who either kindly share this with the writer, or possess another.

"I ain't seen his comin' sail yet; he'll be likely to dodge round among the islands so he'll be the less observed," continued Mrs. Todd. "You can get a dory up the bay, even a clean new painted one, if you know as how, keepin' it against the high land." She stepped to the door and looked off to sea as she spoke. I could see her eye follow the gray shores to and fro, and then a bright light spread over her calm face. "There he comes, and he's strikin' right in across the open bay like a man!" she said with splendid approval. "See, there he comes! Yes, there's William, and he's bent his new sail."

I looked too, and saw the fleck of white no larger than a gull's wing yet, but present to her eager vision.

I was going to France for the whole long summer that

year, and the more I thought of such an absence from these simple scenes the more dear and delightful they became. Santa Teresa says that the true proficiency of the soul is not in much thinking, but in much loving, and sometimes I believed that I had never found love in its simplicity as I had found it at Dunnet Landing in the various hearts of Mrs. Blackett and Mrs. Todd and William. It is only because one came to know them, these three, loving and wise and true, in their own habitations. Their counterparts are in every village in the world, thank heaven, and the gift to one's life is only in its discernment. I had only lived in Dunnet until the usual distractions and artifices of the world were no longer in control, and I saw these simple natures clear. "The happiness of life is in its recognitions. It seems that we are not ignorant of these truths, and even that we believe them; but we are so little accustomed to think of them, they are so strange to us—"

"Well now, deary me!" said Mrs. Todd, breaking into exclamation; "I've got to fly round—I thought he'd have to beat; he can't sail far on that tack, and he won't be in for a good hour yet—I expect he's made every arrangement, but he said he shouldn't go up after Esther unless the weather was good, and I declare it did look doubtful this morning."

I remembered Esther's weather-worn face. She was like a Frenchwoman who had spent her life in the fields. I remembered her pleasant look, her childlike eyes, and thought of the astonishment of joy she would feel now in being taken care of and tenderly sheltered from wind and weather after all these years. They were going to be young again now, she and William, to forget work and care in the spring weather. I could hardly wait for the boat to come to land, I was so eager to see his happy face.

"Cake an' wine I'm goin' to set 'em out!" said Mrs. Todd. "They won't stop to set down for an orderly meal, they'll want to get right out home quick's they can. Yes, I'll give 'em some cake an' wine—I've got a rare plum-cake from my best receipt, and a bottle o' wine that the old Cap'n Denton of all give me, one of two, the day I was married, one we had and one we saved, and I've never touched it till now. He said there wa'n't none like it in the State o' Maine."

It was a day of waiting, that day of spring; the May weather was as expectant as our fond hearts, and one could see the grass grow green hour by hour. The warm air was full of birds, there was a glow of light on the sea instead of the cold shining of chilly weather which had lingered late. There was a look on Mrs. Todd's face which I saw once and could not meet again. She was in her highest mood. Then I went out early for a walk, and when I came back we sat in different rooms for the most part. There was such a thrill in the air that our only conversation was in her most abrupt and incisive manner. She was knitting, I believe, and as for me I dallied with a book. I heard her walking to and fro, and, the door being wide open now, she went out and paced the front walk to the gate as if she walked a quarter-deck.

It is very solemn to sit waiting for the great events of life—most of us have done it again and again—to be expectant of life or expectant of death gives one the same feeling.

But at the last Mrs. Todd came quickly back from the gate, and standing in the sunshine at the door, she beckoned me as if she were a sibyl. *prophetess of Ancient Greece or Rome*

"I thought you comprehended everything the day you was up there," she added with a little more patience in her tone, but I felt that she thought I had lost instead of gained since we parted the autumn before.

"William's made this pretext o' goin' fishin' for the last time. 'T wouldn't done to take notice, 't would 'a scared him to death! but there never was nobody took less comfort out o' forty years courtin'. No, he won't have to make no further pretexts," said Mrs. Todd, with an air of triumph.

"Did you know where he was going that day?" I asked, with a sudden burst of admiration at such discernment.

"I did!" replied Mrs. Todd grandly.

"Oh! but that pennyroyal lotion," I indignantly protested, remembering that under pretext of mosquitoes she had besmeared the poor lover in an awful way—why, it was outrageous! Medea could not have been more conscious of high ultimate purposes.

"Darlin'," said Mrs. Todd, in the excitement of my arrival and the great concerns of marriage, "he's got a beautiful shaped face, and they pison him very unusual—you wouldn't have had him present himself to his lady all lop-sided with a mosquito-bite? Once when we was young I rode up with him, and they set upon him in concert the minute we entered the woods." She stood before me re-proachfully, and I was conscious of deserved rebuke. "Yes, you've come just in the nick of time to advise me about a bunnit. They say large bows on top is liable to be worn."

IV   The period of waiting was one of direct contrast to these high moments of recognition. The very slowness of the morning hours wasted that sense of excitement with which we had begun the day. Mrs. Todd came down from the mount where her face had shone so bright, to the cares of common life, and some acquaintances from Black Island for whom she had little natural preference or liking came, bringing a poor, sickly child to get medical advice. They were noisy women, with harsh, clamorous voices, and they stayed a long time. I heard the clink of teacups, however, and could detect no impatience in the tones of Mrs. Todd's voice; but when they were at last going away, she did not linger unduly over her leave-taking, and returned to me to explain that they were people she had never liked, and they had made an excuse of a friendly visit to save their doctor's bill; but she pitied the poor little child, and knew beside that the doctor was away.

"I had to give 'em the remedies right out," she told me; "they wouldn't have bought a cent's worth o' drugs down to the store for that dwindlin' thing. She needed feedin' up, and I don't expect she gets milk enough; they're great butter-makers down to Black Island, 't is excellent pasturage, but they use no milk themselves, and their butter is heavy laden with salt to make weight, so that you'd think all their ideas come down from Sodom."

She was very indignant and very wistful about the pale little girl. "I wish they'd let me kept her," she said. "I kind of advised it, and her eyes was so wishful in that pinched face when she heard me, so that I could see what was the matter with her, but they said she wa'n't prepared. Pre-pared!" And Mrs. Todd snuffed like an offended war-horse, and departed; but I could hear her still grumbling and talking to herself in high dudgeon an hour afterward.

At the end of that time her arch enemy, Mari' Harris, appeared at the side-door with a gingham handkerchief over her head. She was always on hand for the news, and made some formal excuse for her presence,—she wished to borrow the weekly paper. Captain Littlepage, whose housekeeper she was, had taken it from the post-office in the morning, but had forgotten, being of failing memory, what he had done with it.

"How is the poor old gentleman?" asked Mrs. Todd with solicitude, ignoring the present errand of Maria and all her concerns.

I had spoken the evening before of intended visits to Captain Littlepage and Elijah Tilley, and I now heard Mrs. Todd repeating my inquiries and intentions, and fending off with unusual volubility of her own the curious questions that were sure to come. But at last Maria Harris secured an opportunity and boldly inquired if she had not seen William ashore early that morning.

"I don't say he wasn't," replied Mrs. Todd; "Thu'sday's a very usual day with him to come ashore."

"He was all dressed up," insisted Maria—she really had no sense of propriety. "I didn't know but they was going to be married?"

Mrs. Todd did not reply. I recognized from the sounds that reached me that she had retired to the fastnesses of the kitchen-closet and was clattering the tins.

"I expect they'll marry soon anyway," continued the visitor.

"I expect they will if they want to," answered Mrs. Todd. "I don't know nothin' 't all about it; that's what folks say." And presently the gingham handkerchief retreated past my window.

"I routed her, horse and foot," said Mrs. Todd proudly, coming at once to stand at my door. "Who's comin' now?" as two figures passed inward bound to the kitchen.

They were Mrs. Begg and Johnny Bowden's mother, who were favorites, and were received with Mrs. Todd's usual civilities. Then one of the Mrs. Caplins came with a cup in hand to borrow yeast. On one pretext or another nearly all

our acquaintances came to satisfy themselves of the facts,
and see what Mrs. Todd would impart about the wedding.
But she firmly avoided the subject through the length of
every call and errand, and answered the final leading question of each curious guest with her noncommittal phrase,
"I don't know nothin' 't all about it; that's what folks say!"

She had just repeated this for the fourth or fifth time
and shut the door upon the last comers, when we met in
the little front entry. Mrs. Todd was not in a bad temper,
but highly amused. "I've been havin' all sorts o' social
privileges, you may have observed. They didn't seem to consider that if they could only hold out till afternoon they'd
know as much as I did. There wa'n't but one o' the whole
sixteen that showed real interest, the rest demeaned themselves to ask out o' cheap curiosity; no, there wa'n't but
one showed any real feelin'."

"Miss Maria Harris, you mean?" and Mrs. Todd laughed.

"Certain, dear," she agreed, "how you do understand
poor human natur'!"

A short distance down the hilly street stood a narrow
house that was newly painted white. It blinded one's eyes
to catch the reflection of the sun. It was the house of
the minister, and a wagon had just stopped before it; a man
was helping a woman to alight, and they stood side by side
for a moment, while Johnny Bowden appeared as if by
magic, and climbed to the wagon-seat. Then they went into
the house and shut the door. Mrs. Todd and I stood close
together and watched; the tears were running down her
cheeks. I watched Johnny Bowden, who made light of so
great a moment by so handling the whip that the old white
Caplin horse started up from time to time and was inexo-
rably stopped as if he had some idea of running away. There
was something in the back of the wagon which now and
then claimed the boy's attention; he leaned over as if there
were something very precious left in his charge; perhaps it
was only Esther's little trunk going to its new home.

At last the door of the parsonage opened, and two figures
came out. The minister followed them and stood in the
doorway, delaying them with parting words; he could not
have thought it was a time for admonition.

"He's all alone; his wife's up to Portland to her sister's," said Mrs. Todd aloud, in a matter-of-fact voice. "She's a nice woman, but she might ha' talked too much. There! see, they're comin' here. I didn't know how 't would be. Yes, they're comin' up to see us before they go home. I declare, if William ain't lookin' just like a king!"

Mrs. Todd took one step forward, and we stood and waited. The happy pair came walking up the street, Johnny Bowden driving ahead. I heard a plaintive little cry from time to time to which in the excitement of the moment I had not stopped to listen; but when William and Esther had come and shaken hands with Mrs. Todd and then with me, all in silence, Esther stepped quickly to the back of the wagon, and unfastening some cords returned to us carrying a little white lamb. She gave a shy glance at William as she fondled it and held it to her heart, and then, still silent, we went into the house together. The lamb had stopped bleating. It was lovely to see Esther carry it in her arms.

When we got into the house, all the repression of Mrs. Todd's usual manner was swept away by her flood of feeling. She took Esther's thin figure, lamb and all, to her heart and held her there, kissing her as she might have kissed a child, and then held out her hand to William and they gave each other the kiss of peace. This was so moving, so tender, so free from their usual fetters of self-consciousness, that Esther and I could not help giving each other a happy glance of comprehension. I never saw a young bride half so touching in her happiness as Esther was that day of her wedding. We took the cake and wine of the marriage feast together, always in silence, like a true sacrament, and then to my astonishment I found that sympathy and public interest in so great an occasion were going to have their way. I shrank from the thought of William's possible sufferings, but he welcomed both the first group of neighbors and the last with heartiness; and when at last they had gone, for there were thoughtless loiterers in Dunnet Landing, I made ready with eager zeal and walked with William and Esther to the water-side. It was only a little way, and kind faces nodded reassuringly from the windows, while kind voices spoke from the doors. Esther carried the lamb on one arm; she had found time to tell me that its mother had died that morning and she could not bring herself to the thought of leaving it behind. She kept the other hand on William's arm until we reached the landing. Then he shook hands with me, and looked me full in the face to be sure I understood how happy he was, and stepping into the boat held out his arms to Esther—at last she was his own.

I watched him make a nest for the lamb out of an old sea-cloak at Esther's feet, and then he wrapped her own shawl round her shoulders, and finding a pin in the lapel of his Sunday coat he pinned it for her. She looked at him fondly while he did this, and then glanced up at us, a pretty, girlish color brightening her cheeks.

We stood there together and watched them go far out into the bay. The sunshine of the May day was low now, but there was a steady breeze, and the boat moved well.

"Mother'll be watching for them," said Mrs. Todd. "Yes, mother'll be watching all day, and waiting. She'll be so happy to have Esther come."

We went home together up the hill, and Mrs. Todd said nothing more; but we held each other's hands all the way.

24 *The Backward View* At last it was the time of late summer, when the house was cool and damp in the morning, and all the light seemed to come through green leaves; but at the first step out of doors the sunshine always laid a warm hand on my shoulder, and the clear, high sky seemed to lift quickly as I looked at it. There was no autumnal mist on the coast, nor any August fog; instead of these, the sea, the sky, all the long shore line and the inland hills, with every bush of bay and every fir-top, gained a deeper color and a sharper clearness. There was something shining in the air, and a kind of lustre on the water and the pasture grass,—a northern look that, except at this moment of the year, one must go far to seek. The sunshine of a northern summer was coming to its lovely end.

The days were few then at Dunnet Landing, and I let each of them slip away unwillingly as a miser spends his coins. I wished to have one of my first weeks back again, with those long hours when nothing happened except the growth of herbs and the course of the sun. Once I had not even known where to go for a walk; now there were many delightful things to be done and done again, as if I were in London. I felt hurried and full of pleasant engagements, and the days flew by like a handful of flowers flung to the sea wind.

At last I had to say good-by to all my Dunnet Landing friends, and my homelike place in the little house, and return to the world in which I feared to find myself a foreigner. There may be restrictions to such a summer's happiness, but the ease that belongs to simplicity is charming enough to make up for whatever a simple life may lack, and the gifts of peace are not for those who live in the thick of battle.

I was to take the small unpunctual steamer that went down the bay in the afternoon, and I sat for a while by my window looking out on the green herb garden, with regret for company. Mrs. Todd had hardly spoken all day except in the briefest and most disapproving way; it was as if we were on the edge of a quarrel. It seemed impossible to take my departure with anything like composure. At last I heard a footstep, and looked up to find that Mrs. Todd was standing at the door.

"I've seen to everything now," she told me in an unusually loud and business-like voice. "Your trunks are on the w'arf by this time. Cap'n Bowden he come and took 'em down himself, an' is going to see that they're safe aboard. Yes, I've seen to all your 'rangements," she repeated in a gentler tone. "These things I've left on the kitchen table you'll want to carry by hand; the basket needn't be returned. I guess I shall walk over towards the Port now an' inquire how old Mis' Edward Caplin is."

I glanced at my friend's face, and saw a look that touched me to the heart. I had been sorry enough before to go away.

"I guess you'll excuse me if I ain't down there to stand round on the w'arf and see you go," she said, still trying to be gruff. "Yes, I ought to go over and inquire for Mis' Edward Caplin; it's her third shock, and if mother gets in on Sunday she'll want to know just how the old lady is." With this last word Mrs. Todd turned and left me as if with sudden thought of something she had forgotten, so that I felt sure she was coming back, but presently I heard her go out of the kitchen door and walk down the path toward the gate. I could not part so; I ran after her to say good-by, but she shook her head and waved her hand without looking back when she heard my hurrying steps, and so went away down the street.

When I went in again the little house had suddenly grown lonely, and my room looked empty as it had the day I came. I and all my belongings had died out of it, and I knew how it would seem when Mrs. Todd came back and found her lodger gone. So we die before our own eyes; so we see some chapters of our lives come to their natural end.

I found the little packages on the kitchen table. There was a quaint West Indian basket which I knew its owner had valued, and which I had once admired; there was an affecting provision laid beside it for my seafaring supper, with a neatly tied bunch of southernwood and a twig of bay, and a little old leather box which held the coral pin that Nathan Todd brought home to give to poor Joanna.

There was still an hour to wait, and I went up to the hill just above the schoolhouse and sat there thinking of things, and looking off to sea, and watching for the boat to come in sight. I could see Green Island, small and darkly wooded at that distance; below me were the houses of the village with their apple-trees and bits of garden ground. Presently, as I looked at the pastures beyond, I caught a last glimpse of Mrs. Todd herself, walking slowly in the footpath that led along, following the shore toward the Port. At such a distance one can feel the large, positive qualities that control a character. Close at hand, Mrs. Todd seemed able and warm-hearted and quite absorbed in her bustling industries, but her distant figure looked mateless and appealing, with something about it that was strangely self-possessed and mysterious. Now and then she stooped to pick something, —it might have been her favorite pennyroyal,—and at last I lost sight of her as she slowly crossed an open space on one of the higher points of land, and disappeared again behind a dark clump of juniper and the pointed firs.

As I came away on the little coastwise steamer, there was an old sea running which made the surf leap high on all the rocky shores. I stood on deck, looking back, and watched the busy gulls agree and turn, and sway together down the long slopes of air, then separate hastily and plunge into the waves. The tide was setting in, and plenty of small fish were coming with it, unconscious of the silver flashing of the great birds overhead and the quickness of their fierce beaks. The sea was full of life and spirit, the tops of the waves flew back as if they were winged like the gulls themselves, and like them had the freedom of the wind. Out in the main channel we passed a bent-shouldered old fisherman bound for the evening round among his lobster traps. He was toiling along with short oars, and the dory tossed and sank and tossed again with the steamer's waves. I saw that it was old Elijah Tilley, and though we had so long been strangers we had come to be warm friends, and I wished that he had waited for one of his mates, it was such hard work to row along shore through rough seas and tend the traps alone. As we passed I waved my hand and tried to call to him, and he looked up and answered my farewells by a solemn nod. The little town, with the tall masts of its disabled schooners in the inner bay, stood high above the flat sea for a few minutes, then it sank back into the uniformity of the coast, and became indistinguishable from the other towns that looked as if they were crumbled on the furzy-green stoniness of the shore.

The small outer islands of the bay were covered among the ledges with turf that looked as fresh as the early grass; there had been some days of rain the week before, and the darker green of the sweet-fern was scattered on all the pasture heights. It looked like the beginning of summer ashore, though the sheep, round and warm in their winter wool, betrayed the season of the year as they went feeding along the slopes in the low afternoon sunshine. Presently the wind began to blow, and we struck out seaward to double the long sheltering headland of the cape, and when I looked back again, the islands and the headland had run together and Dunnet Landing and all its coasts were lost to sight.

Almira draws in the
narrator to her nurturing
and kind ways.

1 The woods were already filled with shadows one June evening, just before eight o'clock, though a bright sunset still glimmered faintly among the trunks of the trees. A little girl was driving home her cow, a plodding, dilatory, provoking creature in her behavior, but a valued companion for all that. They were going away from the western light, and striking deep into the dark woods, but their feet were familiar with the path, and it was no matter whether their eyes could see it or not.

There was hardly a night the summer through when the old cow could be found waiting at the pasture bars; on the contrary, it was her greatest pleasure to hide herself away among the high huckleberry bushes, and though she wore a loud bell she had made the discovery that if one stood perfectly still it would not ring. So Sylvia had to hunt for her until she found her, and call Co'! Co'! with never an answering Moo, until her childish patience was quite spent. If the creature had not given good milk and plenty of it, the case would have seemed very different to her owners. Besides, Sylvia had all the time there was, and very little use to make of it. Sometimes in pleasant weather it was a consolation to look upon the cow's pranks as an intelligent attempt to play hide and seek, and as the child had no playmates she lent herself to this amusement with a good deal of zest. Though this chase had been so long that the wary animal herself had given an unusual signal of her whereabouts, Sylvia had only laughed when she came upon Mistress Moolly at the swamp-side, and urged her affectionately homeward with a twig of birch leaves. The old cow was not inclined to wander farther, she even turned in the right direction for once as they left the pasture, and stepped along the road at a good pace. She was quite ready to be milked now, and seldom stopped to browse. Sylvia wondered what her grandmother would say because they were so late. It was a great while since she had left home at half past five o'clock, but everybody knew the difficulty of making this errand a short one. Mrs. Tilley had chased

the hornéd torment too many summer evenings herself to
blame any one else for lingering, and was only thankful as
she waited that she had Sylvia, nowadays, to give such
valuable assistance. The good woman suspected that Syliva
loitered occasionally on her own account; there never was
such a child for straying about out-of-doors since the world
was made! Everybody said that it was a good change for a
little maid who had tried to grow for eight years in a crowded
manufacturing town, but, as for Sylvia herself, it seemed as
if she never had been alive at all before she came to live at
the farm. She thought often with wistful compassion of a
wretched dry geranium that belonged to a town neighbor.

"'Afraid of folks,'" old Mrs. Tilley said to herself, with
a smile, after she had made the unlikely choice of Sylvia
from her daughter's houseful of children, and was returning to the farm. "'Afraid of folks,' they said! I guess she
won't be troubled no great with 'em up to the old place!"
When they reached the door of the lonely house and
stopped to unlock it, and the cat came to purr loudly, and
rub against them, a deserted pussy, indeed, but fat with
young robins, Sylvia whispered that this was a beautiful
place to live in, and she never should wish to go home.

The companions followed the shady woodroad, the cow
taking slow steps, and the child very fast ones. The cows
stopped long at the brook to drink, as if the pasture were
not half a swamp, and Sylvia stood still and waited, letting
her bare feet cool themselves in the shoal water, while the
great twilight moths struck softly against her. She waded
on through the brook as the cow moved away, and listened
to the thrushes with a heart that beat fast with pleasure.
There was a stirring in the great boughs overhead. They
were full of little birds and beasts that seemed to be wide-
awake, and going about their world, or else saying good-
night to each other in sleepy twitters. Sylvia herself felt
sleepy as she walked along. However, it was not much farther to the house, and the air was soft and sweet. She was
not often in the woods so late as this, and it made her feel
as if she were a part of the gray shadows and the moving
leaves. She was just thinking how long it seemed since she
first came to the farm a year ago, and wondering if every-

thing went on in the noisy town just the same as when she was there; the thought of the great red-faced boy who used to chase and frighten her made her hurry along the path to escape from the shadow of the trees.

Suddenly this little woods-girl is horror-stricken to hear a clear whistle not very far away. Not a bird's whistle, which would have a sort of friendliness, but a boy's whistle, determined, and somewhat aggressive. Sylvia left the cow to whatever sad fate might await her, and stepped discreetly aside into the bushes, but she was just too late. The enemy had discovered her, and called out in a very cheerful and persuasive tone, "Halloa, little girl, how far is it to the road?" and trembling Sylvia answered almost inaudibly, "A good ways."

She did not dare to look boldly at the tall young man, who carried a gun over his shoulder, but she came out of her bush and again followed the cow, while he walked alongside.

"I have been hunting for some birds," the stranger said kindly, "and I have lost my way, and need a friend very much. Don't be afraid," he added gallantly. "Speak up and tell me what your name is, and whether you think I can spend the night at your house, and go out gunning early in the morning."

Sylvia was more alarmed than before. Would not her grandmother consider her much to blame? But who could have foreseen such an accident as this? It did not appear to be her fault, and she hung her head as if the stem of it were broken, but managed to answer "Sylvy," with much effort when her companion again asked her name.

Mrs. Tilley was standing in the doorway when the trio came into view. The cow gave a loud moo by way of explanation.

"Yes, you'd better speak up for yourself, you old trial! Where'd she tuck herself away this time, Sylvy?" Sylvia kept an awed silence; she knew by instinct that her grandmother did not comprehend the gravity of the situation. She must be mistaking the stranger for one of the farmer-lads of the region.

The young man stood his gun beside the door, and dropped a heavy game-bag beside it; then he bade Mrs.

Tilley good-evening, and repeated his wayfarer's story, and asked if he could have a night's lodging.

"Put me anywhere you like," he said. "I must be off early in the morning, before day; but I am very hungry, indeed. You can give me some milk at any rate, that's plain."

"Dear sakes, yes," responded the hostess, whose long slumbering hospitality seemed to be easily awakened. "You might fare better if you went out on the main road a mile or so, but you're welcome to what we've got. I'll milk right off, and you make yourself at home. You can sleep on husks or feathers," she proffered graciously. "I raised them all myself. There's good pasturing for geese just below here towards the ma'sh. Now step round and set a plate for the gentleman, Sylvy!" And Sylvia promptly stepped. She was glad to have something to do, and she was hungry herself.

It was a surprise to find so clean and comfortable a little dwelling in this New England wilderness. The young man had known the horrors of its most primitive housekeeping, and the dreary squalor of that level of society which does not rebel at the companionship of hens. This was the best thrift of an old-fashioned farmstead, though on such a small scale that it seemed like a hermitage. He listened eagerly to the old woman's quaint talk, he watched Sylvia's pale face and shining gray eyes with ever growing enthusiasm, and insisted that this was the best supper he had eaten for a month; then, afterward, the new-made friends sat down in the doorway together while the moon came up.

Soon it would be berry-time, and Sylvia was a great help at picking. The cow was a good milker, though a plaguy thing to keep track of, the hostess gossiped frankly, adding presently that she had buried four children, so that Sylvia's mother, and a son (who might be dead) in California were all the children she had left. "Dan, my boy, was a great hand to go gunning," she explained sadly. "I never wanted for pa'tridges or gray squer'ls while he was to home. He's been a great wand'rer, I expect, and he's no hand to write letters. There, I don't blame him, I'd ha' seen the world myself if it had been so I could.

"Sylvia takes after him," the grandmother continued affectionately, after a minute's pause. "There ain't a foot o'

ground she don't know her way over, and the wild creatur's
counts her one o' themselves. Squer'ls she'll tame to come
an' feed right out o' her hands, and all sorts o' birds. Last
winter she got the jay-birds to bangeing here, and I believe
she'd 'a' scanted herself of her own meals to have plenty to
throw out amongst 'em, if I hadn't kep' watch. Anything
but crows, I tell her, I'm willin' to help support,—though
Dan he went an' tamed one o' them that did seem to have
reason same as folks. It was round here a good spell after
he went away. Dan an' his father they didn't hitch,—but
he never held up his head ag'in after Dan had dared him
an' gone off."

The guest did not notice this hint of fam'ly sorrows in
his eager interest in something else.

"So Sylvy knows all about birds, does she?" he exclaimed,
as he looked round at the little girl who sat, very demure
but increasingly sleepy, in the moonlight. "I am making a
collection of birds myself. I have been at it ever since I was
a boy." (Mrs. Tilley smiled.) "There are two or three very
rare ones I have been hunting for these five years. I mean
to get them on my own ground if they can be found."

"Do you cage 'em up?" asked Mrs. Tilley doubtfully,
in response to this enthusiastic announcement.

"Oh, no, they're stuffed and preserved, dozens and dozens of them," said the ornithologist, "and I have shot or
snared every one myself. I caught a glimpse of a white
heron three miles from here on Saturday, and I have followed it in this direction. They have never been found in
this district at all. The little white heron, it is," and he
turned again to look at Sylvia with the hope of discovering
that the rare bird was one of her acquaintances.

But Sylvia was watching a hop-toad in the narrow foot-
path.

"You would know the heron if you saw it," the stranger
continued eagerly. "A queer tall white bird with soft feathers and long thin legs. And it would have a nest perhaps
in the top of a high tree, made of sticks, something like a
hawk's nest."

Sylvia's heart gave a wild beat; she knew that strange
white bird, and had once stolen softly near where it stood
in some bright green swamp grass, away over at the other

side of the woods. There was an open place where the sunshine always seemed strangely yellow and hot, where tall, nodding rushes grew, and her grandmother had warned her that she might sink in the soft black mud underneath and never be heard of more. Not far beyond were the salt marshes and beyond those was the sea, the sea which Sylvia wondered and dreamed about, but never had looked upon, though its great voice could often be heard above the noise of the woods on stormy nights.

"I can't think of anything I should like so much as to find that heron's nest," the handsome stranger was saying. "I would give ten dollars to anybody who could show it to me," he added desperately, "and I mean to spend my whole vacation hunting for it if need be. Perhaps it was only migrating, or had been chased out of its own region by some bird of prey."

Mrs. Tilley gave amazed attention to all this, but Sylvia still watched the toad, not divining, as she might have done at some calmer time, that the creature wished to get to its hole under the doorstep, and was much hindered by the unusual spectators at that hour of the evening. No amount of thought, that night, could decide how many wished-for treasures the ten dollars, so lightly spoken of, would buy.

The next day the young sportsman hovered about the woods, and Sylvia kept him company, having lost her first fear of the friendly lad, who proved to be most kind and sympathetic. He told her many things about the birds and what they knew and where they lived and what they did with themselves. And he gave her a jack-knife, which she thought as great a treasure as if she were a desert-islander. All day long he did not once make her troubled or afraid except when he brought down some unsuspecting singing creature from its bough. Sylvia would have liked him vastly better without his gun; she could not understand why he killed the very birds he seemed to like so much. But as the day waned, Sylvia still watched the young man with loving admiration. She had never seen anybody so charming and delightful; the woman's heart, asleep in the child, was vaguely thrilled by a dream of love. Some premonition of that great power stirred and swayed these young foresters who traversed the solemn woodlands with soft-footed silent care. They stopped to listen to a bird's song; they pressed forward again eagerly, parting the branches,—speaking to each other rarely and in whispers; the young man going first and Sylvia following, fascinated, a few steps behind, with her gray eyes dark with excitement.

She grieved because the longed-for white heron was elusive, but she did not lead the guest, she only followed, and there was no such thing as speaking first. The sound of her own unquestioned voice would have terrified her,—it was hard enough to answer yes or no when there was need of that. At last evening began to fall, and they drove the cow home together, and Sylvia smiled with pleasure when they came to the place where she heard the whistle and was afraid only the night before.

2   Half a mile from home, at the farther edge of the woods, where the land was highest, a great pine-tree stood, the last of its generation. Whether it was left for a boundary mark, or for what reason, no one could say; the woodchoppers who had felled its mates were dead and gone long ago, and a whole forest of sturdy trees, pines and oaks and maples, had grown again. But the stately head of this old pine towered above them all and made a landmark for sea and shore miles and miles away. Sylvia knew it well. She had always believed that whoever climbed to the top of it could see the ocean; and the little girl had often laid her hand on the great rough trunk and looked up wistfully at those dark boughs that the wind always stirred, no matter how hot and still the air might be below. Now she thought of the tree with a new excitement, for why, if one climbed it at break of day, could not one see all the world, and easily discover whence the white heron flew, and mark the place, and find the hidden nest?

What a spirit of adventure, what wild ambition! What fancied triumph and delight and glory for the later morning when she could make known the secret! It was almost too real and too great for the childish heart to bear.

All night the door of the little house stood open, and the whippoorwills came and sang upon the very step. The young sportsman and his old hostess were sound asleep, but Sylvia's great design kept her broad awake and watching. She forgot to think of sleep. The short summer night seemed as long as the winter darkness, and at last when the whippoorwills ceased, and she was afraid the morning would after all come too soon, she stole out of the house and followed the pasture path through the woods, hastening toward the open ground beyond, listening with a sense of comfort and companionship to the drowsy twitter of a half-awakened bird, whose perch she had jarred in passing. Alas, if the great wave of human interest which flooded for the first time this dull little life should sweep away the satisfactions of an existence heart to heart with nature and the dumb life of the forest!

There was the huge tree asleep yet in the paling moonlight, and small and hopeful Sylvia began with utmost bravery to mount to the top of it, with tingling, eager blood coursing the channels of her whole frame, with her bare feet and fingers, that pinched and held like bird's claws to the monstrous ladder reaching up, up, almost to the sky itself. First she must mount the white oak tree that grew alongside, where she was almost lost among the dark branches and the green leaves heavy and wet with dew; a bird fluttered off its nest, and a red squirrel ran to and fro and scolded pettishly at the harmless housebreaker. Sylvia felt her way easily. She had often climbed there, and knew that higher still one of the oak's upper branches chafed against the pine trunk, just where its lower boughs were set close together. There, when she made the dangerous pass from one tree to the other, the great enterprise would really begin.

She crept out along the swaying oak limb at last, and took the daring step across into the old pine-tree. The way was harder than she thought; she must reach far and hold fast, the sharp dry twigs caught and held her and scratched her like angry talons, the pitch made her thin little fingers clumsy and stiff as she went round and round the tree's great stem, higher and higher upward. The sparrows and robins in the woods below were beginning to wake and twitter to the dawn, yet it seemed much lighter there aloft in the pine-tree, and the child knew that she must hurry if her project were to be of any use.

The tree seemed to lengthen itself out as she went up, and to reach farther and farther upward. It was like a great main-mast to the voyaging earth; it must truly have been amazed that morning through all its ponderous frame as it felt this determined spark of human spirit creeping and climbing from higher branch to branch. Who knows how steadily the least twigs held themselves to advantage this light, weak creature on her way! The old pine must have loved his new dependent. More than all the hawks, and bats, and moths, and even the sweet-voiced thrushes, was the brave, beating heart of the solitary gray-eyed child. And the tree stood still and held away the winds that June morning while the dawn grew bright in the east.

Sylvia's face was like a pale star, if one had seen it from the ground, when the last thorny bough was past, and she stood trembling and tired but wholly triumphant, high in the tree-top. Yes, there was the sea with the dawning sun making a golden dazzle over it, and toward that glorious east flew two hawks with slow-moving pinions. How low they looked in the air from that height when before one had only seen them far up, and dark against the blue sky. Their gray feathers were as soft as moths; they seemed only a little way from the tree, and Sylvia felt as if she too could go flying away among the clouds. Westward, the woodlands and farms reached miles and miles into the distance; here and there were church steeples, and white villages; truly it was a vast and awesome world.

The birds sang louder and louder. At last the sun came up bewilderingly bright. Sylvia could see the white sails of ships out at sea, and the clouds that were purple and rose-colored and yellow at first began to fade away. Where was the white heron's nest in the sea of green branches, and was this wonderful sight and pageant of the world the only reward for having climbed to such a giddy height? Now look down again, Sylvia, where the green marsh is set among the shining birches and dark hemlocks; there where you saw the white heron once you will see him again; look, look! a white spot of him like a single floating feather comes up from the dead hemlock and grows larger, and rises, and comes close at last, and goes by the landmark pine with steady sweep of wing and outstretched slender neck and crested head. And wait! wait! do not move a foot or a finger, little girl, do not send an arrow of light and consciousness from your two eager eyes, for the heron has perched on a pine bough not far beyond yours, and cries back to his mate on the nest, and plumes his feathers for the new day!

The child gives a long sigh a minute later when a company of shouting cat-birds comes also to the tree, and vexed by their fluttering and lawlessness the solemn heron goes away. She knows his secret now, the wild, light, slender bird that floats and wavers, and goes back like an arrow presently to his home in the green world beneath. Then Sylvia, well satisfied, makes her perilous way down again, not daring to look far below the branch she stands on, ready to cry sometimes because her fingers ache and her lamed feet slip. Wondering over and over again what the stranger would say to her, and what he would think when she told him how to find his way straight to the heron's nest.

"Sylvy, Sylvy!" called the busy old grandmother again and again, but nobody answered, and the small husk bed was empty, and Sylvia had disappeared.

The guest waked from a dream, and remembering his day's pleasure hurried to dress himself that it might sooner begin. He was sure from the way the shy little girl looked once or twice yesterday that she had at least seen the white heron, and now she must really be persuaded to tell. Here she comes now, paler than ever, and her worn old frock is torn and tattered, and smeared with pine pitch. The grandmother and the sportsman stand in the door together and question her, and the splendid moment has come to speak of the dead hemlock-tree by the green marsh.

But Sylvia does not speak after all, though the old grandmother fretfully rebukes her, and the young man's kind appealing eyes are looking straight in her own. He can make them rich with money; he has promised it, and they are poor now. He is so well worth making happy, and he waits to hear the story she can tell.

No, she must keep silence! What is it that suddenly forbids her and makes her dumb? Has she been nine years growing, and now, when the great world for the first time puts out a hand to her, must she thrust it aside for a bird's sake? The murmur of the pine's green branches is in her ears, she remembers how the white heron came flying through the golden air and how they watched the sea and the morning together, and Sylvia cannot speak; she cannot tell the heron's secret and give its life away.

Dear loyalty, that suffered a sharp pang as the guest went away disappointed later in the day, that could have served and followed him and loved him as a dog loves! Many a night Sylvia heard the echo of his whistle haunting the pasture path as she came home with the loitering cow. She forgot even her sorrow at the sharp report of his gun and the piteous sight of thrushes and sparrows dropping silent to the ground, their songs hushed and their pretty feathers stained and wet with blood. Were the birds better friends than their hunter might have been,—who can tell? Whatever treasures were lost to her, woodlands and summer-time, remember! Bring your gifts and graces and tell your secrets to this lonely country child!

THE FLIGHT OF
BETSEY LANE

1 One windy morning in May, three old women sat together near an open window in the shed chamber of Byfleet
Poor-house. The wind was from the northwest, but their
window faced the southeast, and they were only visited by
an occasional pleasant waft of fresh air. They were close
together, knee to knee, picking over a bushel of beans, and
commanding a view of the dandelion-starred, green yard
below, and of the winding, sandy road that led to the village, two miles away. Some captive bees were scolding
among the cobwebs of the rafters overhead, or thumping
against the upper panes of glass; two calves were bawling
from the barnyard, where some of the men were at work
loading a dump-cart and shouting as if every one were deaf.
There was a cheerful feeling of activity, and even an air of
comfort, about the Byfleet Poor-house. Almost every one
was possessed of a most interesting past, though there was
less to be said about the future. The inmates were by no
means distressed or unhappy; many of them retired to this
shelter only for the winter season, and would go out
presently, some to begin such work as they could still do,
others to live in their own small houses; old age had im-
poverished most of them by limiting their power of en-
durance; but far from lamenting the fact that they were
town charges, they rather liked the change and excitement
of a winter residence on the poor-farm. There was a sharp-
faced, hard-worked young widow with seven children, who
was an exception to the general level of society, because
she deplored the change in her fortunes. The older women
regarded her with suspicion, and were apt to talk about
her in moments like this, when they happened to sit together at their work.

The three bean-pickers were dressed alike in stout brown
ginghams, checked by a white line, and all wore great faded
aprons of blue drilling, with sufficient pockets convenient
to the right hand. Miss Peggy Bond was a very small,

belligerent-looking person, who wore a huge pair of steel-
bowed spectacles, holding her sharp chin well up in air, as if
to supplement an inadequate nose. She was more than half
blind, but the spectacles seemed to face upward instead of
square ahead, as if their wearer were always on the sharp
lookout for birds. Miss Bond had suffered much personal
damage from time to time, because she never took heed
where she planted her feet, and so was always tripping and
stubbing her bruised way through the world. She had fallen
down hatchways and cellarways, and stepped composedly
into deep ditches and pasture brooks; but she was proud
of stating that she was upsighted, and so was her father
before her. At the poor-house, where an unusual malady was
considered a distinction, upsightedness was looked upon as
a most honorable infirmity. Plain rheumatism, such as
afflicted Aunt Lavina Dow, whose twisted hands found even
this light work difficult and tiresome,—plain rheumatism
was something of every-day occurrence, and nobody cared
to hear about it. Poor Peggy was a meek and friendly soul,
who never put herself forward; she was just like other folks,
as she always loved to say, but Mrs. Lavina Dow was a
different sort of person altogether, of great dignity and, occasionally, almost aggressive behavior. The time had been
when she could do a good day's work with anybody: but
for many years now she had not left the town-farm, being
too badly crippled to work; she had no relations or friends
to visit, but from an innate love of authority she could not
submit to being one of those who are forgotten by the
world. Mrs. Dow was the hostess and social lawgiver here,
where she remembered every inmate and every item of interest for nearly forty years, besides an immense amount of
town history and biography for three or four generations
back.

She was the dear friend of the third woman, Betsey Lane;
together they led thought and opinion—chiefly opinion—
and held sway, not only over Byfleet Poor-farm, but also
the selectmen and all others in authority. Betsey Lane had
spent most of her life as aid-in-general to the respected
household of old General Thornton. She had been much
trusted and valued, and, at the breaking up of that once
large and flourishing family, she had been left in good cir-

cumstances, what with legacies and her own comfortable
savings; but by sad misfortune and lavish generosity everything had been scattered, and after much illness, which
ended in a stiffened arm and more uncertainty, the good
soul had sensibly decided that it was easier for the whole
town to support her than for a part of it. She had always
hoped to see something of the world before she died; she
came of an adventurous, seafaring stock, but had never
made a longer journey than to the towns of Danby and
Northville, thirty miles away.

They were all old women; but Betsey Lane, who was
sixty-nine, and looked much older, was the youngest. Peggy
Bond was far on in the seventies, and Mrs. Dow was at
least ten years older. She made a great secret of her years;
and as she sometimes spoke of events prior to the Revolu-
tion with the assertion of having been an eye-witness, she
naturally wore an air of vast antiquity. Her tales were an
inexpressible delight to Betsey Lane, who felt younger by
twenty years because her friend and comrade was so unconscious of chronological limitations.

The bushel basket of cranberry beans was within easy
reach, and each of the pickers had filled her lap from it
again and again. The shed chamber was not an unpleasant
place in which to sit at work, with its traces of seed corn
hanging from the brown crossbeams, its spare churns, and
dusty loom, and rickety wool-wheels, and a few bits of old
furniture. In one far corner was a wide board of dismal use
and suggestion, and close beside it an old cradle. There was
a battered chest of drawers where the keeper of the poor-
house kept his garden-seeds, with the withered remains of
three seed cucumbers ornamenting the top. Nothing beautiful could be discovered, nothing interesting, but there
was something usable and homely about the place. It was
the favorite and untroubled bower of the bean-pickers, to
which they might retreat unmolested from the public apart-
ments of this rustic institution.

Betsey Lane blew away the chaff from her handful of
beans. The spring breeze blew the chaff back again, and
sifted it over her face and shoulders. She rubbed it out of
her eyes impatiently, and happened to notice old Peggy
holding her own handful high, as if it were an oblation,

and turning her queer, up-tilted head this way and that, to look at the beans sharply, as if she were first cousin to a hen.

"There, Miss Bond, 't is kind of botherin' work for you, ain't it?" Betsey inquired compassionately.

"I feel to enjoy it, anything that I can do my own way so," responded Peggy. "I like to do my part. Ain't that old Mis' Fales comin' up the road? It sounds like her step."

The others looked, but they were not farsighted, and for a moment Peggy had the advantage. Mrs. Fales was not a favorite.

"I hope she ain't comin' here to put up this spring. I guess she won't now, it's gettin' so late," said Betsey Lane. "She likes to go rovin' soon as the roads is settled."

"'T is Mis' Fales!" said Peggy Bond, listening with solemn anxiety. "There, do let's pray her by!"

"I guess she's headin' for her cousin's folks up Beech Hill way," said Betsey presently. "If she'd left her daughter's this mornin', she'd have got just about as far as this. I kind o' wish she had stepped in just to pass the time o'day, long's she wa'n't going to make no stop."

There was a silence as to further speech in the shed chamber; and even the calves were quiet in the barnyard. The men had all gone away to the field where corn-planting was going on. The beans clicked steadily into the wooden measure of the pickers' feet. Betsey Lane began to sing a hymn, and the others joined in as best they might, like autumnal crickets; their voices were sharp and cracked, with now and then a few low notes of plaintive tone. Betsey herself could sing pretty well, but the others could only make a kind of accompaniment. Their voices ceased altogether at the higher notes.

"Oh my! I wish I had the means to go to the Centennial," mourned Betsey Lane, stopping so suddenly that the others had to go on croaking and shrilling without her for a moment before they could stop. "It seems to me as if I can't die happy 'less I do," she added; "I ain't never seen nothin' of the world, an' here I be."

"What if you was as old as I be?" suggested Mrs. Dow pompously. "You've got time enough yet, Betsey; don't you go an' despair. I knowed of a woman that went clean round the world four times when she was past eighty, an' enjoyed herself real well. Her folks followed the sea; she had three sons an' a daughter married,—all shipmasters, and she'd been with her own husband when they was young. She was left a widder early, and fetched up her family herself,—a real stirrin', smart woman. After they'd got married off, an' settled, an' was doing well, she come to be lonesome; and first she tried to stick it out alone, but she wa'n't one that could; an' she got a notion she hadn't nothin' before her but her last sickness, and she wa'n't a person that enjoyed havin' other folks do for her. So one on her boys—I guess 't was the oldest—said he was going to take her to sea; there was ample room, an' he was sailin' a good time o' year for the Cape o' Good Hope an' way up to some o' them tea-ports in the Chiny Seas. She was all high to go, but it made a sight o' talk at her age; an' the minister made it a subject o' prayer the last Sunday, and all the folks took a last leave; but she said to some she'd fetch 'em home something real pritty, and so did. An' then they come home t' other way, round the Horn, an' she done so well, an' was such a sight o' company, the other child'n was jealous, an' she promised she'd go a v'y'ge long o' each on 'em. She was as sprightly a person as ever I see; an' could speak well o' what she'd seen."

"Did she die to sea?" asked Peggy, with interest.

"No, she died to home between v'y'ges, or she'd gone to sea again. I was to her funeral. She liked her son George's ship the best; 't was the one she was going on to Callao. They said the men aboard all called her 'gran'ma'am,' an' she kep' 'em mended up, an' would go below and tend to 'em if they was sick. She might 'a' been alive an' enjoyin' of herself a good many years but for the kick of a cow; 't was a new cow out of a drove, a dreadful unruly beast."

Mrs. Dow stopped for breath, and reached down for a new supply of beans; her empty apron was gray with soft chaff. Betsey Lane, still pondering on the Centennial, began to sing another verse of her hymn, and again the old women joined her. At this moment some strangers came driving round into the yard from the front of the house. The turf was soft, and our friends did not hear the horses' steps. Their voices cracked and quavered; it was a funny little concert, and a lady in an open carriage just below listened with sympathy and amusement.

2 "Betsey! Betsey! Miss Lane!" a voice called eagerly at the foot of the stairs that led up from the shed. "Betsey! There's a lady here wants to see you right away."

Betsey was dazed with excitement, like a country child who knows the rare pleasure of being called out of school. "Lor', I ain't fit to go down, be I?" she faltered, looking anxiously at her friends; but Peggy was gazing even nearer to the zenith than usual, in her excited effort to see down into the yard, and Mrs. Dow only nodded somewhat jealously, and said that she guessed 't was nobody would do her any harm. She rose ponderously, while Betsey hesitated, being, as they would have said, all of a twitter. "It is a lady, certain," Mrs. Dow assured her; "'t ain't often there's a lady comes here."

"While there was any of Mis' Gen'ral Thornton's folks left, I wa'n't without visits from the gentry," said Betsey Lane, turning back proudly at the head of the stairs, with a touch of old-world pride and sense of high station. Then she disappeared, and closed the door behind her at the stair-foot with a decision quite unwelcome to the friends above.

"She needn't 'a' been so dreadful 'fraid anybody was goin' to listen. I guess we've got folks to ride an' see us, or had once, if we hain't now," said Miss Peggy Bond, plaintively.

"I expect 't was only the wind shoved it to," said Aunt Lavina. "Betsey is one that gits flustered easier than some. I wish 't was somebody to take her off an' give her a kind of a good time; she's young to settle down 'long of old folks like us. Betsey's got a notion o' rovin' such as ain't my natur', but I should like to see her satisfied. She'd been a very understandin' person, if she had the advantages that some does."

"'T is so," said Peggy Bond, tilting her chin high. "I suppose you can't hear nothin' they're saying? I feel my hearin' ain't up to whar it was. I can hear things close to me well as ever; but there, hearin' ain't everything; 't ain't as if we lived where there was more goin' on to hear. Seems to me them folks is stoppin' a good while."

"They surely be," agreed Lavina Dow.

"I expect it's somethin' particular. There ain't none of the Thornton folks left, except one o' the gran'darters, an' I've often heard Betsey remark that she should never see her more, for she lives to London. Strange how folks feels contented in them strayaway places off to the ends of the airth."

The flies and bees were buzzing against the hot window-panes; the handfuls of beans were clicking into the brown wooden measure. A bird came and perched on the window-sill, and then flitted away toward the blue sky. Below, in the yard, Betsey Lane stood talking with the lady. She had put her blue drilling apron over her head, and her face was shining with delight.

"Lor', dear," she said, for at least the third time, "I remember ye when I first see ye; an awful pritty baby you was, an' they all said you looked just like the old gen'ral. Be you goin' back to foreign parts right away?"

"Yes, I'm going back; you know that all my children are there. I wish I could take you with me for a visit," said the charming young guest. "I'm going to carry over some of the pictures and furniture from the old house; I didn't care half so much for them when I was younger as I do now. Perhaps next summer we shall all come over for a while. I should like to see my girls and boys playing under the pines."

"I wish you re'lly was livin' to the old place," said Betsey Lane. Her imagination was not swift; she needed time to think over all that was being told her, and she could not fancy the two strange houses across the sea. The old Thornton house was to her mind the most delightful and elegant in the world.

"Is there anything I can do for you?" asked Mrs. Strafford kindly,—"anything that I can do for you myself, before I go away? I shall be writing to you, and sending some pictures of the children, and you must let me know how you are getting on."

"Yes, there is one thing, darlin'. If you could stop in the village an' pick me out a pritty, little, small lookin'-glass, that I can keep for my own an' have to remember you by. 'T ain't that I want to set me above the rest o' the folks, but I was always used to havin' my own when I was to your grandma's. There's very nice folks here, some on 'em, and I'm better off than if I was able to keep house; but sence you ask me, that's the only thing I feel cropin' about. What be you goin' right back for? ain't you goin' to see the great fair to Pheladelphy, that everybody talks about?"

"No," said Mrs. Strafford, laughing at this eager and almost convicting question. "No; I'm going back next week. If I were, I believe that I should take you with me. Good-by, dear old Betsey; you make me feel as if I were a little girl again; you look just the same."

For full five minutes the old woman stood out in the sunshine, dazed with delight, and majestic with a sense of her own consequence. She held something tight in her hand, without thinking what it might be; but just as the friendly mistress of the poor-farm came out to hear the news, she tucked the roll of money into the bosom of her brown gingham dress. " 'T was my dear Mis' Katy Strafford," she turned to say proudly. "She come way over from London; she's been sick; they thought the voyage would do her good. She said most the first thing she had on her mind was to come an' find me, and see how I was, an' if I was comfortable; an' now she's goin' right back. She's got two splendid houses; an' said how she wished I was there to look after things,—she remembered I was always her gran'ma's right hand. Oh, it does so carry me back, to see her! Seems if all the rest on 'em must be there together to the old house. There, I must go right up an' tell Mis' Dow an' Peggy."

"Dinner's all ready; I was just goin' to blow the horn for the men-folks," said the keeper's wife. "They'll be right down. I expect you've got along smart with them beans,— all three of you together;" but Betsey's mind roved so high and so far at that moment that no achievements of bean-picking could lure it back.

3 The long table in the great kitchen soon gathered its company of waifs and strays,—creatures of improvidence

and misfortune, and the irreparable victims of old age. The
dinner was satisfactory, and there was not much delay for
conversation. Peggy Bond and Mrs. Dow and Betsey Lane
always sat together at one end, with an air of putting the
rest of the company below the salt. Betsey was still flushed
with excitement; in fact, she could not eat as much as
usual, and she looked up from time to time expectantly,
as if she were likely to be asked to speak of her guest; but
everybody was hungry, and even Mrs. Dow broke in upon
some attempted confidences by asking inopportunely for a
second potato. There were nearly twenty at the table,
counting the keeper and his wife and two children, noisy
little persons who had come from school with the small
flock belonging to the poor widow, who sat just opposite
our friends. She finished her dinner before any one else,
and pushed her chair back; she always helped with the
housework,—a thin, sorry, bad-tempered-looking poor soul,
whom grief had sharpened instead of softening. "I expect
you feel too fine to set with common folks," she said en-
viously to Betsey.

"Here I be a-settin'," responded Betsey calmly. "I don'
know's I behave more unbecomin' than usual." Betsey
prided herself upon her good and proper manners; but the
rest of the company, who would have liked to hear the bit
of morning news, were now defrauded of that pleasure.
The wrong note had been struck; there was a silence after
the clatter of knives and plates, and one by one the cheerful
town charges disappeared. The bean-picking had been
finished, and there was a call for any of the women who felt
like planting corn; so Peggy Bond, who could follow the
line of hills pretty fairly, and Betsey herself, who was still
equal to anybody at that work, and Mrs. Dow, all went out
to the field together. Aunt Lavina labored slowly up the
yard, carrying a light splint-bottomed kitchen chair and
her knitting-work, and sat near the stone wall on a gentle
rise, where she could see the pond and the green country,
and exchange a word with her friends as they came and
went up and down the rows. Betsey vouchsafed a word now
and then about Mrs. Strafford, but you would have thought
that she had been suddenly elevated to Mrs. Strafford's
own cares and the responsibilities attending them, and had

little in common with her old associates. Mrs. Dow and
Peggy knew well that these high-feeling times never lasted
long, and so they waited with as much patience as they
could muster. They were by no means without that true
tact which is only another word for unselfish sympathy.

The strip of corn land ran along the side of a great field;
at the upper end of it was a field-corner thicket of young
maples and walnut saplings, the children of a great nut-
tree that marked the boundary. Once, when Betsey Lane
found herself alone near this shelter at the end of her row,
the other planters having lagged behind beyond the rising
ground, she looked stealthily about, and then put her hand
inside her gown, and for the first time took out the money
that Mrs. Strafford had given her. She turned it over and
over with an astonished look: there were new bank-bills for
a hundred dollars. Betsey gave a funny little shrug of her
shoulders, came out of the bushes, and took a step or two
on the narrow edge of turf, as if she were going to dance;
then she hastily tucked away her treasure, and stepped discreetly down into the soft harrowed and hoed land, and
began to drop corn again, five kernels to a hill. She had seen
the top of Peggy Bond's head over the knoll, and now Peggy
herself came entirely into view, gazing upward to the skies,
and stumbling more or less, but counting the corn by touch
and twisting her head about anxiously to gain advantage
over her uncertain vision. Betsey made a friendly, in-
articulate little sound as they passed; she was thinking that
somebody said once that Peggy's eyesight might be reme-
died if she could go to Boston to the hospital; but that
was so remote and impossible an undertaking that no one
had ever taken the first step. Betsey Lane's brown old face
suddenly worked with excitement, but in a moment more
she regained her usual firm expression, and spoke carelessly
to Peggy as she turned and came alongside.

The high spring wind of the morning had quite fallen; it
was a lovely May afternoon. The woods about the field to
the northward were full of birds, and the young leaves
scarcely hid the solemn shapes of a company of crows that
patiently attended the corn-planting. Two of the men had
finished their hoeing, and were busy with the construction
of a scarecrow; they knelt in the furrows, chuckling, and

looking over some forlorn, discarded garments. It was a time-honored custom to make the scarecrow resemble one of the poor-house family; and this year they intended to have Mrs. Lavina Dow protect the field in effigy; last year it was the counterfeit of Betsey Lane who stood on guard, with an easily recognized quilted hood and the remains of a valued shawl that one of the calves had found airing on a fence and chewed to pieces. Behind the men was the foundation for this rustic attempt at statuary,—an upright stake and bar in the form of a cross. This stood on the highest part of the field; and as the men knelt near it, and the quaint figures of the corn-planters went and came, the scene gave a curious suggestion of foreign life. It was not like New England; the presence of the rude cross appealed strangely to the imagination.

4   Life flowed so smoothly, for the most part, at the By-fleet Poor-farm, that nobody knew what to make, later in the summer, of a strange disappearance. All the elder inmates were familiar with illness and death, and the poor pomp of a town-pauper's funeral. The comings and goings and the various misfortunes of those who composed this strange family, related only through its disasters, hardly served for the excitement and talk of a single day. Now that the June days were at their longest, the old people were sure to wake earlier than ever; but one morning, to the astonishment of every one, Betsey Lane's bed was empty; the sheets and blankets, which were her own, and guarded with jealous care, were carefully folded and placed on a chair not too near the window, and Betsey had flown. Nobody had heard her go down the creaking stairs. The kitchen door was unlocked, and the old watch-dog lay on the step outside in the early sunshine, wagging his tail and looking wise, as if he were left on guard and meant to keep the fugitive's secret.

"Never knowed her to do nothin' afore 'thout talking it over a fortnight, and paradin' off when we could all see her," ventured a spiteful voice. "Guess we can wait till night to hear 'bout it."

Mrs. Dow looked sorrowful and shook her head. "Betsey

had an aunt on her mother's side that went and drownded of herself; she was a pritty-appearing woman as ever you see."

"Perhaps she's gone to spend the day with Decker's folks," suggested Peggy Bond. "She always takes an extra early start; she was speakin' lately o' going up their way;" but Mrs. Dow shook her head with a most melancholy look. "I'm impressed that something's befell her," she insisted. "I heard her a-groanin' in her sleep. I was wakeful the fore-part o' the night,—'t is very unusual with me, too."

"'T wa'n't like Betsey not to leave us any word," said the other old friend, with more resentment than melancholy. They sat together almost in silence that morning in the shed chamber. Mrs. Dow was sorting and cutting rags, and Peggy braided them into long ropes, to be made into mats at a later date. If they had only known where Betsey Lane had gone, they might have talked about it until din-ner-time at noon; but failing this new subject, they could take no interest in any of their old ones. Out in the field the corn was well up, and the men were hoeing. It was a hot morning in the shed chamber, and the woolen rags were dusty and hot to handle.

5 Byfleet people knew each other well, and when this mysteriously absent person did not return to the town-farm at the end of a week, public interest became much excited; and presently it was ascertained that Betsey Lane was neither making a visit to her friends the Deckers on Birch Hill, nor to any nearer acquaintances; in fact, she had dis-appeared altogether from her wonted haunts. Nobody re-membered to have seen her pass, hers had been such an early flitting; and when somebody thought of her having gone away by train, he was laughed at for forgetting that the earliest morning train from South Byfleet, the nearest sta-tion, did not start until long after eight o'clock; and if Betsey had designed to be one of the passengers, she would have started along the road at seven, and been seen and known of all women. There was not a kitchen in that part of Byfleet that did not have windows toward the road. Con-versation rarely left the level of the neighborhood gossip:

to see Betsey Lane, in her best clothes, at that hour in the morning, would have been the signal for much exercise of imagination; but as day after day went by without news, the curiosity of those who knew her best turned slowly into fear, and at last Peggy Bond again gave utterance to the belief that Betsey had either gone out in the early morning and put an end to her life, or that she had gone to the Centennial. Some of the people at table were moved to loud laughter,—it was at supper-time on a Sunday night,— but others listened with great interest.

"She never'd put on her good clothes to drownd herself," said the widow. "She might have thought 't was good as takin' 'em with her, though. Old folks has wandered off an' got lost in the woods afore now."

Mrs. Dow and Peggy resented this impertinent remark, but deigned to take no notice of the speaker. "She wouldn't have wore her best clothes to the Centennial, would she?" mildly inquired Peggy, bobbing her head toward the ceiling. "'T would be a shame to spoil your best things in such a place. An' I don't know of her havin' any money; there's the end o' that."

"You're bad as old Mis' Bland, that used to live neighbor to our folks," said one of the old men. "She was dreadful precise; an' she so begretched to wear a good alapaca dress that was left to her, that it hung in a press forty year, an' baited the moths at last."

"I often seen Mis' Bland a-goin' in to meetin' when I was a young girl," said Peggy Bond approvingly. "She was a good-appearin' woman, an' she left property."

"Wish she'd left it to me, then," said the poor soul opposite, glancing at her pathetic row of children: but it was not good manners at the farm to deplore one's situation, and Mrs. Dow and Peggy only frowned. "Where do you suppose Betsey can be?" said Mrs. Dow, for the twentieth time. "She didn't have no money. I know she ain't gone far, if it's so that she's yet alive. She's b'en real pinched all the spring."

"Perhaps that lady that come one day give her some," the keeper's wife suggested mildly.

"Then Betsey would have told me," said Mrs. Dow, with injured dignity.

6   On the morning of her disappearance, Betsey rose even
before the pewee and the English sparrow, and dressed
herself quietly, though with trembling hands, and stole out
of the kitchen door like a plunderless thief. The old dog
licked her hand and looked at her anxiously; the tortoise-
shell cat rubbed against her best gown, and trotted away
up the yard, then she turned anxiously and came after the
old woman, following faithfully until she had to be driven
back. Betsey was used to long country excursions afoot. She
dearly loved the early morning; and finding that there was
no dew to trouble her, she began to follow pasture paths
and short cuts across the fields, surprising here and there a
flock of sleepy sheep, or a startled calf that rustled out
from the bushes. The birds were pecking their breakfast
from bush and turf; and hardly any of the wild inhabitants
of that rural world were enough alarmed by her presence
to do more than flutter away if they chanced to be in her
path. She stepped along, light-footed and eager as a girl,
dressed in her neat old straw bonnet and black gown, and
carrying a few belongings in her best bundle-handkerchief,
one that her only brother had brought home from the East
Indies fifty years before. There was an old crow perched
as sentinel on a small, dead pine-tree, where he could warn
friends who were pulling up the sprouted corn in a field
close by; but he only gave a contemptuous caw as the adven-
turer appeared, and she shook her bundle at him in revenge, and laughed to see him so clumsy as he tried to keep
his footing on the twigs.

"Yes, I be," she assured him. "I'm a-goin' to Pheladelphy, to the Centennial, same's other folks. I'd jest as soon
tell ye's not, old crow;" and Betsey laughed aloud in pleased
content with herself and her daring, as she walked along.
She had only two miles to go to the station at South Byfleet,
and she felt for the money now and then, and found it safe
enough. She took great pride in the success of her escape,
and especially in the long concealment of her wealth. Not a
night had passed since Mrs. Strafford's visit that she had
not slept with the roll of money under her pillow by night,
and buttoned safe inside her dress by day. She knew that

everybody would offer advice and even commands about the spending or saving of it; and she brooked no interference.

The last mile of the foot-path to South Byfleet was along the railway track; and Betsey began to feel in haste, though it was still nearly two hours to train time. She looked anxiously forward and back along the rails every few minutes, for fear of being run over; and at last she caught sight of an engine that was apparently coming toward her, and took flight into the woods before she could gather courage to follow the path again. The freight train proved to be at a standstill, waiting at a turnout; and some of the men were straying about, eating their early breakfast comfortably in this time of leisure. As the old woman came up to them, she stopped too, for a moment of rest and conversation.

"Where be ye goin'?" she asked pleasantly; and they told her. It was to the town where she had to change cars and take the great through train; a point of geography which she had learned from evening talks between the men at the farm.

"What'll ye carry me there for?"

"We don't run no passenger cars," said one of the young fellows, laughing. "What makes you in such a hurry?"

"I'm startin' for Pheladelphy, an' it's a gre't ways to go."

"So 't is; but you're consid'able early, if you're makin' for the eight-forty train. See here! you haven't got a needle an' thread 'long of you in that bundle, have you? If you'll sew me on a couple o' buttons, I'll give ye a free ride. I'm in a sight o' distress, an' none o' the fellows is provided with as much as a bent pin."

"You poor boy! I'll have you seen to, in half a minute. I'm troubled with a stiff arm, but I'll do the best I can."

The obliging Betsey seated herself stiffly on the slope of the embankment, and found her thread and needle with utmost haste. Two of the train-men stood by and watched the careful stitches, and even offered her a place as spare brakeman, so that they might keep her near; and Betsey took the offer with considerable seriousness, only thinking it necessary to assure them that she was getting most too old to be out in all weathers. An express went by like an

earthquake, and she was presently hoisted on board an
empty box-car by two of her new and flattering acquaintances, and found herself before noon at the end of the first
stage of her journey, without having spent a cent, and
furnished with any amount of thrifty advice. One of the
young men, being compassionate of her unprotected state
as a traveler, advised her to find out the widow of an uncle
of his in Philadelphia, saying despairingly that he couldn't
tell her just how to find the house; but Miss Betsey Lane
said that she had an English tongue in her head, and should
be sure to find whatever she was looking for. This unexpected incident of the freight train was the reason why
everybody about the South Byfleet station insisted that no
such person had taken passage by the regular train that
same morning, and why there were those who persuaded
themselves that Miss Betsey Lane was probably lying at
the bottom of the poor-farm pond.

7   "Land sakes!" said Miss Betsey Lane, as she watched
a Turkish person parading by in his red fez, "I call the
Centennial somethin' like the day o' judgment! I wish I
was goin' to stop a month, but I dare say 't would be the
death o' my poor old bones."

She was leaning against the barrier of a patent pop-corn
establishment, which had given her a sudden reminder of
home, and of the winter nights when the sharp-kerneled
little red and yellow ears were brought out, and Old Uncle
Eph Flanders sat by the kitchen stove, and solemnly filled
a great wooden chopping-tray for the refreshment of the
company. She had wandered and loitered and looked until
her eyes and head had grown numb and unreceptive; but
it is only unimaginative persons who can be really astonished. The imagination can always outrun the possible and
actual sights and sounds of the world; and this plain old
body from Byfleet rarely found anything rich and splendid
enough to surprise her. She saw the wonders of the West
and the splendors of the East with equal calmness and
satisfaction; she had always known that there was an amazing world outside the boundaries of Byfleet. There was a
piece of paper in her pocket on which was marked, in her

clumsy handwriting, "If Betsey Lane should meet with accident, notify the selectmen of Byfleet;" but having made this slight provision for the future, she had thrown herself boldly into the sea of strangers, and then had made the joyful discovery that friends were to be found at every turn.

There was something delightfully companionable about Betsey; she had a way of suddenly looking up over her big spectacles with a reassuring and expectant smile, as if you were going to speak to her, and you generally did. She must have found out where hundreds of people came from, and whom they had left at home, and what they thought of the great show, as she sat on a bench to rest, or leaned over the railings where free luncheons were afforded by the makers of hot waffles and molasses candy and fried potatoes; and there was not a night when she did not return to her lodgings with a pocket crammed with samples of spool cotton and nobody knows what. She had already collected small presents for almost everybody she knew at home, and she was such a pleasant, beaming old country body, so unmistakably appreciative and interested, that nobody ever thought of wishing that she would move on. Nearly all the busy people of the Exhibition called her either Aunty or Grandma at once, and made little pleasures for her as best they could. She was a delightful contrast to the indifferent, stupid crowd that drifted along, with eyes fixed at the same level, and seeing, even on that level, nothing for fifty feet at a time. "What be you making here, dear?" Betsy Lane would ask joyfully, and the most perfunctory guardian hastened to explain. She squandered money as she had never had the pleasure of doing before, and this hastened the day when she must return to Byfleet. She was always inquiring if there were any spectacle-sellers at hand, and received occasional directions; but it was a difficult place for her to find her way about in, and the very last day of her stay arrived before she found an exhibitor of the desired sort, an oculist and instrument-maker.

"I called to get some specs for a friend that's upsighted," she gravely informed the salesman, to his extreme amusement. "She's dreadful troubled, and jerks her head up like a hen a-drinkin'. She's got a blur a-growin' an' spreadin', an' sometimes she can see out to one side on 't, and more times she can't."

"Cataracts," said a middle-aged gentleman at her side; and Betsey Lane turned to regard him with approval and curiosity.

"'T is Miss Peggy Bond I was mentioning, of Byfleet Poor-farm," she explained. "I count on gettin' some glasses to relieve her trouble, if there's any to be found."

"Glasses won't do her any good," said the stranger. "Suppose you come and sit down on this bench, and tell me all about it. First, where is Byfleet?" and Betsey gave the directions at length.

"I thought so," said the surgeon. "How old is this friend of yours?"

Betsey cleared her throat decisively, and smoothed her gown over her knees as if it were an apron; then she turned to take a good look at her new acquaintance as they sat on the rustic bench together. "Who be you, sir, I should like to know?" she asked, in a friendly tone.

"My name's Dunster."

"I take it you're a doctor," continued Betsey, as if they had overtaken each other walking from Byfleet to South Byfleet on a summer morning.

"I'm a doctor; part of one at least," said he. "I know more or less about eyes; and I spend my summers down on the shore at the mouth of your river; some day I'll come up and look at this person. How old is she?"

"Peggy Bond is one that never tells her age; 't ain't come quite up to where she'll begin to brag of it, you see," explained Betsey reluctantly; "but I know her to be nigh to seventy-six, one way or t' other. Her an' Mrs. Mary Ann Chick was same year's child'n, and Peggy knows I know it, an' two or three times when we've be'n in the buryin'-ground where Mary Ann lays an' has her dates right on her headstone, I couldn't bring Peggy to take no sort o' notice. I will say she makes, at times, a convenience of being up-sighted. But there, I feel for her,—everybody does; it keeps her stubbin' an' trippin' against everything, beakin' and gazin' up the way she has to."

"Yes, yes," said the doctor, whose eyes were twinkling. "I'll come and look after her, with your town doctor, this summer,—some time in the last of July or first of August."

"You'll find occupation," said Betsey, not without an air of patronage. "Most of us to the Byfleet Farm has got our ails, now I tell ye. You ain't got no bitters that'll take a dozen years right off an ol' lady's shoulders?"

The busy man smiled pleasantly, and shook his head as he went away. "Dunster," said Betsey to herself, soberly committing the new name to her sound memory. "Yes, I mustn't forget to speak of him to the doctor, as he directed. I do' know now as Peggy would vally herself quite so much accordin' to, if she had her eyes fixed same as other folks. I expect there wouldn't been a smarter woman in town, though, if she'd had a proper chance. Now I've done what I set to do for her, I do believe, an' 't wa'n't glasses, neither. I'll git her a pretty little shawl with that money I laid aside. Peggy Bond ain't got a pretty shawl. I always wanted to have a real good time, an' now I'm havin' it."

8 Two or three days later, two pathetic figures might have been seen crossing the slopes of the poor-farm field, toward the low shores of Byfield pond. It was early in the morning, and the stubble of the lately mown grass was wet with rain and hindering to old feet. Peggy Bond was more blundering and liable to stray in the wrong direction than usual; it was one of the days when she could hardly see at all. Aunt Lavina Dow was unusually clumsy of movement, and stiff in the joints; she had not been so far from the house for three years. The morning breeze filled the gathers of her wide gingham skirt, and aggravated the size of her unwieldy figure. She supported herself with a stick, and trusted beside to the fragile support of Peggy's arm. They were talking together in whispers.

"Oh, my sakes!" exclaimed Peggy, moving her small head from side to side. "Hear you wheeze, Mis' Dow! This may be the death o' you; there, do go slow! You set here on the side-hill, an' le' me go try if I can see."

"It needs more eyesight than you've got," said Mrs. Dow, panting between the words. "Oh! to think how spry I was in my young days, an' here I be now, the full of a door, an' all my complaints so aggravated by my size. 'T is hard! 't

is hard! but I'm a-doin' of all this for pore Betsey's sake. I
know they've all laughed, but I look to see her ris' to the
top o' the pond this day,—'t is just nine days since she departed; an' say what they may, I know she hove herself in.
It run in her family; Betsey had an aunt that done just so,
an' she ain't be'n like herself, a-broodin' an' hivin' away
alone, an' nothin' to say to you an' me that was always sich
good company all together. Somethin' sprung her mind,
now I tell ye, Mis' Bond."

"I feel to hope we sha'n't find her, I must say," faltered
Peggy. It was plain that Mrs. Dow was the captain of this
doleful expedition. "I guess she ain't never thought o'
drownin' of herself, Mis' Dow; she's gone off a-visitin' way
over to the other side o' South Byfleet; some thinks she's
gone to the Centennial even now!"

"She hadn't no proper means, I tell ye," wheezed Mrs.
Dow indignantly; "an' if you prefer that others should find
her floatin' to the top this day, instid of us that's her best
friends, you can step back to the house."

They walked on in aggrieved silence. Peggy Bond trembled with excitement, but her companion's firm grasp never
wavered, and so they came to the narrow, gravelly margin
and stood still. Peggy tried in vain to see the glittering
water and the pond-lilies that starred it; she knew that
they must be there; once, years ago, she had caught fleeting
glimpses of them, and she never forgot what she had once
seen. The clear blue sky overhead, the dark pine-woods beyond the pond, were all clearly pictured in her mind. "Can't
you see nothin'?" she faltered; "I believe I'm wuss'n up-
sighted this day. I'm going to be blind."

"No," said Lavina Dow solemnly; "no, there ain't
nothin' whatever, Peggy. I hope to mercy she ain't"—

"Why, whoever'd expected to find you 'way out here!"
exclaimed a brisk and cheerful voice. There stood Betsey
Lane herself, close behind them, having just emerged from
a thicket of alders that grew close by. She was following the
short way homeward from the railroad.

"Why, what's the matter, Mis' Dow? You ain't over-
doin', be ye? an' Peggy's all of a flutter. What in the name
o' natur' ails ye?"

"There ain't nothin' the matter, as I knows on," responded the leader of this fruitless expedition. "We only thought we'd take a stroll this pleasant mornin'," she added, with sublime self-possession. "Where've you be'n, Betsey Lane?"

"To Pheladelphy, ma'am," said Betsey, looking quite young and gay, and wearing a townish and unfamiliar air that upheld her words. "All ought to go that can; why, you feel's if you'd be'n all round the world. I guess I've got enough to think of and tell ye for the rest o' my days. I've always wanted to go somewheres. I wish you'd be'n there, I do so. I've talked with folks from Chiny an' the back o' Pennsylvany; and I see folks way from Australy that 'peared as well as anybody; an' I see how they made spool cotton, an' sights o' other things; an' I spoke with a doctor that lives down to the beach in the summer, an' he offered to come up 'long in the first of August, an' see what he can do for Peggy's eyesight. There was di'monds there as big as pigeon's eggs; an' I met with Mis' Abby Fletcher from South Byfleet depot; an' there was hogs there that weighed risin' thirteen hunderd"—

"I want to know," said Mrs. Lavina Dow and Peggy Bond, together.

"Well, 't was a great exper'ence for a person," added Lavina, turning ponderously, in spite of herself, to give a last wistful look at the smiling waters of the pond.

"I don't know how soon I be goin' to settle down," proclaimed the rustic sister of Sindbad. "What's for the good o' one's for the good of all. You just wait till we're setting together up in the old shed chamber! You know, my dear Mis' Katy Strafford give me a han'some present o' money that day she come to see me; and I'd be'n a-dreamin' by night an' day o' seein' that Centennial; and when I come to think on 't I felt sure somebody ought to go from this neighborhood, if 't was only for the good o' the rest; and I thought I'd better be the one. I wa'n't goin' to ask the selec'men neither. I've come back with one-thirty-five in money, and I see everything there, an' I fetched ye all a little somethin'; but I'm full o' dust now, an' pretty nigh beat out. I never see a place more friendly than Pheladelphy; but 't ain't natural to a Byfleet person to be always walkin' on a level. There, now, Peggy, you take my bundlehandkercher and the basket, and let Mis' Dow sag on to me. I'll git her along twice as easy."

With this the small elderly company set forth triumphant toward the poor-house, across the wide green field.

To be leaders of society in the town of Dulham was as satisfactory to Miss Dobin and Miss Lucinda Dobin as if Dulham were London itself. Of late years, though they would not allow themselves to suspect such treason, the most ill-bred of the younger people in the village made fun of them behind their backs, and laughed at their treasured summer mantillas, their mincing steps, and the shape of their parasols.

They were always conscious of the fact that they were the daughters of a once eminent Dulham minister; but beside this unanswerable claim to the respect of the First Parish, they were aware that their mother's social position was one of superior altitude. Madam Dobin's grandmother was a Greenaple of Boston. In her younger days she had often visited her relatives, the Greenaples and Hightrees, and in seasons of festivity she could relate to a select and properly excited audience her delightful experiences of town life. Nothing could be finer than her account of having taken tea at Governor Clovenfoot's, on Beacon Street, in company with an English lord, who was indulging himself in a brief vacation from his arduous duties at the Court of St. James.

"He exclaimed that he had seldom seen in England so beautiful and intelligent a company of ladies," Madam Dobin would always say in conclusion. "He was decorated with the blue ribbon of the Knights of the Garter." Miss Dobin and Miss Lucinda thought for many years that this famous blue ribbon was tied about the noble gentleman's leg. One day they even discussed the question openly; Miss Dobin placing the decoration at his knee, and Miss Lucinda locating it much lower down, according to the length of the short gray socks with which she was familiar.

"You have no imagination, Lucinda," the elder sister replied impatiently. "Of course, those were the days of small-clothes and long silk stockings!"—whereat Miss Lucinda was rebuked, but not persuaded.

"I wish that my dear girls could have the outlook upon

society which fell to my portion," Madam Dobin sighed,
after she had set these ignorant minds to rights, and en-
riched them by communicating the final truth about the
blue ribbon. "I must not chide you for the absence of opportunities, but if our cousin Harriet Greenaple were only
living, you would not lack enjoyment or social education."

Madam Dobin had now been dead a great many years. She
seemed an elderly woman to her daughters some time before she left them; they thought later that she had really
died comparatively young, since their own years had come
to equal the record of hers. When they visited her tall
white tombstone in the orderly Dulham burying-ground, it
was a strange thought to both the daughters that they were
older women than their mother had been when she died.
To be sure, it was the fashion to appear older in her day,
—they could remember the sober effect of really youthful
married persons in cap and frisette; but, whether they owed
it to the changed times or to their own qualities, they felt
no older themselves than ever they had. Beside upholding
the ministerial dignity of their father, they were obliged
to give a lenient sanction to the ways of the world for their
mother's sake; and they combined the two duties with
reverence and impartiality.

Madam Dobin was, in her prime, a walking example of
refinement and courtesy. If she erred in any way, it was by
keeping too strict watch and rule over her small kingdom.
She acted with great dignity in all matters of social ad-
ministration and etiquette, but, while it must be owned
that the parishioners felt a sense of freedom for a time
after her death, in their later years they praised and valued
her more and more, and often lamented her generously
and sincerely.

Several of her distinguished relatives attended Madam
Dobin's funeral, which was long considered the most dignified and elegant pageant of that sort which had ever taken
place in Dulham. It seemed to mark the close of a famous
epoch in Dulham history, and it was increasingly difficult
forever afterward to keep the tone of society up to the old
standard. Somehow, the distinguished relatives had one by
one disappeared, though they all had excellent reasons for

the discontinuance of their visits. A few had left this world altogether, and the family circle of the Greenaples and Hightrees was greatly reduced in circumference. Sometimes, in summer, a stray connection drifted Dulham-ward, and was displayed to the townspeople (not to say paraded) by the gratified hostesses. It was a disappointment if the guest could not be persuaded to remain over Sunday and appear at church. When household antiquities became fashionable, the ladies remarked upon a surprising interest in their corner cupboard and best chairs, and some distant relatives revived their almost forgotten custom of paying a summer visit to Dulham. They were not long in finding out with what desperate affection Miss Dobin and Miss Lucinda clung to their mother's wedding china and other inheritances, and were allowed to depart without a single teacup. One graceless descendant of the Hightrees prowled from garret to cellar, and admired the household belongings diligently, but she was not asked to accept even the dislocated cherry-wood footstool that she had discovered in the far corner of the parsonage pew.

Some of the Dulham friends had always suspected that Madam Dobin made a social misstep when she chose the Reverend Edward Dobin for her husband. She was no longer young when she married, and though she had gone through the wood and picked up a crooked stick at last, it made a great difference that her stick possessed an ecclesiastical bark. The Reverend Edward was, moreover, a respectable graduate of Harvard College, and to a woman of her standards a clergyman was by no means insignificant. It was impossible not to respect his office, at any rate, and she must have treated him with proper veneration for the sake of that, if for no other reason, though his early advantages had been insufficient, and he was quite insensible to the claims of the Greenaple pedigree, and preferred an Indian pudding to pie crust that was, without exaggeration, half a quarter high. The delicacy of Madam Dobin's touch and preference in everything, from hymns to cookery, was quite lost upon this respected preacher, yet he was not without pride or complete confidence in his own decisions.

The Reverend Mr. Dobin was never very enlightening in his discourses, and was providentially stopped short by

a stroke of paralysis in the middle of his clerical career. He
lived on and on through many dreary years, but his children
never accepted the fact that he was a tyrant, and served
him humbly and patiently. He fell at last into a condition
of great incapacity and chronic trembling, but was able for
nearly a quarter of a century to be carried to the meetinghouse from time to time to pronounce farewell discourses.
On high days of the church he was always placed in the
pulpit, and held up his shaking hands when the benediction
was pronounced, as if the divine gift were exclusively his
own, and the other minister did but say empty words. Afterward he was usually tired and displeased and hard to cope
with, but there was always a proper notice taken of these
too often recurring events. For old times' and for pity's
sake and from natural goodness of heart, the elder parishioners rallied manfully about the Reverend Mr. Dobin;
and whoever his successor or colleague might be, the Do-
bins were always called the minister's folks, while the active
laborer in that vineyard was only Mr. Smith or Mr. Jones,
as the case might be. At last the poor old man died, to
everybody's relief and astonishment; and after he was
properly preached about and lamented, his daughters, Miss
Dobin and Miss Lucinda, took a good look at life from a
new standpoint, and decided that, now they were no longer
constrained by home duties, they must make themselves of
a great deal more use to the town.

Sometimes there is such a household as this (which has
been perhaps too minutely described), where the parents
linger until their children are far past middle age, and always keep them in a too childish and unworthy state of
subjection. The Misses Dobin's characters were much in-
fluenced by such an unnatural prolongation of the filial relationship, and they were amazingly slow to suspect that
they were not so young as they used to be. There was nothing to measure themselves by but Dulham people and
things. The elm-trees were growing yet, and many of the
ladies of the First Parish were older than they, and called
them, with pleasant familiarity, the Dobin girls. These
elderly persons seemed really to be growing old, and Miss
Lucinda frequently lamented the change in society; she
thought it a freak of nature and too sudden blighting of

earthly hopes that several charming old friends of her mother's were no longer living. They were advanced in age when Miss Lucinda was a young girl, though time and space are but relative, after all.

Their influence upon society would have made a great difference in many ways. Certainly, the new parishioners, who had often enough been instructed to pronounce their pastor's name as if it were spelled with one "b," would not have boldly returned again and again to their obnoxious habit of saying Dobbin. Miss Lucinda might carefully speak to the neighbor and new-comers of "my sister, Miss Do-bin;" only the select company of intimates followed her lead, and at last there was something humiliating about it, even though many persons spoke of them only as "the ladies."

"The name was originally *D'Aubigne*, we think," Miss Lucinda would say coldly and patiently, as if she had already explained this foolish mistake a thousand times too often. It was like the sorrows in many a provincial château in the Reign of Terror. The ladies looked on with increasing dismay at the retrogression in society. They felt as if they were a feeble garrison, to whose lot it had fallen to repulse a noisy, irreverent mob, an increasing band of marauders who would overthrow all landmarks of the past, all etiquette and social rank. The new minister himself was a round-faced, unspiritual-looking young man, whom they would have instinctively ignored if he had not been a minister. The new people who came to Dulham were not like the older residents, and they had no desire to be taught better. Little they cared about the Greenaples or the High-trees; and once, when Miss Dobin essayed to speak of some detail of her mother's brilliant experiences in Boston high life, she was interrupted, and the new-comer who sat next her at the parish sewing society began to talk about something else. We cannot believe that it could have been the tea-party at Governor Clovenfoot's which the rude creature so disrespectfully ignored, but some persons are capable of showing any lack of good taste.

The ladies had an unusual and most painful sense of failure, as they went home together that evening. "I have always made it my object to improve and interest the

people at such times; it would seem so possible to elevate
their thoughts and direct them into higher channels," said
Miss Dobin sadly. "But as for that Woolden woman, there
is no use in casting pearls before swine!"

Miss Lucinda murmured an indignant assent. She had a
secret suspicion that the Woolden woman had heard the
story in question oftener than had pleased her. She was
but an ignorant creature; though she had lived in Dulham
twelve or thirteen years, she was no better than when she
came. The mistake was in treating sister Harriet as if she
were on a level with the rest of the company. Miss Lucinda
had observed more than once, lately, that her sister sometimes repeated herself, unconsciously, a little oftener than
was agreeable. Perhaps they were getting a trifle dull; towards spring it might be well to pass a few days with some
of their friends, and have a change.

"If I have tried to do anything," said Miss Dobin in an
icy tone, "it has been to stand firm in my lot and place,
and to hold the standard of cultivated mind and elegant
manners as high as possible. You would think it had been a
hundred years since our mother's death, so completely has
the effect of her good breeding and exquisite hospitality
been lost sight of, here in Dulham. I could wish that our
father had chosen to settle in a larger and more appreciative
place. They would like to put us on the shelf, too. I can see
that plainly."

"I am sure we have our friends," said Miss Lucinda
anxiously, but with a choking voice. "We must not let
them think we do not mean to keep up with the times,
as we always have. I do feel as if perhaps—our hair"—

And the sad secret was out at last. Each of the sisters
drew a long breath of relief at this beginning of a confession.

It was certain that they must take some steps to retrieve
their lost ascendency. Public attention had that evening
been called to their fast-disappearing locks, poor ladies; and
Miss Lucinda felt the discomfort most, for she had been
the inheritor of the Hightree hair, long and curly, and chestnut in color. There used to be a waviness about it, and
sometimes pretty escaping curls, but these were gone long
ago. Miss Dobin resembled her father, and her hair had

not been luxuriant, so that she was less changed by its absence than one might suppose. The straightness and thinness had increased so gradually that neither sister had quite accepted the thought that other persons would particularly notice their altered appearance.

They had shrunk, with the reticence born of close family association, from speaking of the cause even to each other, when they made themselves pretty little lace and dotted muslin caps. Breakfast caps, they called them, and explained that these were universally worn in town; the young Princess of Wales originated them, or at any rate adopted them. The ladies offered no apology for keeping the breakfast caps on until bedtime, and in spite of them a forward child had just spoken, loud and shrill, an untimely question in the ears of the for once silent sewing society. "Do Miss Dobinses wear them great caps because their heads is cold?" the little beast had said; and everybody was startled and dismayed.

Miss Dobin had never shown better her good breeding and valor, the younger sister thought.

"No, little girl," replied the stately Harriet, with a chilly smile. "I believe that our headdresses are quite in the fashion for ladies of all ages. And you must remember that it is never polite to make such personal remarks." It was after this that Miss Dobin had been reminded of Madam Somebody's unusual headgear at the evening entertainment in Boston. Nobody but the Woolden woman could have interrupted her under such trying circumstances.

Miss Lucinda, however, was certain that the time had come for making some effort to replace her lost adornment. The child had told an unwelcome truth, but had paved the way for further action, and now was the time to suggest something that had slowly been taking shape in Miss Lucinda's mind. A young grand-nephew of their mother and his bride had passed a few days with them, two or three summers before, and the sisters had been quite shocked to find that the pretty young woman wore a row of frizzes, not originally her own, over her smooth forehead. At the time, Miss Dobin and Miss Lucinda had spoken severely with each other of such bad taste, but now it made a great difference that the wearer of the frizzes was not only a relative by marriage and used to good society, but also that she came from town, and might be supposed to know what was proper in the way of toilet.

"I really think, sister, that we had better see about having some—arrangements, next time we go anywhere," Miss Dobin said unexpectedly, with a slight tremble in her voice, just as they reached their own door. "There seems to be quite a fashion for them nowadays. For the parish's sake we ought to recognize"—and Miss Lucinda responded with instant satisfaction. She did not like to complain, but she had been troubled with neuralgic pains in her forehead on suddenly meeting the cold air. The sisters felt a new bond of sympathy in keeping this secret with and for each other; they took pains to say to several acquaintances that they were thinking of going to the next large town to do a few errands for Christmas.

A bright, sunny morning seemed to wish the ladies good-fortune. Old Hetty Downs, their faithful maid-servant and protector, looked after them in affectionate foreboding. "Dear sakes, what devil's wiles may be played on them blessed innocents afore they're safe home again?" she murmured, as they vanished round the corner of the street that led to the railway station.

Miss Dobin and Miss Lucinda paced discreetly side by side down the main street of Westbury. It was nothing like Boston, of course, but the noise was slightly confusing, and the passers-by sometimes roughtly pushed against them. Westbury was a consequential manufacturing town, but a great convenience at times like this. The trifling Christmas gifts for their old neighbors and Sunday-school scholars were purchased and stowed away in their neat Fayal basket before the serious commission of the day was attended to. Here and there, in the shops, disreputable frizzes were displayed in unblushing effrontery, but no such vulgar shopkeeper merited the patronage of the Misses Dobin. They pretended not to observe the unattractive goods, and went their way to a low, one-storied building on a side street, where an old tradesman lived. He had been useful to the minister while he still remained upon the earth and had need of a wig, sandy in hue and increasingly sprinkled with gray, as if it kept pace with other changes of existence. But old Paley's shutters were up, and a bar of rough wood was nailed firmly across the one that had lost its fastening and would rack its feeble hinges in the wind. Old Paley had always been polite and bland; they really had looked forward to a little chat with him; they had heard a year or two before of his wife's death, and meant to offer sympathy. His business of hair-dressing had been carried on with that of parasol and umbrella mending, and the condemned umbrella which was his sign flapped and swung in the rising wind, a tattered skeleton before the closed door. The ladies sighed and turned away; they were beginning to feel tired; the day was long, and they had not met with any pleasures yet. "We might walk up the street a little farther," suggested Miss Lucinda; "that is, if you are not tired," as they stood hesitating on the corner after they had finished a short discussion of Mr. Paley's disappearance. Happily it was only a few minutes before they came to a stop together in front of a new, shining shop, where smirking waxen heads all in a row were decked with the latest fashions of wigs and frizzes. One smiling fragment of a gentleman stared so straight at Miss Lucinda with his black eyes that she felt quite coy and embarrassed, and was obliged to feign not to be conscious of his admiration. But Miss Dobin, after a brief delay, boldly opened the door and entered; it was better to be sheltered in the shop than exposed to public remark as they gazed in at the windows. Miss Lucinda felt her heart beat and her courage give out; she, coward like, left the transaction of their business to her sister, and turned to contemplate the back of the handsome model. It was a slight shock to find that he was not so attractive from this point of view. The wig he wore was well made all round, but his shoulders were roughly finished in a substance that looked like plain plaster of Paris.

"What can I have ze pleasure of showing you, young ladees?" asked a person who advanced; and Miss Lucinda faced about to discover a smiling, middle-aged Frenchman, who rubbed his hands together and looked at his customers, first one and then the other, with delightful deference. He seemed a very civil nice person, the young ladies thought.

"My sister and I were thinking of buying some little arrangements to wear above the forehead." Miss Dobin explained, with pathetic dignity; but the Frenchman spared her any further words. He looked with eager interest at the bonnets, as if no lack had attracted his notice before. "Ah, yes. *Je comprends*; ze high foreheads are not now ze mode. Je prefer them, moi, yes, yes, but ze ladees must accept ze fashion; zay must now cover ze forehead with ze frizzes, ze bangs, you say. As you wis', as you wis'!" and the tactful little man, with many shrugs and merry gestures at such girlish fancies, pulled down one box after another.

It was a great relief to find that this was no worse, to say the least, than any other shopping, though the solemnity and secrecy of the occasion were infringed upon by the great supply of "arrangements" and the loud discussion of the color of some crimps a noisy girl was buying from a young saleswoman the other side of the shop.

Miss Dobin waved aside the wares which were being displayed for her approval. "Something—more simple, if you please,"—she did not like to say "older."

"But these are *très simple*," protested the Frenchman. "We have nothing younger;" and Miss Dobin and Miss Lucinda blushed, and said no more. The Frenchman had his own way; he persuaded them that nothing was so suitable as some conspicuous forelocks that matched their hair as it used to be. They would have given anything rather than leave their breakfast caps at home, if they had known that their proper winter bonnets must come off. They hardly listened to the wig merchant's glib voice as Miss Dobin stood revealed before the merciless mirror at the back of the shop.

He made everything as easy as possible, the friendly creature, and the ladies were grateful to him. Besides, now that the bonnet was on again there was a great improvement in Miss Dobin's appearance. She turned to Miss Lucinda, and saw a gleam of delight in her eager countenance. "It really is very becoming. I like the way it parts over your forehead," said the younger sister, "but if it were long enough to go behind the ears"—"*Non, non*," entreated the Frenchman. "To make her the old woman at once would be cruelty!" And Lucinda, who was wondering how well she would look in her turn, succumbed promptly to such protestations.

Yes, there was no use in being old before their time. Dulham was not quite keeping pace with the rest of the world in these days, but they need not drag behind everybody else, just because they lived there.

The price of the little arrangements was much less than the sisters expected, and the uncomfortable expense of their reverend father's wigs had been, it was proved, a thing of the past. Miss Dobin treated her polite Frenchman with great curtesy; indeed, Miss Lucinda had more than once whispered to her to talk French, and as they were bowed out of the shop the gracious *Bong-sure* of the elder lady seemed to act like the string of a showerbath, and bring down an awesome torrent of foreign phrases upon the two guileless heads. It was impossible to reply; the ladies bowed again, however, and Miss Lucinda caught a last smile from the handsome wax countenance in the window. He appeared to regard her with fresh approval, and she departed down the street with mincing steps.

"I feel as if anybody might look at me now, sister," said gentle Miss Lucinda. "I confess, I have really suffered sometimes, since I knew I looked so distressed."

"Yours is lighter than I thought it was in the shop," remarked Miss Dobin doubtfully, but she quickly added that perhaps it would change a little. She was so perfectly satisfied with her own appearance that she could not bear to dim the pleasure of any one else. The truth remained that she never would have let Lucinda choose that particular arrangement if she had seen it first in a good light. And Lucinda was thinking exactly the same of her companion.

"I am sure we shall have no more neuralgia," said Miss Dobin. "I am sorry we waited so long, dear," and they tripped down the main street of Westbury, confident that nobody would suspect them of being over thirty. Indeed, they felt quite girlish, and unconsciously looked sideways as they went along, to see their satisfying reflections in the windows. The great panes made excellent mirrors, with not too clear or lasting pictures of these comforted passers-by.

The Frenchman in the shop was making merry with his assistants. The two great frisettes had long been out of fashion; he had been lying in wait with them for two unsuspecting country ladies, who could be cajoled into such a purchase.

"Sister," Miss Lucinda was saying, "you know there is still an hour to wait before our train goes. Suppose we take a little longer walk down the other side of the way;" and they strolled slowly back again. In fact, they nearly missed the train, naughty girls! Hetty would have been so worried, they assured each other, but they reached the station just in time.

"Lutie," said Miss Dobin, "put up your hand and part it from your forehead; it seems to be getting a little out of place;" and Miss Lucinda, who had just got breath enough to speak, returned the information that Miss Dobin's was almost covering her eyebrows. They might have to trim them a little shorter; of course it could be done. The darkness was falling; they had taken an early dinner before they started, and now they were tired and hungry after the exertion of the afternoon, but the spirit of youth flamed afresh in their hearts, and they were very happy. If one's heart remains young, it is a sore trial to have the outward appearance entirely at variance. It was the ladies' nature to be girlish, and they found it impossible not to be grateful to the flimsy, ineffectual disguise which seemed to set them right with the world. The old conductor, who had known them for many years, looked hard at them as he took their tickets, and, being a man of humor and compassion, affected not to notice anything remarkable in their appearance. "You ladies never mean to grow old, like the rest of us," he said gallantly, and the sisters fairly quaked with joy. Their young hearts would forever keep them truly unconscious of the cruel thievery of time.

"Bless us!" the obnoxious Mrs. Woolden was saying, at the other end of the car. "There's the old maid Dobbinses, and they've bought 'em some bangs. I expect they wanted to get thatched in a little before real cold weather; but don't they look just like a pair o' poodle dogs."

The little ladies descended wearily from the train. Somehow they did not enjoy a day's shopping as much as they used. They were certainly much obliged to Hetty for sending her niece's boy to meet them, with a lantern; also for having a good warm supper ready when they came in. Hetty took a quick look at her mistresses, and returned to the kitchen. "I knew somebody would be foolin' of 'em," she assured herself angrily, but she had to laugh. Their dear, kind faces were wrinkled and pale, and the great frizzes had lost their pretty curliness, and were hanging down, almost straight and very ugly, into the ladies' eyes. They could not tuck them up under their caps, as they were sure might be done.

Then came a succession of rainy days, and nobody visited the rejuvenated household. The frisettes looked very bright chestnut by the light of day, and it must be confessed that Miss Dobin took the scissors and shortened Miss Lucinda's half an inch, and Miss Lucinda returned the compliment quite secretly, because each thought her sister's forehead lower than her own. Their dear gray eyebrows were honestly displayed, as if it were the fashion not to have them match with wigs. Hetty at last spoke out, and begged her mistresses, as they sat at breakfast, to let her take the frizzes back and change them. Her sister's daughter worked in that very shop, and though in the workroom, would be able to oblige them, Hetty was sure.

But the ladies looked at each other in pleased assurance, and then turned together to look at Hetty, who stood already a little apprehensive near the table, where she had just put down a plateful of smoking drop-cakes. The good creature really began to look old.

"They are worn very much in town," said Miss Dobin. "We think it was quite fortunate that the fashion came in just as our hair was growing a trifle thin. I dare say we may choose those that are a shade duller in color when these are a little past. Oh, we shall not want tea this evening, you remember, Hetty. I am glad there is likely to be such a good night for the sewing circle." And Miss Dobin and Miss Lucinda nodded and smiled.

"Oh, my sakes alive!" the troubled handmaiden groaned. "Going to the circle, be they, to be snickered at! Well, the Dobbin girls they was born, and the Dobbin girls they will remain till they die; but if they ain't innocent Christian babes to those that knows 'em well, mark me down for an idjit myself! They believe them front-pieces has set the

clock back forty year or more, but if they're pleased to think
so, let 'em!"

Away paced the Dulham ladies, late in the afternoon, to
grace the parish occasion, and face the amused scrutiny of
their neighbors. "I think we owe it to society to observe
the fashions of the day," said Miss Lucinda. "A lady cannot afford to be unattractive. I feel now as if we were prepared for anything!"

GOING TO SHREWSBURY

The train stopped at a way station with apparent unwillingness, and there was barely time for one elderly passenger to be hurried on board before a sudden jerk threw her almost off her unsteady old feet and we moved on. At my first glance I saw only a perturbed old countrywoman, laden with a large basket and a heavy bundle tied up in an old-fashioned bundle-handkerchief; then I discovered that she was a friend of mine, Mrs. Peet, who lived on a small farm, several miles from the village. She used to be renowned for good butter and fresh eggs and the earliest cowslip greens; in fact, she always made the most of her farm's slender resources; but it was some time since I had seen her drive by from market in her ancient thorough-braced wagon.

The brakeman followed her into the crowded car, also carrying a number of packages. I leaned forward and asked Mrs. Peet to sit by me; it was a great pleasure to see her again. The brakeman seemed relieved, and smiled as he tried to put part of his burden into the rack overhead; but even the flowered carpet-bag was much too large, and he explained that he would take care of everything at the end of the car. Mrs. Peet was not large herself, but with the big basket, and the bundle-handkerchief, and some possessions of my own we had very little spare room.

"So this 'ere is what you call ridin' in the cars! Well, I do declare!" said my friend, as soon as she had recovered herself a little. She looked pale and as if she had been in tears, but there was the familiar gleam of good humor in her tired old eyes.

"Where in the world are you going, Mrs. Peet?" I asked.

"Can't be you ain't heared about me, dear?" said she. "Well, the world's bigger than I used to think 't was. I've broke up,—'t was the only thing *to* do,—and I'm a-movin' to Shrewsbury."

"To Shrewsbury? Have you sold the farm?" I exclaimed, with sorrow and surprise. Mrs. Peet was too old and too characteristic to be suddenly transplanted from her native soil.

"'T wa'n't mine, the place wa'n't." Her pleasant face hardened slightly. "He was coaxed an' over-persuaded into signin' off before he was taken away. Is'iah, son of his sister that married old Josh Peet, come it over him about his bein' past work and how he'd do for him like an own son, an' we owed him a little somethin'. I'd paid off everythin' but that, an' was fool enough to leave it till the last, on account o' Is'iah's bein' a relation and not needin' his pay much as some others did. It's hurt me to have the place fall into other hands. Some wanted me to go right to law; but 't wouldn't be no use. Is'iah's smarter'n I be about them matters. You see he's got my name on the paper, too; he said 't was somethin' 'bout bein' responsible for the taxes. We was scant o' money, an' I was wore out with watchin' an' being broke o' my rest. After my tryin' hard for risin' forty-five year to provide for bein' past work, here I be, dear, here I be! I used to drive things smart, you remember. But we was fools enough in '72 to put about everythin' we had safe in the bank into that spool factory that come to nothin'. But I tell ye I could ha' kept myself long's I lived, if I could ha' held the place. I'd parted with most o' the woodland, if Is'iah'd coveted it. He was welcome to that, 'cept what might keep me in ovenwood. I've always desired to travel an' see somethin' o' the world, but I've got the chance now when I don't value it no great."

"Shrewsbury is a busy, pleasant place," I ventured to say by way of comfort, though my heart was filled with rage at the trickery of Isaiah Peet, who had always looked like a fox and behaved like one.

"Shrewsbury's be'n held up consid'able for me to smile at," said the poor old soul, "but I tell ye, dear, it's hard to go an' live twenty-two miles from where you've always had your home and friends. It may divert me, but it won't be home. You might as well set out one o' my old apple-trees on the beach, so 't could see the waves come in,—there wouldn't be no please to it."

"Where are you going to live in Shrewsbury?" I asked presently.

"I don't expect to stop long, dear creatur'. I'm 'most

seventy-six year old," and Mrs. Peet turned to look at me with pathetic amusement in her honest wrinkled face. "I said right out to Is'iah, before a roomful o' the neighbors, that I expected it of him to git me home an' bury me when my time come, and do it respectable; but I wanted to airn my livin', if 't was so I could, till then. He'd made sly talk, you see, about my electin' to leave the farm and go 'long some o' my own folks; but"—and she whispered this carefully—"he didn't give me no chance to stay there without hurtin' my pride and dependin' on him. I ain't said that to many folks, but all must have suspected. A good sight on 'em's had money of Is'iah, though, and they don't like to do nothin' but take his part an' be pretty soft spoken, fear it'll git to his ears. Well, well, dear, we'll let it be bygones, and not think of it no more;" but I saw the great tears roll slowly down her cheeks, and she pulled her bonnet forward impatiently, and looked the other way.

"There looks to be plenty o' good farmin' land in this part o' the country," she said, a minute later. "Where be we now? See them handsome farm buildin's; he must be a well-off man." But I had to tell my companion that we were still within the borders of the old town where we had both been born. Mrs. Peet gave a pleased little laugh, like a girl. "I'm expectin' Shrewsbury to pop up any minute. I'm feared to be kerried right by. I wa'n't never aboard of the cars before, but I've so often thought about 'em I don't know but it seems natural. Ain't it jest like flyin' through the air? I can't catch holt to see nothin'. Land! and here's my old cat goin' too, and never mistrustin'. I ain't told you that I'd fetched her."

"Is she in that basket?" I inquired with interest.

"Yis, dear. Truth was, I calc'lated to have her put out o' the misery o' movin', an' spoke to one o' the Barnes boys, an' he promised me all fair; but he wa'n't there in season, an' I kind o' made excuse to myself to fetch her along. She's an old creatur', like me, an' I can make shift to keep her some way or 'nuther; there's probably mice where we're goin', an' she's a proper mouser that can about keep herself if there's any sort o' chance. 'T will be somethin' o' home to see her goin' an' comin', but I expect we're both

on us goin' to miss our old haunts. I'd love to know what
kind o' mousin' there's goin' to be for me."

"You mustn't worry," I answered, with all the bravery
and assurance that I could muster. "Your niece will be
thankful to have you with her. Is she one of Mrs. Winn's
daughters?"

"Oh, no, they ain't able; it's Sister Wayland's darter
Isabella, that married the overseer of the gre't carriage-
shop. I ain't seen her since just after she was married; but
I turned to her first because I knew she was best able to
have me, and then I can see just how the other girls is situated and make me some kind of a plot. I wrote to Isabella,
though she *is* ambitious, and said 't was so I'd got to ask to
come an' make her a visit, an' she wrote back she would
be glad to have me; but she didn't write right off, and her
letter was scented up dreadful strong with some sort o'
essence, and I don't feel heartened about no great of a
welcome. But there, I've got eyes, an' I can see *how* 't is
when I git *where* 't is. Sister Winn's gals ain't married, an'
they've always boarded, an' worked in the shop on trimmin's. Isabella's well off; she had some means from her
father's sister. I thought it all over by night an' day, an'
I recalled that our folks kept Sister Wayland's folks all
one winter, when he'd failed up and got into trouble.
I'm reckonin' on sendin' over to-night an' gittin' the Winn
gals to come and see me and advise. Perhaps some on 'em
may know of somebody that'll take me for what help I
can give about house, or some clever folks that have been
lookin' for a smart cat, any ways; no, I don't know's I
could let her go to strangers.

"There was two or three o' the folks round home that
acted real warm-hearted towards me, an' urged me to come
an' winter with 'em," continued the exile; "an' this mornin'
I wished I'd agreed to, 't was so hard to break away. But
now it's done I feel more'n ever it's best. I couldn't bear
to live right in sight o' the old place, and come spring I
shouldn't 'prove of nothing Is'iah ondertakes to do with
the land. Oh, dear sakes! now it comes hard with me not
to have had no child'n. When I was young an' workin' hard
and into everything, I felt kind of free an' superior to them

that was so blessed, an' their houses cluttered up from mornin' till night, but I tell ye it comes home to me now. I'd be most willin' to own to even Is'iah, mean's he is; but I tell ye I'd took it out of him 'fore he was a grown man, if there'd be'n any virtue in cow-hidin' of him. Folks don't look like wild creatur's for nothin'. Is'iah's got fox blood in him, an' p'rhaps 't is his misfortune. His own mother always favored the looks of an old fox, true's the world; she was a poor tool,—a poor tool! I d' know's we ought to blame him same's we do.

"I've always been a master proud woman, if I was riz among the pastures," Mrs. Peet added, half to herself. There was no use in saying much to her; she was conscious of little beside her own thoughts and the smouldering excitement caused by this great crisis in her simple existence. Yet the atmosphere of her loneliness, uncertainty, and sorrow was so touching that after scolding again at her nephew's treachery, and finding the tears come fast to my eyes as she talked, I looked intently out of the car window, and tried to think what could be done for the poor soul. She was one of the old-time people, and I hated to have her go away; but even if she could keep her home she would soon be too feeble to live there alone, and some definite plan must be made for her comfort. Farms in that neighborhood were not valuable. Perhaps through the agency of the law and quite in secret, Isaiah Peet could be forced to give up his unrighteous claim. Perhaps, too, the Winn girls, who were really no longer young, might have saved something, and would come home again. But it was easy to make such pictures in one's mind, and I must do what I could through other people, for I was just leaving home for a long time. I wondered sadly about Mrs. Peet's future, and the ambitious Isabella, and the favorite Sister Winn's daughters, to whom, with all their kindliness of heart, the care of so old and perhaps so dependent an aunt might seem impossible. The truth about life in Shrewsbury would soon be known; more than half the short journey was already past.

To my great pleasure, my fellow-traveler now began to forget her own troubles in looking about her. She was an alert, quickly interested old soul, and this was a bit of

neutral ground between the farm and Shrewsbury, where
she was unattached and irresponsible. She had lived through
the last tragic moments of her old life, and felt a certain
relief, and Shrewsbury might be as far away as the other
side of the Rocky Mountains for all the consciousness she
had of its real existence. She was simply a traveler for the
time being, and began to comment, with delicious phrases
and shrewd understanding of human nature, on two or three
persons near us who attracted her attention.

"Where do you s'pose they be all goin'?" she asked con-
temptuously. "There ain't none on 'em but what looks kind
o' respectable. I'll warrant they've left work to home they'd
ought to be doin'. I knowed, if ever I stopped to think,
that cars was hived full o' folks, an' wa'n't run to an' fro
for nothin'; but these can't be quite up to the average, be
they? Some on 'em's real thrif'less? guess they've be'n
shoved out o' the last place, an' goin' to try the next one,
—*like me*, I suppose you'll want to say! Jest see that flauntin'
old creatur' that looks like a stopped clock. There! everybody can't be o' one goodness, even preachers."

I was glad to have Mrs. Peet amused, and we were as
cheerful as we could be for a few minutes. She said earnestly
that she hoped to be forgiven for such talk, but there were
some kinds of folks in the cars that she never had seen
before. But when the conductor came to take her ticket
she relapsed into her first state of mind, and was at a loss.

"You'll have to look after me, dear, when we get to
Shrewsbury," she said, after we had spent some distracted
moments in hunting for the ticket, and the cat had almost
escaped from the basket, and the bundle-handkerchief had
become untied and all its miscellaneous contents scattered
about our laps and the floor. It was a touching collection
of the last odds and ends of Mrs. Peet's housekeeping: some
battered books, and singed holders for flatirons, and the
faded little shoulder shawl that I had seen her wear many
a day about her bent shoulders. There were her old tin
match-box spilling all its matches, and a goose-wing for
brushing up ashes, and her much-thumbed Leavitt's Al-
manac. It was most pathetic to see these poor trifles out
of their places. At last the ticket was found in her left-hand

woolen glove, where her stiff, work-worn hand had grown used to the feeling of it.

"I shouldn't wonder, now, if I come to like living over to Shrewsbury first-rate," she insisted, turning to me with a hopeful, eager look to see if I differed. "You see 't won't be so tough for me as if I hadn't always felt it lurking within me to go off some day or 'nother an' see how other folks did things. I do' know but what the Winn gals have laid up somethin' sufficient for us to take a house, with the little mite I've got by me. I might keep house for us all, 'stead o' boardin' round in other folks' houses. That I ain't never been demeaned to, but I dare say I should find it pleasant in some ways. Town folks has got the upper hand o' country folks, but with all their work an' pride they can't make a dandelion. I do' know the times when I've set out to wash Monday mornin's, an' tied out the line betwixt the old pucker-pear tree and the corner o' the barn, an' thought, 'Here I be with the same kind o' week's work right over again.' I'd wonder kind o' f'erce if I couldn't git out of it noways; an' now here I be out of it, and an uprooteder creatur' never stood on the airth. Just as I got to feel I had somethin' ahead come that spool-factory business. There! you know he never was a forehanded man; his health was slim, and he got discouraged pretty nigh before ever he begun. I hope he don't know I'm turned out o' the old place. 'Is'iah's well off; he'll do the right thing by ye,' says he. But my! I turned hot all over when I found out what I'd put my name to,—me that had always be'n counted a smart woman! I did undertake to read it over, but I couldn't sense it. I've told all the folks so when they laid it off on to me some: but hand-writin' is awful tedious readin' and my head felt that day as if the works was gone.

"I ain't goin' to sag on to nobody," she assured me eagerly, as the train rushed along. "I've got more work in me now than folks expects at my age. I may be consid'able use to Isabella. She's got a family, an' I'll take right holt in the kitchen or with the little gals. She had four on 'em, last I heared. Isabella was never one that liked house-work. Little gals! I do' know now but what they must be about grown, time doos slip away so. I expect I shall look outlandish to 'em. But there! everybody knows me to home, an' nobody knows me to Shrewsbury; 't won't make a mite o' difference, if I take holt willin'."

I hoped, as I looked at Mrs. Peet, that she would never be persuaded to cast off the gathered brown silk bonnet and the plain shawl that she had worn so many years; but Isabella might think it best to insist upon more modern fashions. Mrs. Peet suggested, as if it were a matter of little consequence, that she had kept it in mind to buy some mourning; but there were other things to be thought of first, and so she had let it go until winter, any way, or until she should be fairly settled in Shrewsbury.

"Are your nieces expecting you by this train?" I was moved to ask, though with all the good soul's ready talk and appealing manner I could hardly believe that she was going to Shrewsbury for more than a visit; it seemed as if she must return to the worn old farmhouse over by the sheep-lands. She answered that one of the Barnes boys had written a letter for her the day before, and there was evidently little uneasiness about her first reception.

We drew near the junction where I must leave her within a mile of the town. The cat was clawing indignantly at the basket, and her mistress grew as impatient of the car. She began to look very old and pale, my poor fellow-traveler, and said that she felt dizzy, going so fast. Presently the friendly red-cheeked young brakeman came along, bringing the carpet-bag and other possessions, and insisted upon taking the alarmed cat beside, in spite of an aggressive paw that had worked its way through the wicker prison. Mrs. Peet watched her goods disappear with suspicious eyes, and clutched her bundle-handkerchief as if it might be all that she could save. Then she anxiously got to her feet, much too soon, and when I said good-by to her at the car door she was ready to cry. I pointed to the car which she was to take next on the branch line of railway, and I assured her that it was only a few minutes' ride to Shrewsbury, and that I felt certain she would find somebody waiting. The sight of that worn, thin figure adventuring alone across the platform gave my heart a sharp pang as the train carried me away.

Some of the passengers who sat near asked me about my old friend with great sympathy, after she had gone. There was a look of tragedy about her, and indeed it had been impossible not to get a good deal of her history, as she talked straight on in the same tone, when we stopped at a station, as if the train were going at full speed, and some of her remarks caused pity and amusements by turns. At the last minute she said, with deep self-reproach, "Why, I haven't asked a word about your folks; but you'd ought to excuse such an old stray hen as I be."

In the spring I was driving by on what the old people of my native town call the sheep-lands road, and the sight of Mrs. Peet's former home brought our former journey freshly to my mind. I had last heard from her just after she got to Shrewbury, when she had sent me a message.

"Have you ever heard how she got on?" I eagerly asked my companion.

"Didn't I tell you that I met her in Shrewsbury High Street one day?" I was answered. "She seemed perfectly delighted with everything. Her nieces have laid up a good bit of money, and are soon to leave the mill, and most thankful to have old Mrs. Peet with them. Somebody told me that they wished to buy the farm here, and come back to live, but she wouldn't hear of it, and thought they would miss too many privileges. She has been going to concerts and lectures this winter, and insists that Isaiah did her a good turn."

We both laughed. My own heart was filled with joy, for the uncertain, lonely face of this homeless old woman had often haunted me. The rain-blackened little house did certainly look dreary, and a whole lifetime of patient toil had left few traces. The pucker-pear tree was in full bloom, however, and gave a welcome gayety to the deserted dooryard.

A little way beyond we met Isaiah Peet, the prosperous money-lender, who had cheated the old woman of her own. I fancied that he looked somewhat ashamed, as he recognized us. To my surprise, he stopped his horse in most social fashion.

"Old Aunt Peet's passed away," he informed me briskly. "She had a shock, and went right off sudden yisterday forenoon. I'm about now tendin' to the funeral 'rangements. She's be'n extry smart, they say, all winter,—out to meetin' last Sabbath; never enjoyed herself so complete as she has this past month. She'd be'n a very hard-workin' woman. Her folks was glad to have her there, and give her every attention. The place here never was good for nothin'. The old gen'leman,—uncle, you know,—he wore hisself out tryin' to make a livin' off from it."

There was an ostentatious sympathy and half-suppressed excitement from bad news which were quite lost upon us, and we did not linger to hear much more. It seemed to me as if I had known Mrs. Peet better than any one else had known her. I had counted upon seeing her again, and hearing her own account of Shrewsbury life, its pleasures and its limitations. I wondered what had become of the cat and the contents of the faded bundle-handkerchief.

1 Just where the village abruptly ended, and the green mowing fields began, stood Mrs. Bickford's house, looking down the road with all its windows, and topped by two prim chimneys that stood up like ears. It was placed with an end to the road, and fronted southward; you could follow a straight path from the gate past the front door and find Mrs. Bickford sitting by the last window of all in the kitchen, unless she were solemnly stepping about, prolonging the stern duties of her solitary housekeeping.

One day in early summer, when almost every one else in Fairfield had put her house plants out of doors, there were still three flower pots on a kitchen window sill. Mrs. Bickford spent but little time over her rose and geranium and Jerusalem cherry-tree, although they had gained a kind of personality born of long association. They rarely undertook to bloom, but had most courageously maintained life in spite of their owner's unsympathetic but conscientious care. Later in the season she would carry them out of doors, and leave them, until the time of frosts, under the shade of a great apple-tree, where they might make the best of what the summer had to give.

The afternoon sun was pouring in, the Jerusalem cherry-tree drooped its leaves in the heat and looked pale, when a neighbor, Miss Pendexter, came in from the next house but one to make a friendly call. As she passed the parlor with its shut blinds, and the sitting-room, also shaded carefully from the light, she wished, as she had done many times before, that somebody beside the owner might have the pleasure of living in and using so good and pleasant a house. Mrs. Bickford always complained of having so much care, even while she valued herself intelligently upon having the right to do as she pleased with one of the best houses in Fairfield. Miss Pendexter was a cheerful, even gay little person, who always brought a pleasant flurry of excitement, and usually had a genuine though small piece of news to tell, or some new aspect of already received information.

Mrs. Bickford smiled as she looked up to see this sprightly neighbor coming. She had no gift at entertaining herself, and was always glad, as one might say, to be taken off her own hands.

Miss Pendexter smiled back, as if she felt herself to be equal to the occasion.

"How be you to-day?" the guest asked kindly, as she entered the kitchen. "Why, what a sight o' flowers, Mis' Bickford! What be you goin' to do with 'em all?"

Mrs. Bickford wore a grave expression as she glanced over her spectacles. "My sister's boy fetched 'em over," she answered. "You know my sister Parsons's a great hand to raise flowers, an' this boy takes after her. He said his mother thought the gardin never looked handsomer, and she picked me these to send over. They was sendin' a team to West-bury for some fertilizer to put on the land, an' he come with the men, an' stopped to eat his dinner 'long o' me. He's been growin' fast, and looks peakëd. I expect sister 'Liza thought the ride, this pleasant day, would do him good. 'Liza sent word for me to come over and pass some days next week, but it ain't so that I can."

"Why, it's a pretty time of year to go off and make a little visit," suggested the neighbor encouragingly.

"I ain't got my sitting-room chamber carpet taken up yet," sighed Mrs. Bickford. "I do feel condemned. I might have done it to-day, but 't was all at end when I saw Tommy coming. There, he's a likely boy, an' so relished his dinner; I happened to be well prepared. I don't know but he's my favorite o' that family. Only I've been sittin' here thinkin', since he went, an' I can't remember that I ever was so belated with my spring cleaning."

" 'T was owin' to the weather," explained Miss Pendexter. "None of us could be so smart as common this year, not even the lazy ones that always get one room done the first o' March, and brag of it to others' shame, and then never let on when they do the rest."

The two women laughed together cheerfully. Mrs. Bickford had put up the wide leaf of her large table between the windows and spread out the flowers. She was sorting them slowly into three heaps.

"Why, I do declare if you haven't got a rose in bloom

yourself!" exclaimed Miss Pendexter abruptly, as if the bud had not been announced weeks before, and its progress regularly commented upon. "Ain't it a lovely rose? Why, Mis' Bickford!"

"Yes'm, it's out to-day," said Mrs. Bickford, with a somewhat plaintive air. "I'm glad you come in so as to see it."

The bright flower was like a face. Somehow, the beauty and life of it were surprising in the plain room, like a gay little child who might suddenly appear in a doorway. Miss Pendexter forgot herself and her hostess and the tangled mass of garden flowers in looking at the red rose. She even forgot that it was incumbent upon her to carry forward the conversation. Mrs. Bickford was subject to fits of untimely silence which made her friends anxiously sweep the corners of their minds in search of something to say, but any one who looked at her now could easily see that it was not poverty of thought that made her speechless, but an overburdening sense of the inexpressible.

"Goin' to make up all your flowers into bo'quets? I think the short-stemmed kinds is often pretty in a dish," suggested Miss Pendexter compassionately.

"I thought I should make them into three bo'quets. I wish there wa'n't quite so many. Sister Eliza's very lavish with her flowers; she's always been a kind sister, too," said Mrs. Bickford vaguely. She was not apt to speak with so much sentiment, and as her neighbor looked at her narrowly she detected unusual signs of emotion. It suddenly became evident that the three nosegays were connected in her mind with her bereavement of three husbands, and Miss Pendexter's easily roused curiosity was quieted by the discovery that her friend was bent upon a visit to the burying-ground. It was the time of year when she was pretty sure to spend an afternoon there, and sometimes they had taken the walk in company. Miss Pendexter expected to receive the usual invitation, but there was nothing further said at the moment, and she looked again at the pretty rose.

Mrs. Bickford aimlessly handled the syringas and flowering almond sprays, choosing them out of the fragrant heap only to lay them down again. She glanced out of the window; then gave Miss Pendexter a long expressive look.

"I expect you're going to carry 'em over to the burying-ground?" inquired the guest, in a sympathetic tone.

"Yes'm," said the hostess, now well started in conversation and in quite her every-day manner. "You see I was goin' over to my brother's folks to-morrow in South Fairfield, to pass the day; they said they were goin' to send over to-morrow to leave a wagon at the blacksmith's, and they'd hitch that to their best chaise, so I could ride back very comfortable. You know I have to avoid bein' out in the mornin' sun?"

Miss Pendexter smiled to herself at this moment; she was obliged to move from her chair at the window, the May sun was so hot on her back, for Mrs. Bickford always kept the curtains rolled high up, out of the way, for fear of fading and dust. The kitchen was a blaze of light. As for the Sunday chaise being sent, it was well known that Mrs. Bickford's married brothers and sisters comprehended the truth that she was a woman of property, and had neither chick nor child.

"So I thought 't was a good opportunity to just stop an' see if the lot was in good order,—last spring Mr. Wallis's stone hove with the frost; an' so I could take these flowers." She gave a sigh. "I ain't one that can bear flowers in a close room,—they bring on a headache; but I enjoy 'em as much as anybody to look at, only you never know what to put 'em in. If I could be out in the mornin' sun, as some do, and keep flowers in the house, I should have me a gardin, certain," and she sighed again.

"A garden's a sight o' care, but I don't begrudge none o' the care I give to mine. I have to scant on flowers so's to make room for pole beans," said Miss Pendexter gayly. She had only a tiny strip of land behind her house, but she always had something to give away, and made riches out of her narrow poverty. "A few flowers gives me just as much pleasure as more would," she added. "You get acquainted with things when you've only got one or two roots. My sweet-williams is just like folks."

"Mr. Bickford was partial to sweet-williams," said Mrs. Bickford. "I never knew him to take notice of no other sort of flowers. When we'd be over to Eliza's, he'd walk down her gardin, an' he'd never make no comments until he come to them, and then he'd say, 'Those is sweet-williams.' How many times I've heard him!"

"You ought to have a sprig of 'em for his bo'quet," suggested Miss Pendexter.

"Yes, I've put a sprig in," said her companion.

At this moment Miss Pendexter took a good look at the bouquets, and found that they were as nearly alike as careful hands could make them. Mrs. Bickford was evidently trying to reach absolute impartiality.

"I don't know but you think it's foolish to tie 'em up this afternoon," she said presently, as she wound the first with a stout string. "I thought I could put 'em in a bucket o' water out in the shed, where there's a draught o' air, and then I should have all my time in the morning. I shall have a good deal to do before I go. I always sweep the setting-room and front entry Wednesdays. I want to leave everything nice, goin' away for all day so. So I meant to get the flowers out o' the way this afternoon. Why, it's most half past four, ain't it? But I sha'n't pick the rose till mornin'; 't will be blowed out better then."

"The rose?" questioned Miss Pendexter. "Why, are you goin' to pick that, too?"

"Yes, I be. I never like to let 'em fade on the bush. There, that's just what's a-troublin' me," and she turned to give a long, imploring look at the friend who sat beside her. Miss Pendexter had moved her chair before the table in order to be out of the way of the sun. "I don't seem to know which of 'em ought to have it," said Mrs. Bickford despondently. "I do so hate to make a choice between 'em; they all had their good points, especially Mr. Bickford, and I respected 'em all. I don't know but what I think of one on 'em 'most as much as I do of the other."

"Why, 't is difficult for you, ain't it?" responded Miss Pendexter. "I don't know's I can offer advice."

"No, I s'pose not," answered her friend slowly, with a shadow of disappointment coming over her calm face. "I feel sure you would if you could, Abby."

Both of the women felt as if they were powerless before a great emergency.

"There's one thing,—they're all in a better world now," said Miss Pendexter, in a self-conscious and constrained voice; "they can't feel such little things or take note o' slights same's we can."

"No; I suppose 't is myself that wants to be just," answered Mrs. Bickford. "I feel under obligations to my last husband when I look about and see how comfortable he left me. Poor Mr. Wallis had his great projects, an' perhaps if he'd lived longer he'd have made a record; but when he died he'd failed all up, owing to that patent cornsheller he'd put everything into, and, as you know, I had to get along 'most any way I could for the next few years. Life was very disappointing with Mr. Wallis, but he meant well, an' used to be an amiable person to dwell with, until his temper got spoilt makin' so many hopes an' havin' 'em turn out failures. He had consider'ble of an air, an' dressed very handsome when I was first acquainted with him, Mr. Wallis did. I don't know's you ever knew Mr. Wallis in his prime?"

"He died the year I moved over here from North Denfield," said Miss Pendexter, in a tone of sympathy. "I just knew him by sight. I was to his funeral. You know you lived in what we call the Wells house then, and I felt it wouldn't be an intrusion, we was such near neighbors. The first time I ever was in your house was just before that, when he was sick, an' Mary 'Becca Wade an' I called to see if there was anything we could do."

"They used to say about town that Mr. Wallis went to an' fro like a mail-coach an' brought nothin' to pass," announced Mrs. Bickford without bitterness. "He ought to have had a better chance than he did in this little neighborhood. You see, he had excellent ideas, but he never'd learned the machinist's trade, and there was somethin' the matter with every model he contrived. I used to be real narrow-minded when he talked about moving 'way up to Lowell, or some o' them places; I hated to think of leaving my folks; and now I see that I never done right by him. His ideas was good. I know once he was on a jury, and there was a man stopping to the tavern where he was, near the court house, a man that traveled for a firm to Lowell; and they engaged in talk, an' Mr. Wallis let out some o' his notions an' contrivances, an' he said that man wouldn't hardly stop to eat, he was so interested, an' said he'd look for a chance for him up to Lowell. It all sounded so well that I kind of begun to think about goin' myself. Mr. Wallis said we'd close the house here, and go an' board through the winter. But he never heard a word from him, and the disappointment was one he never got over. I think of it now different from what I did then. I often used to be kind of disapproving to Mr. Wallis; but there, he used to be always tellin' over his great projects. Somebody told me once that a man by the same name of the one he met while he was to court had got some patents for the very things Mr. Wallis used to be workin' over; but 't was after he died, an' I don't know's 't was in him to ever really set things up so other folks could ha' seen their value. His machines always used to work kind of rickety, but folks used to come from all round to see 'em; they was curiosities if they wa'n't nothin' else, an' gave him a name."

Mrs. Bickford paused a moment, with some geranium leaves in her hand, and seemed to suppress with difficulty a desire to speak even more freely.

"He was a dreadful notional man," she said at last, regretfully, and as if this fact were a poor substitute for what had just been in her mind. "I recollect one time he worked all through the early winter over my churn, an' got it so it would go three quarters of an hour all of itself if you wound it up; an' if you'll believe it, he went an' spent all that time for nothin' when the cow was dry, an' we was with difficulty borrowin' a pint o' milk a day somewheres in the neighborhood just to get along with." Mrs. Bickford flushed with displeasure, and turned to look at her visitor. "Now what do you think of such a man as that, Miss Pendexter?" she asked.

"Why, I don't know but 't was just as good for an invention," answered Miss Pendexter timidly; but her friend looked doubtful, and did not appear to understand.

"Then I asked him where it was, one day that spring when I'd got tired to death churnin', an' the butter wouldn't come in a churn I'd had to borrow, and he'd gone an' took ours all to pieces to get the works to make some other useless contrivance with. He had no sort of a business turn, but he was well meanin', Mr. Wallis was, an' full o' divertin' talk; they used to call him very good company. I see now that he never had no proper chance. I've always regretted Mr. Wallis," said she who was now the widow Bickford.

"I'm sure you always speak well of him," said Miss Pendexter. "'T was a pity he hadn't got among good business men, who could push his inventions an' do all the business part."

"I was left very poor an' needy for them next few years," said Mrs. Bickford mournfully; "but he never'd give up but what he should die worth his fifty thousand dollars. I don't see now how I ever did get along them next few years without him; but there, I always managed to keep a pig, an' sister Eliza gave me my potatoes, and I made out somehow. I could dig me a few greens, you know, in spring, and then 't would come strawberry-time, and other berries a-followin' on. I was always decent to go to meetin' till within the last six months, an' then I went in bad weather, when folks wouldn't notice; but 't was a rainy summer, an' I managed to get considerable preachin' after all. My clothes looked proper enough when 't was a wet Sabbath. I often think o' them pinched days now, when I'm left so comfortable by Mr. Bickford."

"Yes'm, you've everything to be thankful for," said Miss Pendexter, who was as poor herself at that moment as her friend had ever been, and who could never dream of venturing upon the support and companionship of a pig. "Mr. Bickford was a very personable man," she hastened to say, the confidences were so intimate and interesting.

"Oh, very," replied Mrs. Bickford; "there was something about him that was very marked. Strangers would always ask who he was as he come into meetin'. His words counted; he never spoke except he had to. 'T was a relief at first after Mr. Wallis's being so fluent; but Mr. Wallis was splendid company for winter evenings,—'t would be eight o'clock before you knew it. I didn't use to listen to it all, but he had a great deal of information. Mr. Bickford was dreadful dignified; I used to be sort of meechin' with him along at the first, for fear he'd disapprove of me; but I found out 't wa'n't no need; he was always just that way, an' done everything by rule an' measure. He hadn't the mind of my other husbands, but he was a very dignified appearing man; he used 'most always to sleep in the evenin's, Mr. Bickford did."

"Them is lovely bo'quets, certain!" exclaimed Miss Pendexter. "Why, I couldn't tell 'em apart; the flowers are comin' out just right, aren't they?"

Mrs. Bickford nodded assent, and then, startled by sudden recollection, she cast a quick glance at the rose in the window.

"I always seem to forget about your first husband, Mr. Fraley," Miss Pendexter suggested bravely. "I've often heard you speak of him, too, but he'd passed away long before I ever knew you."

"He was but a boy," said Mrs. Bickford. "I thought the world was done for me when he died, but I've often thought since 't was a mercy for him. He come of a very melancholy family, and all his brothers an' sisters enjoyed poor health; it might have been his lot. Folks said we was as pretty a couple as ever come into church; we was both dark, with black eyes an' a good deal o' color,—you wouldn't expect it to see me now. Albert was one that held up his head, and looked as if he meant to own the town, an' he had a good word for everybody. I don't know what the years might have brought."

There was a long pause. Mrs. Bickford leaned over to pick up a heavy-headed Guelder-rose that had dropped on the floor.

"I expect 't was what they call fallin' in love," she added, in a different tone; "he wa'n't nothin' but a boy, an' I wa'n't nothin' but a girl, but we was dreadful happy. He didn't favor his folks,—they all had hay-colored hair and was faded-looking, except his mother; they was alike, and looked alike, an' set everything by each other. He was just the kind of strong, hearty young man that goes right off if they get a fever. We was just settled on a little farm, an' he'd have done well if he'd had time; as it was, he left debts. He had a hasty temper, that was his great fault, but Albert had a lovely voice to sing; they said there wa'n't no such tenor voice in this part o' the State. I could hear him singin' to himself right out in the field a-ploughin' or hoein', an' he didn't know it half o' the time, no more'n a common bird would. I don't know's I valued his gift as

I ought to, but there was nothin' ever sounded so sweet to me. I ain't one that ever had much fancy, but I knowed Albert had a pretty voice."

Mrs. Bickford's own voice trembled a little, but she held up the last bouquet and examined it critically. "I must hurry now an' put these in water," she said, in a matter of fact tone. Little Miss Pendexter was so quiet and sympathetic that her hostess felt no more embarrassed than if she had been talking only to herself.

"Yes, they do seem to droop some; 't is a little warm for them here in the sun," said Miss Pendexter; "but you'll find they'll all come up if you give them their fill o' water. They'll look very handsome to-morrow; folks'll notice them from the road. You've arranged them very tasty, Mis' Bickford."

"They do look pretty, don't they?" Mrs. Bickford regarded the three in turn. "I want to have them all pretty. You may deem it strange, Abby."

"Why, no, Mis' Bickford," said the guest sincerely, although a little perplexed by the solemnity of the occasion. "I know how 't is with friends,—that having one don't keep you from wantin' another; 't is just like havin' somethin' to eat, and then wantin' somethin' to drink just the same. I expect all friends find their places."

But Mrs. Bickford was not interested in this figure, and still looked vague and anxious as she began to brush the broken stems and wilted leaves into her wide calico apron. "I done the best I could while they was alive," she said, "and mourned 'em when I lost 'em, an' I feel grateful to be left so comfortable now when all is over. It seems foolish, but I'm still at a loss about that rose."

"Perhaps you'll feel sure when you first wake up in the morning," answered Miss Pendexter solicitously. "It's a case where I don't deem myself qualified to offer you any advice. But I'll say one thing, seeing's you've been so friendly spoken and confiding with me. I never was married myself, Mis' Bickford, because it wa'n't so that I could have the one I liked."

"I suppose he ain't livin', then? Why, I wa'n't never aware you had met with a disappointment, Abby," said Mrs. Bickford instantly. None of her neighbors had ever suspected little Miss Pendexter of a romance.

"Yes'm, he's livin'," replied Miss Pendexter humbly. "No'm, I never have heard that he died."

"I want to know!" exclaimed the woman of experience. "Well, I'll tell you this, Abby: you may have regretted your lot, and felt lonesome and hardshipped, but they all have their faults, and a single woman's got her liberty, if she ain't got other blessin's."

" 'T wouldn't have been my choice to live alone," said Abby, meeker than before. "I feel very thankful for my blessin's, all the same. You've always been a kind neighbor, Mis' Bickford."

"Why can't you stop to tea?" asked the elder woman, with unusual cordiality; but Miss Pendexter remembered that her hostess often expressed a dislike for unexpected company, and promptly took her departure after she had risen to go, glancing up at the bright flower as she passed outside the window. It seemed to belong most to Albert, but she had not liked to say so. The sun was low; the green fields stretched away southward into the misty distance.

.2 Mrs. Bickford's house appeared to watch her out of sight down the road, the next morning. She had lost all spirit for her holiday. Perhaps it was the unusual excitement of the afternoon's reminiscences, or it might have been simply the bright moonlight night which had kept her broad awake until dawn, thinking of the past, and more and more concerned about the rose. By this time it had ceased to be merely a flower, and had become a definite symbol and assertion of personal choice. She found it very difficult to decide. So much of her present comfort and well-being was due to Mr. Bickford; still, it was Mr. Wallis who had been most unfortunate, and to whom she had done least justice. If she owed recognition to Mr. Bickford, she certainly owed amends to Mr. Wallis. If she gave him the rose, it would be for the sake of affectionate apology. And then there was Albert, to whom she had no thought of being either indebted or forgiving. But she could not escape from the terrible feeling of indecision.

It was a beautiful morning for a drive, but Mrs. Bickford was kept waiting sometime for the chaise. Her nephew, who was to be her escort, had found much social advantage at the blacksmith's shop, so that it was after ten when she finally started with the three large flat-backed bouquets, covered with a newspaper to protect them from the sun. The petals of the almond flowers were beginning to scatter, and now and then little streams of water leaked out of the newspaper and trickled down the steep slope of her best dress to the bottom of the chaise. Even yet she had not made up her mind; she had stopped trying to deal with such an evasive thing as decision, and leaned back and rested as best she could.

"What an old fool I be!" she rebuked herself from time to time, in so loud a whisper that her companion ventured a respectful "What, ma'am?" and was astonished that she made no reply. John was a handsome young man, but Mrs. Bickford could never cease thinking of him as a boy. He had always been her favorite among the younger members of the family, and now returned this affectionate feeling, being possessed of an instinctive confidence in the sincerities of his prosaic aunt.

As they drove along, there had seemed at first to be something unsympathetic and garish about the beauty of the summer day. After the shade and shelter of the house, Mrs. Bickford suffered even more from a contracted and assailed feeling out of doors. The very trees by the roadside had a curiously fateful, trying way of standing back to watch her, as she passed in the acute agony of indecision, and she was annoyed and startled by a bird that flew too near the chaise in a moment of surprise. She was conscious of a strange reluctance to the movement of the Sunday chaise, as if she were being conveyed against her will; but the companionship of her nephew John grew every moment to be more and more a reliance. It was very comfortable to sit by his side, even though he had nothing to say; he was manly and cheerful, and she began to feel protected.

"Aunt Bickford," he suddenly announced, "I may's well out with it! I've got a piece o' news to tell you, if you won't let on to nobody. I expect you'll laugh, but you know I've set everything by Mary Lizzie Gifford ever since I was a boy. Well, sir!"

"Well, sir!" exclaimed aunt Bickford in her turn, quickly roused into most comfortable self-forgetfulness. "I am really pleased. She'll make you a good, smart wife, John. Ain't all the folks pleased, both sides?"

"Yes, they be," answered John soberly, with a happy, important look that became him well.

"I guess I can make out to do something for you to help along, when the right time comes," said aunt Bickford impulsively, after a moment's reflection. "I've known what it is to be starting out in life with plenty o' hope. You ain't calculatin' on gettin' married before fall,—or be ye?"

"'Long in the fall," said John regretfully. "I wish t' we could set up for ourselves right away this summer. I ain't got much ahead, but I can work well as anybody, an' now I'm out o' my time."

"She's a nice, modest, pretty girl. I thought she liked you, John," said the old aunt. "I saw her over to your mother's, last day I was there. Well, I expect you'll be happy."

"Certain," said John, turning to look at her affectionately, surprised by this outspokenness and lack of embarrassment between them. "Thank you, aunt," he said simply; "you're a real good friend to me;" and he looked away again hastily, and blushed a fine scarlet over his sun-browned face. "She's coming over to spend the day with the girls," he added. "Mother thought of it. You don't get over to see us very often."

Mrs. Bickford smiled approvingly. John's mother looked for her good opinion, no doubt, but it was very proper for John to have told his prospects himself, and in such a pretty way. There was no shilly-shallying about the boy.

"My gracious!" said John suddenly. "I'd like to have drove right by the burying-ground. I forgot we wanted to stop."

Strange as it may appear, Mrs. Bickford herself had not noticed the burying-ground, either, in her excitement and pleasure; now she felt distressed and responsible again, and showed it in her face at once. The young man leaped lightly to the ground, and reached for the flowers.

"Here, you just let me run up with 'em," he said kindly.

"'T is hot in the sun to-day, an' you'll mind it risin' the hill. We'll stop as I fetch you back to-night, and you can go up comfortable an' walk the yard after sundown when it's cool, an' stay as long as you're a mind to. You seem sort of tired, aunt."

"I don't know but what I will let you carry 'em," said Mrs. Bickford slowly.

To leave the matter of the rose in the hands of fate seemed weakness and cowardice, but there was not a moment for consideration. John was a smiling fate, and his proposition was a great relief. She watched him go away with a terrible inward shaking, and sinking of pride. She had held the flowers with so firm a grasp that her hands felt weak and numb, and as she leaned back and shut her eyes she was afraid to open them again at first for fear of knowing the bouquets apart even at that distance, and giving instructions which she might regret. With a sudden impulse she called John once or twice eagerly; but her voice had a thin and piping sound, and the meditative early crickets that chirped in the fresh summer grass probably sounded louder in John's ears. The bright light on the white stones dazzled Mrs. Bickford's eyes; and then all at once she felt light-hearted, and the sky seemed to lift itself higher and wider from the earth, and she gave a sigh of relief as her messenger came back along the path. "I know who I do hope's got the right one," she said to herself. "There, what a touse I be in! I don't see what I had to go and pick the old rose for, anyway."

"I declare, they did look real handsome, aunt," said John's hearty voice as he approached the chaise. "I set 'em up just as you told me. This one fell out, an' I kept it. I don't know's you'll care. I can give it to Lizzie."

He faced her now with a bright, boyish look. There was something gay in his buttonhole,—it was the red rose.

Aunt Bickford blushed like a girl. "Your choice is easy made," she faltered mysteriously, and then burst out laughing, there in front of the burying-ground. "Come, get right in, dear," she said. "Well, well! I guess the rose was made for you; it looks very pretty in your coat, John."

She thought of Albert, and the next moment the tears came into her old eyes. John was a lover, too.

"My first husband was just such a tall, straight young man as you be," she said as they drove along. "The flower he first give me was a rose."

The time of year was April; the place was a small farming town in New Hampshire, remote from any railroad. One by one the lights had been blown out in the scattered houses near Miss Tempy Dent's; but as her neighbors took a last look out-of-doors, their eyes turned with instinctive curiosity toward the old house, where a lamp burned steadily. They gave a little sigh. "Poor Miss Tempy!" said more than one bereft acquaintance; for the good woman lay dead in her north chamber, and the light was a watcher's light. The funeral was set for the next day, at one o'clock.

The watchers were two of the oldest friends, Mrs. Crowe and Sarah Ann Binson. They were sitting in the kitchen, because it seemed less awesome than the unused best room, and they beguiled the long hours by steady conversation. One would think that neither topics nor opinions would hold out, at that rate, all through the long spring night; but there was a certain degree of excitement just then, and the two women had risen to an unusual level of expressiveness and confidence. Each had already told the other more than one fact that she had determined to keep secret; they were again and again tempted into statements that either would have found impossible by daylight. Mrs. Crowe was knitting a blue yarn stocking for her husband; the foot was already so long that it seemed as if she must have forgotten to narrow it at the proper time. Mrs. Crowe knew exactly what she was about, however; she was of a much cooler disposition than Sister Binson, who made futile attempts at some sewing, only to drop her work into her lap whenever the talk was most engaging.

Their faces were interesting,—of the dry, shrewd, quick-witted New England type, with thin hair twisted neatly back out of the way. Mrs. Crowe could look vague and benignant, and Miss Binson was, to quote her neighbors, a little too sharp-set; but the world knew that she had need to be, with the load she must carry of supporting an inefficient widowed sister and six unpromising and unwilling nieces and nephews. The eldest boy was at last placed with a good man to learn the mason's trade. Sarah Ann Binson, for all her sharp, anxious aspect, never defended herself, when her sister whined and fretted. She was told every week of her life that the poor children never would have had to lift a finger if their father had lived, and yet she had kept her steadfast way with the little farm, and patiently taught the young people many useful things, for which, as everybody said, they would live to thank her. However pleasureless her life appeared to outward view, it was brimful of pleasure to herself.

Mrs. Crowe, on the contrary, was well to do, her husband being a rich farmer and an easy-going man. She was a stingy woman, but for all that she looked kindly; and when she gave away anything, or lifted a finger to help anybody, it was thought a great piece of beneficence, and a compliment, indeed, which the recipient accepted with twice as much gratitude as double the gift that came from a poorer and more generous acquaintance. Everybody liked to be on good terms with Mrs. Crowe. Socially she stood much higher than Sarah Ann Binson. They were both old schoolmates and friends of Temperance Dent, who had asked them, one day, not long before she died, if they would not come together and look after the house, and manage everything, when she was gone. She may have had some hope that they might become closer friends in this period of intimate partnership, and that the richer woman might better understand the burdens of the poorer. They had not kept the house the night before; they were too weary with the care of their old friend, whom they had not left until all was over.

There was a brook which ran down the hillside very near the house, and the sound of it was much louder than usual. When there was silence in the kitchen, the busy stream had a strange insistence in its wild voice, as if it tried to make the watchers understand something that related to the past.

"I declare, I can't begin to sorrow for Tempy yet. I am so glad to have her at rest," whispered Mrs. Crowe. "It is strange to set here without her, but I can't make it clear that she has gone. I feel as if she had got easy and dropped off to sleep, and I'm more scared about waking her up than knowing any other feeling."

"Yes," said Sarah Ann, "it's just like that, ain't it? But I tell you we are goin' to miss her worse than we expect. She's helped me through with many a trial, has Temperance. I ain't the only one who says the same, neither."

These words were spoken as if there were a third person listening; somebody beside Mrs. Crowe. The watchers could not rid their minds of the feeling that they were being watched themselves. The spring wind whistled in the window crack, now and then, and buffeted the little house in a gusty way that had a sort of companionable effect. Yet, on the whole, it was a very still night, and the watchers spoke in a half-whisper.

"She was the freest-handed woman that ever I knew," said Mrs. Crowe, decidedly. "According to her means, she gave away more than anybody. I used to tell her 't wa'n't right. I used really to be afraid that she went without too much, for we have a duty to ourselves."

Sister Binson looked up in a half-amused, unconscious way, and then recollected herself.

Mrs. Crowe met her look with a serious face. "It ain't so easy for me to give as it is for some," she said simply, but with an effort which was made possible only by the occasion. "I should like to say, while Tempy is laying here yet in her own house, that she has been a constant lesson to me. Folks are too kind, and shame me with thanks for what I do. I ain't such a generous woman as poor Tempy was, for all she had nothin' to do with, as one may say."

Sarah Binson was much moved at this confession, and was even pained and touched by the unexpected humility. "You have a good many calls on you"—she began, and then left her kind little compliment half finished.

"Yes, yes, but I've got means enough. My disposition's more of a cross to me as I grow older, and I made up my mind this morning that Tempy's example should be my pattern henceforth." She began to knit faster than ever.

" 'T ain't no use to get morbid: that's what Tempy used to say herself," said Sarah Ann, after a minute's silence. "Ain't it strange to say 'used to say'?" and her own voice choked a little. "She never did like to hear folks git goin' about themselves."

" 'T was only because they're apt to do it so as other folks will say 't wasn't so, an' praise 'em up," humbly replied Mrs. Crowe, "and that ain't my object. There wa'n't a child but what Tempy set herself to work to see what she could do to please it. One time my brother's folks had been stopping here in the summer, from Massachusetts. The children was all little, and they broke up a sight of toys, and left 'em when they were going away. Tempy come right up after they rode by, to see if she couldn't help me set the house to rights, and she caught me just as I was going to fling some of the clutter into the stove. I was kind of tired out, starting 'em off in season. 'Oh, give me them!' says she, real pleading; and she wropped 'em up and took 'em home with her when she went, and she mended 'em up and stuck 'em together, and made some young one or other happy with every blessed one. You'd thought I'd done her the biggest favor. 'No thanks to me. I should ha' burnt 'em, Tempy,' says I."

"Some of 'em came to our house, I know," said Miss Binson. "She'd take a lot o' trouble to please a child, 'stead o' shoving of it out o' the way, like the rest of us when we're drove.

"I can tell you the biggest thing she ever done, and I don't know's there's anybody left but me to tell it. I don't want it forgot," Sarah Binson went on, looking up at the clock to see how the night was going. "It was that pretty-looking Trevor girl, who taught the Corners school, and married so well afterwards, out in New York State. You remember her, I dare say?"

"Certain," said Mrs. Crowe, with an air of interest.

"She was a splendid scholar, folks said, and give the school a great start; but she'd overdone herself getting her education, and working to pay for it, and she all broke down one spring, and Tempy made her come and stop with her a while,—you remember that? Well, she had an uncle, her mother's brother, out in Chicago, who was well off and friendly, and used to write to Lizzie Trevor, and I dare say make her some presents; but he was a lively, driving man, and didn't take time to stop and think about his folks. He hadn't seen her since she was a little girl. Poor Lizzie was so pale and weakly that she just got through the term o' school. She looked as if she was just going straight off in a decline. Tempy, she cosseted her up a while, and then, next thing folks knew, she was tellin' round how Miss Trevor had gone to see her uncle, and meant to visit Niagary Falls on the way, and stop over night. Now I happened to know, in ways I won't dwell on to explain, that the poor girl was in debt for her schoolin' when she come here, and her last quarter's pay had just squared it off at last, and left her without a cent ahead, hardly; but it had fretted her thinking of it, so she paid it all; those might have dunned her that she owed it to. An' I taxed Tempy about the girl's goin' off on such a journey till she owned up, rather'n have Lizzie blamed, that she'd given her sixty dollars, same's if she was rolling in riches, and sent her off to have a good rest and vacation."

"Sixty dollars!" exclaimed Mrs. Crowe. "Tempy only had ninety dollars a year that came in to her; rest of her livin' she got by helpin' about, with what she raised off this little piece o' ground, sand one side an' clay the other. An' how often I've heard her tell, years ago, that she'd rather see Niagary than any other sight in the world!"

The women looked at each other in silence; the magnitude of the generous sacrifice was almost too great for their comprehension.

"She was just poor enough to do that!" declared Mrs. Crowe at last, in an abandonment of feeling. "Say what you may, I feel humbled to the dust," and her companion ventured to say nothing. She never had given away sixty dollars at once, but it was simply because she never had it to give. It came to her very lips to say in explanation, "Tempy was so situated;" but she checked herself in time, for she would not betray her own loyal guarding of a dependent household.

"Folks say a great deal of generosity, and this one's being public-sperited, and that one free-handed about giving," said Mrs. Crowe, who was a little nervous in the silence. "I suppose we can't tell the sorrow it would be to some folks not to give, same's 't would be to me not to save. I seem kind of made for that, as if 't was what I'd got to do. I should feel sights better about it if I could make it evident what I was savin' for. If I had a child, now, Sarah Ann," and her voice was a little husky,—"if I had a child, I should think I was heapin' of it up because he was the one trained by the Lord to scatter it again for good. But here's Mr. Crowe and me, we can't do anything with money, and both of us like to keep things same's they've always been. Now Priscilla Dance was talking away like a mill-clapper, week before last. She'd think I would go right off and get one o' them new-fashioned gilt-and-white papers for the best room, and some new furniture, an' a marble-top table. And I looked at her, all struck up. 'Why,' says I, 'Priscilla, that nice old velvet paper ain't hurt a mite. I shouldn't feel 't was my best room without it. Dan'el says 't is the first thing he can remember rubbin' his little baby fingers on to it, and how splendid he thought them red roses was.' I maintain," continued Mrs. Crowe stoutly, "that folks wastes sights o' good money doin' just such foolish things. Tearin' out the insides o' meetin'-houses, and fixin' the pews different; 't was good enough as 't was with mendin'; then times come, an' they want to put it all back same's 't was before."

This touched upon an exciting subject to active members of that parish. Miss Binson and Mrs. Crowe belonged to opposite parties, and had at one time come as near hard feelings as they could, and yet escape them. Each hastened to speak of other things and to show her untouched friendliness.

"I do agree with you," said Sister Binson, "that few of us know what use to make of money, beyond every-day necessities. You've seen more o' the world than I have, and know what's expected. When it comes to taste and judgment about such things, I ought to defer to others;" and with this modest avowal the critical moment passed when there might have been an improper discussion.

In the silence that followed, the fact of their presence in a house of death grew more clear than before. There was something disturbing in the noise of a mouse gnawing at the dry boards of a closet wall near by. Both the watchers looked up anxiously at the clock; it was almost the middle of the night, and the whole world seemed to have left them alone with their solemn duty. Only the brook was awake.

"Perhaps we might give a look up-stairs now," whispered Mrs. Crowe, as if she hoped to hear some reason against their going just then to the chamber of death; but Sister Binson rose, with a serious and yet satisfied countenance, and lifted the small lamp from the table. She was much more used to watching than Mrs. Crowe, and much less affected by it. They opened the door into a small entry with a steep stairway; they climbed the creaking stairs, and entered the cold upper room on tiptoe. Mrs. Crowe's heart began to beat very fast as the lamp was put on a high bureau, and made long, fixed shadows about the walls. She went hesitatingly toward the solemn shape under its white drapery, and felt a sense of remonstrance as Sarah Ann gently, but in a business-like way, turned back the thin sheet.

"Seems to me she looks pleasanter and pleasanter," whispered Sarah Ann Binson impulsively, as they gazed at the white face with its wonderful smile. "To-morrow 't will all have faded out. I do believe they kind of wake up a day or two after they die, and it's then they go." She replaced the light covering, and they both turned quickly away; there was a chill in this upper room.

" 'T is a great thing for anybody to have got through, ain't it?" said Mrs. Crowe softly, as she began to go down the stairs on tiptoe. The warm air from the kitchen beneath met them with a sense of welcome and shelter.

"I don' know why it is, but I feel as near again to Tempy down here as I do up there," replied Sister Binson. "I feel as if the air was full of her, kind of. I can sense things, now and then, that she seems to say. Now I never was one to take up with no nonsense of sperits and such, but I declare I felt as if she told me just now to put some more wood into the stove."

Mrs. Crowe preserved a gloomy silence. She had suspected before this that her companion was of a weaker and more credulous disposition than herself. " 'T is a great thing to have got through," she repeated, ignoring definitely all that had last been said. "I suppose you know as well as I that Tempy was one that always feared death. Well, it's all put behind her now; she knows what 't is." Mrs. Crowe gave a little sigh, and Sister Binson's quick sympathies were stirred toward this other old friend, who also dreaded the great change.

"I'd never like to forgit almost those last words Tempy spoke plain to me," she said gently, like the comforter she truly was. "She looked up at me once or twice, that last afternoon after I come to set by her, and let Mis' Owen go home; and I says, 'Can I do anything to ease you, Tempy?' and the tears come into my eyes so I couldn't see what kind of a nod she give me. 'No, Sarah Ann, you can't, dear,' says she; and then she got her breath again, and says she, looking at me real meanin', 'I'm only a-gettin' sleepier and sleepier; that's all there is,' says she, and smiled up at me kind of wishful, and shut her eyes. I knew well enough all she meant. She'd been lookin' out for a chance to tell me, and I don' know's she ever said much afterwards."

Mrs. Crowe was not knitting; she had been listening too eagerly. "Yes, 't will be a comfort to think of that sometimes," she said, in acknowledgment.

"I know that old Dr. Prince said once, in evenin' meetin', that he'd watched by many a dyin' bed, as we well knew, and enough o' his sick folks had been scared o' dyin' their whole lives through; but when they come to the last, he'd never seen one but was willin', and most were glad, to go. ''T is as natural as bein' born or livin' on,' he said. I don't know what had moved him to speak that night. You know he wa'n't in the habit of it, and 't was the monthly concert of prayer for foreign missions anyways," said Sarah Ann; "but 't was a great stay to the mind to listen to his words of experience."

"There never was a better man," responded Mrs. Crowe, in a really cheerful tone. She had recovered from her feeling of nervous dread, the kitchen was so comfortable with lamplight and firelight; and just then the old clock began to tell the hour of twelve with leisurely whirring strokes.

Sister Binson laid aside her work, and rose quickly and went to the cupboard. "We'd better take a little to eat," she explained. "The night will go fast after this. I want to know if you went and made some o' your nice cupcake, while you was home to-day?" she asked, in a pleased tone; and Mrs. Crowe acknowledged such a gratifying piece of

thoughtfulness for this humble friend who denied herself
all luxuries. Sarah Ann brewed a generous cup of tea, and
the watchers drew their chairs up to the table presently,
and quelled their hunger with good country appetites. Sister Binson put a spoon into a small, old-fashioned glass of
preserved quince, and passed it to her friend. She was most
familiar with the house, and played the part of hostess.
"Spread some o' this on your bread and butter," she said
to Mrs. Crowe. "Tempy wanted me to use some three or
four times, but I never felt to. I know she'd like to have
us comfortable now, and would urge us to make a good
supper, poor dear."

"What excellent preserves she did make!" mourned Mrs.
Crowe. "None of us has got her light hand at doin' things
tasty. She made the most o' everything, too. Now, she only
had that one old quince-tree down in the far corner of the
piece, but she'd go out in the spring and tend to it, and
look at it so pleasant, and kind of expect the old thorny
thing into bloomin'."

"She was just the same with folks," said Sarah Ann.
"And she'd never git more'n a little apernful o' quinces,
but she'd have every mite o' goodness out o' those, and
set the glasses up onto her best-room closet shelf, so pleased.
'T wa'n't but a week ago to-morrow mornin' I fetched her
a little taste o' jelly in a teaspoon; and she says 'Thank ye,'
and took it, an' the minute she tasted it she looked up at
me as worried as could be. 'Oh, I don't want to eat that,'
says she. 'I always keep that in case o' sickness.' 'You're
goin' to have the good o' one tumbler yourself,' says I.
'I'd just like to know who's sick now, if you ain't!' An' she
couldn't help laughin', I spoke up so smart. Oh, dear me,
how I shall miss talkin' over things with her! She always
sensed things, and got just the p'int you meant."

"She didn't begin to age until two or three years ago,
did she?" asked Mrs. Crowe. "I never saw anybody keep
her looks as Tempy did. She looked young long after I
begun to feel like an old woman. The doctor used to say
't was her young heart, and I don't know but what he was
right. How she did do for other folks! There was one spell
she wasn't at home a day to a fortnight. She got most of
her livin' so, and that made her own potatoes and things

last her through. None o' the young folks could get married without her, and all the old ones was disappointed if she wa'n't round when they was down with sickness and had to go. An' cleanin', or tailorin' for boys, or rug-hookin',— there was nothin' but what she could do as handy as most. 'I do love to work,'—ain't you heard her say that twenty times a week?"

Sarah Ann Binson nodded, and began to clear away the empty plates. "We may want a taste o' somethin' more towards mornin'," she said. "There's plenty in the closet here; and in case some comes from a distance to the funeral, we'll have a little table spread after we get back to the house."

"Yes, I was busy all the mornin'. I've cooked up a sight o' things to bring over," said Mrs. Crowe. "I felt 't was the last I could do for her."

They drew their chairs near the stove again, and took up their work. Sister Binson's rocking-chair creaked as she rocked; the brook sounded louder than ever. It was more lonely when nobody spoke, and presently Mrs. Crowe returned to her thoughts of growing old.

"Yes, Tempy aged all of a sudden. I remember I asked her if she felt as well as common, one day, and she laughed at me good. There, when Mr. Crowe begun to look old, I couldn't help feeling as if somethin' ailed him, and like as not 't was somethin' he was goin' to git right over, and I dosed him for it stiddy, half of one summer."

"How many things we shall be wanting to ask Tempy!" exclaimed Sarah Ann Binson, after a long pause. "I can't make up my mind to doin' without her. I wish folks could come back just once, and tell us how 't is where they've gone. Seems then we could do without 'em better."

The brook hurried on, the wind blew about the house now and then; the house itself was a silent place, and the supper, the warm fire, and an absence of any new topics for conversation made the watchers drowsy. Sister Binson closed her eyes first, to rest them for a minute; and Mrs. Crowe glanced at her compassionately, with a new sympathy for the hard-worked little woman. She made up her mind to let Sarah Ann have a good rest, while she kept watch alone; but in a few minutes her own knitting was dropped, and she, too, fell asleep. Overhead, the pale shape of Tempy Dent, the outworn body of that generous, loving-hearted, simple soul, slept on also in its white raiment. Perhaps Tempy herself stood near, and saw her own life and its surroundings with new understanding. Perhaps she herself was the only watcher.

Later, by some hours, Sarah Ann Binson woke with a start. There was a pale light of dawn outside the small windows. Inside the kitchen, the lamp burned dim. Mrs. Crowe awoke, too.

"I think Tempy'd be the first to say 't was just as well we both had some rest," she said, not without a guilty feeling.

Her companion went to the outer door, and opened it wide. The fresh air was none too cold, and the brook's voice was not nearly so loud as it had been in the midnight darkness. She could see the shapes of the hills, and the great shadows that lay across the lower country. The east was fast growing bright.

" 'T will be a beautiful day for the funeral," she said, and turned again, with a sigh, to follow Mrs. Crowe up the stairs.

MARTHA'S LADY

1 One day, many years ago, the old Judge Pyne house wore an unwonted look of gayety and youthfulness. The high-fenced green garden was bright with June flowers. Under the elms in the large shady front yard you might see some chairs placed near together, as they often used to be when the family were all at home and life was going on gayly with eager talk and pleasure-making; when the elder judge, the grandfather, used to quote that great author, Dr. Johnson, and say to his girls, "Be brisk, be splendid, and be public."

One of the chairs had a crimson silk shawl thrown carelessly over its straight back, and a passer-by, who looked in through the latticed gate between the tall gate-posts with their white urns, might think that this piece of shining East Indian color was a huge red lily that had suddenly bloomed against the syringa bush. There were certain windows thrown wide open that were usually shut, and their curtains were blowing free in the light wind of a summer afternoon; it looked as if a large household had returned to the old house to fill the prim best rooms and find them full of cheer.

It was evident to every one in town that Miss Harriet Pyne, to use the village phrase, had company. She was the last of her family, and was by no means old; but being the last, and wonted to live with people much older than herself, she had formed all the habits of a serious elderly person. Ladies of her age, something past thirty, often wore discreet caps in those days, especially if they were married, but being single, Miss Harriet clung to youth in this respect, making the one concession of keeping her waving chestnut hair as smooth and stiffly arranged as possible. She had been the dutiful companion of her father and mother in their latest years, all her elder brothers and sisters having married and gone, or died and gone, out of the old house. Now that she was left alone it seemed quite the best thing frankly to accept the fact of age, and to turn more resolutely than ever to the companionship of duty and serious books. She was more serious and given to routine than her elders themselves, as sometimes happened when the daughters of New England gentlefolks were brought up wholly in the society of their elders. At thirty-five she had more reluctance than her mother to face an unforeseen occasion, certainly more than her grandmother, who had preserved some cheerful inheritance of gayety and worldliness from colonial times.

There was something about the look of the crimson silk shawl in the front yard to make one suspect that the sober customs of the best house in a quiet New England village were all being set at defiance, and once when the mistress of the house came to stand in her own doorway, she wore the pleased but somewhat apprehensive look of a guest. In these days New England life held the necessity of much dignity and discretion of behavior; there was the truest hospitality and good cheer in all occasional festivities, but it was sometimes a self-conscious hospitality, followed by an inexorable return to asceticism both of diet and of behavior. Miss Harriet Pyne belonged to the very dullest days of New England, those which perhaps held the most priggishness for the learned professions, the most limited interpretation of the word "evangelical," and the pettiest indifference to large things. The outbreak of a desire for larger religious freedom caused at first a most determined reaction toward formalism, especially in small and quiet villages like Ashford, intently busy with their own concerns. It was high time for a little leaven to begin its work, in this moment when the great impulses of the war for liberty had died away and those of the coming war for patriotism and a new freedom had hardly yet begun.

The dull interior, the changed life of the old house, whose former activities seemed to have fallen sound asleep, really typified these larger conditions, and a little leaven had made its easily recognized appearance in the shape of a light-hearted girl. She was Miss Harriet's young Boston cousin, Helena Vernon, who, half-amused and half-impatient at the unnecessary sober-mindedness of her hostess and of Ashford in general, had set herself to the difficult task of gayety. Cousin Harriet looked on at a succession of ingenious and, on the whole, innocent attempts at pleasure, as she might have looked on at the frolics of a kitten who easily substitutes a ball of yarn for the uncertainties of a bird or a wind-blown leaf, and who may at any moment ravel the fringe of a sacred curtain-tassle in preference to either.

Helena, with her mischievous appealing eyes, with her enchanting old songs and her guitar, seemed the more delightful and even reasonable because she was so kind to everybody, and because she was a beauty. She had the gift of most charming manners. There was all the unconscious lovely ease and grace that had come with the good breeding of her city home, where many pleasant people came and went; she had no fear, one had almost said no respect, of the individual, and she did not need to think of herself. Cousin Harriet turned cold with apprehension when she saw the minister coming in at the front gate, and wondered in agony if Martha were properly attired to go to the door, and would by any chance hear the knocker; it was Helena who, delighted to have anything happen, ran to the door to welcome the Reverend Mr. Crofton as if he were a congenial friend of her own age. She could behave with more or less propriety during the stately first visit, and even contrive to lighten it with modest mirth, and to extort the confession that the guest had a tenor voice, though sadly out of practice; but when the minister departed a little flattered, and hoping that he had not expressed himself too strongly for a pastor upon the poems of Emerson, and feeling the unusual stir of gallantry in his proper heart, it was Helena who caught the honored hat of the late Judge Pyne from its last resting-place in the hall, and holding it securely in both hands, mimicked the minister's self-conscious entrance. She copied his pompous and anxious expression in the dim parlor in such delicious fashion that Miss Harriet, who could not always extinguish a ready spark of the original sin of humor, laughed aloud.

"My dear!" she exclaimed severely the next moment, "I am ashamed of your being so disrespectful!" and then laughed again, and took the affecting old hat and carried it back to its place.

"I would not have had any one else see you for the

world," she said sorrowfully as she returned, feeling quite
self-possessed again, to the parlor doorway; but Helena still
sat in the minister's chair, with her small feet placed as his
stiff boots had been, and a copy of his solemn expression
before they came to speaking of Emerson and of the guitar.
"I wish I had asked him if he would be so kind as to climb
the cherry-tree," said Helena, unbending a little at the
discovery that her cousin would consent to laugh no more.
"There are all those ripe cherries on the top branches. I
can climb as high as he, but I can't reach far enough from
the last branch that will bear me. The minister is so long
and thin"—

"I don't know what Mr. Crofton would have thought of
you; he is a very serious young man," said cousin Harriet,
still ashamed of her laughter. "Martha will get the cherries
for you, or one of the men. I should not like to have Mr.
Crofton think you were frivolous, a young lady of your opportunities"—but Helena had escaped through the hall
and out at the garden door at the mention of Martha's
name. Miss Harriet Pyne sighed anxiously, and then smiled,
in spite of her deep convictions, as she shut the blinds and
tried to make the house look solemn again.

The front door might be shut, but the garden door at
the other end of the broad hall was wide open upon the
large sunshiny garden, where the last of the red and white
peonies and the golden lilies, and the first of the tall blue
larkspurs lent their colors in generous fashion. The straight
box borders were all in fresh and shining green of their
new leaves, and there was a fragrance of the old garden's in-
most life and soul blowing from the honeysuckle blossoms
on a long trellis. It was now late in the afternoon, and the
sun was low behind great apple-trees at the garden's end,
which threw their shadows over the short turf of the bleaching-green. The cherry-trees stood at one side in full sunshine,
and Miss Harriet, who presently came to the garden steps to
watch like a hen at the water's edge, saw her cousin's pretty
figure in its white dress of India muslin hurrying across
the grass. She was accompanied by the tall, ungainly shape
of Martha the new maid, who, dull and indifferent to every
one else, showed a surprising willingness and allegiance to
the young guest.

"Martha ought to be in the dining-room, already, slow as she is; it wants but half an hour of tea-time," said Miss Harriet, as she turned and went into the shaded house. It was Martha's duty to wait at table, and there had been many trying scenes and defeated efforts toward her education. Martha was certainly very clumsy, and she seemed the clumsier because she had replaced her aunt, a most skillful person, who had but lately married a thriving farm and its prosperous owner. It must be confessed that Miss Harriet was a most bewildering instructor, and that her pupil's brain was easily confused and prone to blunders. The coming of Helena had been somewhat dreaded by reason of this incompetent service, but the guest took no notice of frowns or futile gestures at the first tea-table, except to establish friendly relations with Martha on her own account by a reassuring smile. They were about the same age, and next morning, before cousin Harriet came down, Helena showed by a word and a quick touch the right way to do something that had gone wrong and been impossible to understand the night before. A moment later the anxious mistress came in without suspicion, but Martha's eyes were as affectionate as a dog's, and there was a new look of hopefulness on her face; this dreaded guest was a friend after all, and not a foe come from proud Boston to confound her ignorance and patient efforts.

The two young creatures, mistress and maid, were hurrying across the bleaching-green.

"I can't reach the ripest cherries," explained Helena politely, "and I think that Miss Pyne ought to send some to the minister. He has just made us a call. Why, Martha, you haven't been crying again!"

"Yes'm," said Martha sadly. "Miss Pyne always loves to send something to the minister," she acknowledged with interest, as if she did not wish to be asked to explain these latest tears.

"We'll arrange some of the best cherries in a pretty dish. I'll show you how, and you shall carry them over to the parsonage after tea," said Helena cheerfully, and Martha accepted the embassy with pleasure. Life was beginning to hold moments of something like delight in the last few days.

"You'll spoil your pretty dress, Miss Helena," Martha gave shy warning, and Miss Helena stood back and held up her skirts with unusual care while the country girl, in her heavy blue checked gingham, began to climb the cherry-tree like a boy.

Down came the scarlet fruit like bright rain into the green grass.

"Break some nice twigs with the cherries and leaves together; oh, you're a duck, Martha!" and Martha, flushed with delight, and looking far more like a thin and solemn blue heron, came rustling down to earth again, and gathered the spoils into her clean apron.

That night at tea, during her handmaiden's temporary absence, Miss Harriet announced, as if by way of apology, that she thought Martha was beginning to understand something about her work. "Her aunt was a treasure, she never had to be told anything twice; but Martha has been as clumsy as a calf," said the precise mistress of the house. "I have been afraid sometimes that I never could teach her anything. I was quite ashamed to have you come just now, and find me so unprepared to entertain a visitor."

"Oh, Martha will learn fast enough because she cares so much," said the visitor eagerly. "I think she is a dear good girl. I do hope that she will never go away. I think she does things better every day, cousin Harriet," added Helena pleadingly, with all her kind young heart. The china-closet door was open a little way, and Martha heard every word. From that moment, she not only knew what love was like, but she knew love's dear ambitions. To have come from a stony hill-farm and a bare small wooden house, was like a cave-dweller's coming to make a permanent home in an art museum, such had seemed the elaborateness and elegance of Miss Pyne's fashion of life; and Martha's simple brain was slow enough in its processes and recognitions. But with this sympathetic ally and defender, this exquisite Miss Helena who believed in her, all difficulties appeared to vanish.

Later that evening, no longer homesick or hopeless, Martha returned from her polite errand to the minister, and stood with a sort of triumph before the two ladies, who were sitting in the front doorway, as if they were waiting for visi-

tors, Helena still in her white muslin and red ribbons, and
Miss Harriet in a thin black silk. Being happily self-forget-
ful in the greatness of the moment, Martha's manners were
perfect, and she looked for once almost pretty and quite as
young as she was.

"The minister came to the door himself, and returned
his thanks. He said that cherries were always his favorite
fruit, and he was much obliged to both Miss Pyne and
Miss Vernon. He kept me waiting a few minutes, while he
got this book ready to send to you, Miss Helena."

"What are you saying, Martha? I have sent him nothing!" exclaimed Miss Pyne, much astonished. "What does
she mean, Helena?"

"Only a few cherries," explained Helena. "I thought
Mr. Crofton would like them after his afternoon of parish
calls. Martha and I arranged them before tea, and I sent
them with our compliments."

"Oh, I am very glad you did," said Miss Harriet, wondering, but much relieved. "I was afraid"—

"No, it was none of my mischief," answered Helena
daringly. "I did not think that Martha would be ready to go
so soon. I should have shown you how pretty they looked
among their green leaves. We put them in one of your
best white dishes with the openwork edge. Martha shall
show you to-morrow; mamma always likes to have them
so." Helena's fingers were busy with the hard knot of a
parcel.

"See this, cousin Harriet!" she announced proudly, as
Martha disappeared round the corner of the house, beaming with the pleasures of adventure and success. "Look!
the minister has sent me a book: Sermons on *what?* Sermons—it is so dark that I can't quite see."

"It must be his 'Sermons on the Seriousness of Life;' they
are the only ones he has printed, I believe," said Miss
Harriet, with much pleasure. "They are considered very fine
discourses. He pays you a great compliment, my dear. I
feared that he noticed your girlish levity."

"I behaved beautifully while he stayed," insisted Helena. "Ministers are only men," but she blushed with pleasure. It was certainly something to receive a book from its
author, and such a tribute made her of more value to the

whole reverent household. The minister was not only a
man, but a bachelor, and Helena was at the age that
best loves conquest; it was at any rate comfortable to be
reinstated in cousin Harriet's good graces.

"Do ask the kind gentleman to tea! He needs a little
cheering up," begged the siren in India muslin, as she laid
the shiny black volume of sermons on the stone doorstep
with an air of approval, but as if they had quite finished
their mission.

"Perhaps I shall, if Martha improves as much as she
has within the last day or two," Miss Harriet promised
hopefully. "It is something I always dread a little when I
am all alone, but I think Mr. Crofton likes to come. He
converses so elegantly."

2   These were the days of long visits, before affectionate
friends thought it quite worth while to take a hundred
miles' journey merely to dine or to pass a night in one another's houses. Helena lingered through the pleasant weeks
of early summer, and departed unwillingly at last to join
her family at the White Hills, where they had gone, like
other households of high social station, to pass the month
of August out of town. The happy-hearted young guest
left many lamenting friends behind her, and promised each
that she would come back again next year. She left the
minister a rejected lover, as well as the preceptor of the
academy, but with their pride unwounded, and it may have
been with wider outlooks upon the world and a less narrow
sympathy both for their own work in life and for their
neighbors' work and hindrances. Even Miss Harriet Pyne
herself had lost some of the unnecessary provincialism and
prejudice which had begun to harden a naturally good and
open mind and affectionate heart. She was conscious of
feeling younger and more free, and not so lonely. Nobody
had ever been so gay, so fascinating, or so kind as Helena,
so full of social resource, so simple and undemanding in her
friendliness. The light of her young life cast no shadow
on either young or old companions, her pretty clothes never
seemed to make other girls look dull or out of fashion.
When she went away up the street in Miss Harriet's car-

riage to take the slow train toward Boston and the gayeties of the new Profile House, where her mother waited impatiently with a group of Southern friends, it seemed as if there would never be any more picnics or parties in Ashford, and as if society had nothing left to do but to grow old and get ready for winter.

Martha came into Miss Helena's bedroom that last morning, and it was easy to see that she had been crying; she looked just as she did in that first sad week of homesickness and despair. All for love's sake she had been learning to do many things, and to do them exactly right; her eyes had grown quick to see the smallest chance for personal service. Nobody could be more humble and devoted; she looked years older than Helena, and wore already a touching air of caretaking.

"You spoil me, you dear Martha!" said Helena from the bed. "I don't know what they will say at home, I am so spoiled."

Martha went on opening the blinds to let in the brightness of the summer morning, but she did not speak.

"You are getting on splendidly, aren't you?" continued the little mistress. "You have tried so hard that you make me ashamed of myself. At first you crammed all the flowers together, and now you make them look beautiful. Last night cousin Harriet was so pleased when the table was so charming, and I told her that you did everything yourself, every bit. Won't you keep the flowers fresh and pretty in the house until I come back? It's so much pleasanter for Miss Pyne, and you'll feed my little sparrows, won't you? They're growing so tame."

"Oh, yes, Miss Helena!" and Martha looked almost angry for a moment, then she burst into tears and covered her face with her apron. "I couldn't understand a single thing when I first came. I never had been anywhere to see anything, and Miss Pyne frightened me when she talked. It was you made me think I could ever learn. I wanted to keep the place, 'count of mother and the little boys; we're dreadful hard pushed. Hepsy has been good in the kitchen; she said she ought to have patience with me, for she was awkward herself when she first came."

Helena laughed; she looked so pretty under the tasseled white curtains.

"I dare say Hepsy tells the truth," she said. "I wish you had told me about your mother. When I come again, some day we'll drive up country, as you call it, to see her. Martha! I wish you would think of me sometimes after I go away. Won't you promise?" and the bright young face suddenly grew grave. "I have hard times myself; I don't always learn things that I ought to learn, I don't always put things straight. I wish you wouldn't forget me ever, and would just believe in me. I think it does help more than anything."

"I won't forget," said Martha slowly. "I shall think of you every day." She spoke almost with indifference, as if she had been asked to dust a room, but she turned aside quickly and pulled the little mat under the hot water jug quite out of its former straightness; then she hastened away down the long white entry, weeping as she went.

3   To lose out of sight the friend whom one has loved and lived to please is to lose joy out of life. But if love is true, there comes presently a higher joy of pleasing the ideal, that is to say, the perfect friend. The same old happiness is lifted to a higher level. As for Martha, the girl who stayed behind in Ashford, nobody's life could seem duller to those who could not understand; she was slow of step, and her eyes were almost always downcast as if intent upon incessant toil; but they startled you when she looked up, with their shining light. She was capable of the happiness of holding fast to a great sentiment, the ineffable satisfaction of trying to please one whom she truly loved. She never thought of trying to make other people pleased with herself; all she lived for was to do the best she could for others, and to conform to an ideal, which grew at last to be like a saint's vision, a heavenly figure painted upon the sky.

On Sunday afternoons in summer, Martha sat by the window of her chamber, a low-storied little room, which looked into the side yard and the great branches of an elm-tree. She never sat in the old wooden rocking-chair except on Sundays like this; it belonged to the day of rest and to happy meditation. She wore her plain black dress and a clean white apron, and held in her lap a little wooden box, with a brass ring on top for a handle. She was past sixty years of age and looked even older, but there was the same look on her face that it had sometimes worn in girlhood. She was the same Martha; her hands were old-looking and work-worn, but her face still shone. It seemed like yesterday that Helena Vernon had gone away, and it was more than forty years.

War and peace had brought their changes and great anxieties, the face of the earth was furrowed by floods and fire, the faces of mistress and maid were furrowed by smiles and tears, and in the sky the stars shone on as if nothing had happened. The village of Ashford added a few pages to its unexciting history, the minister preached, the people listened; now and then a funeral crept along the street, and now and then the bright face of a little child rose above the horizon of a family pew. Miss Harriet Pyne lived on in the large white house, which gained more and more distinction because it suffered no changes, save successive repaintings and a new railing about its stately roof. Miss Harriet herself had moved far beyond the uncertainties of an anxious youth. She had long ago made all her decisions, and settled all necessary questions; her scheme of life was as faultless as the miniature landscape of a Japanese garden, and as easily kept in order. The only important change she would ever be capable of making was the final change to another and a better world; and for that nature itself would gently provide, and her own innocent life.

Hardly any great social event had ruffled the easy current of life since Helena Vernon's marriage. To this Miss Pyne had gone, stately in appearance and carrying gifts of some old family silver which bore the Vernon crest, but not without some protest in her heart against the uncertainties of married life. Helena was so equal to a happy independence and even to the assistance of other lives grown strangely dependent upon her quick sympathies and instinctive decisions, that it was hard to let her sink her personality in the affairs of another. Yet a brilliant English match was not without its attractions to an old-fashioned gentlewoman like Miss Pyne, and Helena herself was amazingly

happy; one day there had come a letter to Ashford, in which
her very heart seemed to beat with love and self-forgetfulness, to tell cousin Harriet of such new happiness and high
hope. "Tell Martha all that I say about my dear Jack,"
wrote the eager girl; "please show my letter to Martha,
and tell her that I shall come home next summer and bring
the handsomest and best man in the world to Ashford. I
have told him all about the dear house and the dear garden;
there never was such a lad to reach for cherries with his
six-foot-two." Miss Pyne, wondering a little, gave the letter
to Martha, who took it deliberately and as if she wondered
too, and went away to read it slowly by herself. Martha
cried over it, and felt a strange sense of loss and pain; it
hurt her heart a little to read about the cherry-picking. Her
idol seemed to be less her own since she had become the
idol of a stranger. She never had taken such a letter in her
hands before, but love at last prevailed, since Miss Helena
was happy, and she kissed the last page where her name
was written, feeling overbold, and laid the envelope on
Miss Pyne's secretary without a word.

The most generous love cannot but long for reassurance,
and Martha had the joy of being remembered. She was not
forgotten when the day of the wedding drew near, but she
never knew that Miss Helena had asked if cousin Harriet
would not bring Martha to town; she should like to have
Martha there to see her married. "She would help about the
flowers," wrote the happy girl; "I know she will like to
come, and I'll ask mamma to plan to have some one take
her all about Boston and make her have a pleasant time
after the hurry of the great day is over."

Cousin Harriet thought it was very kind and exactly like
Helena, but Martha would be out of her element; it was
most imprudent and girlish to have thought of such a thing.
Helena's mother would be far from wishing for any unnecessary guest just then, in the busiest part of her household, and it was best not to speak of the invitation. Some
day Martha should go to Boston if she did well, but not
now. Helena did not forget to ask if Martha had come, and
was astonished by the indifference of the answer. It was the
first thing which reminded her that she was not a fairy princess having everything her own way in that last day before

the wedding. She knew that Martha would have loved to be near, for she could not help understanding in that moment of her own happiness the love that was hidden in another heart. Next day this happy young princess, the bride, cut a piece of a great cake and put it into a pretty box that had held one of her wedding presents. With eager voices calling her, and all her friends about her, and her mother's face growing more and more wistful at the thought of parting, she still lingered and ran to take one or two trifles from her dressing-table, a little mirror and some tiny scissors that Martha would remember, and one of the pretty handkerchiefs marked with her maiden name. These she put in the box too; it was half a girlish freak and fancy, but she could not help trying to share her happiness, and Martha's life was so plain and dull. She whispered a message, and put the little package into cousin Harriet's hand for Martha as she said good-by. She was very fond of cousin Harriet. She smiled with a gleam of her old fun; Martha's puzzled look and tall awkward figure seemed to stand suddenly before her eyes, as she promised to come again to Ashford. Impatient voices called to Helena, her lover was at the door, and she hurried away, leaving her old home and her girlhood gladly. If she had only known it, as she kissed cousin Harriet good-by, they were never going to see each other again until they were old women. The first step that she took out of her father's house that day, married, and full of hope and joy, was a step that led her away from the green elms of Boston Common and away from her own country and those she loved best, to a brilliant, much-varied foreign life, and to nearly all the sorrows and nearly all the joys that the heart of one woman could hold or know.

On Sunday afternoons Martha used to sit by the window in Ashford and hold the wooden box which a favorite young brother, who afterward died at sea, had made for her, and she used to take out of it the pretty little box with a gilded cover that had held the piece of wedding-cake, and the small scissors, and the blurred bit of a mirror in its silver case; as for the handkerchief with the narrow lace edge, once in two or three years she sprinkled it as if it were a flower, and spread it out in the sun on the old bleaching-green, and sat near by in the shrubbery to watch lest some bold robin or cherry-bird should seize it and fly away.

4   Miss Harriet Pyne was often congratulated upon the good fortune of having such a helper and friend as Martha. As time went on this tall, gaunt woman, always thin, always slow, gained a dignity of behavior and simple affectionateness of look which suited the charm and dignity of the ancient house. She was unconsciously beautiful like a saint, like the picturesqueness of a lonely tree which lives to shelter unnumbered lives and to stand quietly in its place. There was such rustic homeliness and constancy belonging to her, such beautiful powers of apprehension, such reticence, such gentleness for those who were troubled or sick; all these gifts and graces Martha hid in her heart. She never joined the church because she thought she was not good enough, but life was such a passion and happiness of service that it was impossible not to be devout, and she was always in her humble place on Sundays, in the back pew next the door. She had been educated by a remembrance; Helena's young eyes forever looked at her reassuringly from a gay girlish face. Helena's sweet patience in teaching her own awkwardness could never be forgotten.

"I owe everything to Miss Helena," said Martha, half aloud, as she sat alone by the window; she had said it to herself a thousand times. When she looked in the little keepsake mirror she always hoped to see some faint reflection of Helena Vernon, but there was only her own brown old New England face to look back at her wonderingly.

Miss Pyne went less and less often to pay visits to her friends in Boston; there were very few friends left to come to Ashford and make long visits in the summer, and life grew more and more monotonous. Now and then there came news from across the sea and messages of remembrance, letters that were closely written on thin sheets of paper, and that spoke of lords and ladies, of great journeys, of the death of little children and the proud successes of boys at school, of the wedding of Helena Dysart's only daughter; but even that had happened years ago. These things seemed far away and vague, as if they belonged to a story and not to life itself; the true links with the past were quite different. There was the unvarying flock of ground-sparrows that Helena had begun to feed; every morning Martha scattered crumbs for them from the side doorsteps while Miss Pyne watched from the dining-room window, and they were counted and cherished year by year.

Miss Pyne herself had many fixed habits, but little ideality or imagination, and so at last it was Martha who took thought for her mistress, and gave freedom to her own good taste. After a while, without any one's observing the change, the every-day ways of doing things in the house came to be the stately ways that had once belonged only to the entertainment of guests. Happily both mistress and maid seized all possible chances for hospitality, yet Miss Harriet nearly always sat alone at her exquisitely served table with its fresh flowers, and the beautiful old china which Martha handled so lovingly that there was no good excuse for keeping it hidden on closet shelves. Every year when the old cherry-trees were in fruit, Martha carried the round white old English dish with a fretwork edge, full of pointed green leaves and scarlet cherries, to the minister, and his wife never quite understood why every year he blushed and looked so conscious of the pleasure, and thanked Martha as if he had received a very particular attention. There was no pretty suggestion toward the pursuit of the fine art of housekeeping in Martha's limited acquaintance with newspapers that she did not adopt; there was no refined old custom of the Pyne housekeeping that she consented to let go. And every day, as she had promised, she thought of Miss Helena,—oh, many times in every day: whether this thing would please her, or that be likely to fall in with her fancy or ideas of fitness. As far as was possible the rare news that reached Ashford through an occasional letter or the talk of guests was made part of Martha's own life, the history of her own heart. A worn old geography often stood open at the map of Europe on the lightstand in her room, and a little old-fashioned gilt button, set with a bit of glass like a ruby, that had broken and fallen from the trimming of one of Helena's dresses, was used to mark the city of her dwelling-place. In the changes of a diplomatic life Martha followed her lady all about the map. Sometimes the button was at Paris, and sometimes at Madrid; once, to her great anxiety, it remained long at St. Petersburg. For such a slow scholar Martha was not unlearned at last, since everything about life in these foreign towns was of interest to her faithful heart. She satisfied her own mind as she threw crumbs to the tame sparrows; it was all part of the same thing and for the same affectionate reasons.

5   One Sunday afternoon in early summer Miss Harriet Pyne came hurrying along the entry that led to Martha's room and called two or three times before its inhabitant could reach the door. Miss Harriet looked unusually cheerful and excited, and she held something in her hand. "Where are you, Martha?" she called again. "Come quick, I have something to tell you!"

"Here I am, Miss Pyne," said Martha, who had only stopped to put her precious box in the drawer, and to shut the geography.

"Who do you think is coming this very night at half-past six? We must have everything as nice as we can; I must see Hannah at once. Do you remember my cousin Helena who has lived abroad so long? Miss Helena Vernon,—the Honorable Mrs. Dysart, she is now."

"Yes, I remember her," answered Martha, turning a little pale.

"I knew that she was in this country, and I had written to ask her to come for a long visit," continued Miss Harriet, who did not often explain things, even to Martha, though she was always conscientious about the kind messages that were sent back by grateful guests. "She telegraphs that she means to anticipate her visit by a few days and come to me at once. The heat is beginning in town, I suppose. I daresay, having been a foreigner so long, she does not mind traveling on Sunday. Do you think Hannah will be prepared? We must have tea a little later."

"Yes, Miss Harriet," said Martha. She wondered that she could speak as usual, there was such a ringing in her ears. "I shall have time to pick some fresh strawberries; Miss Helena is so fond of our strawberries."

"Why, I had forgotten," said Miss Pyne, a little puzzled by something quite unusual in Martha's face. "We must expect to find Mrs. Dysart a good deal changed, Martha; it is a great many years since she was here; I have not seen her since her wedding, and she has had a great deal of trouble, poor girl. You had better open the parlor chamber, and make it ready before you go down."

"It is all ready," said Martha. "I can carry some of those little sweet-brier roses upstairs before she comes."

"Yes, you are always thoughtful," said Miss Pyne, with unwonted feeling.

Martha did not answer. She glanced at the telegram wistfully. She had never really suspected before that Miss Pyne knew nothing of the love that had been in her heart all these years; it was half a pain and half a golden joy to keep such a secret; she could hardly bear this moment of surprise.

Presently the news gave wings to her willing feet. When Hannah, the cook, who never had known Miss Helena, went to the parlor an hour later on some errand to her old mistress, she discovered that this stranger guest must be a very important person. She had never seen the tea-table look exactly as it did that night, and in the parlor itself there were fresh blossoming boughs in the old East India jars, and lilies in the paneled hall, and flowers everywhere, as if there were some high festivity.

Miss Pyne sat by the window watching, in her best dress, looking stately and calm; she seldom went out now, and it was almost time for the carriage. Martha was just coming in from the garden with the strawberries, and with more flowers in her apron. It was a bright cool evening in June, the golden robins sang in the elms, and the sun was going down behind the apple-trees at the foot of the garden. The beautiful old house stood wide open to the long-expected guest.

"I think that I shall go down to the gate," said Miss Pyne, looking at Martha for approval, and Martha nodded and they went together slowly down the broad front walk.

There was a sound of horses and wheels on the roadside turf: Martha could not see at first; she stood back inside the gate behind the white lilac-bushes as the carriage came. Miss Pyne was there; she was holding out both arms and taking a tired, bent little figure in black to her heart. "Oh, my Miss Helena is an old woman like me!" and Martha gave a pitiful sob; she had never dreamed it would be like this; this was the one thing she could not bear.

"Where are you, Martha?" called Miss Pyne. "Martha will bring these in; you have not forgotten my good Martha, Helena?" Then Mrs. Dysart looked up and smiled just as she used to smile in the old days. The young eyes were there still in the changed face, and Miss Helena had come.

That night Martha waited in her lady's room just as she used, humble and silent, and went through with the old unforgotten loving services. The long years seemed like days. At last she lingered a moment trying to think of something else that might be done, then she was going silently away, but Helena called her back. She suddenly knew the whole story and could hardly speak.

"Oh, my dear Martha!" she cried, "won't you kiss me good-night? Oh, Martha, have you remembered like this, all these long years!"

THE GUESTS OF
MRS. TIMMS

1 Mrs. Persis Flagg stood in her front doorway taking
leave of Miss Cynthia Pickett, who had been making a long
call. They were not intimate friends. Miss Pickett always
came formally to the front door and rang when she paid
her visits, but, the week before, they had met at the county
conference, and happened to be sent to the same house for
entertainment, and so had deepened and renewed the pleasures of acquaintance.

It was an afternoon in early June; the syringa-bushes were
tall and green on each side of the stone doorsteps, and were
covered with their lovely white and golden flowers. Miss
Pickett broke off the nearest twig, and held it before her
prim face as she talked. She had a pretty childlike smile
that came and went suddenly, but her face was not one
that bore the marks of many pleasures. Mrs. Flagg was a
tall, commanding sort of person, with an air of satisfaction
and authority.

"Oh, yes, gather all you want," she said stiffly, as Miss
Pickett took the syringa without having asked beforehand;
but she had an amiable expression, and just now her large
countenance was lighted up by pleasant anticipation.

"We can tell early what sort of a day it's goin' to be,"
she said eagerly. "There ain't a cloud in the sky now. I'll
stop for you as I come along, or if there should be anything
unforeseen to detain me, I'll send you word. I don't expect
you'd want to go if it wa'n't so that I could?"

"Oh my sakes, no!" answered Miss Pickett discreetly,
with a timid flush. "You feel certain that Mis' Timms
won't be put out? I shouldn't feel free to go unless I went
'long o' you."

"Why, nothin' could be plainer than her words," said
Mrs. Flagg in a tone of reproval. "You saw how she urged
me, an' had over all that talk about how we used to see
each other often when we both lived to Longport, and told
how she'd been thinkin' of writin', and askin' if it wa'n't

so I should be able to come over and stop three or four days as soon as settled weather come, because she couldn't make no fire in her best chamber on account of the chimbley smokin' if the wind wa'n't just right. You see how she felt toward me, kissin' of me comin' and goin'? Why, she even asked me who I employed to do over my bonnet, Miss Pickett, just as interested as if she was a sister; an' she remarked she should look for us any pleasant day after we all got home, an' were settled after the conference."

Miss Pickett smiled, but did not speak, as if she expected more arguments still.

"An' she seemed just about as much gratified to meet with you again. She seemed to desire to meet you again very particular," continued Mrs. Flagg. "She really urged us to come together an' have a real good day talkin' over old times—there, don't le' 's go all over it again! I've always heard she'd made that old house of her aunt Bascoms' where she lives look real handsome. I once heard her best parlor carpet described as being an elegant carpet, different from any there was round here. Why, nobody couldn't be more cordial, Miss Pickett; you ain't goin' to give out just at the last?"

"Oh, no!" answered the visitor hastily; "no, 'm! I want to go full as much as you do, Mis' Flagg, but you see I never was so well acquainted with Mis' Cap'n Timms, an' I always seem to dread putting myself for'ard. She certain was very urgent, an' she said plain enough to come any day next week, an' here 't is Wednesday, though of course she wouldn't look for us either Monday or Tuesday. 'T will be a real pleasant occasion, an' now we've been to the conference it don't seem near so much effort to start."

"Why, I don't think nothin' of it," said Mrs. Flagg proudly. "We shall have a grand good time, goin' together an' all, I feel sure."

Miss Pickett still played with her syringa flower, tapping her thin cheek, and twirling the stem with her fingers. She looked as if she were going to say something more, but after a moment's hesitation she turned away.

"Good-afternoon, Mis' Flagg," she said formally, looking up with a quick little smile; "I enjoyed my call; I hope I ain't kep' you too late; I don't know but what it's 'most tea-time. Well, I shall look for you in the mornin'."

"Good-afternoon, Miss Pickett; I'm glad I was in when you came. Call again, won't you?" said Mrs. Flagg. "Yes; you may expect me in good season," and so they parted. Miss Pickett went out at the neat clicking gate in the white fence, and Mrs. Flagg a moment later looked out of her sitting-room window to see if the gate were latched, and felt the least bit disappointed to find that it was. She sometimes went out after the departure of a guest, and fastened the gate herself with a loud, rebuking sound. Both of these Woodville women lived alone, and were very precise in their way of doing things.

2 The next morning dawned clear and bright, and Miss Pickett rose even earlier than usual. She found it most difficult to decide which of her dresses would be best to wear. Summer was still so young that the day had all the freshness of spring, but when the two friends walked away together along the shady street, with a chorus of golden robins singing high overhead in the elms, Miss Pickett decided that she had made a wise choice of her second-best black silk gown, which she had just turned again and freshened. It was neither too warm for the season nor too cool, nor did it look overdressed. She wore her large cameo pin, and this, with a long watch-chain, gave an air of proper mural decoration. She was a straight, flat little person, as if, when not in use, she kept herself, silk dress and all, between the leaves of a book. She carried a noticeable parasol with a fringe, and a small shawl, with a pretty border, neatly folded over her left arm. Mrs. Flagg always dressed in black cashmere, and looked, to hasty observers, much the same one day as another; but her companion recognized the fact that this was the best black cashmere of all, and for a moment quailed at the thought that Mrs. Flagg was paying such extreme deference to their prospective hostess. The visit turned for a moment into an unexpectedly solemn formality, and pleasure seemed to wane before Cynthia Pickett's eyes, yet with great courage she never slackened a

single step. Mrs. Flagg carried a somewhat worn black leather handbag, which Miss Pickett regretted; it did not give the visit that casual and unpremeditated air which she felt to be more elegant.

"Sha'n't I carry your bag for you?" she asked timidly. Mrs. Flagg was the older and more important person.

"Oh, dear me, no," answered Mrs. Flagg. "My pocket's so remote, in case I should desire to sneeze or anything, that I thought 't would be convenient for carrying my handkerchief and pocket-book; an' then I just tucked in a couple o' glasses o' my crab-apple jelly for Mis' Timms. She used to be a great hand for preserves of every sort, an' I thought 't would be a kind of an attention, an' give rise to conversation. I know she used to make excellent drop-cakes when we was both residin' to Longport; folks used to say she never would give the right receipt, but if I get a real good chance, I mean to ask her. Or why can't you, if I start talkin' about receipts—why can't you say, sort of innocent, that I have always spoken frequently of her drop-cakes, an' ask for the rule? She would be very sensible to the compliment, and could pass it off if she didn't feel to indulge us. There, I do so wish you would!"

"Yes, 'm," said Miss Pickett doubtfully; "I'll try to make the opportunity. I'm very partial to drop-cakes. Was they flour or rye, Mis' Flagg?"

"They was flour, dear," replied Mrs. Flagg approvingly; "crisp an' light as any you ever see."

"I wish I had thought to carry somethin' to make it pleasant," said Miss Pickett, after they had walked a little farther; "but there, I don't know's 't would look just right, this first visit, to offer anything to such a person as Mis' Timms. In case I ever go over to Baxter again I won't forget to make her some little present, as nice as I've got. 'T was certain very polite of her to urge me to come with you. I did feel very doubtful at first. I didn't know but she thought it behooved her, because I was in your company at the conference, and she wanted to save my feelin's, and yet expected I would decline. I never was well acquainted with her; our folks wasn't well off when I first knew her; 't was before uncle Cap'n Dyer passed away an' remembered mother an' me in his will. We couldn't make no han'some companies in them days, so we didn't go to none, an' kep' to ourselves; but in my grandmother's time, mother always said, the families was very friendly. I shouldn't feel like goin' over to pass the day with Mis' Timms if I didn't mean to ask her to return the visit. Some don't think o' these things, but mother was very set about not bein' done for when she couldn't make no return."

"'When it rains porridge hold up your dish,'" said Mrs. Flagg; but Miss Pickett made no response beyond a feeble "Yes, 'm," which somehow got caught in her pale-green bonnet-strings.

"There, 't ain't no use to fuss too much over all them things," proclaimed Mrs. Flagg, walking along at a good pace with a fine sway of her skirts, and carrying her head high. "Folks walks right by an' forgits all about you; folks can't always be going through with just so much. You'd had a good deal better time, you an' your ma, if you'd been freer in your ways; now don't you s'pose you would? 'T ain't what you give folks to eat so much as 't is makin' 'em feel welcome. Now, there's Mis' Timms; when we was to Longport she was dreadful methodical. She wouldn't let Cap'n Timms fetch nobody home to dinner without lettin' of her know, same's other cap'ns' wives had to submit to. I was thinkin', when she was so cordial over to Danby, how she'd softened with time. Years do learn folks somethin'! She did seem very pleasant an' desirous. There, I am so glad we got started; if she'd gone an' got up a real good dinner to-day, an' then not had us come till to-morrow, 't would have been real too bad. Where anybody lives alone such a thing is very tryin'."

"Oh, so 't is!" said Miss Pickett. "There, I'd like to tell you what I went through with year before last. They come an' asked me one Saturday night to entertain the minister, that time we was having candidates"—

"I guess we'd better step along faster," said Mrs. Flagg suddenly. "Why, Miss Pickett, there's the stage comin' now! It's dreadful prompt, seems to me. Quick! there's folks awaitin', an' I sha'n't get to Baxter in no state to visit Mis' Cap'n Timms if I have to ride all the way there backward!"

3   The stage was not full inside. The group before the store proved to be made up of spectators, except one man, who climbed at once to a vacant seat by the driver. Inside there was only one person, after two passengers got out, and she preferred to sit with her back to the horses, so that Mrs. Flagg and Miss Pickett settled themselves comfortably in the coveted corners of the back seat. At first they took no notice of their companion, and spoke to each other in low tones, but presently something attracted the attention of all three and engaged them in conversation.

"I never was over this road before," said the stranger. "I s'pose you ladies are well acquainted all along."

"We have often traveled it in past years. We was over this part of it last week goin' and comin' from the county conference," said Mrs. Flagg in a dignified manner.

"What persuasion?" inquired the fellow-traveler, with interest.

"Orthodox," said Miss Pickett quickly, before Mrs. Flagg could speak. "It was a very interestin' occasion; this other lady an' me stayed through all the meetin's."

"I ain't Orthodox," announced the stranger, waiving any interest in personalities. "I was brought up amongst the Freewill Baptists."

"We're well acquainted with several of that denomination in our place," said Mrs. Flagg, not without an air of patronage. "They've never built 'em no church; there ain't but a scattered few."

"They prevail where I come from," said the traveler. "I'm goin' now to visit with a Freewill lady. We was to a conference together once, same's you an' your friend, but 't was a state conference. She asked me to come some time an' make her a good visit, and I'm on my way now. I didn't seem to have nothin' to keep me to home."

"We're all goin' visitin' to-day, ain't we?" said Mrs. Flagg sociably; but no one carried on the conversation.

The day was growing very warm; there was dust in the sandy road, but the fields of grass and young growing crops looked fresh and fair. There was a light haze over the hills, and birds were thick in the air. When the stage-horses stopped to walk, you could hear the crows caw, and the bobolinks singing, in the meadows. All the farmers were busy in their fields.

"It don't seem but little ways to Baxter, does it?" said Miss Pickett, after a while. "I felt we should pass a good deal o' time on the road, but we must be pretty near halfway there a'ready."

"Why, more'n half!" exclaimed Mrs. Flagg. "Yes; there's Beckett's Corner right ahead, an' the old Beckett house. I haven't been on this part of the road for so long that I feel kind of strange. I used to visit over here when I was a girl. There's a nephew's widow owns the place now. Old Miss Susan Beckett willed it to him, an' he died; but she resides there an' carries on the farm, an unusual smart woman, everybody says. Ain't it pleasant here, right out among the farms!"

"Mis' Beckett's place, did you observe?" said the stranger, leaning forward to listen to what her companions said. "I expect that's where I'm goin'—Mis' Ezra Beckett's?"

"That's the one," said Miss Pickett and Mrs. Flagg together, and they both looked out eagerly as the coach drew up to the front door of a large old yellow house that stood close upon the green turf of the roadside.

The passenger looked pleased and eager, and made haste to leave the stage with her many bundles and bags. While she stood impatiently tapping at the brass knocker, the stage-driver landed a large trunk, and dragged it toward the door across the grass. Just then a busy-looking middle-aged woman made her appearance, with floury hands and a look as if she were prepared to be somewhat on the defensive.

"Why, how do you do, Mis' Beckett?" exclaimed the guest. "Well, here I be at last. I didn't know's you thought I was ever comin'. Why, I do declare, I believe you don't recognize me, Mis' Beckett."

"I believe I don't," said the self-possessed hostess. "Ain't you made some mistake, ma'am?"

"Why, don't you recollect we was together that time to the state conference, an' you said you should be pleased to have me come an' make you a visit some time, an' I said I would certain. There, I expect I look more natural to you now."

Mrs. Beckett appeared to be making the best possible effort, and gave a bewildered glance, first at her unexpected visitor, and then at the trunk. The stage-driver, who watched this encounter with evident delight, turned away with reluctance. "I can't wait all day to see how they settle it," he said, and mounted briskly to the box, and the stage rolled on.

"He might have waited just a minute to see," said Miss Pickett indignantly, but Mrs. Flagg's head and shoulders were already far out of the stage window—the house was on her side. "She ain't got in yet," she told Miss Pickett triumphantly. "I could see 'em quite a spell. With that trunk, too! I do declare, how inconsiderate some folks is!"

" 'T was pushin' an acquaintance most too far, wa'n't it?" agreed Miss Pickett. "There, 't will be somethin' laughable to tell Mis' Timms. I never see anything more divertin'. I shall kind of pity that woman if we have to stop an' git her as we go back this afternoon."

"Oh, don't let's forgit to watch for her," exclaimed Mrs. Flagg, beginning to brush off the dust of travel. "There, I feel an excellent appetite, don't you? And we ain't got more'n three or four miles to go, if we have that. I wonder what Mis' Timms is likely to give us for dinner; she spoke of makin' a good many chicken-pies, an' I happened to remark how partial I was to 'em. She felt above most of the things we had provided for us over to the conference. I know she was always counted the best o' cooks when I knew her so well to Longport. Now, don't you forget, if there's a suitable opportunity, to inquire about the drop-cakes;" and Miss Pickett, a little less doubtful than before, renewed her promise.

4   "My gracious, won't Mis' Timms be pleased to see us! It's just exactly the day to have company. And ain't Baxter a sweet pretty place?" said Mrs. Flagg, as they walked up the main street. "Cynthy Pickett, now ain't you proper glad you come? I felt sort o' calm about it part o' the time yesterday, but I ain't felt so like a girl for a good while. I do believe I'm goin' to have a splendid time."

Miss Pickett glowed with equal pleasure as she paced

along. She was less expansive and enthusiastic than her companion, but now that they were fairly in Baxter, she lent herself generously to the occasion. The social distinction of going away to spend a day in company with Mrs. Flagg was by no means small. She arranged the folds of her shawl more carefully over her arm so as to show the pretty palm-leaf border, and then looked up with great approval to the row of great maples that shaded the broad sidewalk. "I wonder if we can't contrive to make time to go an' see old Miss Nancy Fell?" she ventured to ask Mrs. Flagg. "There ain't a great deal o' time before the stage goes at four o'clock; 't will pass quickly, but I should hate to have her feel hurt. If she was one we had visited often at home, I shouldn't care so much, but such folks feel any little slight. She was a member of our church; I think a good deal of that."

"Well, I hardly know what to say," faltered Mrs. Flagg coldly. "We might just look in a minute; I shouldn't want her to feel hurt."

"She was one that always did her part, too," said Miss Pickett, more boldly. "Mr. Cronin used to say that she was more generous with her little than many was with their much. If she hadn't lived in a poor part of the town, and so been occupied with a different kind of people from us, 't would have made a difference. They say she's got a comfortable little home over here, an' keeps house for a nephew. You know she was to our meeting one Sunday last winter, and 'peared dreadful glad to get back; folks seemed glad to see her, too. I don't know as you were out."

"She always wore a friendly look," said Mrs. Flagg indulgently. "There, now, there's Mis' Timms's residence; it's handsome, ain't it, with them big spruce-trees? I expect she may be at the window now, an' see us as we come along. Is my bonnet on straight, an' everything? The blinds looks open in the room this way; I guess she's to home fast enough."

The friends quickened their steps, and with shining eyes and beating hearts hastened forward. The slightest mists of uncertainty were now cleared away; they gazed at the house with deepest pleasure; the visit was about to begin.

They opened the front gate and went up the short walk,

noticing the pretty herringbone pattern of the bricks, and as they stood on the high steps Cynthia Pickett wondered whether she ought not to have worn her best dress, even though there was lace at the neck and sleeves, and she usually kept it for the most formal of tea-parties and exceptional parish festivals. In her heart she commended Mrs. Flagg for that familiarity with the ways of a wider social world which had led her to wear the very best among her black cashmeres.

"She's a good while coming to the door," whispered Mrs. Flagg presently. "Either she didn't see us, or else she's slipped upstairs to make some change, an' is just goin' to let us ring again. I've done it myself sometimes. I'm glad we come right over after her urgin' us so; it seems more cordial than to keep her expectin' us. I expect she'll urge us terribly to remain with her over-night."

"Oh, I ain't prepared," began Miss Pickeft, but she looked pleased. At that moment there was a slow withdrawal of the bolt inside, and a key was turned, the front door opened, and Mrs. Timms stood before them with a smile. Nobody stopped to think at that moment what kind of smile it was.

"Why, if it ain't Mis' Flagg," she exclaimed politely, "an' Miss Pickett too! I am surprised!"

The front entry behind her looked well furnished, but not exactly hospitable; the stairs with their brass rods looked so clean and bright that it did not seem as if anybody had ever gone up or come down. A cat came purring out, but Mrs. Timms pushed her back with a determined foot, and hastily closed the sitting-room door. Then Miss Pickett let Mrs. Flagg precede her, as was becoming, and they went into a darkened parlor, and found their way to some chairs, and seated themselves solemnly.

" 'T is a beautiful day, ain't it?" said Mrs. Flagg, speaking first. "I don't know's I ever enjoyed the ride more. We've been having a good deal of rain since we saw you at the conference, and the country looks beautiful."

"Did you leave Woodville this morning? I thought I hadn't heard you was in town," replied Mrs. Timms formally. She was seated just a little too far away to make things seem exactly pleasant. The darkness of the best room seemed to retreat somewhat, and Miss Pickett looked over by the door, where there was a pale gleam from the side-lights in the hall, to try to see the pattern of the carpet; but her effort failed.

"Yes, 'm," replied Mrs. Flagg to the question. "We left Woodville about half past eight, but it is quite a ways from where we live to where you take the stage. The stage does come slow, but you don't seem to mind it such a beautiful day."

"Why, you must have come right to see me first!" said Mrs. Timms, warming a little as the visit went on. "I hope you're going to make some stop in town. I'm sure it was very polite of you to come right an' see me; well, it's very pleasant, I declare. I wish you'd been in Baxter last Sabbath; our minister did give us an elegant sermon on faith an' works. He spoke of the conference, and gave his views on some o' the questions that came up, at Friday evenin' meetin'; but I felt tired after getting home, an' so I wasn't out. We feel very much favored to have such a man amon'st us. He's building up the parish very considerable. I understand the pew-rents come to thirty-six dollars more this quarter than they did last."

"We also feel grateful in Woodville for our pastor's ef-forts," said Miss Pickett; but Mrs. Timms turned her head away sharply, as if the speech had been untimely, and trembling Miss Pickett had interrupted.

"They're thinking here of raisin' Mr. Barlow's salary an-other year," the hostess added; "a good many of the old parishioners have died off, but every one feels to do what they can. Is there much interest among the young people in Woodville, Mis' Flagg?"

"Considerable at this time, ma'am," answered Mrs. Flagg, without enthusiasm, and she listened with unusual silence to the subsequent fluent remarks of Mrs. Timms.

The parlor seemed to be undergoing the slow processes of a winter dawn. After a while the three women could begin to see one another's faces, which aided them some-what in carrying on a serious and impersonal conversation. There were a good many subjects to be touched upon, and Mrs. Timms said everything that she should have said, ex-cept to invite her visitors to walk upstairs and take off their bonnets. Mrs. Flagg sat her parlor-chair as if it were a throne, and carried her banner of self-possession as high as she knew how, but toward the end of the call even she began to feel hurried.

"Won't you ladies take a glass of wine an' a piece of cake after your ride?" inquired Mrs. Timms, with an air of hospitality that almost concealed the fact that neither cake nor wine was anywhere to be seen; but the ladies bowed and declined with particular elegance. Altogether it was a visit of extreme propriety on both sides, and Mrs. Timms was very pressing in her invitation that her guests should stay longer.

"Thank you, but we ought to be going," answered Mrs. Flagg, with a little show of ostentation, and looking over her shoulder to be sure that Miss Pickett had risen too. "We've got some little ways to go," she added with dignity. "We should be pleased to have you call an' see us in case you have occasion to come to Woodville," and Miss Pickett faintly seconded the invitation. It was in her heart to add, "Come any day next week," but her courage did not rise so high as to make the words audible. She looked as if she were ready to cry; her usual smile had burnt itself out into gray ashes; there was a white, appealing look about her mouth. As they emerged from the dim parlor and stood at the open front door, the bright June day, the golden-green trees, almost blinded their eyes. Mrs. Timms was more smiling and cordial than ever.

"There, I ought to have thought to offer you fans; I am afraid you was warm after walking," she exclaimed, as if to leave no stone of courtesy unturned. "I have so enjoyed meeting you again, I wish it was so you could stop longer. Why, Mis' Flagg, we haven't said one word about old times when we lived to Longport. I've had news from there, too, since I saw you; my brother's daughter-in-law was here to pass the Sabbath after I returned."

Mrs. Flagg did not turn back to ask any questions as she stepped stiffly away down the brick walk. Miss Pickett followed her, raising the fringed parasol; they both made ceremonious little bows as they shut the high white gate behind them. "Good-by," said Mrs. Timms finally, as she stood in the door with her set smile; and as they departed she came out and began to fasten up a rosebush that climbed a narrow white ladder by the steps.

"Oh, my goodness alive!" exclaimed Mrs. Flagg, after they had gone some distance in aggrieved silence, "if I haven't gone and forgotten my bag! I ain't goin' back, whatever happens. I expect she'll trip over it in that dark room and break her neck!"

"I brought it; I noticed you'd forgotten it," said Miss Pickett timidly, as if she hated to deprive her companion of even that slight consolation.

"There, I'll tell you what we'd better do," said Mrs. Flagg gallantly; "we'll go right over an' see poor old Miss Nancy Fell; 't will please her about to death. We can say we felt like goin' somewhere to-day an' 't was a good many years since either one of us had seen Baxter, so we come just for the ride, an' to make a few calls. She'll like to hear all about the conference; Miss Fell was always one that took a real interest in religious matters."

Miss Pickett brightened, and they quickened their step. It was nearly twelve o'clock, they had breakfasted early, and now felt as if they had eaten nothing since they were grown up. An awful feeling of tiredness and uncertainty settled down upon their once buoyant spirits.

"I can forgive a person," said Mrs. Flagg, once, as if she were speaking to herself; "I can forgive a person, but when I'm done with 'em, I'm done."

5   "I do declare, 't was like a scene in Scriptur' to see that poor good-hearted Nancy Fell run down her walk to open the gate for us!" said Mrs. Persis Flagg later that afternoon, when she and Miss Pickett were going home in the stage. Miss Pickett nodded her head approvingly.

"I had a good sight better time with her than I should have had at the other place," she said with fearless honesty. "If I'd been Mis' Cap'n Timms, I'd made some apology or just passed us the compliment. If it wa'n't convenient, why couldn't she just tell us so after all her urgin' and sayin' how she should expect us?"

"I thought then she'd altered from what she used to be," said Mrs. Flagg. "She seemed real sincere an' open away

from home. If she wa'n't prepared to-day, 't was easy enough
to say so; we was reasonable folks, an' should have gone
away with none but friendly feelin's. We did have a grand
good time with Nancy. She was as happy to see us as if we'd
been queens."

" 'T was a real nice little dinner," said Miss Pickett grate-
fully. "I thought I was goin' to faint away just before we
got to the house, and I didn't know how I should hold
out if she undertook to do anything extra, and keep us a-
waitin'; but there, she just made us welcome, simple-
hearted, to what she had. I never tasted such dandelion
greens; an' that nice little piece o' pork and new biscuit,
why, they was just splendid. She must have an excellent
good cellar, if 't is such a small house. Her potatoes was
truly remarkable for this time o' year. I myself don't deem
it necessary to cook potatoes when I'm goin' to have dandelion greens. Now, didn't it put you in mind of that verse
in the Bible that says, 'Better is a dinner of herbs where love
is'? An' how desirous she'd been to see somebody that
could tell her some particulars about the conference!"

"She'll enjoy tellin' folks about our comin' over to see
her. Yes, I'm glad we went; 't will be of advantage every
way, an' our bein' of the same church an' all, to Woodville.
If Mis' Timms hears of our bein' there, she'll see we had
reason, an' knew of a place to go. Well, I needn't have
brought this old bag!"

Miss Pickett gave her companion a quick resentful glance,
which was followed by one of triumph directed at the dust
that was collecting on the shoulders of the best black cashmere; then she looked at the bag on the front seat, and suddenly felt illuminated with the suspicion that Mrs. Flagg
had secretly made preparations to pass the night in Baxter.
The bag looked plump, as if it held much more than the
pocket-book and the jelly.

Mrs. Flagg looked up with unusual humility. "I did
think about that jelly," she said, as if Miss Pickett had
openly reproached her. "I was afraid it might look as if I
was tryin' to pay Nancy for her kindness."

"Well, I don't know," said Cynthia; "I guess she'd been
pleased. She'd thought you just brought her over a little
present: but I do' know as 't would been any good to her

after all; she'd thought so much of it, comin' from you, that she'd kep' it till 't was all candied." But Mrs. Flagg didn't look exactly pleased by this unexpected compliment, and her fellow-traveler colored with confusion and a sudden feeling that she had shown undue forwardness.

Presently they remembered the Beckett house, to their great relief, and, as they approached, Mrs. Flagg reached over and moved her hand-bag from the front seat to make room for another passenger. But nobody came out to stop the stage, and they saw the unexpected guest sitting by one of the front windows comfortably swaying a palm-leaf fan, and rocking to and fro in calm content. They shrank back into their corners, and tried not to be seen. Mrs. Flagg's face grew very red.

"She got in, didn't she?" said Miss Pickett, snipping her words angrily, as if her lips were scissors. Then she heard a call, and bent forward to see Mrs. Beckett herself appear in the front doorway, very smiling and eager to stop the stage.

The driver was only too ready to stop his horses. "Got a passenger for me to carry back, ain't ye?" said he facetiously. "Them's the kind I like; carry both ways, make somethin' on a double trip," and he gave Mrs. Flagg and Miss Pickett a friendly wink as he stepped down over the wheel. Then he hurried toward the house, evidently in a hurry to put the baggage on; but the expected passenger still sat rocking and fanning at the window.

"No, sir; I ain't got any passengers," exclaimed Mrs. Beckett, advancing a step or two to meet him, and speaking very loud in her pleasant excitement. "This lady that come this morning wants her large trunk with her summer things that she left to the depot in Woodville. She's very desirous to git into it, so don't you go an' forgit; ain't you got a book or somethin', Mr. Ma'sh? Don't you forget to make a note of it; here's her check, an' we've kep' the number in case you should mislay it or anything. There's things in the trunk she needs; you know how you overlooked stoppin' to the milliner's for my bunnit last week."

"Other folks disremembers things as well's me," grumbled Mr. Marsh. He turned to give the passengers another wink more familiar than the first, but they wore an offended

air, and were looking the other way. The horses had backed
a few steps, and the guest at the front window had ceased
the steady motion of her fan to make them a handsome
bow, and been puzzled at the lofty manner of their acknowledgment.

"Go 'long with your foolish jokes, John Ma'sh!" Mrs.
Beckett said cheerfully, as she turned away. She was a comfortable, hearty person, whose appearance adjusted the
beauties of hospitality. The driver climbed to his seat,
chuckling, and drove away with the dust flying after the
wheels.

"Now, she's a friendly sort of a woman, that Mis' Beckett," said Mrs. Flagg unexpectedly, after a few moments
of silence, when she and her friend had been unable to
look at each other. "I really ought to call over an' see her
some o' these days, knowing her husband's folks as well as
I used to, an' visitin' of 'em when I was a girl." But Miss
Pickett made no answer.

"I expect it was all for the best, that woman's comin',"
suggested Mrs. Flagg again hopefully. "She looked like a
willing person who would take right hold. I guess Mis'
Beckett knows what she's about, and must have had her
reasons. Perhaps she thought she'd chance it for a couple o'
weeks anyway, after the lady'd come so fur, an' bein' one
o' her own denomination. Hayin'-time'll be here before we
know it. I think myself, gen'rally speakin', 't is just as well
to let anybody know you're comin'."

"Them seemed to be Mis' Cap'n Timms's views," said
Miss Pickett in a low tone; but the stage rattled a good
deal, and Mrs. Flagg looked up inquiringly, as if she had
not heard.

Mrs. William Trimble and Miss Rebecca Wright were driving along Hampden east road, one afternoon in early spring. Their progress was slow. Mrs. Trimble's sorrel horse was old and stiff, and the wheels were clogged by clay mud. The frost was not yet out of the ground, although the snow was nearly gone, except in a few places on the north side of the woods, or where it had drifted all winter against a length of fence.

"There must be a good deal o' snow to the nor'ard of us yet," said weather-wise Mrs. Trimble. "I feel it in the air; 't is more than the ground-damp. We ain't goin' to have real nice weather till the upcountry snow's all gone."

"I heard say yesterday that there was good sleddin' yet, all up through Parsley," responded Miss Wright. "I shouldn't like to live in them northern places. My cousin Ellen's husband was a Parsley man, an' he was obliged, as you may have heard, to go up north to his father's second wife's funeral; got back day before yesterday. 'T was about twenty-one miles, an' they started on wheels; but when they'd gone nine or ten miles, they found 't was no sort o' use, an' left their wagon an' took a sleigh. The man that owned it charged 'em four an' six, too. I shouldn't have thought he would; they told him they was goin' to a funeral; an' they had their own buffaloes an' everything."

"Well, I expect it's a good deal harder scratchin', up that way; they have to git money where they can; the farms is very poor as you go north," suggested Mrs. Trimble kindly. "'T ain't none too rich a country where we be, but I've always been grateful I wa'n't born up to Parsley."

The old horse plodded along, and the sun, coming out from the heavy spring clouds, sent a sudden shine of light along the muddy road. Sister Wright drew her large veil forward over the high brim of her bonnet. She was not used to driving, or to being much in the open air; but Mrs. Trimble was an active business woman, and looked after her own affairs herself, in all weathers. The late Mr. Trimble had left her a good farm, but not much ready money, and it was often said that she was better off in the end than if he had lived. She regretted his loss deeply, however; it was impossible for her to speak of him, even to intimate friends, without emotion, and nobody had ever hinted that this emotion was insincere. She was most warm-hearted and generous, and in her limited way played the part of Lady Bountiful in the town of Hampden.

"Why, there's where the Bray girls lives, ain't it?" she exclaimed, as, beyond a thicket of witch-hazel and scrub-oak, they came in sight of a weather-beaten, solitary farm-house. The barn was too far away for thrift or comfort, and they could see long lines of light between the shrunken boards as they came nearer. The fields looked both stony and sodden. Somehow, even Parsley itself could be hardly more forlorn.

"Yes'm," said Miss Wright, "that's where they live now, poor things. I know the place, though I ain't been up here for years. You don't suppose, Mis' Trimble—I ain't seen the girls out to meetin' all winter. I've re'lly been cov-etin' "—

"Why, yes, Rebecca, of course we could stop," answered Mrs. Trimble heartily. "The exercises was over earlier 'n I expected, an' you're goin' to remain over night long o' me, you know. There won't be no tea till we git there, so we can't be late. I'm in the habit o' sendin' a basket to the Bray girls when any o' our folks is comin' this way, but I ain't been to see 'em since they moved up here. Why, it must be a good deal over a year ago. I know 't was in the late winter they had to make the move. 'T was cruel hard, I must say, an' if I hadn't been down with my pleurisy fever I'd have stirred round an' done somethin' about it. There was a good deal o' sickness at the time, an'—well, 't was kind o' rushed through, breakin' of 'em up, an' lots o' folks blamed the selec'*men*; but when 't was done, 't was done, an' nobody took holt to undo it. Ann an' Mandy looked same 's ever when they come to meetin', 'long in the sum-mer,—kind o' wishful, perhaps. They've always sent me word they was gittin' on pretty comfortable."

"That would be their way," said Rebecca Wright. "They never was any hand to complain, though Mandy's less cheer-ful than Ann. If Mandy'd been spared such poor eyesight, an' Ann hadn't got her lame wrist that wa'n't set right, they'd kep' off the town fast enough. They both shed tears when they talked to me about havin' to break up, when I went to see 'em before I went over to brother Asa's. You see we was brought up neighbors, an' we went to school together, the Brays an' me. 'T was a special Providence brought us home this road, I've been so covetin' a chance to git to see 'em. My lameness hampers me."

"I'm glad we come this way, myself," said Mrs. Trimble.

"I'd like to see just how they fare," Miss Rebecca Wright continued. "They give their consent to goin' on the town because they knew they'd got to be dependent, an' so they felt 't would come easier for all than for a few to help 'em. They acted real dignified an' right-minded, contrary to what most do in such cases, but they was dreadful anxious to see who would bid 'em off, town-meeting day; they did so hope 't would be somebody right in the village. I just sat down an' cried good when I found Abel Janes's folks had got hold of 'em. They always had the name of bein' slack an' poor-spirited, an' they did it just for what they got out o' the town. The selectmen this last year ain't what we have had. I hope they've been considerate about the Bray girls."

"I should have be'n more considerate about fetchin' of you over," apologized Mrs. Trimble. "I've got my horse, an' you're lame-footed; 't is too far for you to come. But time does slip away with busy folks, an' I forgit a good deal I ought to remember."

"There's nobody more considerate than you be," protested Miss Rebecca Wright.

Mrs. Trimble made no answer, but took out her whip and gently touched the sorrel horse, who walked considerably faster, but did not think it worth while to trot. It was a long, round-about way to the house, farther down the road and up a lane.

"I never had any opinion of the Bray girls' father, leavin' 'em as he did," said Mrs. Trimble.

"He was much praised in his time, though there was always some said his early life hadn't been up to the mark," explained her companion. "He was a great favorite of our then preacher, the Reverend Daniel Longbrother. They

did a good deal for the parish, but they did it their own
way. Deacon Bray was one that did his part in the repairs
without urging. You know 't was in his time the first repairs
was made, when they got out the old soundin'-board an'
them handsome square pews. It cost an awful sight o'
money, too. They hadn't done payin' up that debt when
they set to alter it again an' git the walls frescoed. My
grandmother was one that always spoke her mind right out,
an' she was dreadful opposed to breakin' up the square pews
where she'd always set. They was countin' up what 't would
cost in parish meetin', an' she riz right up an' said 't
wouldn't cost nothin' to let 'em stay, an' there wa'n't a
house carpenter left in the parish that could do such nice
work, an' time would come when the great-grandchildren
would give their eye-teeth to have the old meetin'-house
look just as it did then. But haul the inside to pieces they
would and did."

"There come to be a real fight over it, didn't there?"
agreed Mrs. Trimble soothingly. "Well, 't wa'n't good
taste. I remember the old house well. I come here as a
child to visit a cousin o' mother's, an' Mr. Trimble's folks
was neighbors, an' we was drawed to each other then, young
's we was. Mr. Trimble spoke of it many's the time,—that
first time he ever see me, in a leghorn hat with a feather;
't was one that mother had, an' pressed over."

"When I think of them old sermons that used to be
preached in that old meetin'-house of all, I'm glad it's
altered over, so's not to remind folks," said Miss Rebecca
Wright, after a suitable pause. "Them old brimstone discourses, you know, Mis' Trimble. Preachers is far more reasonable, nowadays. Why, I set an' thought, last Sabbath,
as I listened, that if old Mr. Longbrother an' Deacon Bray
could hear the difference they'd crack the ground over 'em
like pole beans, an' come right up 'long side their head-
stones."

Mrs. Trimble laughed heartily, and shook the reins three
or four times by way of emphasis. "There's no gitting round
you," she said, much pleased. "I should think Deacon Bray
would want to rise, any way, if 't was so he could, an' knew
how his poor girls was farin'. A man ought to provide for
his folks he's got to leave behind him, specially if they're

women. To be sure, they had their little home; but we've seen how, with all their industrious ways, they hadn't means to keep it. I s'pose he thought he'd got time enough to lay by, when he give so generous in collections; but he didn't lay by, an' there they be. He might have took lessons from the squirrels: even them little wild creatur's makes them their winter hoards, an' menfolks ought to know enough if squirrels does. 'Be just before you are generous:' that's what was always set for the B's in the copy-books, when I was to school, and it often runs through my mind."

"'As for man, his days are as grass,'—that was for A; the two go well together," added Miss Rebecca Wright soberly. "My good gracious, ain't this a starved-lookin' place? It makes me ache to think them nice Bray girls has to brook it here."

The sorrel horse, though somewhat puzzled by an unexpected deviation from his homeward way, willingly came to a stand by the gnawed corner of the door-yard fence, which evidently served as hitching-place. Two or three ragged old hens were picking about the yard, and at last a face appeared at the kitchen window, tied up in a hand-kerchief, as if it were a case of toothache. By the time our friends reached the side door next this window, Mrs. Janes came disconsolately to open it for them, shutting it again as soon as possible, though the air felt more chilly inside the house.

"Take seats," said Mrs. Janes briefly. "You'll have to see me just as I be. I have been suffering these four days with the ague, and everything to do. Mr. Janes is to court, on the jury. 'T was inconvenient to spare him. I should be pleased to have you lay off your things."

Comfortable Mrs. Trimble looked about the cheerless kitchen, and could not think of anything to say; so she smiled blandly and shook her head in answer to the invitation. "We'll just set a few minutes with you, to pass the time o' day, an' then we must go in an' have a word with the Miss Brays, bein' old acquaintance. It ain't been so we could git to call on 'em before. I don't know 's you're acquainted with Miss R'becca Wright. She's been out of town a good deal."

"I heard she was stopping over to Plainfields with her

brother's folks," replied Mrs. Janes, rocking herself with irregular motion, as she sat close to the stove. "Got back some time in the fall, I believe?"

"Yes'm," said Miss Rebecca, with an undue sense of guilt and conviction. "We've been to the installation over to the East Parish, an' thought we'd stop in; we took this road home to see if 't was any better. How is the Miss Brays gettin' on?"

"They're well's common," answered Mrs. Janes grudgingly. "I was put out with Mr. Janes for fetchin' of 'em here, with all I've got to do, an' I own I was kind o' surly to 'em 'long to the first of it. He gits the money from the town, an' it helps him out; but he bid 'em off for five dollars a month, an' we can't do much for 'em at no such price as that. I went an' dealt with the selec'men, an' made 'em promise to find their firewood an' some other things extra. They was glad to get rid o' the matter the fourth time I went, an' would ha' promised 'most anything. But Mr. Janes don't keep me half the time in oven-wood, he's off so much, an' we was cramped o' room, any way. I have to store things up garrit a good deal, an' that keeps me trampin' right through their room. I do the best for 'em I can, Mis' Trimble, but 't ain't so easy for me as 't is for you, with all your means to do with."

The poor woman looked pinched and miserable herself, though it was evident that she had no gift at house or home keeping. Mrs. Trimble's heart was wrung with pain, as she thought of the unwelcome inmates of such a place; but she held her peace bravely, while Miss Rebecca again gave some brief information in regard to the installation.

"You go right up them back stairs," the hostess directed at last. "I'm glad some o' you church folks has seen fit to come an' visit 'em. There ain't been nobody here this long spell, an' they've aged a sight since they come. They always send down a taste out of your baskets, Mis' Trimble, an' I relish it, I tell you. I'll shut the door after you, if you don't object. I feel every draught o' cold air."

"I've always heard she was a great hand to make a poor mouth. Wa'n't she from somewheres up Parsley way?" whispered Miss Rebecca, as they stumbled in the half-light.

"Poor meechin' body, wherever she come from," replied Mrs. Trimble, as she knocked at the door.

There was silence for a moment after this unusual sound; then one of the Bray sisters opened the door. The eager guests stared into a small, low room, brown with age, and gray, too, as if former dust and cobwebs could not be made wholly to disappear. The two elderly women who stood there looked like captives. Their withered faces wore a look of apprehension, and the room itself was more bare and plain than was fitting to their evident refinement of character and self-respect. There was an uncovered small table in the middle of the floor, with some crackers on a plate; and, for some reason or other, this added a great deal to the general desolation.

But Miss Ann Bray, the elder sister, who carried her right arm in a sling, with piteously drooping fingers, gazed at the visitors with radiant joy. She had not seen them arrive.

The one window gave only the view at the back of the house, across the fields, and their coming was indeed a surprise. The next minute she was laughing and crying together. "Oh, sister!" she said, "if here ain't our dear Mis' Trimble!—an' my heart o' goodness, 't is 'Becca Wright, too! What dear good creatur's you be! I've felt all day as if something good was goin' to happen, an' was just sayin' to myself 't was most sundown now, but I wouldn't let on to Mandany I'd give up hope quite yet. You see, the scissors stuck in the floor this very mornin' an' it's always a reliable sign. There, I've got to kiss ye both again!"

"I don't know where we can all set," lamented sister Mandana. "There ain't but the one chair an' the bed; t' other chair's too rickety; an' we've been promised another these ten days; but first they've forgot it, an' next Mis' Janes can't spare it,—one excuse an' another. I am goin' to git a stump o' wood an' nail a board on to it, when I can git outdoor again," said Mandana, in a plaintive voice. "There, I ain't goin' to complain o' nothin', now you've come," she added; and the guests sat down, Mrs. Trimble, as was proper, in the one chair.

"We've sat on the bed many's the time with you, 'Becca, an' talked over our girl nonsense, ain't we? You know where 't was—in the little back bedroom we had when we was

girls, an' used to peek out at our beaux through the strings
o' mornin'-glories," laughed Ann Bray delightedly, her thin
face shining more and more with joy. "I brought some o'
them mornin'-glory seeds along when we come away, we'd
raised 'em so many years; an' we got 'em started all right,
but the hens found 'em out. I declare I chased them poor
hens, foolish as 't was; but the mornin'-glories I'd counted
on a sight to remind me o' home. You see, our debts was so
large, after my long sickness an' all, that we didn't feel 't
was right to keep back anything we could help from the
auction."

It was impossible for any one to speak for a moment or
two; the sisters felt their own uprooted condition afresh,
and their guests for the first time really comprehended the
piteous contrast between that neat little village house,
which now seemed a palace of comfort, and this cold, unpainted upper room in the remote Janes farmhouse. It was
an unwelcome thought to Mrs. Trimble that the well-to-do
town of Hampden could provide no better for its poor than
this, and her round face flushed with resentment and the
shame of personal responsibility. "The girls shall be well
settled in the village before another winter, if I pay their
board myself," she made an inward resolution, and took
another almost tearful look at the broken stove, the miserable bed, and the sisters' one hair-covered trunk, on which
Mandana was sitting. But the poor place was filled with a
golden spirit of hospitality.

Rebecca was again discoursing eloquently of the installation; it was so much easier to speak of general subjects, and
the sisters had evidently been longing to hear some news.
Since the late summer they had not been to church, and
presently Mrs. Trimble asked the reason.

"Now, don't you go to pouring out our woes, Mandy!"
begged little old Ann, looking shy and almost girlish, and as
if she insisted upon playing that life was still all before
them and all pleasure. "Don't you go to spoilin' their visit
with our complaints! They know well's we do that changes
must come, an' we'd been so wonted to our home things
that this come hard at first; but then they felt for us, I
know just as well's can be. 'T will soon be summer again, an'
't is real pleasant right out in the fields here, when there

ain't too hot a spell. I've got to know a sight o' singin' birds since we come."

"Give me the folks I've always known," sighed the younger sister, who looked older than Miss Ann, and less even-tempered. "You may have your birds, if you want 'em. I do re'lly long to go to meetin' an' see folks go by up the aisle. Now, I will speak of it, Ann, whatever you say. We need, each of us, a pair o' good stout shoes an' rubbers,— ours are all wore out; an' we've asked an' asked, an' they never think to bring 'em, an' "—

Poor old Mandana, on the trunk, covered her face with her arms and sobbed aloud. The elder sister stood over her, and patted her on the thin shoulder like a child, and tried to comfort her. It crossed Mrs. Trimble's mind that it was not the first time one had wept and the other had comforted. The sad scene must have been repeated many times in that long, drear winter. She would see them forever after in her mind as fixed as a picture, and her own tears fell fast.

"You didn't see Mis' Janes's cunning little boy, the next one to the baby, did you?" asked Ann Bray, turning round quickly at last, and going cheerfully on with the conversation. "Now, hush, Mandy, dear; they'll think you're childish! He's a dear, friendly little creatur', an' likes to stay with us a good deal, though we feel 's if it was too cold for him, now we are waitin' to get us more wood."

"When I think of the acres o' woodland in this town!" groaned Rebecca Wright. "I believe I'm goin' to preach next Sunday, 'stead o' the minister, an' I'll make the sparks fly. I've always heard the saying, 'What's everybody's business is nobody's business,' an' I've come to believe it."

"Now, don't you, 'Becca. You've happened on a kind of a poor time with us, but we've got more belongings than you see here, an' a good large cluset, where we can store those things there ain't room to have about. You an' Mis' Trimble have happened on a kind of poor day, you know. Soon's I git me some stout shoes an' rubbers, as Mandy says, I can fetch home plenty o' little dry boughs o' pine; you remember I was always a great hand to roam in the woods? If we could only have a front room, so 't we could look out on the road an' see passin', an' was shod for meetin', I don' know's we should complain. Now we're just

goin' to give you what we've got, an' make out with a good
welcome. We make more tea 'n we want in the mornin',
an' then let the fire go down, since 't has been so mild.
We've got a *good* cluset" (disappearing as she spoke), "an'
I know this to be good tea, 'cause it's some o' yourn, Mis'
Trimble. An' here's our sprigged chiny cups that R'becca
knows by sight, if Mis' Trimble don't. We kep' out four of
'em, an' put the even half dozen with the rest of the auction
stuff. I've often wondered who'd got 'em, but I never asked,
for fear 't would be somebody that would distress us. They
was mother's, you know."

The four cups were poured, and the little table pushed
to the bed, where Rebecca Wright still sat, and Mandana,
wiping her eyes, came and joined her. Mrs. Trimble sat in
her chair at the end, and Ann trotted about the room in
pleased content for a while, and in and out of the closet, as
if she still had much to do; then she came and stood opposite Mrs. Trimble. She was very short and small, and
there was no painful sense of her being obliged to stand.
The four cups were not quite full of cold tea, but there
was a clean old tablecloth folded double, and a plate with
three pairs of crackers neatly piled, and a small—it must
be owned, a very small—piece of hard white cheese. Then,
for a treat, in a glass dish, there was a little preserved peach,
the last—Miss Rebecca knew it instinctively—of the household stores brought from their old home. It was very sugary,
this bit of peach; and as she helped her guests and sister
Mandy, Miss Ann Bray said, half unconsciously, as she often
had said with less reason in the old days, "Our preserves
ain't so good as usual this year; this is beginning to candy."
Both the guests protested, while Rebecca added that the
taste of it carried her back, and made her feel young again.
The Brays had always managed to keep one or two peach-
trees alive in their corner of a garden. "I've been keeping
this preserve for a treat," said her friend. "I'm glad to have
you eat some, 'Becca. Last summer I often wished you was
home an' could come an' see us, 'stead o' being away off
to Plainfields."

The crackers did not taste too dry. Miss Ann took the
last of the peach on her own cracker; there could not have
been quite a small spoonful, after the others were helped,

but she asked them first if they would not have some more. Then there was a silence, and in the silence a wave of tender feeling rose high in the hearts of the four elderly women. At this moment the setting sun flooded the poor plain room with light; the unpainted wood was all of a golden-brown, and Ann Bray, with her gray hair and aged face, stood at the head of the table in a kind of aureole. Mrs. Trimble's face was all aquiver as she looked at her; she thought of the text about two or three being gathered together, and was half afraid.

"I believe we ought to 've asked Mis' Janes if she wouldn't come up," said Ann. "She's real good feelin', but she's had it very hard, an gits discouraged. I can't find that she's ever had anything real pleasant to look back to, as we have. There, next time we'll make a good heartenin' time for her too."

The sorrel horse had taken a long nap by the gnawed fence-rail, and the cool air after sundown made him impatient to be gone. The two friends jolted homeward in the gathering darkness, through the stiffening mud, and neither Mrs. Trimble nor Rebecca Wright said a word until they were out of sight as well as out of sound of the Janes house. Time must elapse before they could reach a more familiar part of the road and resume conversation on its natural level.

"I consider myself to blame," insisted Mrs. Trimble at last. "I haven't no words of accusation for nobody else, an' I ain't one to take comfort in calling names to the board o' selec'*men*. I make no reproaches, an' I take it all on my own shoulders; but I'm goin' to stir about me, I tell you! I shall begin early to-morrow. They're goin' back to their own house,—it's been standin' empty all winter,—an' the town's goin' to give 'em the rent an' what firewood they need; it won't come to more than the board's payin' out now. An' you an' me'll take this same horse an' wagon, an' ride an' go afoot by turns, an' git means enough together to buy back their furniture an' whatever was sold at that plaguey auction; an' then we'll put it all back, an' tell 'em they've got to move to a new place, an' just carry 'em right back again where they come from. An' don't you never tell,

R'becca, but here I be a widow woman, layin' up what I make from my farm for nobody knows who, an' I'm goin' to do for them Bray girls all I'm a mind to. I should be sca't to wake up in heaven, an' hear anybody there ask how the Bray girls was. Don't talk to me about the town o' Hampden, an' don't ever let me hear the name o' town poor! I'm ashamed to go home an' see what's set out for supper. I wish I'd brought 'em right along."

"I was goin' to ask if we couldn't git the new doctor to go up an' do somethin' for poor Ann's arm," said Miss Rebecca. "They say he's very smart. If she could get so's to braid straw or hook rugs again, she'd soon be earnin' a little somethin'. An' may be he could do somethin' for Mandy's eyes. They did use to live so neat an' ladylike. Somehow I couldn't speak to tell 'em there that 't was I bought them six best cups an' saucers, time of the auction; they went very low, as everything else did, an' I thought I could save it some other way. They shall have 'em back an' welcome. You're real whole-hearted, Mis' Trimble. I expect Ann'll be sayin' that her father's child'n wa'n't goin' to be left desolate, an' that all the bread he cast on the water's comin' back through you."

"I don't care what she says, dear creatur'!" exclaimed Mrs. Trimble. "I'm full o' regrets I took time for that installation, an' set there seepin' in a lot o' talk this whole day long, except for its kind of bringin' us to the Bray girls. I wish to my heart 't was to-morrow mornin' a'ready, an' I a-startin' for the selec'*men*."

THE HILTONS' HOLIDAY

1 There was a bright, full moon in the clear sky, and the sunset was still shining faintly in the west. Dark woods stood all about the old Hilton farmhouse, save down the hill, westward, where lay the shadowy fields which John Hilton, and his father before him, had cleared and tilled with much toil,—the small fields to which they had given the industry and even affection of their honest lives.

John Hilton was sitting on the doorstep of his house. As he moved his head in and out of the shadows, turning now and then to speak to his wife, who sat just within the doorway, one could see his good face, rough and somewhat unkempt, as if he were indeed a creature of the shady woods and brown earth, instead of the noisy town. It was late in the long spring evening, and he had just come from the lower field as cheerful as a boy, proud of having finished the planting of his potatoes.

"I had to do my last row mostly by feelin'," he said to his wife. "I'm proper glad I pushed through, an' went back an' ended off after supper. 'T would have taken me a good part o' to-morrow mornin', an' broke my day."

" 'T ain't no use for ye to work yourself all to pieces, John," answered the woman quickly. "I declare it does seem harder than ever that we couldn't have kep' our boy; he'd been comin' fourteen years old this fall, most a grown man, and he'd work right 'longside of ye now the whole time."

" 'T was hard to lose him; I do seem to miss little John," said the father sadly. "I expect there was reasons why 't was best. I feel able an' smart to work; my father was a girt strong man, an' a monstrous worker afore me. 'T ain't that; but I was thinkin' by myself to-day what a sight o' company the boy would ha' been. You know, small's he was, how I could trust to leave him anywheres with the team, and how he'd beseech to go with me wherever I was goin'; always right in my tracks I used to tell 'em. Poor little John, for all he was so young he had a great deal o' judgment; he'd ha' made a likely man."

The mother sighed heavily as she sat within the shadow.

"But then there's the little girls, a sight o' help an' company," urged the father eagerly, as if it were wrong to dwell upon sorrow and loss. "Katy, she's most as good as a boy, except that she ain't very rugged. She's a real little farmer, she's helped me a sight this spring; an' you've got Susan Ellen, that makes a complete little housekeeper for ye as far as she's learnt. I don't see but we're better off than most folks, each on us having a work-mate."

"That's so, John," acknowledged Mrs. Hilton wistfully, beginning to rock steadily in her straight, splint-bottomed chair. It was always a good sign when she rocked.

"Where be the little girls so late?" asked their father. " 'T is gettin' long past eight o'clock. I don't know when we've all set up so late, but it's so kind o' summer-like an' pleasant. Why, where be they gone?"

"I've told ye; only over to Becker's folks," answered the mother. "I don't see myself what keeps 'em so late; they beseeched me after supper till I let 'em go. They're all in a dazzle with the new teacher; she asked 'em to come over. They say she's unusual smart with 'rethmetic, but she has a kind of a gorpen look to me. She's goin' to give Katy some pieces for her doll, but I told Katy she ought to be ashamed wantin' dolls' pieces, big as she's gettin' to be. I don't know's she ought, though; she ain't but nine this summer."

"Let her take her comfort," said the kind-hearted man. "Them things draws her to the teacher, an' makes them acquainted. Katy's shy with new folks, more so 'n Susan Ellen, who's of the business kind. Katy's shy-feelin' and wishful."

"I don't know but she is," agreed the mother slowly. "Ain't it sing'lar how well acquainted you be with that one, an' I with Susan Ellen? 'T was always so from the first. I'm doubtful sometimes our Katy ain't one that'll be like to get married—anyways not about here. She lives right with herself, but Susan Ellen ain't nothin' when she's alone, she's always after company; all the boys is waitin' on her a'ready. I ain't afraid but she'll take her pick when the time comes. I expect to see Susan Ellen well settled,—she feels grown up now,—but Katy don't care one mite 'bout none o' them things. She wants to be rovin' out o' doors. I do believe she'd stand an' hark to a bird the whole forenoon."

"Perhaps she'll grow up to be a teacher," suggested John Hilton. "She takes to her book more 'n the other one. I should like one on 'em to be a teacher same's my mother was. They're good girls as anybody's got."

"So they be," said the mother, with unusual gentleness, and the creak of her rocking-chair was heard, regular as the ticking of a clock. The night breeze stirred in the great woods, and the sound of a brook that went falling down the hillside grew louder and louder. Now and then one could hear the plaintive chirp of a bird. The moon glittered with whiteness like a winter moon, and shone upon the low-roofed house until its small window-panes gleamed like silver, and one could almost see the colors of a blooming bush of lilac that grew in a sheltered angle by the kitchen door. There was an incessant sound of frogs in the lowlands.

"Be you sound asleep, John?" asked the wife presently.

"I don't know but what I was a'most," said the tired man, starting a little. "I should laugh if I was to fall sound asleep right here on the step; 't is the bright night, I expect, makes my eyes feel heavy, an' 't is so peaceful. I was up an' dressed a little past four an' out to work. Well, well!" and he laughed sleepily and rubbed his eyes. "Where's the little girls? I'd better step along an' meet 'em."

"I wouldn't just yet; they'll get home all right, but 't is late for 'em certain. I don't want 'em keepin' Mis' Becker's folks up neither. There, le' 's wait a few minutes," urged Mrs. Hilton.

"I've be'n a-thinkin' all day I'd like to give the child'n some kind of a treat," said the father, wide awake now. "I hurried up my work 'cause I had it so in mind. They don't have the opportunities some do, an' I want 'em to know the world, an' not stay right here on the farm like a couple o' bushes."

"They're a sight better off not to be so full o' notions as some is," protested the mother suspiciously.

"Certain," answered the farmer; "but they're good, bright child'n, an' commencin' to take a sight o' notice. I

want 'em to have all we can give 'em. I want 'em to see
how other folks does things."

"Why, so do I,"—here the rocking-chair stopped omi-
nously,—"but so long 's they're contented"—

"Contented ain't all in this world; hopper-toads may
have that quality an' spend all their time a-blinkin'. I don't
know's bein' contented is all there is to look for in a child.
Ambition 's somethin' to me."

"Now you've got your mind on to some plot or other."
(The rocking-chair began to move again.) "Why can't you
talk right out?"

" 'T ain't nothin' special," answered the good man, a
little ruffled; he was never prepared for his wife's mysterious
powers of divination. "Well there, you do find things out
the master! I only thought perhaps I'd take 'em to-morrow,
an' go off somewhere if 't was a good day. I've been promisin' for a good while I'd take 'em to Topham Corners;
they've never been there since they was very small."

"I believe you want a good time yourself. You ain't never
got over bein' a boy." Mrs. Hilton seemed much amused.
"There, go if you want to an' take 'em; they've got their
summer hats an' new dresses. I don't know o' nothin' that
stands in the way. I should sense it better if there was a
circus or anythin' to go to. Why don't you wait an' let the
girls pick 'em some strawberries or nice ros'berries, and then
they could take an' sell 'em to the stores?"

John Hilton reflected deeply. "I should like to get me
some good yellow-turnip seed to plant late. I ain't more
'n satisfied with what I've been gettin' o' late years o' Ira
Speed. An' I'm goin' to provide me with a good hoe; mine's
gettin' wore out an' all shackly. I can't seem to fix it good."

"Them's excuses," observed Mrs. Hilton, with friendly
tolerance. "You just cover up the hoe with somethin', if you
get it—I would. Ira Speed's so jealous he'll remember it of
you this twenty year, your goin' an' buyin' a new hoe o'
anybody but him."

"I've always thought 't was a free country," said John
Hilton soberly. "I don't want to vex Ira neither; he favors
us all he can in trade. 'T is difficult for him to spare a cent,
but he's as honest as daylight."

At this moment there was a sudden sound of young

voices, and a pair of young figures came out from the
shadow of the woods into the moonlighted open space. An
old cock crowed loudly from his perch in the shed, as if he
were a herald of royalty. The little girls were hand in hand,
and a brisk young dog capered about them as they came.

"Wa'n't it dark gittin' home through the woods this time
o' night?" asked the mother hastily, and not without re-
proach.

"I don't love to have you gone so late; mother an' me
was timid about ye, and you've kep' Mis' Becker's folks up,
I expect," said their father regretfully. "I don't want to have
it said that my little girls ain't got good manners."

"The teacher had a party," chirped Susan Ellen, the
elder of the two children. "Goin' home from school she
asked the Grover boys, an' Mary an' Sarah Speed. An' Mis'
Becker was real pleasant to us: she passed round some cake,
an' handed us sap sugar on one of her best plates, an' we
played games an' sung some pieces too. Mis' Becker thought
we did real well. I can pick out most of a tune on the cabinet
organ; teacher says she'll give me lessons."

"I want to know, dear!" exclaimed John Hilton.

"Yes, an' we played Copenhagen, an' took sides spellin',
an' Katy beat everybody spellin' there was there."

Katy had not spoken; she was not so strong as her sister,
and while Susan Ellen stood a step or two away addressing
her eager little audience, Katy had seated herself close to
her father on the doorstep. He put his arm around her
shoulders, and drew her close to his side, where she stayed.

"Ain't you got nothin' to tell, daughter?" he asked, looking down fondly; and Katy gave a pleased little sigh for
answer.

"Tell 'em what's goin' to be the last day o' school, and
about our trimmin' the schoolhouse," she said; and Susan
Ellen gave the programme in most spirited fashion.

" 'T will be a great time," said the mother, when she had
finished. "I don't see why folks wants to go trapesin' off to
strange places when such things is happenin' right about
'em." But the children did not observe her mysterious air.
"Come, you must step yourselves right to bed!"

They all went into the dark, warm house; the bright

moon shone upon it steadily all night, and the lilac flowers were shaken by no breath of wind until the early dawn.

2   The Hiltons always waked early. So did their neighbors, the crows and song-sparrows and robins, the light-footed foxes and squirrels in the woods. When John Hilton waked, before five o'clock, an hour later than usual because he had sat up so late, he opened the house door and came out into the yard, crossing the short green turf hurriedly as if the day were too far spent for any loitering. The magnitude of the plan for taking a whole day of pleasure confronted him seriously, but the weather was fair, and his wife, whose disapproval could not have been set aside, had accepted and even smiled upon the great project. It was inevitable now, that he and the children should go to Topham Corners. Mrs. Hilton had the pleasure of waking them, and telling the news.

In a few minutes they came frisking out to talk over the great plans. The cattle were already fed, and their father was milking. The only sign of high festivity was the wagon pulled out into the yard, with both seats put in as if it were Sunday; but Mr. Hilton still wore his every-day clothes, and Susan Ellen suffered instantly from disappointment.

"Ain't we goin', father?" she asked complainingly; but he nodded and smiled at her, even though the cow, impatient to get to pasture, kept whisking her rough tail across his face. He held his head down and spoke cheerfully, in spite of this vexation.

"Yes, sister, we're goin' certain', an' goin' to have a great time too." Susan Ellen thought that he seemed like a boy at that delightful moment, and felt new sympathy and pleasure at once. "You go an' help mother about breakfast an' them things; we want to get off quick 's we can. You coax mother now, both on ye, an' see if she won't go with us."

"She said she wouldn't be hired to," responded Susan Ellen. "She says it's goin' to be hot, an' she's laid out to go over an' see how her aunt Tamsen Brooks is this afternoon."

The father gave a little sigh; then he took heart again.

The truth was that his wife made light of the contemplated pleasure, and, much as he usually valued her companionship and approval, he was sure that they should have a better time without her. It was impossible, however, not to feel guilty of disloyalty at the thought. Even though she might be completely unconscious of his best ideals, he only loved her and the ideals the more, and bent his energies to satisfying her indefinite expectations. His wife still kept much of that youthful beauty which Susan Ellen seemed likely to reproduce.

An hour later the best wagon was ready, and the great expedition set forth. The little dog sat apart, and barked as if it fell entirely upon him to voice the general excitement. Both seats were in the wagon, but the empty place testified to Mrs. Hilton's unyielding disposition. She had wondered why one broad seat would not do, but John Hilton meekly suggested that the wagon looked better with both. The little girls sat on the back seat dressed alike in their Sunday hats of straw with blue ribbons, and their little plaid shawls pinned neatly about their small shoulders. They wore gray thread gloves, and sat very straight. Susan Ellen was half a head the taller, but otherwise, from behind, they looked much alike. As for their father, he was in his Sunday best,— a plain black coat, and a winter hat of felt, which was heavy and rusty-looking for that warm early summer day. He had it in mind to buy a new straw hat at Topham, so that this with the turnip seed and the hoe made three important reasons for going.

"Remember an' lay off your shawls when you get there, an' carry them over your arms," said the mother, clucking like an excited hen to her chickens. "They'll do to keep the dust off your new dresses goin' an' comin'. An' when you eat your dinners don't get spots on you, an' don't point at folks as you ride by, an' stare, or they'll know you come from the country. An' John, you call into Cousin Ad'line Marlow's an' see how they all be, an' tell her I expect her over certain to stop awhile before hayin'. It always eases her phthisic to git up here on the highland, an' I've got a new notion about doin' over her best-room carpet sence I see her that'll save rippin' one breadth. An' don't come home all wore out; an', John, don't you go an' buy me no kickshaws to fetch home. I ain't a child, an' you ain't got no money to waste. I expect you'll go, like 's not, an' buy you some kind of a foolish boy's hat; do look an' see if it's reasonable good straw, an' won't splinter all off round the edge. An' you mind, John"—

"Yes, yes, hold on!" cried John impatiently; then he cast a last affectionate, reassuring look at her face, flushed with the hurry and responsibility of starting them off in proper shape. "I wish you was goin' too," he said, smiling. "I do so!" Then the old horse started, and they went out at the bars, and began the careful long descent of the hill. The young dog, tethered to the lilac-bush, was frantic with piteous appeals; the little girls piped their eager good-bys again and again, and their father turned many times to look back and wave his hand. As for their mother, she stood alone and watched them out of sight.

There was one place far out on the high-road where she could catch a last glimpse of the wagon, and she waited what seemed a very long time until it appeared and then was lost to sight again behind a low hill. "They're nothin' but a pack o' child'n together," she said aloud; and then felt lonelier than she expected. She even stooped and patted the unresigned little dog as she passed him, going into the house.

The occasion was so much more important than any one had foreseen that both the little girls were speechless. It seemed at first like going to church in new clothes, or to a funeral; they hardly knew how to behave at the beginning of a whole day of pleasure. They made grave bows at such persons of their acquaintance as happened to be straying in the road. Once or twice they stopped before a farmhouse, while their father talked an inconsiderately long time with some one about the crops and the weather, and even dwelt upon town business and the doings of the selectmen, which might be talked of at any time. The explanations that he gave of their excursion seemed quite unnecessary. It was made entirely clear that he had a little business to do at Topham Corners, and thought he had better give the little girls a ride; they had been very steady at school, and he had finished planting, and could take the day as well as not. Soon, however, they all felt as if such an excursion were an every-day affair, and Susan Ellen began to ask eager questions, while Katy silently sat apart enjoying herself as she never had done before. She liked to see the strange houses, and the children who belonged to them; it was delightful to find flowers that she knew growing all along the road, no matter how far she went from home. Each small homestead looked its best and pleasantest, and shared the exquisite beauty that early summer made,—shared the luxury of greenness and floweriness that decked the rural world. There was an early peony or a late lilac in almost every dooryard.

It was seventeen miles to Topham. After a while they seemed very far from home, having left the hills far behind, and descended to a great level country with fewer tracts of woodland, and wider fields where the crops were much more forward. The houses were all painted, and the roads were smoother and wider. It had been so pleasant driving along that Katy dreaded going into the strange town when she first caught sight of it, though Susan Ellen kept asking with bold fretfulness if they were not almost there. They counted the steeples of four churches, and their father presently showed them the Topham Academy, where their grandmother once went to school, and told them that perhaps some day they would go there too. Katy's heart gave a strange leap; it was such a tremendous thing to think of, but instantly the suggestion was transformed for her into one of the certainties of life. She looked with solemn awe at the tall belfry, and the long rows of windows in the front of the academy, there where it stood high and white among the clustering trees. She hoped that they were going to drive by, but something forbade her taking the responsibility of saying so.

Soon the children found themselves among the crowded village houses. Their father turned to look at them with affectionate solicitude.

"Now sit up straight and appear pretty," he whispered to them. "We're among the best people now, an' I want folks to think well of you."

"I guess we're as good as they be," remarked Susan Ellen, looking at some innocent passers-by with dark suspicion, but Katy tried indeed to sit straight, and folded her hands

prettily in her lap, and wished with all her heart to be
pleasing for her father's sake. Just then an elderly woman
saw the wagon and the sedate party it carried, and smiled
so kindly that it seemed to Katy as if Topham Corners
had welcomed and received them. She smiled back again
as if this hospitable person were an old friend, and entirely
forgot that the eyes of all Topham had been upon her.

"There, now we're coming to an elegant house that I
want you to see; you'll never forget it," said John Hilton.
"It's where Judge Masterson lives, the great lawyer; the
handsomest house in the county, everybody says."

"Do you know him, father?" asked Susan Ellen.

"I do," answered John Hilton proudly. "Him and my
mother went to school together in their young days, and
were always called the two best scholars of their time. The
judge called to see her once; he stopped to our house to
see her when I was a boy. An' then, some years ago—you've
heard me tell how I was on the jury, an' when he heard
my name spoken he looked at me sharp, and asked if I
wa'n't the son of Catharine Winn, an' spoke most beautiful of your grandmother, an' how well he remembered
their young days together."

"I like to hear about that," said Katy.

"She had it pretty hard, I'm afraid, up on the old farm.
She was keepin' school in our district when father married
her—that's the main reason I backed 'em down when they
wanted to tear the old schoolhouse all to pieces," confided
John Hilton, turning eagerly. "They all say she lived longer
up here on the hill than she could anywhere, but she never
had her health. I wa'n't but a boy when she died. Father
an' me lived alone afterward till the time your mother
come; 't was a good while, too; I wa'n't married so young
as some. 'T was lonesome, I tell you; father was plumb discouraged losin' of his wife, an' her long sickness an' all set
him back, an' we'd work all day on the land an' never
say a word. I s'pose 't is bein' so lonesome early in life
that makes me so pleased to have some nice girls growin'
up round me now."

There was a tone in her father's voice that drew Katy's
heart toward him with new affection. She dimly understood,
but Susan Ellen was less interested. They had often heard

this story before, but to one child it was always new and to the other old. Susan Ellen was apt to think it tiresome to hear about her grandmother, who, being dead, was hardly worth talking about.

"There's Judge Masterson's place," said their father in an every-day manner, as they turned a corner, and came into full view of the beautiful old white house standing behind its green trees and terraces and lawns. The children had never imagined anything so stately and fine, and even Susan Ellen exclaimed with pleasure. At that moment they saw an old gentleman, who carried himself with great dignity, coming slowly down the wide box-bordered path toward the gate.

"There he is now, there's the judge!" whispered John Hilton excitedly, reining his horse quickly to the green roadside. "He's goin' down-town to his office; we can wait right here an' see him. I can't expect him to remember me; it's been a good many years. Now you are goin' to see the great Judge Masterson!"

There was a quiver of expectation in their hearts. The judge stopped at his gate, hesitating a moment before he lifted the latch, and glanced up the street at the country wagon with its two prim little girls on the back seat, and the eager man who drove. They seemed to be waiting for something; the old horse was nibbling at the fresh roadside grass. The judge was used to being looked at with interest, and responded now with a smile as he came out to the sidewalk, and unexpectedly turned their way. Then he suddenly lifted his hat with grave politeness, and came directly toward them.

"Good-morning, Mr. Hilton," he said. "I am very glad to see you, sir;" and Mr. Hilton, the little girls' own father, took off his hat with equal courtesy, and bent forward to shake hands.

Susan Ellen cowered and wished herself away, but little Katy sat straighter than ever, with joy in her father's pride and pleasure shining in her pale, flower-like little face.

"These are your daughters, I am sure," said the old gentleman kindly, taking Susan Ellen's limp and reluctant hand; but when he looked at Katy, his face brightened. "How she recalls your mother!" he said with great feeling.

"I am glad to see this dear child. You must come to see me with your father, my dear," he added, still looking at her. "Bring both the little girls, and let them run about the old garden; the cherries are just getting ripe," said Judge Masterson hospitably. "Perhaps you will have time to stop this afternoon as you go home?"

"I should call it a great pleasure if you would come and see us again some time. You may be driving our way, sir," said John Hilton.

"Not very often in these days," answered the old judge. "I thank you for the kind invitation. I should like to see the fine view again from your hill westward. Can I serve you in any way while you are in town? Good-by, my little friends!"

Then they parted, but not before Katy, the shy Katy, whose hand the judge still held unconsciously while he spoke, had reached forward as he said good-by, and lifted her face to kiss him. She could not have told why, except that she felt drawn to something in the serious, worn face. For the first time in her life the child had felt the charm of manners; perhaps she owned a kinship between that which made him what he was, and the spark of nobleness and purity in her own simple soul. She turned again and again to look back at him as they drove away.

"Now you have seen one of the first gentlemen in the country," said their father. "It was worth comin' twice as far"—but he did not say any more, nor turn as usual to look in the children's faces.

In the chief business street of Topham a great many country wagons like the Hiltons' were fastened to the posts, and there seemed to our holiday-makers to be a great deal of noise and excitement.

"Now I've got to do my errands, and we can let the horse rest and feed," said John Hilton. "I'll slip his head-stall right off, an' put on his halter. I'm goin' to buy him a real good treat o' oats. First we'll go an' buy me my straw hat; I feel as if this one looked a little past to wear in Topham. We'll buy the things we want, an' then we'll walk all along the street, so you can look in the windows an' see the han'some things, same's your mother likes to. What was it mother told you about your shawls?"

"To take 'em off an' carry 'em over our arms," piped Susan Ellen, without comment, but in the interest of alighting and finding themselves afoot upon the pavement the shawls were forgotten. The children stood at the doorway of a shop while their father went inside, and they tried to see what the Topham shapes of bonnets were like, as their mother had advised them; but everything was exciting and confusing, and they could arrive at no decision. When Mr. Hilton came out with a hat in his hand to be seen in a better light, Katy whispered that she wished he would buy a shiny one like Judge Masterson's; but her father only smiled and shook his head, and said that they were plain folks, he and Katy. There were dry-goods for sale in the same shop, and a young clerk who was measuring linen kindly pulled off some pretty labels with gilded edges and gay pictures, and gave them to the little girls, to their exceeding joy. He may have had small sisters at home, this friendly lad, for he took pains to find two pretty blue boxes besides, and was rewarded by their beaming gratitude.

It was a famous day; they even became used to seeing so many people pass. The village was full of its morning activity, and Susan Ellen gained a new respect for her father, and an increased sense of her own consequence, because even in Topham several persons knew him and called him familiarly by name. The meeting with an old man who had once been a neighbor seemed to give Mr. Hilton the greatest pleasure. The old man called to them from a house doorway as they were passing, and they all went in. The children seated themselves wearily on the wooden step, but their father shook his old friend eagerly by the hand, and declared that he was delighted to see him so well and enjoying the fine weather.

"Oh, yes," said the old man, in a feeble, quavering voice, "I'm astonishin' well for my age. I don't complain, John, I don't complain."

They talked long together of people whom they had known in the past, and Katy, being a little tired, was glad to rest, and sat still with her hands folded, looking about the front yard. There were some kinds of flowers that she never had seen before.

"This is the one that looks like my mother," her father said, and touched Katy's shoulder to remind her to stand up and let herself be seen. "Judge Masterson saw the resemblance; we met him at his gate this morning."

"Yes, she certain does look like your mother, John," said the old man, looking pleasantly at Katy, who found that she liked him better than at first. "She does, certain; the best of young folks is, they remind us of the old ones. 'T is nateral to cling to life, folks say, but for me, I git impatient at time. Most everybody's gone now, an' I want to be goin'. 'T is somethin' before me, an' I want to have it over with. I want to be there 'long o' the rest o' the folks. I expect to last quite a while though; I may see ye couple o' times more, John."

John Hilton responded cheerfully, and the children were urged to pick some flowers. The old man awed them with his impatience to be gone. There was such a townful of people about him, and he seemed as lonely as if he were the last survivor of a former world. Until that moment they had felt as if everything were just beginning.

"Now I want to buy somethin' pretty for your mother," said Mr. Hilton, as they went soberly away down the street, the children keeping fast hold of his hands. "By now the old horse will have eat his dinner and had a good rest, so pretty soon we can jog along home. I'm goin' to take you round by the academy, and the old North Meetinghouse where Dr. Barstow used to preach. Can't you think o' somethin' that your mother'd want?" he asked suddenly, confronted by a man's difficulty of choice.

"She was talkin' about wantin' a new pepper-box, one day; the top o' the old one won't stay on," suggested Susan Ellen, with delightful readiness. "Can't we have some candy, father?"

"Yes, ma'am," said John Hilton, smiling and swinging her hand to and fro as they walked. "I feel as if some would be good myself. What's all this?" They were passing a photographer's doorway with its enticing array of portraits. "I do declare!" he exclaimed excitedly, "I'm goin' to have our pictures taken; 't will please your mother more 'n a little."

This was, perhaps, the greatest triumph of the day, except the delightful meeting with the judge; they sat in a row, with the father in the middle, and there was no doubt as to the excellence of the likeness. The best hats had to be taken off because they cast a shadow, but they were not missed, as their owners had feared. Both Susan Ellen and Katy looked their brightest and best; their eager young faces would forever shine there; the joy of the holiday was mirrored in the little picture. They did not know why their father was so pleased with it; they would not know until age had dowered them with the riches of association and remembrance.

Just at nightfall the Hiltons reached home again, tired out and happy. Katy had climbed over into the front seat beside her father, because that was always her place when they went to church on Sundays. It was a cool evening, there was a fresh sea wind that brought a light mist with it, and the sky was fast growing cloudy. Somehow the children looked different; it seemed to their mother as if they had grown older and taller since they went away in the morning, and as if they belonged to the town now as much as to the country. The greatness of their day's experience had left her far behind; the day had been silent and lonely without them, and she had had their supper ready, and been watching anxiously, ever since five o'clock. As for the children themselves they had little to say at first—they had eaten their luncheon early on the way to Topham. Susan Ellen was childishly cross, but Katy was pathetic and wan. They could hardly wait to show the picture, and their mother was as much pleased as everybody had expected.

"There, what did make you wear your shawls?" she exclaimed a moment afterward, reproachfully. "You ain't been an' wore 'em all day long? I wanted folks to see how pretty your new dresses was, if I did make 'em. Well, well! I wish more'n ever now I'd gone an' seen to ye!"

"An' here's the pepper-box!" said Katy, in a pleased, unconscious tone.

"That really is what I call beautiful," said Mrs. Hilton, after a long and doubtful look. "Our other one was only tin. I never did look so high as a chiny one with flowers, but I can get us another any time for every day. That's a proper hat, as good as you could have got, John. Where's your new hoe?" she asked as he came toward her from the barn, smiling with satisfaction.

"I declare to Moses if I didn't forget all about it," meekly acknowledged the leader of the great excursion. "That an' my yellow-turnip seed, too; they went clean out o' my head, there was so many other things to think of. But 't ain't no sort o' matter; I can get a hoe just as well to Ira Speed's."

His wife could not help laughing. "You an' the little girls have had a great time. They was full o' wonder to me about everything, and I expect they'll talk about it for a week. I guess we was right about havin' 'em see somethin' more o' the world."

"Yes," answered John Hilton, with humility, "yes, we did have a beautiful day. I didn't expect so much. They looked as nice as anybody, and appeared so modest an' pretty. The little girls will remember it perhaps by an' by. I guess they won't never forget this day they had 'long o' father."

It was evening again, the frogs were piping in the lower meadows, and in the woods, higher up the great hill, a little owl began to hoot. The sea air, salt and heavy, was blowing in over the country at the end of the hot bright day. A lamp was lighted in the house, the happy children were talking together, and supper was waiting. The father and mother lingered for a moment outside and looked down over the shadowy fields; then they went in, without speaking. The great day was over, and they shut the door.

1 "No," said Mrs. Hand, speaking wistfully,—"no, we never were in the habit of keeping Christmas at our house. Mother died when we were all young; she would have been the one to keep up with all new ideas, but father and grandmother were old-fashioned folks, and—well, you know how 't was then, Miss Pendexter: nobody took much notice of the day except to wish you a Merry Christmas."

"They didn't do much to make it merry, certain," answered Miss Pendexter. "Sometimes nowadays I hear folks complainin' o' bein' overtaxed with all the Christmas work they have to do."

"Well, others think that it makes a lovely chance for all that really enjoys givin'; you get an opportunity to speak your kind feelin' right out," answered Mrs. Hand, with a bright smile. "But there! I shall always keep New Year's Day, too; it won't do no hurt to have an extra day kept an' made pleasant. And there's many of the real old folks have got pretty things to remember about New Year's Day."

"Aunt Cynthy Dallett's just one of 'em," said Miss Pendexter. "She's always very reproachful if I don't get up to see her. Last year I missed it, on account of a light fall o' snow that seemed to make the walkin' too bad, an' she sent a neighbor's boy 'way down from the mount'in to see if I was sick. Her lameness confines her to the house altogether now, an' I have her on my mind a good deal. How anybody does get thinkin' of those that lives alone, as they get older! I waked up only last night with a start, thinkin' if Aunt Cynthy's house should get afire or anything, what she would do, 'way up there all alone. I was half dreamin', I s'pose, but I couldn't seem to settle down until I got up an' went upstairs to the north garret window to see if I could see any light; but the mountains was all dark an' safe, same's usual. I remember noticin' last time I was there that her chimney needed pointin', and I spoke to her about it,—the bricks looked poor in some places."

"Can you see the house from your north gable window?" asked Mrs. Hand, a little absently.

"Yes'm; it's a great comfort that I can," answered her companion. "I have often wished we were near enough to have her make me some sort o' signal in case she needed help. I used to plead with her to come down and spend the winters with me, but she told me one day I might as well try to fetch down one o' the old hemlocks, an' I believe 't was true."

"Your aunt Dallett is a very self-contained person," observed Mrs. Hand.

"Oh, very!" exclaimed the elderly niece, with a pleased look. "Aunt Cynthy laughs, an' says she expects the time will come when age'll compel her to have me move up an' take care of her; and last time I was there she looked up real funny, an' says, 'I do' know, Abby; I'm most afeard sometimes that I feel myself beginnin' to look for'ard to it!' 'T was a good deal, comin' from Aunt Cynthy, an' I so esteemed it."

"She ought to have you there now," said Mrs. Hand. "You'd both make a savin' by doin' it; but I don't expect she needs to save as much as some. There! I know just how you both feel. I like to have my own home an' do everything just my way too." And the friends laughed, and looked at each other affectionately.

"There was old Mr. Nathan Dunn,—left no debts an' no money when he died," said Mrs. Hand. "'T was over to his niece's last summer. He had a little money in his wallet, an' when the bill for funeral expenses come in there was just exactly enough; some item or other made it come to so many dollars an' eighty-four cents, and, lo an' behold! there was eighty-four cents in a little separate pocket beside the neat fold o' bills, as if the old gentleman had known beforehand. His niece couldn't help laughin', to save her; she said the old gentleman died as methodical as he lived. She didn't expect he had any money, an' was prepared to pay for everything herself; she's very well off."

"'T was funny, certain," said Miss Pendexter. "I expect he felt comfortable, knowin' he had that money by him. 'T is a comfort, when all's said and done, 'specially to folks that's gettin' old."

A sad look shadowed her face for an instant, and then she smiled and rose to take leave, looking expectantly at her hostess to see if there were anything more to be said.

"I hope to come out square myself," she said, by way of farewell pleasantry; "but there are times when I feel doubtful."

Mrs. Hand was evidently considering something, and waited a moment or two before she spoke. "Suppose we both walk up to see your aunt Dallett, New Year's Day, if it ain't too windy and the snow keeps off?" she proposed. "I couldn't rise the hill if 't was a windy day. We could take a hearty breakfast an' start in good season; I'd rather walk than ride, the road's so rough this time o' year."

"Oh, what a person you are to think o' things! I did so dread goin' 'way up there all alone," said Abby Pendexter. "I'm no hand to go off alone, an' I had it before me, so I really got to dread it. I do so enjoy it after I get there, seein' Aunt Cynthy, an' she's always so much better than I expect to find her."

"Well, we'll start early," said Mrs. Hand cheerfully; and so they parted. As Miss Pendexter went down the foot-path to the gate, she sent grateful thoughts back to the little sitting-room she had just left.

"How doors are opened!" she exclaimed to herself. "Here I've been so poor an' distressed at beginnin' the year with nothin', as it were, that I couldn't think o' even goin' to make poor old Aunt Cynthy a friendly call. I'll manage to make some kind of a little pleasure too, an' somethin' for dear Mis' Hand. 'Use what you've got,' mother always used to say when every sort of an emergency come up, an' I may only have wishes to give, but I'll make 'em good ones!"

2 The first day of the year was clear and bright, as if it were a New Year's pattern of what winter can be at its very best. The two friends were prepared for changes of weather, and met each other well wrapped in their winter cloaks and shawls, with sufficient brown barége veils tied securely over their bonnets. They ignored for some time the plain truth that each carried something under her arm; the shawls were rounded out suspiciously, especially Miss Pendexter's, but each respected the other's air of secrecy. The narrow road was frozen in deep ruts, but a smooth-

trodden little foot-path that ran along its edge was very inviting to the wayfarers. Mrs. Hand walked first and Miss Pendexter followed, and they were talking busily nearly all the way, so that they had to stop for breath now and then at the tops of the little hills. It was not a hard walk; there were a good many almost level stretches through the woods, in spite of the fact that they should be a very great deal higher when they reached Mrs. Dallett's door.

"I do declare, what a nice day 't is, an' such pretty footin'!" said Mrs. Hand, with satisfaction. "Seems to me as if my feet went o' themselves; gener'lly I have to toil so when I walk that I can't enjoy nothin' when I get to a place."

"It's partly this beautiful bracin' air," said Abby Pendexter. "Sometimes such nice air comes just before a fall of snow. Don't it seem to make anybody feel young again and to take all your troubles away?"

Mrs. Hand was a comfortable, well-to-do soul, who seldom worried about anything, but something in her companion's tone touched her heart, and she glanced sidewise and saw a pained look in Abby Pendexter's thin face. It was a moment for confidence.

"Why, you speak as if something distressed your mind, Abby," said the elder woman kindly.

"I ain't one that has myself on my mind as a usual thing, but it does seem now as if I was goin' to have it very hard," said Abby. "Well, I've been anxious before."

"Is it anything wrong about your property?" Mrs. Hand ventured to ask.

"Only that I ain't got any," answered Abby, trying to speak gayly. "'T was all I could do to pay my last quarter's rent, twelve dollars. I sold my hens, all but this one that had run away at the time, an' now I'm carryin' her up to Aunt Cynthy, roasted just as nice as I know how."

"I thought you was carrying somethin'," said Mrs. Hand, in her usual tone. "For me, I've got a couple o' my mince pies. I thought the old lady might like 'em; one we can eat for our dinner, and one she shall have to keep. But weren't you unwise to sacrifice your poultry, Abby? You always need eggs, and hens don't cost much to keep."

"Why, yes, I shall miss 'em," said Abby; "but, you see,

I had to do every way to get my rent-money. Now the shop's shut down I haven't got any way of earnin' anything, and I spent what little I've saved through the summer."

"Your aunt Cynthy ought to know it an' ought to help you," said Mrs. Hand. "You're a real foolish person, I must say. I expect you do for her when she ought to do for you."

"She's old, an' she's all the near relation I've got," said the little woman. "I've always felt the time would come when she'd need me, but it's been her great pleasure to live alone an' feel free. I shall get along somehow, but I shall have it hard. Somebody may want help for a spell this winter, but I'm afraid I shall have to give up my house. 'T ain't as if I owned it. I don't know just what to do, but there'll be a way."

Mrs. Hand shifted her two pies to the other arm, and stepped across to the other side of the road where the ground looked a little smoother.

"No, I wouldn't worry if I was you, Abby," she said. "There, I suppose if 't was me I should worry a good deal more! I expect I should lay awake nights." But Abby answered nothing, and they came to a steep place in the road and found another subject for conversation at the top.

"Your aunt don't know we're coming?" asked the chief guest of the occasion.

"Oh, no, I never send her word," said Miss Pendexter. "She'd be so desirous to get everything ready, just as she used to."

"She never seemed to make any trouble o' havin' company; she always appeared so easy and pleasant, and let you set with her while she made her preparations," said Mrs. Hand, with great approval. "Some has such a dreadful way of making you feel inopportune, and you can't always send word you're comin'. I did have a visit once that's always been a lesson to me; 't was years ago; I don't know's I ever told you?"

"I don't believe you ever did," responded the listener to this somewhat indefinite prelude.

"Well, 't was one hot summer afternoon. I set forth an' took a great long walk 'way over to Mis' Eben Fulham's, on the crossroad between the cranberry ma'sh and Staples's Corner. The doctor was drivin' that way, an' he give me a

a lift that shortened it some at the last; but I never should
have started, if I'd known 't was so far. I had been promisin'
all summer to go, and every time I saw Mis' Fulham, Sundays, she'd say somethin' about it. We wa'n't very well
acquainted, but always friendly. She moved here from Bed-
ford Hill."

"Oh, yes; I used to know her," said Abby, with interest.

"Well, now, she did give me a beautiful welcome when
I got there," continued Mrs. Hand. "'T was about four
o'clock in the afternoon, an' I told her I'd come to accept
her invitation if 't was convenient, an' the doctor had been
called several miles beyond and expected to be detained,
but he was goin' to pick me up as he returned about seven;
't was very kind of him. She took me right in, and she did
appear so pleased, an' I must go right into the best room
where 't was cool, and then she said she'd have tea early,
and I should have to excuse her a short time. I asked her
not to make any difference, and if I couldn't assist her; but
she said no, I must just take her as I found her; and she
give me a large fan, and off she went.

"There. I was glad to be still and rest where 't was cool,
an' I set there in the rockin'-chair an' enjoyed it for a while,
an' I heard her clacking at the oven door out beyond, an'
gittin' out some dishes. She was a brisk-actin' little woman,
an' I thought I'd caution her when she come back not to
make up a great fire, only for a cup o' tea, perhaps. I started
to go right out in the kitchen, an' then somethin' told me
I'd better not, we never'd been so free together as that; I
didn't know how she'd take it, an' there I set an' set. 'T was
sort of a greenish light in the best room, an' it begun to feel
a little damp to me,—the s'rubs outside grew close up to the
windows. Oh, it did seem dreadful long! I could hear her
busy with the dishes an' beatin' eggs an' stirrin', an' I knew
she was puttin' herself out to get up a great supper, and I
kind o' fidgeted about a little an' even stepped to the door,
but I thought she'd expect me to remain where I was. I
saw everything in that room forty times over, an' I did
divert myself killin' off a brood o' moths that was in a
worsted-work mat on the table. It all fell to pieces. I never
saw such a sight o' moths to once. But occupation failed
after that, an' I begun to feel sort o' tired an' numb. There

was one o' them late crickets got into the room an' begun to chirp, an' it sounded kind o' fallish. I couldn't help sayin' to myself that Mis' Fulham had forgot all about my bein' there. I thought of all the beauties of hospitality that ever I see!"—

"Didn't she ever come back at all, not whilst things was in the oven, nor nothin'?" inquired Miss Pendexter, with awe.

"I never see her again till she come beamin' to the parlor door an' invited me to walk out to tea," said Mrs. Hand. " 'T was 'most a quarter past six by the clock; I thought 't was seven. I'd thought o' everything, an' I'd counted, an' I'd trotted my foot, an' I'd looked more'n twenty times to see if there was any more moth-millers."

"I s'pose you did have a very nice tea?" suggested Abby, with interest.

"Oh, a beautiful tea! She couldn't have done more if I'd been the Queen," said Mrs. Hand. "I don't know how she could ever have done it all in the time, I'm sure. The table was loaded down; there was cup-custards and custard pie, an' cream pie, an' two kinds o' hot biscuits, an' black tea as well as green, an' elegant cake,—one kind she'd just made new, and called it quick cake; I've often made it since —an' she'd opened her best preserves, two kinds. We set down together, an' I'm sure I appreciated what she'd done; but 't wa'n't no time for real conversation whilst we was to the table, and before we got quite through the doctor come hurryin' along, an' I had to leave. He asked us if we'd had a good talk, as we come out, an' I couldn't help laughing to myself; but she said quite hearty that she'd had a nice visit from me. She appeared well satisfied, Mis' Fulham did; but for me, I was disappointed; an' early that fall she died."

Abby Pendexter was laughing like a girl; the speaker's tone had grown more and more complaining. "I do call that a funny experience," she said. " 'Better a dinner o' herbs.' I guess that text must ha' risen to your mind in connection. You must tell that to Aunt Cynthy, if conversation seems to fail." And she laughed again, but Mrs. Hand still looked solemn and reproachful.

"Here we are; there's Aunt Cynthy's lane right ahead,

there by the great yellow birch," said Abby. "I must say,
you've made the way seem very short, Mis' Hand."

3   Old Aunt Cynthia Dallett sat in her high-backed rocking-chair by the little north window, which was her favorite
dwelling-place.

"New Year's Day again," she said, aloud,—"New Year's
Day again!" And she folded her old bent hands, and looked
out at the great woodland view and the hills without
really seeing them, she was lost in so deep a reverie. "I'm
gittin' to be very old," she added, after a little while.

It was perfectly still in the small gray house. Outside in
the apple-trees there were some blue-jays flitting about and
calling noisily, like schoolboys fighting at their games. The
kitchen was full of pale winter sunshine. It was more like
late October than the first of January, and the plain little
room seemed to smile back into the sun's face. The outer
door was standing open into the green dooryard, and a fat
small dog lay asleep on the step. A capacious cupboard
stood behind Mrs. Dallett's chair and kept the wind away
from her corner. Its doors and drawers were painted a clean
lead-color, and there were places round the knobs and buttons where the touch of hands had worn deep into the
wood. Every braided rug was straight on the floor. The
square clock on its shelf between the front windows looked
as if it had just had its face washed and been wound up for
a whole year to come. If Mrs. Dallett turned her head she
could look into the bedroom, where her plump feather bed
was covered with its dark blue homespun winter quilt. It
was all very peaceful and comfortable, but it was very
lonely. By her side, on a light-stand, lay the religious newspaper of her denomination, and a pair of spectacles whose
jointed silver bows looked like a funny two-legged beetle
cast helplessly upon its back.

"New Year's Day again," said old Cynthia Dallett. Time
had left nobody in her house to wish her a Happy New
Year,—she was the last one left in the old nest. "I'm gittin'
to be very old," she said for the second time; it seemed to
be all there was to say.

She was keeping a careful eye on her friendly clock, but

it was hardly past the middle of the morning, and there was no excuse for moving; it was the long hour between the end of her slow morning work and the appointed time for beginning to get dinner. She was so stiff and lame that this hour's rest was usually most welcome, but to-day she sat as if it were Sunday, and did not take up her old shallow splint basket of braiding-rags from the side of her footstool.

"I do hope Abby Pendexter'll make out to git up to see me this afternoon as usual," she continued. "I know 't ain't so easy for her to get up the hill as it used to be, but I do seem to want to see some o' my own folks. I wish 't I'd thought to send her word I expected her when Jabez Hooper went back after he came up here with the flour. I'd like to have had her come prepared to stop two or three days."

A little chickadee perched on the window-sill outside and bobbed his head sideways to look in, and then pecked impatiently at the glass. The old woman laughed at him with childish pleasure and felt companioned; it was pleasant at that moment to see the life in even a bird's bright eye.

"Sign of a stranger," she said, as he whisked his wings and flew away in a hurry. "I must throw out some crumbs for 'em; it's getting to be hard pickin' for the stayin'-birds." She looked past the trees of her little orchard now with seeing eyes, and followed the long forest slopes that led downward to the lowland country. She could see the two white steeples of Fairfield Village, and the map of fields and pastures along the valley beyond, and the great hills across the valley to the westward. The scattered houses looked like toys that had been scattered by children. She knew their lights by night, and watched the smoke of their chimneys by day. Far to the northward were higher mountains, and these were already white with snow. Winter was already in sight, but to-day the wind was in the south, and the snow seemed only part of a great picture.

"I do hope the cold'll keep off a while longer," thought Mrs. Dallett. "I don't know how I'm going to get along after the deep snow comes."

The little dog suddenly waked, as if he had had a bad dream, and after giving a few anxious whines he began to bark outrageously. His mistress tried, as usual, to appeal to his better feelings.

" 'T ain't nobody, Tiger," she said. "Can't you have some patience? Maybe it's some foolish boys that's rangin' about with their guns." But Tiger kept on, and even took the trouble to waddle in on his short legs, barking all the way. He looked warningly at her, and then turned and ran out again. Then she saw him go hurrying down to the bars, as if it were an occasion of unusual interest.

"I guess somebody is comin'; he don't act as if 't were a vagrant kind o' noise; must really be somebody in our lane." And Mrs. Dallett smoothed her apron and gave an anxious housekeeper's glance round the kitchen. None of her state visitors, the minister or the deacons, ever came in the morning. Country people are usually too busy to go visiting in the forenoons.

Presently two figures appeared where the road came out of the woods,—the two women already known to the story, but very surprising to Mrs. Dallett; the short, thin one was easily recognized as Abby Pendexter, and the taller, stout one was soon discovered to be Mrs. Hand. Their old friend's heart was in a glow. As the guests approached they could see her pale face with its thin white hair framed under the close black silk handkerchief.

"There she is at her window smilin' away!" exclaimed Mrs. Hand; but by the time they reached the doorstep she stood waiting to meet them.

"Why, you two dear creatur's!" she said, with a beaming smile. "I don't know when I've ever been so glad to see folks comin'. I had a kind of left-all-alone feelin' this mornin', an' I didn't even make bold to be certain o' you, Abby, though it looked so pleasant. Come right in an' set down. You're all out o' breath, ain't you, Mis' Hand?"

Mrs. Dallett led the way with eager hospitality. She was the tiniest little bent old creature, her handkerchiefed head was quick and alert, and her eyes were bright with excitement and feeling, but the rest of her was much the worse for age; she could hardly move, poor soul, as if she had only a make-believe framework of a body under a shoulder-shawl and thick petticoats. She got back to her chair again, and the guests took off their bonnets in the bedroom, and returned discreet and sedate in their black woolen dresses. The lonely kitchen was blest with society at last, to its mistress's heart's content. They talked as fast as possible about the weather, and how warm it had been walking up the mountain, and how cold it had been a year ago, that day when Abby Pendexter had been kept at home by a snowstorm and missed her visit. "And I ain't seen you now, aunt, since the twenty-eighth of September, but I've thought of you a great deal, and looked forward to comin' more'n usual," she ended, with an affectionate glance at the pleased old face by the window.

"I've been wantin' to see you, dear, and wonderin' how you was gettin' on," said Aunt Cynthy kindly. "And I take it as a great attention to have you come to-day, Mis' Hand," she added, turning again towards the more distinguished guest. "We have to put one thing against another. I should hate dreadfully to live anywhere except on a high hill farm, 'cordin' as I was born an' raised. But there ain't the chance to neighbor that townfolks has, an' I do seem to have more lonely hours than I used to when I was younger. I don't know but I shall soon be gittin' too old to live alone." And she turned to her niece with an expectant, lovely look, and Abby smiled back.

"I often wish I could run in an' see you every day, aunt," she answered. "I have been sayin' so to Mrs. Hand."

"There, how anybody does relish company when they don't have but a little of it!" exclaimed Aunt Cynthia. "I am all alone to-day; there is going to be a shootin'-match somewhere the other side o' the mountain, an' Johnny Foss, that does my chores, begged off to go when he brought the milk unusual early this mornin'. Gener'lly he's about here all the fore part of the day; but he don't go off with the boys very often, and I like to have him have a little sport; 't was New Year's Day, anyway; he's a good, stiddy boy for my wants."

"Why, I wish you Happy New Year, aunt!" said Abby, springing up with unusual spirit. "Why, that's just what we come to say, and we like to have forgot all about it!" She kissed her aunt, and stood a minute holding her hand with a soft, affectionate touch. Mrs. Hand rose and kissed Mrs. Dallett too, and it was a moment of ceremony and deep feeling.

"I always like to keep the day," said the old hostess, as

they seated themselves and drew their splint-bottomed
chairs a little nearer together than before. "You see, I was
brought up to it, and father made a good deal of it; he said
he liked to make it pleasant and give the year a fair start. I
can see him now, how he used to be standing there by the
fireplace when we came out o' the two bedrooms early in
the morning, an' he always made out, poor 's he was, to give
us some little present, and he'd heap 'em up on the corner
o' the mantelpiece, an' we'd stand front of him in a row,
and mother be bustling about gettin' breakfast. One year
he give me a beautiful copy o' the 'Life o' General La-
fayette,' in a green cover,—I've got it now, but we child'n
'bout read it to pieces,—an' one year a nice piece o' blue
ribbon, an' Abby—that was your mother, Abby—had a pink
one. Father was real kind to his child'n. I thought o' them
early days when I first waked up this mornin', and I
couldn't help lookin' up then to the corner o' the shelf
just as I used to look."

"There's nothin' so beautiful as to have a bright childhood to look back to," said Mrs. Hand. "Sometimes I think
child'n has too hard a time now,—all the responsibility is
put on to 'em, since they take the lead o' what to do an'
what they want, and get to be so toppin' an' knowin'. 'T
was happier in the old days, when the fathers an' mothers
done the rulin'."

"They say things have changed," said Aunt Cynthy; "but
staying right here, I don't know much of any world but my
own world."

Abby Pendexter did not join in this conversation, but sat
in her straight-backed chair with folded hands and the air
of a good child. The little old dog had followed her in,
and now lay sound asleep again at her feet. The front
breadth of her black dress looked rusty and old in the sunshine that slanted across it, and the aunt's sharp eyes saw
this and saw the careful darns. Abby was as neat as wax, but
she looked as if the frost had struck her. "I declare, she's
gittin' along in years," thought Aunt Cynthia compassionately. "She begins to look sort o' set and dried up, Abby
does. She oughtn't to live all alone; she's one that needs
company."

At this moment Abby looked up with new interest.

"Now, aunt," she said, in her pleasant voice, "I don't want you to forget to tell me if there ain't some sewin' or mendin' I can do whilst I'm here. I know your hands trouble you some, an' I may 's well tell you we're bent on stayin' all day an' makin' a good visit, Mis' Hand an' me."

"Thank ye kindly," said the old woman; "I do want a little sewin' done before long, but 't ain't no use to spile a good holiday." Her face took a resolved expression. "I'm goin' to make other arrangements," she said. "No, you needn't come up here to pass New Year's Day an' be put right down to sewin'. I make out to do what mendin' I need, an' to sew on my hooks an' eyes. I get Johnny Foss to thread me up a good lot o' needles every little while, an' that helps me a good deal. Abby, why can't you step into the best room an' bring out the rockin'-chair? I seem to want Mis' Hand to have it."

"I opened the window to let the sun in awhile," said the niece, as she returned. "It felt cool in there an' shut up."

"I thought of doin' it not long before you come," said Mrs. Dallett, looking gratified. Once the taking of such a liberty would have been very provoking to her. "Why, it does seem good to have somebody think o' things an' take right hold like that!"

"I'm sure you would, if you were down at my house," said Abby, blushing. "Aunt Cynthy, I don't suppose you could feel as if 't would be best to come down an' pass the winter with me,—just durin' the cold weather, I mean. You'd see more folks to amuse you, an'—I do think of you so anxious these long winter nights."

There was a terrible silence in the room, and Miss Pendexter felt her heart begin to beat very fast. She did not dare to look at her aunt at first.

Presently the silence was broken. Aunt Cynthia had been gazing out of the window, and she turned towards them a little paler and older than before, and smiling sadly.

"Well, dear, I'll do just as you say," she answered. "I'm beat by age at last, but I've had my own way for eighty-five years, come the month o' March, an' last winter I did use to lay awake an' worry in the long storms. I'm kind o' humble now about livin' alone to what I was once." At this moment a new light shone in her face. "I don't expect you'd be willin' to come up here an' stay till spring,—not if I had Foss's folks stop for you to ride to meetin' every pleasant Sunday, an' take you down to the Corners plenty o' other times besides?" she said beseechingly. "No, Abby, I'm too old to move now; I should be homesick down to the village. If you'll come an' stay with me, all I have shall be yours. Mis' Hand hears me say it."

"Oh, don't you think o' that; you're all I've got near to me in the world, an' I'll come an' welcome," said Abby, though the thought of her own little home gave a hard tug at her heart. "Yes, Aunt Cynthy, I'll come, an' we'll be real comfortable together. I've been lonesome some-times"—

"'T will be best for both," said Mrs. Hand judicially. And so the great question was settled, and suddenly, without too much excitement, it became a thing of the past.

"We must be thinkin' o' dinner," said Aunt Cynthia gayly. "I wish I was better prepared; but there's nice eggs an' pork an' potatoes, an' you girls can take hold an' help." At this moment the roast chicken and the best mince pies were offered and kindly accepted, and before another hour had gone they were sitting at their New Year feast, which Mrs. Dallett decided to be quite proper for the Queen.

Before the guests departed, when the sun was getting low, Aunt Cynthia called her niece to her side and took hold of her hand.

"Don't you make it too long now, Abby," said she. "I shall be wantin' ye every day till you come; but you mustn't forgit what a set old thing I be."

Abby had the kindest of hearts, and was always longing for somebody to love and care for; her aunt's very age and helplessness seemed to beg for pity.

"This is Saturday; you may expect me the early part of the week; and thank you, too, aunt," said Abby.

Mrs. Hand stood by with deep sympathy. "It's the proper thing," she announced calmly. "You'd both of you be a sight happier; and truth is, Abby's wild an' reckless, an' needs somebody to stand right over her, Mis' Dallett. I guess she'll try an' behave, but there—there's no knowin'!" And they all laughed. Then the New Year guests said fare-

well and started off down the mountain road. They looked
back more than once to see Aunt Cynthia's face at the
window as she watched them out of sight. Miss Abby
Pendexter was full of excitement; she looked as happy as a
child.

"I feel as if we'd gained the battle of Waterloo," said
Mrs. Hand. "I've really had a most beautiful time. You
an' your aunt mustn't forgit to invite me up some time
again to spend another day."